This special edition of
'Strathcarnage'
is limited to 100 slipcased copies
signed by the author and illustrator.
This is copy number: 29/100

Matt Hamilton

Chris Odgers

# STRATHCARNAGE

# STRATHCARNAGE

## Matt Hamilton

*Illustrated by Chris Odgers*

Copyright © 2009 Matt Hamilton

The moral right of the author has been asserted.

Apart from any fair dealing for the purposes of research or private study,
or criticism or review, as permitted under the Copyright, Designs and Patents
Act 1988, this publication may only be reproduced, stored or transmitted, in
any form or by any means, with the prior permission in writing of the
publishers, or in the case of reprographic reproduction in accordance with
the terms of licences issued by the Copyright Licensing Agency. Enquiries
concerning reproduction outside those terms should be sent to the publishers.

Matador
5 Weir Road
Kibworth Beauchamp
Leicester LE8 0LQ, UK
Tel: (+44) 116 279 2299
Email: books@troubador.co.uk
Web: www.troubador.co.uk/matador

ISBN 9781848761438

Typeset in 11pt Baskerville by Troubador Publishing Ltd, Leicester, UK
Printed in the UK by TJ International, Padstow, Cornwall

**Matador** is an imprint of Troubador Publishing Ltd

Through Me One Goes To The Sorrowful City,
Through Me One Goes To Eternal Suffering.
Through Me One Goes Amongst Lost People....
Abandon All Hope, Ye Who Enter !

*Divina Commedia, Inferno,*
Dante Alighieri (1265-1321)

For everyone who invested time, patience, love, belief and trust in me – you know who you are and I thank you from the bottom of my heart.

And to Chris Odgers for sharing his advice, friendship and his genius.

# CONTENTS

|  | Prologue | 1 |
|---|---|---|
| 1. | The Statement Begins | 4 |
| 2. | Journey to the Hut | 13 |
| 3. | Roman Holiday | 23 |
| 4. | The Garage | 40 |
| 5. | Yoyo | 53 |
| 6. | Christmas Tales | 72 |
| 7. | The Pubic Modeller | 83 |
| 8. | The Clairvoyant | 101 |
| 9. | Country and Western | 115 |
| 10. | The Defective Detective | 137 |
| 11. | The Pensioner's Brothel | 150 |
| 12. | Roadkill | 168 |
| 13. | School Days | 181 |
| 14. | The Mau Chang Fighters | 198 |
| 15. | The Wooden Fuhrer | 226 |
| 16. | The Final Half Chapter | 250 |
| 17. | The Tale's End | 263 |
| 18. | The Stranger Arrives | 265 |
| 19. | Barvas Arrives | 276 |
| 20. | Barvas Reacts | 284 |
| 21. | The Men React | 291 |
| 22. | Footnote | 293 |

# Prologue

In an anonymous room, deep within the basement corridors of an unremarkable police station in a long forgotten coastal town, three policemen stand in an ominous dark line. The trinity of figures are unmoving, their shapes silhouetted from behind by a single bulb suspended from the ceiling on a dusty wire. Three distorted shadows projected onto white painted brick are demonic outlines looming over a single man sitting at a table. The men stand silent, staring at the stranger, waiting.

A single eye looks out from beneath a chair in the corner of the room, watching and blinking occasionally in the shadows.

No one speaks, the silence filling the room as the stranger scans slowly along the line. Finding no emotion in the three pairs of eyes staring back at him, he lowers his own gaze back to the table, wiping beads of sweat from his bruised brow with the back of his hand as he studies the chipped paint of the surface.

The stranger detects a sudden movement in the room and his gaze flashes upward in fear. The middle figure of the line, a huge scowling man with an untidy dark moustache, slowly peels off his black policeman's jacket and turns to hang it over a single rusted nail, hammered into the featureless white wall.

The stranger's eyes settle on the shadow of sweat spread across the back of the man's white shirt. The stain runs the length of his enormous rounded body, spreads outward from the folds of flesh bulging over a dirty collar, down over the massive expanse of back before it disappears beneath the wrinkled cotton displaced by his movement to reveal a pale roll of marbled fat, escaping over his waistband. As the huge man hangs the jacket and goes back to his original position, the seated man returns his gaze back at the table.

No-one in this room is yet noteworthy. For the moment these are ordinary men drawn together by the promise of hearing extraordinary events. Within the featureless room, this line of silent figures waits to hear the details of their new visitor's story. In direct contrast to this most unremarkable location, the stranger has gathered this ordinary group together in order to bear witness to a most extraordinary tale.

They will not be disappointed, for his is a story so incredible that it is unlikely to be forgotten by any person who hears it told. Indeed, this is a tale so potent and powerful that everyone present in the room into men destined to be subjects of grand legends of their own.

Yet for such events we must wait, since we all still remain ignorant of the astonishing contents of the stranger's promised revelation. In order that we may later share, join and understand, we too must begin here, at the beginning.

Anxious to unburden himself of the weight of his story, the seated man decides it is time to break the oppressive silence. Still staring at the table top while picking off little petals of decaying paint with his broken, dirt encrusted nails, he speaks.

"Gentlemen, I am ready to begin whenever you are."

Having spoken, the stranger looks up and meets the gaze of the tall man who is unmistakably the senior of the group. After a moment staring motionless at the stranger with his pale blue eyes, the oldest nods his agreement and all three men stir from their positions and spread out silently around the room.

The youngest of the three sits at the end of the table, head bowed, careful not to catch the visitor's eye as he brushes his untidy blond hair out of his line of vision. His white teeth chew and gnaw at his sharpened pencil while he pats into place his already tidy pile of paper, anxious to begin his task in his assigned role as recorder.

Across the room the huge jacketless policeman lowers his stout frame into a well worn leather office chair. As he eases himself down he releases a deep sigh of effort, his low groan mixing with a resigned metallic squealing and creaking from beneath as the construction takes his familiar weight; the chair only recently prodded all the way along a corridor from another room by lazy kicks from his shining black shoe, especially for this strange occasion.

Seemingly content with his position, the fat man slides thick fingers deep into a trouser pocket and emerges with a single sweet which he unwraps and slides between wet lips with his nicotine stained fingers, before smiling to himself in distracted satisfaction. The stranger can smell mint and hear the dull crunch of sweet ground against the large man's uneven yellow teeth.

The most senior policeman of the three stands in the corner of the room watching over the scene, expressionless. This thin older man extracts a cigarette from the shapeless packet drawn from the inside pocket of his grey tweed jacket and after some searching of pockets, lights it with a worn brass petrol lighter. The sweet smell of the fuel mixes with fresh smoke as he clinks the lid closed and returns the lighter to a pocket and waits for the other men to settle. Finally, once everyone is in position, he walks slowly across the stone floor and sits himself at the table, directly opposite the visitor.

As another plume of pale smoke escapes from the corner of the older man's lined mouth, his unusually blue eyes stare straight through the man opposite, as if attempting to bore into the very depths of the stranger's soul.

With an almost imperceptible nod, he indicates to the visitor they are ready. The unkempt stranger swallows hard and nods once to indicate his understanding, clearing his throat and wiping more sweat from his brow before beginning to speak.

"Since we are ready, then I shall begin. Unless you find good reason to bring me to a halt, I ask that you allow me to share my entire story with as little interruption as is possible, otherwise I may easily lose track and forget some significant detail or other. Is that acceptable?"

The policeman opposite nods once.

Readying his pencil, the young officer holds the gnawed wood between his pale thin fingers, ready to begin his task of filling the clean pages before him.

As the stranger begins to speak, the sharpened lead begins to dance and scrape across the empty white paper.

# CHAPTER 1

## The Statement Begins

"The extraordinary series of events I am about to recount to you began on a snowy evening a number of weeks ago. On the evening in question the Scottish winter wind was rattling my windows as it whipped the falling snow past the cottage, across the open hillside. I rubbed rough grains of drunken sleep from my eyes as I gazed idly from the windows, surveying the bare landscape and watching the snow fall in the twilight, the rancid stench of dead decaying flesh sitting heavy in the room.

My cottage lay isolated, the painted white stone an insignificant speck against the vast waves of soaring hills for which the area is famous, dwarfed by the epic countryside all around. My home was situated miles from the nearest soul by careful selection, my unspoilt outlook from the window that of rolling empty emerald landscape framed only by sky and a thin band of navy sea in the distance.

I had, as I said, selected such solitude for myself, searching long and hard for precisely the detachment and isolation the cottage location had presented me. To further my desire to remain resolutely alone I also remain totally unconnected to either phone or electricity. What little power I required was provided by a small rusting petrol generator, my heat from burning logs and peat on the open fire and on my wood burning stove, and my only light taken from candles. My single remaining connection to the outside world was my rusting pick up truck, used only occasionally to negotiate the unmarked confusion of farm tracks to the nearest town for those supplies I could neither hunt nor grow and gather by my own hand.

The rattle from the windows of my cottage was the result of both age and neglect, the sickly odour of rotting flesh the outcome of my inept endeavours to pickle trapped squirrels for winter storage. It was an unintelligent move to attempt pickling squirrels whilst intoxicated on the cheap whisky I drink plentifully to ease my intense frustration at yet another long disabling episode of writer's block. Earlier that day my slowed, drunken hands had lost their grip while skinning the red squirrel cadaver and the clumsy attempt to catch the slippery corpse had only served to catapult the little body into the dark gorge between cooker and fridge. After that incident I may possibly have passed out for a time on the kitchen floor. I must have slept the afternoon away since it was growing dark when I awoke.

As I now steadied myself on the sill and gazed outward, I concluded that rancid meaty odour had been caused by the heat from the stove affecting the partially skinned animal meat while I had slept. On rousing, the sickly odour of death had become cloying and unmistakable, causing my stomach to lurch terribly and forcing me to drag myself from my drunken sleeping position to open the window.

Dragging the stiff window frame open with a protesting squeal of wood and drawing in a deep lungful of wintry unsullied air, I returned to the kitchen to engage in another arduous assault on the rotting little body, a second and more sober attempt to manoeuvre the small rotting corpse from the chasm.

It was while engaged in this exercise that I suddenly became aware of an eager knocking at the front door. The unexpected clamour startled me and again I dropped the squirrel, which irritated me deeply since I had a first-rate grip on his half skinned leg with the long kitchen tongs. Since it was growing dark and the house is accessible only along a maze of little used snow-covered tracks, any visitor to my isolated home was an enormous surprise to me.

Before I could fully stand upright from my contorted position, the sharp knocking had begun again, even more insistent than before. I announced with an angry shout that I was on my way, and headed along the hall for the door.

An icy blast of air met me as I swung the door open into the growing darkness. As I pushed the door wider I was faced not only with the fierce twilight chill, but with the equally unsettling outline of a dark stooped human figure.

"Good evening, how may I help you?" I asked, swallowing hard against my surprise.

Due to the weather becoming so unsympathetic, and the lateness of the hour, this visitor could not have merely been a chance passer by. I craned my neck and looked behind the dark shape for the presence of a vehicle, but there was nothing to be seen. The visitor was on foot.

As the hooded figure lifted its head I observed that my visitor was a bent, elderly lady whose wrinkled face was scarcely visible in the evening light beneath folds of dark grey material. In her skeletal hand a long thin staff had the unmistakable organic appearance of bone, all flesh long stripped from its gently curved white form, and now tipped with ornate silver ends. Behind her outline, the snow was now falling heavily, the thick covering illuminated by the pale candlelight spilling out through open door and window.

Whatever the purpose of the old lady, she seemed committed to her cause. Her journey to my door was a protracted hike from anything deserving the title of a main road. The nearest property from which she could have started her trek was a number of miles away.

Her head tilted and rose as she spoke from under the hood.

"Are you The Writer?"

The old woman queried of my occupation with a strange emphasis. This wasn't an appeal for a general writer, but for one she was looking for in particular.

"Yes, I am a writer, how can I help you?"

"No, no. Are you *THE* Writer?"

I felt confused; this made no sense to me at all. I worked as a writer, but knew of no motivation that would consent to me making a claim of such a definitive nature. I was unsure if perhaps I needed to know more, to dispute my merit to her emphatic reasoning. I invited her to come inside to rest a moment from the cold evening air outside. She refused, with a slow shake of the head, before an abrupt and immediate repetition of her question.

"Are you *The* Writer?"

The identical question, asked with the same stress of the definitive.

I remained unable to think of just reason not to answer positively or to satisfy this insistent request for confirmation. Since my cottage is in a thinly populated area, it made some logical sense to me, at that instant, that any local knowledge of my work had somehow made me deserving of such definitive identification from the local population. To them I most probably was the only person they knew engaged in the occupation of writing. The emphasis therefore made some sense.

"Yes, I am a writer, *The* Writer if you will."

The wrinkled mouth twisted slightly at the corner in response. In a younger person it may have been a smile, but in this ancient and partially hidden face, there was little else to suggest any emotion. The hooded head remained bowed and the face remained mostly hidden from me in the darkness, but something told me her eyes were staring impassively at my face. I remained confused.

"Please. Come inside, it's a bitter night, you'll freeze. Sit and explain what you require of me. If I can help, then you have my word I will. To paraphrase the old saying, 'I'll try anything once, except incest and Morris dancing'."

My attempts at lightening the mood were met with the same empty silent stare.

I moved aside and held the door open further, to offer the woman entry into to the warmth of the cottage with my hand extended inside.

Suddenly I felt the bony fingers of her hand grip on my arm, pressing like five thin wires against my shirt sleeve.

"No. There is no time to rest. I must insist that you must come now, without delay. It is of the gravest importance."

She moved closer and raised her head fully. Standing nearer to the light in order to retain her firm grip on my arm, the detail of her face became apparent for the first time. And the scar. Previously hidden under the hood's shadow, and now dreadfully visible in the warm glow of the flickering candlelight, my eyes traced the path of the deep, purple line running upwards from close to her thin lips, over and through the long scar where an eye once lay, ending somewhere beneath the white hair scarce seen beneath her hood. I felt a mixture of sadness and of dread at the bizarre sight.

The shock of the scar caused questions to all at once topple from my mouth.

"Where have you come from madam? What is the affair with which you seem to think I may help? What, pray, is so urgent?"

Her thin grip tightened on my arm.

"Please, come now, immediately. I will tell you of the matter as we walk. My house is not too far from here, but we must leave here now."

It was not only the urgency of her voice and the desperate grip of her hand which informed me of the significance of her mission. Something about the set of her face and body betrayed a deep impatient yearning, urging me with her every movement to follow her. It seemed somehow crucial to her that I did, utterly vital that I followed her insistent desire, conveyed to me by a face lined with grave unspoken desperation.

"Ok, ok, I'll just get my jacket and shoes. Please at least come inside while I get ready."

My decision to help seemed to ease the most obvious and extreme signs of her anxiousness, her bony hand releasing me as she stepped back into the snowy night.

"Thank you. I'll wait here."

I was baffled by her resolve to remain outside. It was bitterly cold and the wind gusting off the nearby sea across the open fields was buffeting the cape around the woman's slight shape, the temperature continuing to drop quickly as the day dissolved into to darkness. I wondered what harm a few minutes of warmth would have done our mission.

Then, all at once, I felt a cold chill run the length of my spine as a sudden thought gripped me. What if this very house held some ancient power, or was the base of some local historical curse which she could feel instinctively? Maybe her desperate insistence was due to a desire to save me without scaring me. I swiftly found the most evil visions rampaging through my mind and grew instantly terrified, terrified enough to blurt out the question.

"Am I in danger from some ancient supernatural force?"

She gazed up at me from under her hood, her single eye staring directly at me before leaving my face and darting around at the view through the open door behind me. I followed her gaze nervously, craning my neck, trying to see some indication of a long hidden curse or the sight of onrushing demons. The old face turned towards me with a look of barely concealed repulsion.

"I cannot cross your threshold."

I swallowed hard. "Is there some dark malevolence at work here, in my home madam? Is there some depraved evil stopping you?"

She nodded slowly. My throat grew dry and my stomach sank, as if dropping into the very wells of the earth. I grew almost hysterical.

"Pray tell, old woman, tell me what it is. Am I in danger?"

She shook her head slowly. "Not right at this moment."

I looked around quickly; convinced now I could clearly feel the onset of some evil force rushing silently toward me. "Then tell me! Tell me what it is!" I screamed.

Her eye slid slowly back and forth in its socket, looking around the house again, and then the face leaned towards me to speak. "I think its rotting meat, it's turning my stomach."

I looked at her impassively. Suddenly she extended her tongue, motioned with two long fingers to her mouth and pulled a 'vomiting' face before turning and moving away from the door and off slightly into the darkness, all the while wafting her thin hand under her nose.

I threw on my long tweed walking jacket and fastened it securely against the chill, checking the fire was low enough to leave safely and extinguishing most of the candles before pulling the door closed behind me and joining the old woman outside. As we moved off into the ever-increasing darkness, away from the thin light flickering from the cottage windows, it was not long before I could barely make out even the outline of the old lady moving in front of me. The wind was now driving snow directly into my face and in that stinging assault from the coldness it was hard to keep focus on her shape. She was already moving steadily ahead before me on the dark snow-covered path.

Her bent figure glanced around and beckoned me to follow with a wide sweep of her long white stick and a flap of her cape. I looked downwards to shelter my eyes against the wind and snow, deciding my best method of keeping pace was to follow her footprints. Searching the ground before me in the direction of the slowly moving shape before me, I looked for her foot falls, only to find there were none.

As I closed in and walked directly behind the blurred outline, what I thought I saw, or failed to see on the fresh snow before me, must have been some trick of the quickly failing light or a consequence of her long cloak trailing on the soft ground removing all sign of her footsteps. Then I noticed the long staff propelling her thin outline bent over along against the wind and snow, digging into the ground beside her.

No sooner had the silver covered tip dug in and then emerged from the snow than the small broken hole seemed to close and vanish. I stopped and gazed at the point of contact, trying to make sense of the impossible sight. The snow was falling heavily, but this was an instantaneous reforming of matter, cancelling out all sign of any previous marks. I pressed a hole with the end of my walking stick. It remained perfectly visible.

The old woman must have sensed my hesitancy, halting her onward march and returning to the place where I stood transfixed, staring at the unmarked white surface next to the hole I myself had made. I looked up at her face, now barely visible beneath her hood in the failing twilight. I swear I caught the corners of her mouth twist as she began smiling slightly as she caught my gaze.

"I shall explain later. Hurry, we have little time."

She turned on her heel and again set off again into the darkness. I looked down at the spot. No marks.

I debated then whether to continue following this mysterious old woman who left no marks behind. I contemplated turning on my heels and heading straight home, locking the door forever against this strangeness, but I could find neither the resolve nor the character. Now, gentlemen, hearing this tale as policemen, you may well question what drew me to continue into the snowy night, carrying onward without either rational explanation or reason.

As a writer, my curiosity is easily engaged and I was now profoundly intrigued by the whole mystery and the sheer spontaneous excitement of what was happening. I felt some fear, of course, but that too was over-ridden by my selfish delight at being at the centre of a real life mysterious adventure and my adopting the role of some potential hero, a fundamental figure in helping minister to the insistent needs of the elderly lady who had gone to so much trouble to seek out my talents.

So, while I fully realised I was being drawn into a mystery, my head was spinning with fresh ideas and potential material, and I chose readily to go on, confident that this strange occurrence would remain significant. Also, for the first time in years, I felt wanted and needed. I felt useful to someone. That feeling was perhaps the most selfish, but also the most persuasive. Anyways, what possible danger, I reasoned logically, could such a fragile old lady pose to me, a grown man?

Given the events that followed, a day never passes where I don't question that judgment. But right there, being implored onward in the snow, I felt it was right to continue my own personal adventure, an event presenting itself as if an answer to my prayers at my lowest point as a writer. I felt both noble and impulsive, filled with ideas streaming into my brain at the excitement of coming to the rescue in an unspoken emergency. Any small doubts I had, I quickly shuffled to the back of my mind and gladly stepped forward once more, to follow the shape in front of me.

I pushed on and gradually caught up with the steadily moving outline of the woman. Presently, as I drew alongside her, my footsteps crumpling below as I paced onwards on the fresh snow, she abruptly pulled away, moving suddenly and without warning, off of what I knew to be the path of the track. Before I could shout a warning, her hand again swung high in the air holding her stick, the thin arm winged by the shape of her cape like that of a bat.

She was heading overland now, toward the ominous dark trees of the huge forest that lay to the left of the track, black oppressive shapes that disappeared into darkness far into the distance. Was this some hidden path? Some local trail I had missed on my regular and far-reaching walks along this very same landscape? I had covered every inch of this land regularly over the years, how could I have missed any such paths and trails?

Once we reached the margin of the trees it became evident that any opening the old lady was attempting to use was to me totally invisible, even here on foot and with the closest of examination a few short yards away from the forest. As we passed through the thick branches of the first line of trees at the forest edge, there appeared little more than a small gap leading to a dead end. On stepping through this latest barrier of branches, and taking a few further steps and numerous sudden turns, we reached another unseen opening.

After entering this latest gap, I was soon through those first few trees and onto a wide clear path. This trail appeared barely used but clearly one that had been created and not accidental. As we walked on, the path almost immediately grew wide enough for two people to walk abreast, gradually opening out yet further into an impressive high corridor, roofed by the arched interlocked branches of the thick pines high above and giving the eerie sense of being somehow indoors in some vast vaulted hall. The ground beneath was suddenly dry and free from snow, now a soft fragrant carpet of pine needles. There was now not even the briefest breeze of wind and the temperature had noticeably warmed. Even with the obvious shelter from above, this was such a sudden state of affairs that I not only found startling, but which immediately helped speed our progress onwards, now rushing forward ever deeper into the black heart of the forest.

I also began to notice that some other outlandish phenomenon was improving the quality of the light. Although we had walked silently for quite a time on a steadily darkening winter evening, a soft illumination around us had steadily improved. The further we moved onward, the more clearly I could now see the hooded figure walking ahead of me, moving steadily along our route.

I looked up towards the sky, thinking perhaps the snow had suddenly cleared or expecting the presence of a bright winter moon, but I saw nothing but the same thick arched roof of branches knotted and interwoven high above us. Yet there remained a slight glow around the entire place, subtle and calming. I wanted to ask the old woman what it was, but she drove on in front of me so intently that I had decided to leave the enquiry for when we halted, wherever that may be.

I had already tried attempting dialogue, repeatedly directing breathy enquiries to the old lady as we marched. I asked recurring questions of our destination and made frequent requests for any clues as to the nature of our emergency, trying to extract any sense of purpose for our adventure as we journeyed onward. Each question was answered with either a slight shake of the head or a hissed 'later'. The old woman seemed consumed by an intense concentration, pulling us both forward over the sweet smelling pine needles towards our goal. I was judging whether to attempt further enquiries when her shadowy figure halted and hunched over on the path.

I stopped immediately and watched in shock as the dark silhouette threw her arms wide and began to emit a low throaty groan.

Raising her staff and lightly rubbing the silver end against her chest, she began to emit a long deep moaning sound. The surrounding trees started rustling ominously and I again began to feel a primal fear rising within. As suddenly as she had begun, she stopped, lowering the staff from her chest. I awaited the next part of the ritual. She turned toward me, her face contorted into a harsh grimace, and began nodding slowly before she shared with me the knowledge of what was happening.

"Heartburn. Big lunch."

Then she turned and set off, once more propelling herself quickly along the path in front of me, aided by her staff. We had walked on a short distance when, quite without warning, the old woman executed a sudden change of route and turned away from what seemed to be the more obvious curving path heading away from us into the thick trees. Rushing forward to stay close, I kept to her path as she turned and twisted toward and then through another seemingly random curtain of thick trees. Concentrating hard at not losing her I twisted and turned behind her only to be surprised when I found myself suddenly outside the protection of the thick forest and again buffeted by the wind.

Still following the dark shape, this time down a well worn path on a small grassy incline, away from the trees and toward what appeared in the near dark to be some huge black abyss. I felt the unmistakable salt breeze of sea on my face, my body stiffening as I suddenly sensed from the deep noise of distant crashing far below that we were now in a most high, precarious place.

I had never been through the forest before, but had explored around the furthest edges of that sinister area of trees during long summer walks. I recalled the edges of the forest came to a sudden halt at the ragged edge of colossal sea cliffs. Realising where I must be, I stopped suddenly dead in my tracks. We were now standing almost at the very edge of that most spectacular and lethal drop. I would have been terrified to be anywhere near those cliffs in the calm summer light of a still day. In the strong wind and black darkness of a wild winter's night, I was frozen to the spot.

The old woman stopped some distance ahead of me, sensing my fear and calling me onwards with a flick of her white stick. Then I noticed something else. Out of the trees and on open featureless ground, the dim glow of light from the forest had gone. Looking upward I could see now only the darkness of the night sky, the moon momentarily appearing between grey clouds scudding quickly across the black. I composed myself and walked carefully onwards, glad the occasional pale moonlight made visible the outline of the woman ahead, allowing me to follow her course.

We carried on in silence for another short period before she stopped suddenly and spun around to face me.

"Heartburn again?" I asked.

She shook her head slowly. "This final part of the journey holds much danger. Please stay close to me and be very careful."

I was observant of the word 'danger', especially used with reference to any activity I was undertaking in darkness, near high cliffs, on a windy night. I made a heavily underlined mental note to stay close and to obey all forthcoming instructions to the letter.

Before I had time to voice my intention, the old woman's dark shape had stepped forward again, but on seeing her move steadily nearer to the deep darkness of what I assumed now was the cliff edge, I now stubbornly refused to follow any further. A short distance ahead, she halted again and motioned back at me to continue, but this time I shook my head and remained resolutely where I was, motionless and utterly gripped by fear. The old woman returned to my position, her expression that of someone ready to bark another set of instructions to hurry me along. However on seeing my obviously terrorised face, her own look softened.

"I understand that you are afraid. You know something of where you are and this troubles you greatly. You are also worried about the task that awaits you ahead. I have no time to explain here, but I promise I shall soon, once we are safe and again indoors. There is danger ahead, but if you stay close to me and follow behind, all shall be well. Of that I give you my word. This is but a short trial. I cannot force you to follow but I promise this to you. Once you find the courage to trust me, hear those tales I will share with you, and witness those sights I shall show you, for as long as you live after this day you shall never again be short of subjects to write about. On that I give you my most solemn and loyal vow. Please, I beg, follow closely; I give you my word I will not allow you to come to any harm, for as long as I am alive."

Again I saw in her face the utter desperation of her task, but it was now joined for the first time by a sudden gentleness and a deep honesty which even here, on this most dangerous spot, made me somehow unquestioningly trust her. I was of course fascinated too at the promise of this final reward, this sworn vow of never again suffering the continual hideous desperation of being unable to muster either plot or story. What could she mean?

Did she somehow know of the utter frustration of a barren imagination? Was she using this as some trick or blackmail to somehow provoke me onward into danger?

Yet even still, with uncertainty all around I could not resist such grand promises; I had to finish my task, whatever it turned out to be. I trusted her vow to keep me safe and now my curiosity would not allow me to turn back. I also realised that I had no idea where to go even if I wanted to find escape. Ten steps in the wrong direction were sure to kill me. I had little choice. I undertook to complete the remainder of the journey. I nodded my decision to her and followed slowly as she again turned and led me on.

It was not long before I saw the danger to which she had referred.

At the bottom of the gradually descending path we were on, the conditions underfoot changed suddenly from soft grass to solid but uneven rock, the hard surface sloping slightly away from me towards a darkness as complete as I had ever sensed. There was no snow lying here thankfully, but the rock was wet underfoot.

Again I heard the sound of the sea below, now closer, unseen titanic waves thundering and breaking on broken jagged toothed rocks far below me. I knew now we were at the very edge of the sheer vast drop of the cliffs. I had witnessed their height from both land and sea, and knew well of their reputation for claiming lives. Locals referred to the sheer black rock only as the 'Cliffs of Death'.

The old woman kept moving along the very edge of the sudden endless darkness, casually swinging her stick at the sturdy bushes growing from the cracks in the flat grey rock, nature surviving somehow in the fierce sea winds whipping up and across the cliff edge. The crashing sea below was growing ever louder and ever more brutal, far beneath and out of sight but yet I was sensing it closer with every step. I was terror-stricken now, retaining some thin strand of comfort from the steadily moving shape of the old woman in front, knowing that she would be the first to encounter any danger. I would be safe if I kept concentrated, kept carefully watching her path and following her every step closely. I moved a little further forward and drew a little closer to her dark outline.

Then, without a sound, the old woman vanished right before me, dropping away suddenly and without a sound over the black void of the cliff edge..."

## CHAPTER 2

## Journey to the Hut

I stopped dead in my tracks and fell to my knees, frozen to the spot by utter terror. The old woman had vanished, dropping into the black abyss to a certain death. I shouted hysterically after her, petrified, afraid to move in case I followed her over the edge myself.

Then, between the crashing noise of the waves below and the roar of the buffeting wind, I heard the faint sound of a chilling laugh floating toward me over the rocks. At first I supposed it was a trick of the wind, the night air whistling as it was forced through the sharp rocks on the cliff edge. I listened intently and heard it again, louder and more frenzied.

Then suddenly, a voice. "Will you please hurry?"

I bellowed into the wind, my eyes darting around while shouting enquiries as to where she was and whether she had fallen and lay trapped, hanging somewhere close below me and gripping tightly on some ledge with her thin fingers in some life and death struggle to remain alive. If I could only find where she lay trapped, I might somehow be able to help. The only answer to my frenzied requests was the sound of more hysterical laughter. Then, from out the twilight before me, the sight of the white bony walking stick, waved in the air a few feet closer to the jagged edge of the cliff, the moonlight glinting off the silver tip. I crawled slowly forward toward the spot, each movement careful, slow and measured.

As I drew closer, a bony arm became visible from the edge, thin fingers curled and imploring me nearer. I reached and locked my hand with the thin fingers and to my surprise and terror found them not waiting to be pulled upward to safety, but gripping mine and pulling me forward, closer to the abyss. When I reached what I knew was the edge, I narrowed my eyes against the spray driven upward by the wind gusting through the chasm, salt water forced upward onto my face from the crashing waves far below.

The hand was pulling me closer to the edge, then, suddenly, over the edge.

My heart nearly stopped as with closed eyes I was pulled over the ridge of rock into the darkness. But as my foot moved downward from the lip of the rocks above, instead of spiralling into the black nothingness of a last final drop, it jarred onto firm ground, thumping onto solid flat stone.

Confident I wasn't falling downward, I opened my eyes a fraction. Below me was the old woman, standing silent and slowly shaking her head at my caution and expressions of confusion.

When I dared to fully open my eyes I discovered to my amazement that I was now standing on the flat top platform of a long row of descending steps, hewn and carved into the side of the cliff. I could feel the solid stone under my feet, worn into a slight curve from years of footfalls like my own, but otherwise level and flat. And safe.

This was an impossible place to stumble upon had you not known it existed right here, hidden as it was, directly below the overhanging edge of the cliff. No visible marker betrayed the existence of this place from the rock above. I could sense the sea far below was now only on one side and I instinctively pushed myself in the opposite direction, searching for the safety of a solid object. Once my hand felt the cold surface of a jagged wall of rock, I moved across and hugged myself against the cliff face. The old woman pulled my hand gently forward from the step below, and I searched ahead with my foot in the darkness, my body still pressed against the safety of the stone. For the first time I risked looking away from the rock next to my face and looked downwards.

Stretching out below was the next in a series of stone steps, curving away from us then disappearing into a thin swirling sea mist. The old woman, confident I had calmed down and would remain steady on my feet, released my hand and set off downwards in front of me. Petrified, I may be, but I had no choice but to follow.

We continued our slow descent, the mist occasionally clearing just enough to reveal additional steps leading further down the cliff into the darkness. I continued deliberately but cautiously, each foot making sure it was firmly supported by solid stone before I risked my full weight and went edging onwards.

I descended slowly and deliberately in this fashion for a number of anxious minutes, constantly aware of the black emptiness of the drop to my side. Then the steps changed direction slightly, following the contours of the cliff to which I was still hugging my body. As I followed the curve round, the noise of the sea began to grow fainter and my own steps began to echo; the thin moonlight that gathered and faded around us now dissolved totally into complete darkness. From the change in sound I knew we had passed into an enclosed tunnel in the rock of the cliff wall. I carefully reached out my hand and felt uneven damp rock on my other side, where previously there had been a long drop to certain death. I relaxed slightly in the safety of the enclosed space and continued walking downwards, more confident now in trusting my steps and feeling the spacing of the even stone platforms under my feet. As I found my rhythm I marginally accelerated my descent.

After a few more minutes of downward progress through the echoing dampness, I noticed an arch of faint light ahead. Drawing closer, I could make out the familiar outline of the figure silhouetted against the opening, pacing impatiently to and fro, waiting for me to reach her. I imagined it was still night but again an unexplained glow of something other than moonlight was growing as I neared the opening, more visible now in the sudden contrast to the tunnel blackness. I stepped out through the opening, onto an expanse of open flat ground. It was soft, and grassy, and I dropped to my knees and thanked God for my continued existence. I felt the old bony hand grasp mine and slowly pull me upward and back to my feet. It was then I looked up fully for the first time and gasped at the sight before me.

I stood inside what looked like an immense natural chasm, a vast flat floor covered by grass but yet somehow enclosed inside the rock. Surrounding me on all sides were huge faces of stone, stretching high above me and curving into a large chamber sheltering almost the whole space. For a moment I thought I was in a dark cave, but in the distance, on one side, I noticed what looked like a rough arch leading to what appeared to be the start of some sort of passageway or tunnel. Through that opening came the same ghostly light as in the forest, not cold and blue like the moonlight but a warmer glow, just enough to illuminate the scene and allow examination of the spectacular ragged walls of this strange but beautiful space.

I looked upwards again at the curved banks of stone arching high above me. They almost enclosed the place entirely, but far above there was another long open section, revealing a thin line of moonlit cloud tumbling past to uncover some stars of the night sky. As my eyes adjusted I saw a final dark opening far ahead, a massive ragged hole in the rock looking out to the darkness where I presumed the sea must lie far below.

Yet it was the glowing light from the passageway which had allowed me to make out the dim shape of some building in the distance, some way off along the flat grass floor of this cathedral of rock. The building looked quite large and from this distance appeared windowless. It appeared to be a tight and skilful arrangement of piled stones, with odd angles of small sticks jutting from gaps between larger stones in the walls. My guide was already moving in the direction the building on a well worn path across the grass. I joined the trail and followed.

Only when nearing the structure did I realise the random building was actually a roofed cottage home, not dissimilar in size to my own. Moving onward, it was with steadily mounting horror that I realised what I had initially mistaken for the branches and curved stones of the walls were in fact bones and skulls. The house itself had once been alive.

The old woman stopped at the door of the cottage as I walked, evermore slowly towards her, my gaze transfixed by the sight of the thousands of bones piled and interlocked into thick solid walls. Although disturbed by the sight, I was increasingly aware of my exhaustion and my desperate craving for warmth and an opportunity to relax after the night's high tension. I held an exhausted silence, keeping any enquiries for later. It was hard to gauge exactly just how long we had been walking, but as the adrenaline rush ebbed away, I felt too deeply fatigued to fully engage my curiosity. Yet I still had a huge number of questions tumbling through my head and forcing themselves to the front of my mind. Tired or not, I had many things I was desperate to ask. I was about to start when she raised her thin hand in front of my face, anticipating my queries.

"Please, ask me nothing now. All shall become clear. Before I allow you to cross the threshold and enter the cottage, I must ask that you give your word that whatever might occur within these walls, you will swear a solemn oath to never speak of it again to another soul, under any circumstances. Of that I must insist."

What strange situation was I becoming involved in, growing even more confused as each fresh new aspect of this mystery unfolded before me? Too exhausted now to ponder the matter further, I nodded agreement. In those moments I admit I was tempted more by the greater promise of warmth and somewhere to lie down than possible consequences relating to any weak threats issued by some frail old woman about secrecy and repercussion.

She took my hand in hers and squeezed it tightly until I felt every sinew of her thin bony fingers between mine, reading to me the oath of secrecy I was to repeat, this time slower and with more deliberation, as if making sure I understood the gravity of the situation. I nodded agreement and she shook her head.

"You must swear by your kin and everything that you hold dear that you agree to an eternal silence of what is spoken of inside the walls of this building. Only then can we begin. Do you agree? If you do, I need you to repeat the oath, to bind you eternally to your word. Should you ever break this vow, you, and whoever you inform, shall remain cursed and destined to remain held by this place forever. Do you understand?"

I nodded.

We joined hands and repeated some superstitious Latin oath together at the cottage door, the exact words or meaning of which I cannot directly recall. I remember that after finishing this first oath I had to swear another, to promise to obey my solemn bond to uphold such secrecy on pain of this curse, binding both me and anyone whomsoever I should pass the information on to. I am no believer in such superstitious mumbo jumbo of myth and mysticism, but I was happy to humour the old lady, increasingly anxious to get inside out of the cold night.

"And so it shall be. You have sworn."

We nodded final agreement and then, suddenly, she stepped back, away from the door into the moonlight falling onto the grassy surface and proceeded to break the still night air with a thunderous belch, her head rising towards the sky as she did so like a howling wolf. The deep blast echoed around the huge rock chamber.

Her face creased in confusion and surprise when I stepped forward and repeated the action, straining until my face began to colour and my eyes glaze as I squeezed out a thin wet burble of a burp. The old woman looked confused.

"I was just releasing some wind. That wasn't part of the oath."

"Oh."

She shook her head slowly with a disappointed look as she moved past me and opened the door to the cottage. A warm light bathed us both as I followed her inside.

Squinting at the sudden brightness of light inside the building, my mouth fell open as I looked around. The interior of the cottage was a revelation. The stark outer walls of bone hid a warm and welcoming interior packed with many ornate delights.

The building was both well lit and heated by a huge open fire at one end of the room, flames twisting and dancing with a delightful earthy aroma, the bare stone floor of the long room filled with the comforting heat and shimmering orange light. Strewn over floors and chairs were various fluffy animal skins, with further pelts strewn around on furniture. At the far end of the room, just past an ancient blackened stone stove, the walls were lined with dark wooden shelves, packed from floor to ceiling with books and curious objects and enclosing three sides of a sturdy wooden table. The space smelt homely and welcoming and I felt immediately at ease in the house, my body relaxing as the warmth from the fire began to creep slowly into me.

The old woman walked unhurriedly across the room towards the table, halting only to remove her hooded cloak and hang it on a hooked claw attached to the wall that looked like it came from some ancient mythical creature. She pulled a heavy wooden chair from under the table, sat, and motioned across at me to join her. I walked slowly toward the table, all the while running my curious gaze across the rich collection of strange and fascinating objects scattered around the room.

There were bizarre stuffed animals and unidentifiable fish in glass display cases, lumps of sparkling minerals that appeared to glow, small curious mechanical objects and devices which appeared to be from another world, shining pieces of strange metal weapons, and, as I drew closer, I noticed the hundreds upon hundreds of thin leather bound books carefully filed around the whole span of the shelves which surrounded the table on three sides. I was utterly fascinated. I wandered across and cautiously drew one of the slender volumes from the shelves, noticing the embossed title on the narrow spine. It read "Thatticus Wheen 1869 - 1957". I held it up in the direction of the seated lady.

"Is this a novel? I've never heard of it, who wrote it?"

"I wrote that book. I wrote all of the books you see before you. Thatticus Wheen himself supplied the content for that volume, but I wrote the words. Although that one, admittedly, was a simple task, for he was but a simple man."

I turned and looked at the old lady, amazed. She had given no indication that she herself was a writer, let alone one so prolific. I opened it and marvelled at the handwritten pages, interspersed throughout with beautiful and haunting illustrations.

"But there must be over two thousand books here. You mean to tell me you wrote and illustrated them all?"

"Two thousand, four hundred and sixty three, were you curious enough to count. And yes, I created them all. It's my job."

"Your job? Are you a novelist?"

The old woman laughed.

"No. Well maybe, of sorts, but these books are all fact, not fiction. Consider me more a bookkeeper."

I thought I understood.

"Biographies?"

"Of sorts. These are the death books. They contain the stories, memories and events of generations now gone. When the time comes near, I visit the person, hear their story, and then write their book, so that the person may pass, knowing he may live on into eternity, his deeds and actions remembered forever. What you see before you on these shelves are the many stories of these people."

"But how....." I faltered, confused.

"I am called when I feel death is nearby. I bear witness to the stories of lives almost at an end and then place their testimony in the books. Then the person may pass in peace from the village with their lives recorded forever. It's simple enough."

"The village? What village? There's no village within 30 miles of here? Where are all these people from? And how, where, around these parts did you manage to get these bound so well?"

I ran my fingers again over the soft leather and close, neat stitching of the spines.

"I've never seen bindings so soft and beautiful. They are exquisite examples of the craft."

"Oh, that's easily enough done. I do them myself."

I was amazed at her craftsmanship. She smiled back and continued.

"Anyway, all the volumes are bound in the owner's skin."

I immediately dropped the book to the floor, my hand recoiling from the soft human leather of the cover.

"Well," said the old lady, "they are, after all, the death books, of the dead. What else would you suggest that was more appropriate?"

I steadied myself at the table edge and looked aghast at the elderly smiling face watching me. Even with the scar, she now seemed so quiet and innocent bathed in the glow from the fire. I felt the questions rising inside me again and a cold chill embrace me at a single thought, creeping to the front of my mind.

"My god, is that what am I doing here? Is it time for my death book? Am I to die?"

She smiled and shook her head slowly.

"No, you are safely alive and shall remain so. I hear no calling for you. Yet you are correct that it has now come time for another book to be written. Mine own."

I moved backwards unsteadily, the back of the chair hitting me behind the knees and causing me to fall gently backwards into it without protest as I listened.

"I was born The Writer for the village, so the task falls on me to choose who I wish to write my book. By the ancient traditions I am not permitted to write my own. I remain now the last in a long line and so, as is written, I have chosen you. And now so you must write and bear witness. I am weary and almost at my end. I require you to finish these final few books as I myself am too weak and of failing eyesight now to complete them all. And then, once this is done, to write the final one, of me."

"What? But how? Have I inherited some job? You don't mean I have somehow become the one that writes all these things, do you?"

She smiled warmly at the humour of my suggestion.

"No, you can relax. Just these few unfinished volumes, and then my own. My powers are weakening now, but the runes dictate that my successor will not arrive until after I have died. Since I am still alive then these final few are the only such books you shall be required to write. Once this duty is finished your work for me is done. This is my final responsibility as the death book keeper. You are only helping me fulfil my final task. Then it is over for us both. Strathcarnage must find itself a new keeper of the books."

At the mention of the word Strathcarnage I started violently, only to find the old woman's single eye staring at me intently across the table in the candlelight. I recall laughing at her. It was an uncertain, faltering laugh, a mixture or nervousness and fear. It seemed to anger her. Her brow furrowed into a deep scowl, the skin around her scar puckering. I began to grow irritated at this deceit, evidently the victim of some intricate practical joke.

"Strathcarnage doesn't exist. It has never existed. It's some atrocious and horrible ancient myth. There is no such place, never has been. It's an ancient folk legend designed to fill slow, gullible superstitious Highland folks with fear. What is this deceit?"

The old lady kept staring angrily, then suddenly her face softened and she smiled.

"I see you doubt. You think I am just a mad old lady? Sitting here lonely and spending my time making up tales of a place you believe is but a myth and has never existed, except in fabricated old stories? But look around you, look at the books, each one the life and recollections of a resident of the ancient village of Strathcarnage. I can assure you that I am not mad, merely feeble and running out of time. I need you to record these tales, so you may bear witness to my own life as a resident of the village. Doubt me not."

I stared at the old face, waiting for some sign to break over the features, or some change of expression to tell me I was being teased or tested with a joke. The face remained smiling and then grew again deadly serious.

"Please, come with me, for I see you still doubt."

The old lady rose from the table and moved slowly towards the door.

"Come, I have something I must show you to convince you completely of my honesty before we can begin."

Opening the door and beckoning me to follow behind her with a wave of her thin hand, we moved again outside the cottage and into the stone cavern. The light in the cavern was beginning to change slowly into daylight, illuminating the walls of the massive chasm where the cottage of bone lay. The old woman walked slowly across the space towards the small opening from where the glowing light was still visible, the light I had witnessed on first entering this space by the long stairs.

I followed behind closely and, drawing closer to the aperture, I followed the old woman inside. As I walked along the carved passageway the warm glowing light illuminated the rough arched walls, light and shadow showing the tool marks and hammer blows that had dug this tunnel out the rock face of the cliff. I followed, wordlessly, for around five minutes, walking at a steady pace, footsteps echoing on the rock as I found the need to dip my head occasionally as the tunnel twisted and wound untidily along a rock seam.

Then we were out of the tunnel and into a smaller cave with numerous dark doorways to other passages leading off on invisible journeys. These did not however grab my attention, since this small rectangular cave had only three sides. One side was missing, and that was where the glow was coming from.

She moved towards the opening, passed through and stopped, turning silently with her arms extended and a broad smile, obviously an invitation to join her and share the view. As I walked forward and got close to the door I was able to peer outward at some flat stone platform extending away from the old woman. I joined her on the flat slab of rock. As my eyes followed her gaze I witnessed a wondrous but chilling sight that filled me with the deepest, most profound, horror I have ever experienced; an unfathomable terror I shall never again be able to fully describe to another living soul as long as I live.

Far below my position, inside the towering cliffs of what appeared to be a massive cave, there appeared far below the haunting sight of thousands of flickering distant lights and the outlines of hundreds of tightly packed buildings. Strange dark angular shapes and thin twisting streets appeared to me at that moment, mere outlines in a retreating mist. Above the collection of buildings, the granite of the cliff pushed upward and inward, hanging curved over the entire apparition, hiding the entire view totally from anyone except us in this spot. The mass of buildings below were piled raggedly around the edges across the entire floor of the gigantic cavern, an untidy mess in the glowing half light. I watched the lights shimmering in the distance and now knew the source of the glow I had witnessed earlier.

I needed ask no questions, for I knew what exactly what I was looking at.

I was looking down upon the town of Strathcarnage.

I looked at the old woman, utterly incredulous at the sight far below. She simply smiled and began to walk back through the doorway into the tunnel that led back towards the house.

"Come," she called out as the sound echoed on the rock around me, "we have much to record."

Over the next thirteen days and nights I sat inside that cottage, writing down every word unquestioningly, transcribing them energetically like a dutiful schoolchild. I never left my position, except at night, when I left the cottage of bone to walk through that glowing tunnel and sit on that flat platform of rock to stare silently down upon that mythical sight far below.

These tales I was faithfully copying were fantastical and horrible stories of events and lives from the mythical place below, never once deviating from the strange and bizarre. Such tales were recounted to me hour after hour by the frail old woman, as if she were overtaken by some sort of trance, her increasingly failing voice slowly and deliberately unfolding to me these stories of individual residents of Strathcarnage far below.

Tales that I wish to pass on to you all.

Please listen carefully and write down all I shall now tell, just as they were told to me, for these statements you shall write shall remain a final record of the bizarre testaments of some of those who live in the very much real and very much alive village of Strathcarnage."

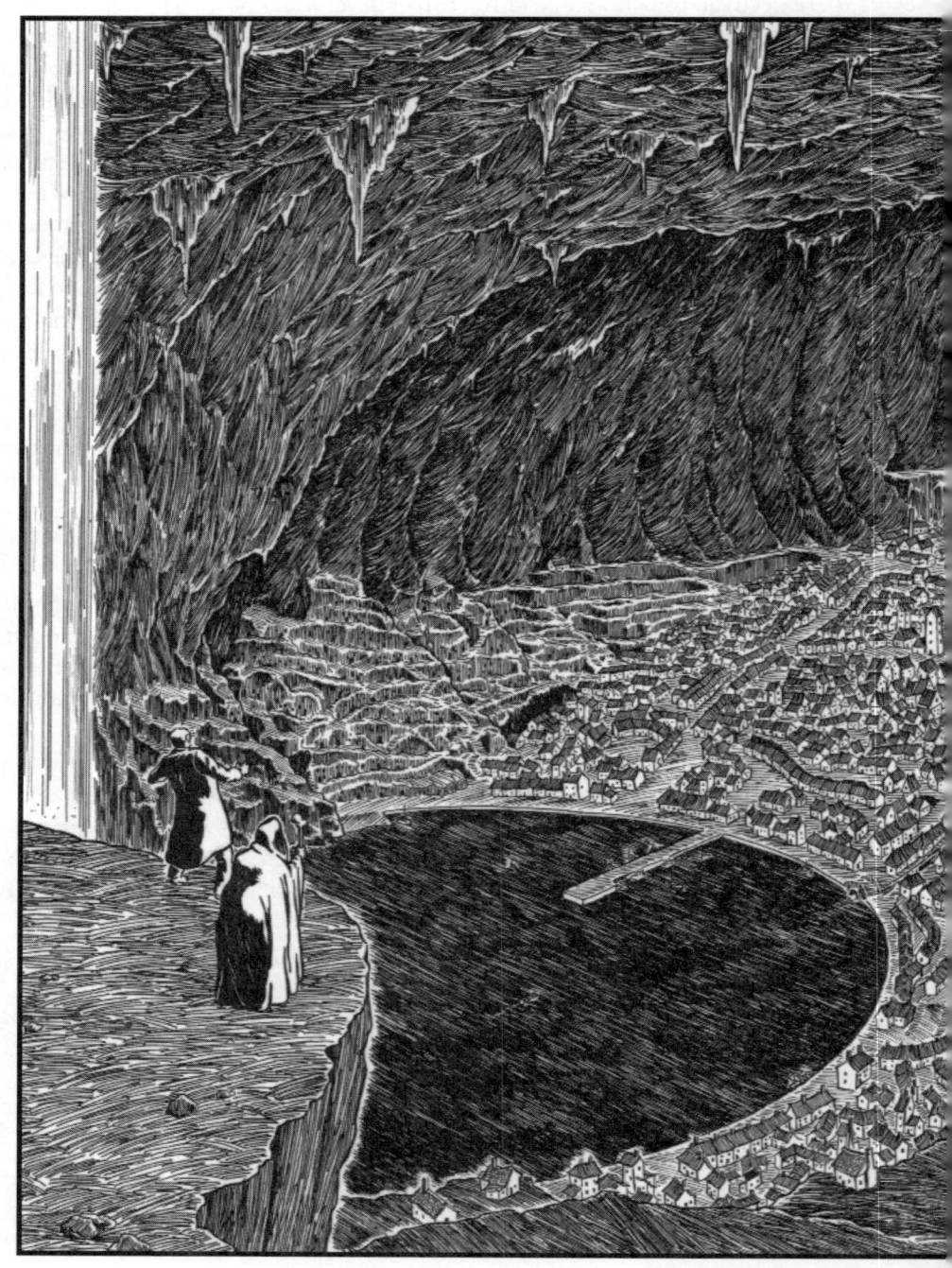

# CHAPTER 3

## Day One – Roman Holiday

Lord Strathcarnage eased himself back against the cold granite wall of his penthouse balcony and sucked on his fat Cuban cigar, the amber glow illuminating his thick moustache in the darkness. The black silhouette of the hotel rose behind him, the building clinging almost impossibly to the face of one of the steep olive green hills overlooking Rome. Strathcarnage exhaled, a steady elongated stream of grey smoke floating away into the night air as he stood gazing out across the striking view of the city before him. The renaissance dome of St Peters Basilica stood illuminated in the distance, standing like a beacon above the distant lights of the Eternal City, shimmering and glistening in the summer heat like a poorly fitted glass eye caught in the candles of an orphan's birthday cake. The epic spectacle of the Italian capital always brought a smile to his face.

With a sudden movement Lord Strathcarnage transformed his expression and shifted position, drawing his foot upwards to rest on the raised decorative granite of the balcony. With a slight grunt of effort, the portly man unleashed a roaring, ear splitting fart which broke the still Roman night and echoed round the surrounding hill like a rifle shot.

"Excellent sir," called Kwok, the Lord's personal butler, registering his approval from inside the main suite, together with an exaggerated round of applause, the clapping floating from the open doors out across the stone balcony. The soft light from the suite interior spilled through the entrance onto the stone, throwing long fingers of light over the scene as the Lord returned his bulk upright.

Strathcarnage smiled and nodded slowly to himself, quietly pleased with both his volume and pitch. As the smell began issuing around him in an invisible putrid cloud he realised he had produced, as he had heard such matters described in the lower classes, a veritable 'blocked sewer' of an aroma. He resisted his sudden urge to enter the suite and pull Kwok outdoors to record a score for the noxious fumes. There would be, he knew from experience, plenty more where that came from. Anyway, holding his manservant's head in the putrid aftermath of his expulsions was a birthright best kept for indoors, since the light Italian breeze had made the speed required to ensure accurate recording and marking far too much effort for the huge man to entertain.

Strathcarnage was proud of his accomplished capacity for breaking wind at immense volume and intensity, generally in the perfectly reproduced key of E Major. The Lord had trained himself over a number of years to master the accurate set of his buttocks, tensing his muscles in just the particular position to replicate the note as Kwok remained stationed dutifully behind sounding a tuning fork as the nobleman braced himself and forced out repeated explosions of soiled air.

As Strathcarnage inhaled deeply, he cupped the warm spoiled evening air towards his nose with the broad paddles of his hands. Closing his eyes and smiling in deep satisfaction at the unexpected potency of the lingering odour, he reminisced over the tumultuous standing ovation he had received on attending breakfast in the oak panelled dining room of Hong Kong's finest hotel a number of years earlier.

That spontaneous show of reverence from the assembled diners had been earned by a particularly strident ear-splitting anal outburst during the stillness of the previous night's stay. The sheer ferocity of that legendary event was of a volume he had yet to surpass, the thunderous eruption waking the entire East wing of the hotel and causing a minor nervous collapse of the hotel owner's pet King Charles spaniel, Rusty.

Nonetheless Strathcarnage knew he was unable to stand amongst the heady mix of self produced methane and cigar smoke all evening. He was in Rome on a mission and had no time to luxuriate in these sights and farmyard smells of the countryside. He had to prepare. Lord Strathcarnage drew himself upright, took a final long hit from his cigar and nonchalantly flicked the lit remnant over the balcony.

The sound of an isolated scream drifted upwards from the darkness far below, as Strathcarnage spun on his hand-sewn Spanish brogues and moved towards the lit doors, his fat lips still set in a broad smile of satisfaction. As the heavily built aristocrat lumbered slowly toward the welcoming light of the suite, his manservant Kwok stood in silhouette at the open door waiting for his master, grinning inanely, before bowing low.

Kwok worked devotedly in his role as the poorly valued manservant of the Strathcarnage dynasty. Indeed the loyal oriental had been serving the family in some capacity his entire life, ever since his birth within the family seat of Haversack Hall a couple of decades before.

Kwok's mother had been a proud, leather faced Chinese woman, won outright by Lord Strathcarnage's father during a ferocious hand of bridge many years previously. The Chinese woman had mysteriously fallen pregnant after a short period employed in the Hall kitchens, and, as such events follow an unavoidable biological path, had given birth a number of months later.

It had been the manner of the birth which was unusual enough to be worthy of mention, producing the offspring as she did suddenly on the gravel driveway of the Hall whilst delivering the opening courses for a lavish anniversary dinner. Those dinner guests present on the fateful evening had been impressed by the woman's stamina as she continued to serve on impassively throughout the evening, the gravel encrusted newborn skittering around on the polished wooden floor behind as she continued to deliver and serve course after course.

Whispered rumours that Kwok was the result of an illicit backstairs liaison between the Chinese kitchen maid and Lord Strathcarnage abounded, and many in the nearby village supposed that the slim oriental manservant's unshakable and almost suicidal devotion to his master lay firmly rooted in a son's simple loyalty to his father.

However those present at the meal in Haversack Hall that fateful evening of Kwok's birth had noted no hint of reaction from the Lord as the newborn child scraped around the floor scattering thin trails of gravel to every corner of the dining room. Indeed, those in attendance noted Lord Strathcarnage had been as indifferent to the affair as to order the woman back to the downstairs kitchen to bring the gathering a second tureen of steaming badger broth in the flickering candlelight. The host had failed completely to acknowledge the new addition to the gathering, the child rotating now on a cord between the bowed legs of the oriental woman staggering around the vast room beneath the roasting hot burden of the colossal carved silver tureen.

As it was, the introduction of the young Kwok to the numerous idiosyncrasies of Haversack Hall was to prove good experience for a hard career in service to the Strathcarnage family. As Kwok had created a furrowed trench across the gravel driveway as he was repeatedly dragged en route from the kitchen block to the dining hall, his mother had continued delivering the remaining courses of a full five course evening meal, with wine. Only once the service was complete, plates cleared and brandy and cigars served in the study, did the proud Chinese politely request to be excused from the room to finally cut the cord.

Lord Strathcarnage must have grown alert to the situation by this stage, since he gave a distracted wave of consent with his fat cigar, burning a hole in the dress of the nearby harbourmaster's wife. The Lord had added abruptly as an afterthought that the undertaking was to be completed without bringing into play any of the family silver carving cutlery.

The unfortunate Kwok also had a brother, Kwai, born later in a more traditional manner amongst the horse dung covered floor of the Hall's stables. Kwai often worked alongside his brother, the pair sharing the often hazardous duty of attending Lord Strathcarnage. Yet Kwai was fated to miss this Roman business trip owing to an unfortunate accident when the Lord, whilst drunk, reversed his carriage over Kwai at speed , driving the vehicle backwards straight over the oriental servant crouched behind securing luggage for the trip onto the lower racks.

Kwok had known better than to interrupt the day's schedule with offhand enquiries concerning his brother's wellbeing, but was delighted to have discovered his sibling had not been mortally wounded in the incident. As the coach had swung round and departed, Kwok glanced back to examine Kwai's outline pressed flat into the driveway, risking a thin smile of relief as he observed the twisted hand lift from its embedded position in the bloodied gravel and offer a limp wave in the general direction of his brother. The coach continued onward without a pause, out through the grand iron gates and down the steep tree lined avenue leading from the Hall, out through the town towards the small boat moored in the town harbour waiting to set sail for Italy.

Kwok had prepared his master's heavy velvet blazer for his return from the balcony. As Lord Strathcarnage entered the room, Kwok held the warmed and pressed scarlet blazer wide for the Lord to slide his expansive frame inside. The efficient manservant had also polished and readied the favourite hunting shoes of his master, the brown brogues leant against the wooden dressing stand shining and ready for his master's huge feet once the jacket was wrestled onto the Lord's heavily built frame.

Lord Strathcarnage maintained a grand standard of dress, even while working alone in the dead of night in the silent Roman streets. Strathcarnage plunged his enormous arms into the sleeves of the garment, wriggling his stout body as the thin oriental servant fought to manoeuvre the blazer around his master's bulk, before relaxing as Kwok carefully removed any marks of the struggle with a soft brush. On the polished walnut stand stood a massive crystal tumbler of brandy and ice, which the Lord lifted and began to gulp down.

The Lord stood silent, the ice clinking gently against the crystal. The huge man was lost in thoughts of his plans for the night ahead, eagerly hoping this trip would prove as rewarding as his previous exotic business expeditions. Strathcarnage had been dutifully measuring and noting the weather for the entire month of his stay and, as Kwok picked at any lingering flecks of fluff, the Lord gazed over the shining black hair of his manservant toward the open doors of the suite to examine current outdoor conditions.

He nodded in a deliberate manner; satisfied that the warm, dry, moonless circumstances were ideal conditions for stalking his prey around the capital's narrow streets. As Kwok knelt and helped the Lord into his hunting shoes, the dapper Strathcarnage whistled piercingly out of tune, dreaming about a successful outcome to his mission. The sound of Kwok's fingers cracking underfoot like dry twigs threw the huge man back to reality.

Kwok screamed.

"You break...you break bad," shouted Kwok, his face a twisted mask of pain, beads of sweat already forming on his heavily furrowed oriental forehead.

Lord Strathcarnage sipped at his drink, shook his head slowly and let out a low sigh of disappointment as he looked downwards, the hand of Kwok firmly trapped under the massive leather sole of his brogue. Kwok's mouth stretched open silently in a grimace of intense pain.

Strathcarnage hated the sloppiness of misused language, and had made it a personal crusade to confront such matters head on.

"My dear Kwok, the phrase you are searching for is not 'you break', since that is *obviously* present tense. Quaint and rustic though it may sound to your uncultured ear, the phrase you are searching for is actually 'you broke', which is in the past tense, since your fingers have now passed into the time after the event and are already no doubt broken. Indeed, technically speaking, your preferred utterance would be 'you have broke', since you are addressing me directly as the breaker. However, this still remains grammatically flawed because even though 'broke' is indeed in the past tense and technically correct, we generally use the form 'you have broken'. Now, let's try it again my little man. "

Strathcarnage nodded at Kwok with a thin smile, satisfied he had nipped this misuse of the English language and confusion of tense firmly in the bud. The Lord saw his role of educating and correcting of the numerous linguistic flaws of his manservant as a constant battle.

Kwok had now turned a paler shade of grey and his heavily contorting face was now a shining mask of perspiration. As Strathcarnage drained the last of his brandy and decided on a refill, he lifted his weight off the foot trapping the twisted hand, Kwok grasped at his limp appendage and muttered "You have broken...you have broken."

Strathcarnage cheered and gave a series of small claps of his huge hands, content that this incident had served as yet another small step in his passionate crusade to deliver correct English grammar and usage to the ill educated unfortunates of the world.

While Kwok sat cradling and rubbing his already discoloured and rapidly swelling hand, Strathcarnage strolled off across the room to pour himself another huge measure of brandy from the sparkling crystal decanter on the sideboard. Taking another huge mouthful, he moved forward to stand before a mysterious square object towering over him in the corner of the room, completely covered by a purple velvet blanket embroidered in gold with the Strathcarnage family crest. Beneath the cover was hidden the object of his secret delight, that which had brought him to on this present trip to Italy. Contained within this ornate cage was the passion which had totally consumed his life for the past twenty years.

The Lord wound his fat fingers round the gold fabric rope tied to the soft cloth and pulled, standing back as the heavy velvet slid effortlessly to the floor to reveal its secret.

Strathcarnage lifted his chins proudly and gazed in appreciation at the construction towering above him. He smiled at the huge wooden cage, overwhelmed anew at its natural beauty. The huge edifice sat on the deep pile of the hotel carpet like an oversized bird cage, a work of elegant and intricate craftsmanship, expertly built with no expense spared by a specialist carpenter in Liverpool. The large rectangular enclosure stood slightly taller than the Lord's six foot frame, carved from solid dark mahogany and with a lockable front gate made of perfectly spaced bars of the finest bamboo, the whole construction trimmed with ornate designs polished and fixed in place by the delicate hand of craftsmen. Strathcarnage nodded his deep admiration at the beauty of the cage, running his hands slowly and lovingly across the wooden bars. As he stood back to admire the artistry Strathcarnage watched as a number of grimy children's faces slowly revealed themselves behind the exquisitely finished bars.

The Lord observed the soft pink ovals pressing against the ornate frame, the dirty faces squinting hard against the sudden light. Strathcarnage smiled as he watched the innocent tiny hands stretched out towards him between the bamboo gaps, grasping the air, most probably looking for some food. He was still smiling broadly as he brought his thick cane down heavily on the tiny grasping hands, the swift blow from the heavy silver topped cane bringing a high pitched scream and an instant withdrawal back toward the rear of the cage in fear.

These dirt streaked faces were destined to become Strathcarnage show children, and their training in the expected behaviour required of such fortunate a position was never to be begun too soon. He laughed and poked at the cowering shapes inside the cage with his stick, turning to Kwok to share the amusement. Kwok was still clutching his hand, but managed to look up and force a thin smile through his pained expression, offering a faint nod in the general direction of the cage.

To best examine those circumstances in which the passionate excitement of showing children for competition had infected the Lord, it is useful to first briefly examine the family history of the Strathcarnage line. Such details may better explain events leading us to the point where we begin our tale, with the present Lord Strathcarnage in Rome on a mission to capture further specimens, anxious to consolidate his standing as a respected authority in the field.

A short perusal of Strathcarnage's background can offer us clues to the dedication and driving forces behind *the* world leader in child show competition and the man now standing in a Roman hotel suite only a few short weeks away from his expectation of securing his unequalled third World Championship crown.

Lord Strathcarnage had been born St John Winston Tallisker McAllister, collecting his current title of Lord only upon the unfortunate and premature death of his father. The title of Lord Strathcarnage had been inherited by the oldest male child of each generation, in a tradition leading back to the first Lord Strathcarnage. He had been Anton McAllister, the captain of the shipwrecked and ruined craft whose destruction on the rocks off the coast of the current village of Strathcarnage had led to its formation.

The McAllister family had gone on to carve a long, noble tradition in the theatre of military action, leaving the safety of the village to take up arms at the first hint of any conflict abroad. As a result, generations of holders of the title Lord Strathcarnage had held great prestige as a much respected guest around the dinner tables of the very highest echelons of the upper classes.

Such was the lust for violence of the family that Lord Strathcarnage's grandfather, Elthenor P. McAllister had, within living memory, secretly fled the village to fight valiantly in numerous military campaigns. Indeed the nobleman had only miraculously escaped an untimely death in the last few days of The Battle of the Somme.

A crack German sniper had shot his grandfather in the middle of the chest on the foggy French battlefield, but by some miracle of fate the bullet had struck a miniature leather bound album of hand-painted Indian pornography given to him by his weeping mother for luck on the day he had cycled off down the tree lined avenue from Haversack Hall to war. The brass bullet had hit cleanly in the centre of his chest, but had become embedded in the book of lurid hand-drawn depictions of unspeakable acts of sexual degeneracy. The bullet had only missed his heart, it was later calculated by army ballistics experts, by around six acts of oral pleasuring and a particularly well rendered example of elephant bestiality.

On discovering this great fortune and escape from death on the battlefield, Lord Strathcarnage's grandfather had run immediately to inform his commanding officer, hoping the chance nature of his remarkable escape might serve to lift the morale of the other men. As he neared the command post however, he was run over and killed instantly by a horse drawn supply truck carrying three tons of boxed ammunition.

The devastating news had come as an appalling blow to the family, and as a direct result of the shock Strathcarnage's father immediately left Haversack Hall and took to wandering the town wearing women's clothing and calling himself Susan. It was an unusual state of affairs, and one that remained in place right up until his death. However, as the local saying goes, every wreck has an unclaimed cargo, and it was during this period of grief in petticoats and lacy underclothes that his father had first met his mother, a chance meeting whilst the grief stricken transvestite nobleman was chairing a Women's Guild gathering at a church hall in the village.

Strathcarnage's mother was a mountainous lumpy muscled woman, who had an encyclopaedic practical and theoretical knowledge of bare-knuckle boxing, and who liked to be addressed only by the name Graham. For all the bewilderment and village society whispering their initial courtship generated, Lord Strathcarnage's mother and father remained ferociously happy together throughout all their years of marriage. The present Lord Strathcarnage often looked back with great fondness to those early years of his childhood. Many in the village remained convinced that it was during these formative, and frequently maniacal years, that the young Lord had developed those unpleasant personality traits which were to later make him a most ruthless and dedicated master of the child show.

At age fifteen however, events again conspired towards another change for the young Strathcarnage heir. Shortly after the occasion of his birthday, the young nobleman's father had been busying himself around the family farm on the surrounding plateaus of Haversack Hall, administering heavy and senseless beatings to some of the farm workmen when tragedy again dragged its black nails down the family blackboard.

His father, Susan, had been helping discipline the men bringing in the harvest when tragedy occurred. By some unexplained freak mishap, one of the men Strathcarnage's father had been heavily beating with a pitchfork handle had accidentally fallen against the heavily made up and long skirted man, throwing his soft upper class frame into the thunderous steel blades of the farm's horse drawn threshing machine. Strathcarnage's father had been instantly torn to ribbons by the flashing steel blades. He was ripped into pieces, it was later discovered, no bigger than a half crown coin. Witnesses had reported him disappearing suddenly into the machines noisy innards and then immediately reappearing at the other end in a nauseating wet blast of freshly diced offal, dispersed over an area the size of a modest cricket pitch.

His mother, Graham, must have been distraught by the news but had somehow managed to put on a remarkable show of bravery in the face of obvious shock and anguish. It was she who decided within hours that no formal funeral should take place; instead opting for her beloved husband to remain scattered in smallish slices, in exactly the position where they had been thrown by the blood soaked exit cylinder of the huge machine. It was to many in the town a curious decision. However her wish was granted and he lay undisturbed where he fell, whereupon the farm's ferocious blackface sheep herd ate him slowly over a period of days.

Fortunately the young Lord Strathcarnage had not witnessed the fatal parent threshing episode first hand, but it was he who had narrowly averted further tragedy on that blackest of days. On rushing to the field on receiving news of the accident,

Strathcarnage instantly recognised that the poor farm hand whose simple unfortunate accident had caused his father to be thrown into the rotating steel jaws of the thresher was himself in the gravest danger.

The unfortunate worker in question was being held far above the ground, over the heads of his fellow farm hands, all of whom were cheering and singing wildly. It had soon became obvious to the young Lord these men were in the grip of some sort of deep and traumatic shock brought on by the grief of the recent event, an incident causing them to form themselves an uncontrollable singing lynch mob. The sudden appearance of the new Lord Strathcarnage had fortunately managed to quieten the men, the gathering obviously driven close to madness by raw grief and by their love and respect for his father. It was a fortunate conclusion, since even in this darkest hour the staff were unable to stop smiling and laughing. It was a heartbreakingly sad sight to see so many men affected so hideously by such recent sorrow.

Young Strathcarnage was unsure how to deal with such hysterical outpourings but fortunately he had been helped by the sudden appearance of his mother. News had been relayed to Haversack Hall of the tragedy and she rushed to the scene as quickly as she could. The poor distraught woman, herself clearly suffering greatly, appeared to be in the grip of a similar manifestation of shock and grief to the other men. As she approached the group she had let out a loud cheering noise, before leading the entire mourning group to a local pub in the town, singing and clapping loudly as their heartbreaking procession of grief moved off.

The young Strathcarnage admired the quick thinking displayed by his mother, even while in the grip of her own obvious distress at the incident. It was to her credit that she had discovered somewhere deep within the strength and personal courage to force such a convincing illusion of hysterical happiness upon herself, thus bonding with the group and averting further tragedy.

In order to help dull the young man's heartache at the unfortunate death of his father, his mother had compassionately arranged for him to be smuggled away out the town on an Albanian fishing boat to stay on the mainland with his distant Uncle, Lord Otis Clamshawe. His mother bravely stayed on in the village, coming to terms with her unexpected loss in her own reflective way, a task helped greatly by her decision to move a large number of the younger and more handsome farm hands involved in the fatal accident into her home at Haversack Hall. Strathcarnage thought it a typical charitable gesture and greatly admired her attempts to exorcise her pain and grief by embarking on a nightly series of raucous parties. The young man was happy to leave knowing his mother was overcoming her hurt in her own way.

Once his new housemate had arrived, Lord Otis had wasted no time in deciding upon his preferred course of action in order to take the young Strathcarnage mind off the whole tragic affair. Otis decided that his best course of recovering the spirits of the young man was to fully involve the youngster in his own beloved hobby: that of showing children. The young Strathcarnage was to prove a keen and bright protégé.

Lord Otis had long been a most fanatical child show competitor, and had collected around him every known example of the numerous books written on the subject. In addition he also held current subscriptions to the entire range of specialist journals, the books lining the walls of the massive library collected and bound in heavy leather volumes. It was later to be the considered opinion of many that the young Lord's time with his beloved distant Uncle had been without doubt the foundation of the passion that had infected Strathcarnage in his later life.

However, for all the dedication and work Otis put into studying childshow theory and his long hours training and grooming his groups of competitive children, he was rarely even close to being placed in competition. The pair would repeatedly return silent and cheerless from numerous competitions around the country, the covered cage of defeated children bouncing around in the back of the carriage. Often on the journey the two men would venture opinions on where they had gone wrong, discussing the matter while driving the long miles home disconsolate and defeated. These regular disappointments and the painful sight of his sad tearful Uncle Otis during such dialogue were just the motivation Strathcarnage required to learn even more in order to help the pair do better, to improve, to win.

Uncle Otis was a fanatical enthusiast and an expert in child showing theory but viewed the numerous competitions merely as a hobby. Otis was without aspiration, only taking part in the many small scale local and regional child shows in order to further his knowledge and confirm his theories. The surrounding grey town halls and village market places of the depressing small town competition circuit were their weekly battleground, the crumbling church hall interiors frustrating the young Lord as he read in the journals of sunlit high profile competitions in more glamorous locations.

Strathcarnage wanted to branch out further afield and craved a chance to become a more professional and prepared competitor. The young Lord had the vision to see that the way forward was to compete in a wider arena; in the regional, national and ultimately world competitions. The young man began to cultivate a serious desire to win. It soon became obvious to the ambitious young man that he needed to break free from his Uncle Otis, since his numerous lengthy and frustrating attempts to persuade the older man of his wider vision had been quickly dismissed as excessively ambitious. Uncle Otis was a knowledgeable man but lacked the confidence and tough competitive edge to make his mark on the child show circuit. It was to be another hideously twisted knife of tragedy in the back of family life that would furnish Strathcarnage with the chance to take that extra leap.

Strathcarnage's mother Graham had been a very loving woman but often a difficult one to live with. Strathcarnage often recalled times as a young boy when family fist fights would suddenly erupt as his mother violently turned over furniture and screamed terse allegations of cheating during attempts to play various board games. His father had installed an elaborate series of emergency alarms around the house and when the frequent explosions of anger from his mother appeared, the family often sat hidden behind barricades of furniture until specially trained servants arrived to drag the demented Lady Strathcarnage off to be subdued.

Lord Strathcarnage recalled tenderly the occasion of a domestic brawl over a tense game of Scrabble which had occurred when he was twelve. It was a brutal and violent incident which had left eight people critical in the local hospital and saw the young man suffer a broken jaw after an ill-advised attempt to place the word 'maniac' on the board.

There were also fond remembrances of weekly childhood gatherings where mother would stage bare knuckle fight nights in the sitting room, taking on all comers in bloody fistfights for cash prizes. These were exciting nights for the young boy, often spent with a large boisterous crowd of his mother's sailor friends. However these events would inevitably end with the arrival of the town's law men and medical staff, when mother had again gotten out of hand in the heat of battle and had equipped herself with various weapons. Ironically it was the occasion of one of these intimate family soirees that was to cruelly rob the young man of his mother and bring the adolescent Lord home to Strathcarnage.

The old fisherman who had been secretly dispatched from the town arrived in the rainy darkness at his Uncle's home to tell the young Lord of the death of his mother. He was unable, or perhaps unwilling, to offer any detailed facts about events leading to her demise. Sitting uneasily in the warmth of the library wearing a sympathetic face and yellow oilskins, the man had passed on only the briefest of details. He told Strathcarnage the village law men who had attended the incident believed that an initial argument had started over the origin of one of his mother's tattoos, and that his mother, being his mother, had then attempted to take a bare-knuckle fighter known as the Athens Gypsy in a choke hold.

It was his mother's specialist move the young man remembered fondly, lost in tears as he listened to the few details unfold. Indeed many evenings had been enjoyed by the family around the fireside as his mother squeezed the air from his windpipe in demonstration, his father Susan lovingly punching her full in the face in an attempt to restore some breath to the faint child.

As the inevitable fight had escalated in Haversack Hall, the law men believed she had finally been felled by a thrown Regency chest of drawers, the sudden impact and splintering leading to a fatal internal injury. It appeared, the old fisherman explained, to be a terrible accident, brought about by high-spirited fun. Strathcarnage was sad to lose her, but drew comfort from the fact she had died happy in the company of her close friends and whilst engaged in the pastime she loved.

Strathcarnage had begun the trip home to Haversack Hall by boat that very night, sailing slowly up the coast under the veil of darkness. As he sat and looked out across the dark waves, the young orphan wondered how to begin the slow process of making the family seat of Haversack Hall his home again. He began to plan for his new future. The young man knew that as the only child of the tempestuous and often vicious marriage, it was now down to him alone to continue the Strathcarnage name.

Reaching his home after a silent journey through the dark village, he immediately lit the Hall's gas lamps and began to clear up the bloody shards of the smashed Regency drawers of death with a steely determination, avowed to remember his parents by succeeding in the only activity he now knew well enough to undertake with confidence. The young Lord had decided to join the show child circuit.

The first modest sign of progress in competition came after sailing off from the village with a small cage of local children, to appear in an open tournament in distant Manchester. It was his first show success and the small victory came in the form of an unkempt young Irish deckhand won in a game of gin rummy from a visiting Polish child smuggler who had called at Haversack Hall a number of weeks previously to offer condolences about his mother's recent death.

The scruffy child had been in the lead throughout the standing and walking sections of the show, only finally losing his lead in the speaking and balancing part of the evening. A hairy Albanian girl with the beginnings of a black wiry moustache and a bearing a quite extravagant squint had narrowly forced the gypsy boy into second place in the very last round of competition.

Strathcarnage was bitterly disappointed but had entered the Irish child unaware of the current fashion for heavily squinted children. On reflection he knew now that the sallow shaven frame of the Irish deckhand could not compete with such a striking and heavy set girl. This, after all, was a child whose violent and extreme eye dislocation had won her the vital extra votes for victory. Strathcarnage remained quietly contented with a podium placing and as he absentmindedly pinned the second place rosette through the skin on the Irish child's bare chest, he smiled in contentment he was at least beginning to make a mark in the competitive world of showing.

Lord Strathcarnage got his first outright victory only a few weeks later, with a club footed Spanish fisherman's son in a ranked show in Norfolk. The boy had limped unstoppably to victory in the 'Slight Seconds' category, going on to win the overall title with a display of unsteady walking that had the judges in raptures. The young Lord had then followed this victory up by taking the 'Broad Faced Child of The Year' title in Great Yarmouth, providing him with his first front page in a newspaper. He often laughed as he recalled the event, the local newspaper having to print the photo sideways on due to the dimensions of the child's uncommonly oblong face, the auspicious result of a childhood farmyard accident to his heavily pregnant mother.

Strathcarnage soon began to show and to win all over the country, quickly moving to competing solely in ranking events, leading him to his first British Title with a bright eyed double-jointed ginger girl with pigtails called Sophie.

The standard of competition was intense at this level. Strathcarnage soon took the professional decision that he would catch and train his own children, instead of frequenting the numerous expensive and untrustworthy brokers in the bigger cities. The reliance on corrupt dealers who often held the best children aside for those able to afford extortionate bribes, he had noted, was one of the many points where his Uncle Otis had gone wrong.

A self caught and trained child cut down hugely on costs and often provided the jaded child show crowds with the thrill of previously unseen delights. Many of the overexposed professionally traded children on the circuit were often marked down by tired judges, over familiar with the same tired collection of children.

Strathcarnage knew his children were unique and fresh, their individual talents exciting both crowds and judges alike. Strathcarnage set out to trap and cage his own prospective competition entrants, allowing him to groom and work with the raw talent at his own pace in the privacy and solitude afforded by the grand open spaces of Haversack Hall.

After some initial problems with transport and smuggling caught children onto boats to bring back to the village, Strathcarnage had begun to gather and train a large stable of prospects. With some hard work the children were soon of a sufficient standard to compete at the very highest level. However, even with this rich stable of self trapped and selected youngsters, Lord Strathcarnage's attempts to capture his first World Championship had ended in disaster.

Strathcarnage had decided his best chance of success at the most prestigious World Championship event lay with his decision to enter the competition with an inordinately fat child called Thomas, who he had captured using drugged steak pies on an recent evening hunting expedition on the North Pier in Blackpool.

The boy was quite perversely rotund, but his swollen features and puffy folds of eyes retained an atmospheric quality that Strathcarnage knew the judges often marked high. Alas the World Championships of that year were to be held in an arena attached to a luxury hotel in Kowloon, and due to an atmospheric anomaly in the region which had unfortunately combined with a local power strike which had shut down the hotel air conditioning, temperatures had reached 47 degrees inside the hall even before the show had commenced.

Things had started well, with Thomas jiggling and swinging his pink rolls of flab around beneath his t-shirt to a musical accompaniment, gathering huge ovations from the knowledgeable sell out crowd. However, just as Thomas was waddling to the end of the 'walking' section, the boy had begun to slow and move lethargically as he neared his last figure of eight.

Strathcarnage had been watching carefully from the side of the stage, angrily noticing the boy's uncomfortable grimace and rapidly reddening face becoming bathed in sweat. The Lord wound the leather handle of the stiff riding crop around his hand, readying himself for the fat child coming offstage.

Yet, at that very moment, Thomas had suddenly halted. Still as a statue in the centre of his manoeuvre, the boy had taken on a pained appearance and then clutched his corpulent fingers hard into his stomach, sinking them deep into the soft flesh curved across his substantial gut. Before Strathcarnage could taunt the boy to continue with a silently raised crop from the side of the stage, Thomas had let out a series of peircing high pitched screams and then exploded.

The child had disintegrated with an ear-splitting bang, spraying the crowd and three of the five judging panel with a heated fermenting assortment of Blackpool pie offal and half digested scotch eggs. Strathcarnage had been both distraught at losing such a good lead and embarrassed at causing organisers such a headache in cleaning up the fleshy mess. Thomas had been a close second favourite with local bookmakers and was heavily backed by several professional experts from the major child show journals to place highly in his first World event. It was, for all concerned, a disaster.

The post-mortem event panel which always convened to discuss sudden show based deaths had later found the explosive events had been triggered by a massive build up of heated stomach gas in the child's yawning internal spaces. This, they decided, combined with the unusually high temperatures in the packed show arena, had caused the mixture to ferment and the freak accident to so occur so unexpectedly.

Although Strathcarnage had been distraught at losing face in such a high profile event, and in such a careless manner, he had learned a vital lesson about fat children and trapped gas, and was never again to risk overly obese children in one of the majors.

All of the above historical events lead us here to Rome, and to Lord Strathcarnage standing in a penthouse suite high above the city staring at a bamboo cage filled with children. He had made the long journey to the city in order to concentrate on restocking his cages at Haversack Hall for a fresh attempt at the latest World Championships.

Some experts thought the olive skinned Roman children a little wiry for competition, but Strathcarnage knew he could soon put meat on their bones and bring them up to show standard by embarking on a combination of force-feeding, overworking them to the point of hallucinating and issuing a prolonged series of scientifically premeditated beatings. He stared through the bars at the children he had captured so far on his trip, content in the knowledge that within the ornate cage, there stared back at him the dirty tear-streaked faces of a numerous potential champions.

The Lord had already dispatched a number of cages of highly abnormal Italian children back to Haversack Hall for the annual charity 'Broken Biscuits' Show, an invitation only event always packed with misshapen delights. Indeed on the very afternoon of his arrival in the city he had caught a chance newsflash on the local Roman radio of a large train crash and just outside the city and had rushed immediately to the scene together with Kwok to extract a few prime specimens of badly damaged children from the twisted wreckage before the arrival of the emergency services. These were quickly patched up and dispatched via sea for home and the show.

The 'Broken Biscuits' show, organised, staged and funded by Lord Strathcarnage, concentrated on the stranger shapes and types of children and had become a showpiece highlight at the end of the year's child show calendar. It was a non competitive trade event where the competitors and professionals associated with child showing from around the world gathered together in a casual atmosphere for some light relief and to raise money for animal charities.

Lord Strathcarnage had made the trip to Italy to capture genetically vandalised children for various choreographed performances right through the show, most notably the show's closing epic showpiece, where Strathcarnage hoped this year to direct a child show musical explosives laden re-enactment of The Battle of The Somme, staged as a memorial to his grandfather.

It was just at that moment, as The Lord stood idly daydreaming of this upcoming extravaganza, that a fresh and most sudden tragedy had visited the Strathcarnage line.

There was much speculation in the press in the following days as to just what had actually occurred in the Roman hotel suite which lead to such a dreadful devastating explosion.

Some experts ventured the opinion that Strathcarnage had learned nothing from the Kowloon incident and been experimenting with overfeeding a collection of fat Italian children stored in overheated conditions. The Daily Mail suspected some manner of foul play from the heavily charred and smouldering oriental gentleman found wandering at the scene clutching a broken hand and repeating the words "You have broken" over and over again to members of the attending emergency services.

Other investigators examined a possible link to a carelessly discarded cigar, citing as their evidence earlier reports of the sudden appearance of the lit object descending from the balcony shortly before the loud screams of what sounded like a fight in the suite. The cigar had landed in and immediately set fire to the hair, and subsequently the dress and dining companion, of an elderly Swiss lady enjoying dinner in the outdoor hotel restaurant. A link was never proven between the two incidents and the Swiss lady had soon returned home to Zurich, bald and nursing a face like a burnt crocodile handbag.

Uncle Otis too was questioned extensively as a possible suspect, but was quickly released owing to his unshakable alibi of being out with friends on the hills around his Scottish home gassing badgers and shooting wildlife with a crossbow, for stuffing and mounting on the walls of his home. This fresh hobby had become the newfound obsession of Otis, one which had taken over from that of the child showing, spurred on by an eventual realisation that his pastime would never bring him happiness.

Other competitors from the child showing circuit were also grilled by increasingly confused Italian detectives investigating the potential motive of professional jealousy. However, as suspected, each member of the child show community questioned by Italian police in turn professed a deep admiration for the dapper, highly respected Lord. None wanted him dead. Fellow competitors found the huge man always polite, friendly and yet retaining the fierce will to win and a keen eye for a crowd pleasing disfigurement.

After a few months' intensive but fruitless investigations, the case was quietly downgraded and eventually closed after a poorly attended public enquiry, with no solution to the cause of explosive events ever having been decided upon.

What had happened? Well, we may only speculate, but here is another, more probable turn of events, and one partially confirmed by Kwok once he regained the power of speech.

The previous year, during a child showing competition in the sleepy German town of Hanover, Lord Strathcarnage had been suddenly laid low with a violent attack of an unidentified stomach illness.

Having only eaten some hotel prepared veal and a small side salad, together with 18 pints of strong German lager, half a bottle of French brandy, a Magnum of pink champagne, and a selection of liqueurs, Strathcarnage was carried to bed by Kwok complaining of intense cramps, where he remained in state of some distress for a number of days. It had quickly become apparent to the Lord that the veal was undoubtedly to blame, and that somehow the meat must have been badly prepared by the untrustworthy German hotel staff. From that day forward the huge man had refused to eat anything while abroad other than tinned squirrel chilli, shipped on each expedition in great quantities from home. He would ensure great towering crates of the traditional highly spiced Strathcarnage mixture followed them wherever he went, to be prepared as required by his manservant Kwok on a portable gas cooking appliance.

Given these circumstances, the events leading to the subsequent explosion were less sinister and somewhat easier to explain.

Lord Strathcarnage had just finished dressing, breaking Kwok's hand in the process. Kwok had been caught up in the pain of his fractured hand and had unsurprisingly forgotten about the preparation of his master's regular evening feast of the squirrel chilli, generally served immediately after the ritual of dressing and brandy.

Although Kwok had become distracted by his severe pain and had failed to fully prepare and serve the meal, he had already lit the gas cooking stove in ever efficient anticipation, and it had sat burning away quietly on a small coffee table in the hotel suite, unnoticed in the greater commotion of events.

Lord Strathcarnage, whilst relaxing and daydreaming about his past and future glories in front of the ornate cage of children, had absentmindedly cocked his leg on the bamboo cage door, from which position he strained and unleashed another explosive emission of foul gas from his rear. This backdoor tornado, discharged violently but again in a note perfect E major, had rushed outward, the foul air driven over the still burning gas flame.

Without warning the anal emission had ignited, the noxious gas catching in a whooshing blue ribbon of flame, flashing through the room mid-air straight back to its source, causing both Lord Strathcarnage, his brandy and the cooking gas canister to instantaneously detonate with a ferocity Italian Police sources later claimed was visible in the night sky from the distant streets of Rome itself.

Little evidence remained thereafter to identify the body of Lord Strathcarnage, given the power and partially internal nature of the enormous blast. However a search of the piles of rubble from the largely demolished upper floor of the hotel revealed frayed remains of a smoking crimson blazer and a single hand sewn Spanish brogue shoe with the charred lower leg still attached. This evidence was to prove adequate to complete identification formalities.

The fortunate Kwok, who had been in the relative shelter of the bathroom applying ice and bandages to his hand at the point of ignition, was afterwards able to offer an additional positive identification of the dead Lord's body by means of a small piece of charred tattoo of a naked woman with the name 'Graham' still readable on the carbonised flesh. This ornate inkwork had remained legible through the melted silk sock still fused to the section of leg later recovered floating in a nearby resident's ornamental garden pond, blown there by the force of the explosion.

The badly burned children were also saved, protected from serious injury from the piles of falling brickwork and masonry by the strength of the ornate show cage, although most were hideously burned in the initial inferno.

In an ironic final twist to the tale, the surviving children were the toast of the final Broken Biscuits Child Show later that year, held as a fitting memorial and as a remembrance of the glittering child show career of the 23$^{rd}$ Lord Strathcarnage.

The display was an appropriate tribute to the Lord. Following a moving introduction by a tearful Uncle Otis, a small knot of charred Italian children presented a reconstruction of events in the hotel suite as a show finale. Their serene performances and the subsequent incendiary climax of the show, involving the children once more being set alight in the bamboo cage, provided a fit and sober finale to the show and the spectacle ensured not a dry eye remained in the audience as both flesh and bamboo crackled long into the night.

Some present still maintain, when pressed, that the thick smoke thrown out by the burning flesh was to blame for most of the evening's weeping.

Uncle Otis returned again to child showing following the event as a tribute to his distant nephew's memory, but as both crowds and enthusiasm for the sport waned following the Roman accident, opportunities to show began slowly but surely to tail off.

In a final twist of fate, Lord Otis Clamshawe won his first ever event in the very last ever recorded child show, hosted by the Reverend Aubery Whisp in Strathcarnage church hall in 1988. This final winning exhibit was a slender, gruesomely disfigured girl called Abigail, who was later released into the wild after receiving her victory rosette. She is believed to have remained in the village.

Lord Otis Clamshawe died of a self inflicted gunshot wound in 1989, his passion finally fulfilled.

The 23$^{rd}$ Lord Strathcarnage 1923 – 1978

# CHAPTER 4

# Day Two – The Garage

Godwin Clawcunte had been employed in the local garage ever since his recent departure from the local school. Careers for young men were hard to come across in the small town of Strathcarnage and Godwin's mother had fought ferociously to guarantee the job prospect for her son. Indeed the fight to secure employment was not merely a metaphorical figure of speech, Godwin's mother only just defeating Giuseppe DeLauro, the local garage proprietor in the yearly annual knife fight on the village green in which Strathcarnage parents undertook to secure a job for their offspring.

The ceremony was cruel and often brutal, but proud village parents traditionally massed on the first Tuesday of June on the small circular village green that marked the centre of the town to engage local businessmen in the long-established ritual of armed combat. The often bloody hand to hand exchanges were a historical tradition, begun long ago to ensure that only the strongest and most genetically dominant families were engaged in the key jobs of the town.

Strathcarnage had been founded by the survivors of a wrecked ship packed with mentally unbalanced asylum inmates being transported south, and at one time the ritual had been vital to ensure only the strongest minds and bodies of the shabby shipwrecked group had been engaged in the then vital task of quickly planning and building the new town at the secret location inside the steep walled cliff caves. The tradition had stuck.

Godwin had visited his mother in hospital once the heavily wounded woman had regained consciousness after the traditional afternoon battle, and the young man remembered fondly the swell of pride on hearing his mother's voice filling the room as he entered, joyous even through muffled through the bandages.

"Hallelujah ! My son will be working with spunk".

Godwin was profoundly moved as a tear escaped his mother's sole visible and heavily swollen eye, the wetness soaking into the bloody bandages below. The young man had been surprised yet touched by his mother's show of emotion, since the woman only very rarely cried.

His mother had been raised during harder times in the village and seldom displayed her feelings. Indeed the last occasion on which Godwin had witnessed the woman remotely tearful was the regrettable afternoon when she had inadvertently cut his father completely in half with a chainsaw while chopping driftwood behind the small family home. Godwin's mother had recovered herself quickly though, and had still made his afternoon shift at the small whale meat factory at the edge of the town.

Godwin's mother was a tough woman, and to observe her open joy at securing his son a job with spunk was a deeply stirring experience. The young man often smiled distractedly as he remembered the family tale of his mother losing an arm in one of the large whale skinning machines at the factory. The woman had been shocked by the loss of a limb, but had kicked the blood-spattered appendage under the strafing machine and finished the remainder of her shift. So important was his mother's intense pride in her work that she had only been reminded of the unfortunate incident when she had gone to lift her traditional post work pint of whisky. The realisation that she was unable to hold her pipe at the same time as her full glass reminded her of the recent upper limb deficit. Only then did the proud woman grudgingly seek medical attention, and even then not before she had finished her drink.

To see a woman like his mother weeping openly over spunk was a poignant moment for any son.

Godwin had proudly embraced the prospect of working with spunk as a full time occupation. In the interests of accuracy, it may be more proper to give 'S.P.U.N.K.' its correct emphasis, given the full title of the complex engine tuning process which lead to the regrettable acronym was Specialist Performance Utilising Natural Knowledge. Strathcarnage Garage was proud of its lengthy association with S.P.U.N.K. and those few citizens of Strathcarnage lucky enough to have motorised vehicles had long been heavy consumers, once they had experienced the numerous benefits.

Local residents appreciated S.P.U.N.K. You could see it all over their faces.

Godwin worked hard in the job his mother had fought so violently for with her carefully sharpened kitchen knives. 'It was well worth the ear,' his mother had whispered as she hugged her son close as he left their home on that first day, the older woman's reading glasses swinging partially unanchored from one side of her face. There was no doubt that Godwin treasured his new position, but events at his new place of employment were soon to change his life forever.

Late one cold November evening, one of his fellow workmates, Burton Harris, had exploded with a deafening scream from the outside toilet cubicle far across the yard. Burton was prone to emitting sudden outbursts from the cubicle, so when the fresh burst of noise came, none of the other men in the large garage shed paid much attention. Even Big Nancy Caldicott the garage engine lifter, the nervous woman most commonly affected by such sudden shouts, continued dragging the oily carcass of a truck engine across the floor without any noticeable sign of surprise.

Burton was the boss's nephew and did very little work, trading his nepotistic good fortune for the opportunity to spend most of the day in the dark outdoor bathroom, pouring over his extensive collection of pornography. He always had a fine selection to hand, exchanged frequently with fly-by-night fishermen and local smugglers in the dockside bars.

The exchange deal suited both Burton and the visiting seamen. Three long weeks of being tossed around the fierce North Sea with only other men for company quickly took a heavy toll on the visual appeal and potential loin provoking qualities of the only reading material aboard. Therefore jaded crews gladly refreshed stocks once they had reached the clandestine harbour of Strathcarnage, with Burton the local connoisseur in providing them with fresh and previously unseen depictions of the flesh. It was a symbiotic relationship erected on the resolute foundation of bare breasts and unspeakable acts of depravity.

The other members of the garage workforce had no problem with Burton's solitary activities, partly because his toilet base was outside on the distant and windswept far corner of the yard. Indeed, on the numerous colder days with the wind raking through the town from the rough seas that lay beyond the waterfall, it was always agreeable to have a pre-warmed seat waiting on arrival.

The other key reason for any lack of resentment lay in the fact that Burton was so hopeless working in the dangerous environment of the garage. It was agreed that they should actively encourage his pastime, for the simple reason that his presence inside the main building, near the heavy machinery, frequently became a liability. He was much better kept well out of the way, locked away literally pleasing himself for large portions of the day inside his toiletry onanism HQ.

Garage procedure regarding the use of toilet facilities was intricate. If usage of the facility was required, the needy individual walked across to the hut, gave the door a firm knock and announced in a loud clear voice to the constant resident inside both the estimated time of arrival and the nature of proposed bodily expulsion. This advance warning system then gave Burton a chance to "finish off" his activities, vacate the premises and wander aimlessly around outside until the toiletry matter in hand was concluded, whereupon he would sprint back inside and hastily re-bolt the door.

The system functioned well and had the added benefit of improving the collective bowel control of the workers. This mutually agreed system worked for everyone apart from Big Nancy, who, as far as anyone who could tell, had never visited the toilet once in her eight years at the garage.

However, on this day, although the workers still remained blissfully unaware, Burton's scream was destined to have greater effect on their existence than usual.

Burton had come across, in a literal as well as a figurative sense, a competition in a newly acquired issue of one of his fleshy periodicals. The competition in question offered one lucky reader of "Ein Handy Schpanker" a chance to win a visit from the celebrated Danish porn star Lottie, whose talents were spread, again literally, across the colourful magazine pages.

The stripped Scandinavian was Burton's much loved favourite onanist muse and the walls of his distant base were generously covered by images of the great Dane in various states of action and undress. The dream prize also presented the winner with an opportunity to have a set of tasteless souvenir pornographic photos taken posed with the Danish beauty, before spending the evening in her company on a fully paid dinner date.

Burton had carefully picked through the article with a slow moving sticky finger, silently mouthing the words as he wrestled understanding from the message buried within. On finally grasping a sufficient level of comprehension, Burton found he was unable to contain his excitement, releasing his elation and explosive enthusiasm in the ferocity of his aforementioned scream.

Seconds after the scream erupted, Burton exploded through the door of his base, sprinting wide eyed and trouserless across the yard before coming to a halt and breathily informing the entire workforce of the competition details. Nancy turned her attention to the truck engine she had been dragging, her eyes averted away from the most obvious sign of Burton's exhilaration. Excitement at the retelling was too much for the man to bear and no sooner had he shared the briefest gasped details of the prize than he returned to his regular base at a rate of knots, to celebrate privately in his own inimitable style.

The other garage workers gathered and discussed events as they watched the small hut rock violently to and fro in the distance, the wooden structure now moving slowly across the yard as if under its own power. After some discussion by the group they decided that they should assist Burton on his competitive quest. Although seldom seen, many in the garage had a soft spot for the workmate eternally but harmlessly groaning inside the toilet and they wanted to help their friend fulfil his tawdry dream.

The competition was in two distinct parts. The first was a "Spot the Difference" section, with two photos featuring the naked object of Burton's desires involved in a particularly sordid sex act. After painstakingly examining the two images, the group helped Burton identify and list the six differences required. The group had some trouble with the last two, but it was Big Nancy who eventually noticed the missing testicle and a partially hidden zip on one of the gentlemen friend's leather masks. There was confusion too when some examining the images thought they had discovered a total of seven mistakes, however on closer examination of the photo it was revealed that a thin trail of white fluid observed on the exposed Dane's thighs was not actually part of the original printing process, but a later addition.

Godwin had helped complete the entry form for Burton, since long term exertions in his toilet base had left him with partially paralysed writing arm and a hideously clawed hand, frozen in position and quite incapable of gripping anything of any shape or volume other than that of his own member. On good days he could just about grasp a spanner, but maintaining hold of a pen was quite out of the question.

It should, however, be noted that Burton was unable to write, so his physical disabilities served merely as a supplementary obstacle to that of his mental deficiencies. Although his co-workers had gladly filled in the enclosed form, Burton's lack of intellect left the group with another, more fundamental problem.

In order to finalize his entry, Burton had to complete a sentence in fifteen words or less stating clearly his chosen reason for his wanting to meet Lottie. The incomplete phrase proved to be a major stumbling block to Burton's ambitions.

The sentence read "I think I should have the chance to dine with the luscious Lottie because..." and provoked a number of responses from Burton which swiftly informed the gathering that urgent coaching may be required not only in coming up with a suitable answer, but also with the eventual prize, should he somehow win.

Burton's first few suggested answers were somewhat more creative and degenerate than it was imagined even the hard-nosed competition judges were after.

A number of the suggested responses were also deemed technically illegal and against the laws of not only nature but of both human decency and morality.

Burton grew increasingly exasperated when informed of the unsuitability of his vivid depictions of despicable perversions being visited upon the female model concerned. Even after some advice, he remained confused that the content of a number of his suggestions may have proved a 'bridge too far' for the judging panel.

Indeed his vivid suggestion related directly to Lottie's rear entrance was not only liable to be a bridge too far, but likely to bring the aforementioned construction collapsing into the river. This soon became not only a question merely of content, but as Burton closed his eyes and kept talking, hostility was soon voiced to the simple technical inaccuracy of Burton using over thirty five extra words during the joyous outburst of enthusiasm in answering.

It was decided that Godwin should compose a suitable ending, given not only that he seemed capable of the most measured answers, but also because he was the only member of the group of garage workers identified as able to write. For bearing this educational cross and for once being discovered reading an actual book, he had henceforth had to put up with being christened "Professor of Languages".

Over the next few days, Godwin had been allowed thinking time by the others to hopefully formulate a winning answer. In a respectful show of Burton's appreciation, Godwin was even sanctioned an extended period in the dark warmth of the toilet cubicle.

It was a strange experience entering the hut not first having knocked and given shouted notice of "Two and a half minutes, back door, solids ", but Godwin soon set to work. After numerous abandoned drafts Godwin eventually arrived at what he thought was the perfect answer. Appearing from the cubicle door beaming, the young man marched across the yard and gathered the rest of the group together for approval.

The final submission read, "I think I should have the chance to dine with the Luscious Lottie because it would excite me to see such a beautiful young woman assisting with my S.P.U.N.K." Godwin hoped the clever linkage of work environment with a play on words would attract the judge's attention. He included a copy of the S.P.U.N.K. engine system marketing literature to better demonstrate the link and to avoid the answer being dismissed out of hand for being overly risqué.

Even Giuseppe, the scarred garage boss, mumbled his incomprehensible approval from his misshapen, knife-ravaged mouth, before gurgling and slamming his fist repeatedly into the desk in a more recognisable show of approval.

The entry was duly sent off for posting on the mainland with a trusted crewman on Russian freighter, and nothing was heard for a number of weeks. Burton had soon recovered from the excitement of his short-lived taste of the outside world and had once more returned himself to sweating and groaning concealed out of sight in his "office". His recovery period was helped greatly by a fresh new batch of magazines, swapped with German haddock trawler crew the previous week.

The other garage staff too had soon settled back to daily routine and had largely forgotten the potential excitement of any possible competition victory. It was to be over four weeks after the competition closing date when the Strathcarnage postman arrived bearing news destined to change Burton's life forever.

Alexei the postman was the public face of a recent program by the Strathcarnage elders to encourage disabled residents out of the shadowy ghettos at the edges of the town and back into work. Alexei was a thin, good-natured Russian man, found washed up on the rocky shoreline after a storm a number of years before by a group of village drug smugglers on a training weekend. Alexei always appeared with a great sense of humour and, as a direct result of his mother's colossal self brewed Vodka intake during pregnancy, two extremely short arms.

Traditionally the workforce greeted his appearance with a torrent of good natured abusive remarks. There was usually a shouted "I see you're late Alex. Are you working short handed?" from some fellow worker, upon which everyone laughed energetically as Alexei sorted through his mail and raised a distracted middle finger in the general direction of the hysterical gathering.

Big Nancy often added to the hilarity with a lusty shout of "Leave him alone guys, he's 'armless'", to which the group again dissolved with mirth. Alexei took the remarks well as always, flicking another stunted finger to the now hysterical masses while muttering Russian curses and insults in their general direction. Subsequently Alexei took revenge on the local remarks about his disability by making a point of opening every item of village mail, before duly practising his English by writing crude and often abusive messages in pencil on the contents. He treasured the educational element of his job.

Today Alexei looked more excited than normal. Having opened the letter to scrawl his customary message of abuse, he had read the letter with increasingly wide eyes as he discovered the news contained within.

However, even though largely uninterested in printed pornography, Alexei had found his interest piqued by the enclosed colour photos in the package, detailing the visit to Strathcarnage of a woman who managed to look both knee weakeningly filthy yet somehow managing at the same time to maintain a somewhat undeserved innocent girl next-door familiar face. Alexei had been impressed and found himself strangely moved by the photos, somehow unwilling to scrawl his traditional daily abuse across such a pretty face, although he had later relented and added some abusive commentary and a detailed drawing of an erect male member to the outer envelope.

News of the letter's arrival travelled fast and the garage workers pressed around Godwin in expectation of hearing the young man read out the contents. As the group gathered, the sound of a piercing female scream made the group jump. Big Nancy had hurriedly pushed the toilet door open to tell Burton of the letter's arrival, fatally forgetting to knock. Burton had later claimed unconscious biological response at the unexpected shock of the opening door, the direct result of which precipitated Big Nancy into a change of overalls. Once everyone was changed and finally assembled, Godwin cleared his throat and began to read.

"To those fine men of Strathcarnage working with 'SPUNK', it gives me great pleasure to announce to you that I, Lottie Savage, will be CUMming to visit you.

Your entry has been chosen as the winner in our CUMpetition, and I look forward meeting Mr Burton Harris and getting to know him *a lot* better. All my love Lottie xxx"

The letter was sealed by a huge lipstick kiss and a simple handwritten letter 'L', which Godwin absent-mindedly mused to be less of an intimate greeting and more the potential result of illiteracy. Next to the signature was the simple drawing of a male member and a quite touching "Galloping Fuck!" of scrawled appreciation from our postman.

Upon hearing the letter's contents, Big Nancy had turned to find Burton standing directly behind her with a remorseful look on his face, an apologetic glance asking for forgiveness at having become excessively excited by the fresh news. Nancy smiled at Burton, lacking the heart to be angry at this moment of celebration and moved silently off to complete another enforced change of overalls.

Inside the envelope with the handwritten note were a number of naked photographs of Lottie and a brief itinerary of her proposed visit to Strathcarnage. She would visit secretly, it stated, with a small entourage made up from a personal make-up artist, publicity staff and a photographer. This small group would be joined by a couple of trained security men to protect the party during Lottie's stay. All this would occur in complete secrecy, agreed after some liaison with The Ox, the local TV station head and an old college friend of the magazine owner.

Posed photos would be taken in the garage premises and then Lottie's entourage would slip away quietly with Burton, to prepare for photographing the intimate romantic dinner in a local restaurant. Burton would follow Lottie in a separate car accompanied by the pair of security guards, the make-up staff, the lighting crew and three photographers. The understated intimacy and romance of the occasion was almost too much to bear.

Also enclosed in the letter was a twenty four page list of conditions. The list ranged from detailing the minimum distance the winner was to be allowed near her genital area during the period of naked exposure, to an extensive list of clauses ruling out bodily contact of any description, together with a number of precise demands for the provision and supply of preferred brands and quantities of baby oil. As Godwin read through the seemingly endless list of extra demands to the gathering, Burton had quickly lost interest in the details, grabbed the enclosed photographs and had hurriedly returned to the safety of his toilet enclosure where he could be heard groaning over the ongoing sound of Goodwin reading the small print aloud to the group.

As the weeks passed, and news of the event spread, anticipation of the visit grew around the village, right up until the day eventually dawned. The Strathcarnage Porcupine, the village newspaper, had published a special souvenir twelve-page colour edition on the visit, together with a free glossy fold out poster and TV guide, the poster featuring Lottie being graphically rear-ended by a huge black man called Clay Roy.

The eagerness greeting the visit owed much to the fact that Lottie was to be the first sighting of a celebrity in Strathcarnage since a local drug mule had appeared in an unplanned walk on role in a national soap opera whilst on a trip outside the town smuggling heroin.

Her eight second appearance, looking gormless whilst attempting to buy sanitary products in the background of a shop scene, had led to the event marked in the town by a 'Sanitary Towel Through The Ages' exhibition in the local museum. The display featured the scene looped on big screens, a framed selection of products and a working display of mechanised and costumed wax models handing over change in a perfect reconstruction of the moment. Sadly the local woman herself had missed the exhibition having been captured shortly afterwards and jailed for thirty years.

As the new celebrity party arrived by the boat specially sent by The Ox, catching the high tide and sailing up the jagged rocky channel leading to hidden harbour behind the town's waterfall, crowds of locals lined the narrow quay walls and clambered onto rock ledges around the mouth of the cave to cheer. Lottie and her entourage had been amazed by the both the size of the welcome and the town's stunning location, leading the topless woman to lean out of the window of the ship's bridge and blow kisses to the crowd. This continued as she sailed towards the quayside, before she disembarked and was met by a specially decorated car.

As the vehicle made its way through the narrow crowd lined streets from the harbour and drew, still backfiring, into the garage forecourt, Giuseppe flicked on a giant neon sign blinking the letters 'SPUNK' on and off above the cheering assembly of invited local schoolchildren. Giuseppe was a man who knew the value of advertising.

The local school had allowed children a special day off to attend the event, and there was to be a presentation from a specially chosen group of the most trusted local primary school pupils. The children had spent weeks on a project to mark the visit, fashioning a giant vulva in the visitor's honour, sculpted from papier-mâché and given a stunning biological realism by children collecting clipped hair donated from local horses. Such was the intense dedication of the pupils that the majority of the town's horses, and some of their parents, now travelled the streets almost bald.

As Lottie stepped from the car, an enormous cheer rose from the assembled crowd, masking a startled scream from Burton, caught short by the sudden excitement and forced to hurriedly change his newly bought khaki waterproof trousers. He had shown a rare foresight, ordering five extra pairs and wearing underneath a small specially welded steel harness designed and hand tooled by children in the school metalwork department, designed especially to avoid him "rising" visibly in company.

Godwin had to admit that Lottie looked wonderful in her chosen PVC outfit, tailored specifically to expose both nipples and the majority of her backside to the cheering crowd. After the unveiling and presentation of the children's model vulva there was a brief photo opportunity for proud parents, before the small group moved inside the garage so the main photographic session of the prize could begin in private. It was during the preparation for the shoot that things started to go wrong.

Godwin had awoken the previous day, swinging his legs out of the bed only to find his feet planted in a fresh lukewarm bowel movement. His cat Clutchbag had found the litter tray full and had taken it upon himself to decorate the bedroom floor in a show of direct action. Finding the local store completely sold out of cat litter and not due another ocean delivery for a few weeks, Godwin had asked about acquiring numerous copies of the local newspaper from the local newsagent. After some good-natured prodding from a bony finger in the chest over his capacity to actually read, it was discovered that some extra copies could be gathered for him by the next morning.

Godwin felt a little subconscious with the newspapers under his arm, and could hear disgusted mumblings at this brazen show of learnedness from some elements of the crowd. Even though Godwin was enjoying the occasion, he wanted to get home to Clutchbag as quickly as possible to both lessen the discovery of random and no doubt extensive feline bowel movements around his home, and to free himself from the open distrust his reading ability was breeding amongst locals.

Thankfully the high-pitched cheers of school children masked the worst of the muttered comments, and Godwin had managed slip unnoticed into the garage to better concentrate his full attention on events. He sidled further away from the crowd during the ceremonial formalities and was glad when he found himself alone inside the large garage shed.

Shortly after Godwin was joined by the rest of the party and before long Lottie was stripped naked with her team of make up artists working furiously to make her look her most wanton, moist and appealing. The photographic team had asked to meet Burton to evaluate he was ready for the photographic session, however he had since retreated to his cubicle again, out of sight and already three pairs of new trousers down on the day and trying hard to preserve the final two for the shoot itself.

The garage staff watched on intently from a distance while Big Nancy, who appeared to be strangely familiar with the proceedings, kept everyone duly informed of what exactly was going on. Suddenly, the door leading from the lavatory swung open, and there stood Burton, wide eyed and breathing heavily. Nancy went to retrieve the ashen faced man and try to calm him on his approach to the naked Lottie.

Burton was led slowly and carefully by Big Nancy across the empty yard and through the large garage doors, ready to meet the object of so many hours of his bathroom based toil. Without warning the Dane was there before him, draped naked over the bonnet of an electric blue Ford Capri, but partially hidden from Burton's gaze behind her entourage and a local photographer trying to catch an iconic image of her shimmering pink adornments for the late edition of the Strathcarnage paper. It was then, as the small group finished its artistic task and parted for the first time that the splayed vision of Lottie was revealed fully to the heavily perspiring Burton. That was the moment when horror struck.

Big Nancy had led a visibly awed Burton slowly towards the scene, but owing to the position of her mountainous frame, it was only as she finally moved aside and pushed the man forward that the highly excited Burton caught his first ever glimpse of a real woman's pudenda.

Events unfolded so suddenly that it was initially unclear just exactly what had occurred. There had been a sudden muffled detonation and screams, followed by a flurry of onrushing security guards diving on someone before the sound of violent blows and further screams. Godwin had been standing behind the group glancing distractedly through his newspaper and had missed the furore entirely. It was only later that the order of events became clear.

On seeing the welcoming unclad spread of Lottie, Burton's abrupt swell of excitement had placed an immeasurable strain on his concealed steel harness, causing him to immediately realise something in his groin area was about to give. Burton had attempted to reach the pressure release valve of the device, but had found his weak arm and clawed hand unable to unzip his trousers with the speed required to reach the creaking harness in time. Deciding to try to manipulate the rapidly swelling area with his other, stronger hand, after some manoeuvring his rigid member had almost freed itself from the harness and into the clutch of his hand, just as the harness finally failed.

Big Nancy received light shrapnel wounds at the point of explosion when the steel contraption gave way, since she was closest to the sexual detonation's epicentre. The hospital informed her afterwards that had it not been for the sudden torrent of liquid following the explosion, she might have received a number of severe burns from the red hot metal. Burton had sensed the oncoming detonation and looked down just in time to witness the contraption's disintegration, his entire genetalia suddenly shorn free from his body by the malfunctioning metal frame of the mechanised restraining harness.

The unexpected commotion stunned Lottie, equally astonished members of her entourage sudden launching themselves onto her naked frame spread on the car bonnet. In the excitement, a number of local photographers and Giuseppe grasped the chance opportunity to provide first aid to the model by adding themselves immediately to the melee atop her naked frame. Lottie eventually wriggled free from the still growing pile of saviours and was hurriedly wiped down, wrapped in a fur coat and rushed inside her car to be whisked away from the emergency. The special competition winner edition of the magazine was ruined, the planned eighteen page feature a disaster.

Or was it?

The magazine's editor, anxious to retrieve something from the shoot, recalled noticing earlier a man reading a large pile of newspapers. His heart sang. He knew that if he could base his entire competition winner feature around someone with an academic slant he could fulfil his long desired ambition to give his magazine some class and himself some kudos as its editor. He would be able to salvage the day and in a single stroke give himself a chance to foster the literary ambitions he had always held for himself. After a frantic search amongst the chaos, he found Godwin in the crowd and barked an order at the remaining security men to shove the young man through the open door of the car and inside with Lottie.

Godwin was amazed. Firstly the surprise explosion and then suddenly, in the clamour, he finds himself suddenly dragged away and bundled inside the tight space in the back of a car. Before he knew what was occurring, Godwin found himself sitting with a naked model and the overly excited editor of one of the biggest porn magazines in Europe.

Godwin began immediately to protest and ask questions, but found himself quickly silenced with a dramatic wave of the editor's jewellery laden hand and told to pay attention to the plan. The young man was to be the switched into the role of winner of the competition and the whole entourage would immediately relocate from the scene of the recent explosive chaos to the restaurant, where a photo shoot of the pair would hastily be arranged. The magazine would pay to clear up all the mess at the garage and construct some later pre-explosion shots in the studio to make the feature look genuine.

"Everything," Godwin was told by the narrow eyed editor through a shifty smile, "will be just fine."

The car sped off, out through the narrow streets of the main town, backfiring and billowing thick black smoke as it headed towards the harbour side restaurant. During the journey, the thick necked driver kept glancing at his rear view mirror and announced in a deep voice that, although it sounded strange, it appeared they were being followed by a ghostly driverless post van.

However the seemingly empty van wasn't some supernatural apparition. The car driver was unable to see the hidden figure of Alexei driving hunched over, his body twisted below the dashboard as his tiny hands gripped the wheel, driving the route blind using the intuition gained from years delivering post along the same familiar twisting village roads.

The smiling editor chose to overlook the event as the actions of another fanatical fan in a strange town, ordering the driver to speed up and lose the pursuer. Lottie was often plagued by obsessive fans wherever she went, and the editor decided another single episode posed the highly trained security team in the car behind no significant problems. With some quick turns and a burst of speed, the ghostly post van was lost.

Godwin discovered on arrival that the chosen location for the romantic meal was the small restaurant owned by the elderly Richard L'Arribo, once a chef in some of the finest hotels in Europe, but arriving to live and work in Strathcarnage after escaping huge gambling debts and some personal disagreements with the Sicilian mafia. Only as Godwin climbed out of the limo and glanced up at the swinging sign did he realise the irony of the restaurant's name. The owner had named the property after his flamboyant speciality of cooking fresh tableside crepes. The swinging wooden sign creaking above them in the sea breeze read "Tossing Dicks"

Back some distance along the harbour side road, Alexei stared out from one of the harbour side lanes, having parked up his van. His eyes began searching along the huge arc of the harbourside, his gaze eventually falling on the outline of the car parked far ahead in front of the lonely restaurant building that sat against the rugged cave wall in the distance.

The postman had been unsure at first, but as Lottie had run past him naked under the open fur coat he had suddenly had a flash of naked familiarity. He hated pornography, but he had known there was something peculiarly well-known to him about this girl. Now it had become clear to him why, he slammed the van door closed with his stumpy arm and set off along the road towards the gathering outside the small isolated building.

The photographer had suggested some exciting location shots on the cliff side rocks just along from the restaurant, featuring both Godwin and Lottie, before moving the pair inside for more intimate internal shots over the meal.

Godwin was feeling profound guilt for denying Burton this chance of meeting his esteemed Lottie, but as he undressed he comforted himself with the recollection that it was, after all, technically his answer that had won the competition. He smiled and pulled in the excess of his soft gut as the naked body of Lottie draped herself over him, relaxing his bare body back against the cold rocks as he watched the camera flash repeatedly.

The sound of running feet and the sight of the onrushing figure of Alexei the postman brought him abruptly back to reality.

Godwin twisted his naked torso round to see Alexei being restrained by Lottie's colossal minders, tears streaming down his face as he watched the pair posing naked atop the rocks.

Godwin was taken aback by sheer level of the man's distress, wondering absent-mindedly if the postman could have technically managed to reach his pocket for a handkerchief to wipe his wet face. Then the postman began shouting in Russian, angry desperation in his voice as he struggled manfully to stop the minders dragging him further away from the scene. The short armed man fought with a power and strength Godwin did not think his slight frame capable of. Suddenly, twisting and breaking free from the grip of the large men, Alexei ran forward and shouted again.

"Lilas? Is it you Lilas?"

Lottie suddenly stopped pouting toward the camera, closed her legs and turned towards him with her hand clamped firmly to her mouth in shock.

"My god!! Alexei? Is it you?" stuttered an unmistakably shaken Lottie.

"Yes, my novotchka, yes. I thought I'd never see you again!" Alexei screamed.

The whole gathering of people looked around at each other, faces knotted in confusion and utter bewilderment.

Then Lottie smiled warmly and began to climb along the rocks, towards Alexei, all the time weeping loudly with happiness. For Alexei knew Lottie by her real name, Lilas Dontrevski.

Lilas had known Alexei in the Moscow orphanage while both were interred there as youths. As young children Lilas had shown him great affection and the pair had formed a deep bond of companionship, at a time when both fellow inmates and staff at the home had cruelly mocked the deformed boy and had treated him brutally. Many evenings had been spent alone with only each other for company, sheltering against the evil world under threadbare orphanage blankets, her caressing his small arms, whispering glorious tales of their future lives together and gazing contentedly into each others eyes. She had promised never to leave him and to be with him always.

However when the home had burned down, and Lilas had been relocated during the night to a new facility for females outside the city, Alexei had been driven to the coast and thrown heartbroken into the sea, due an absence of beds and the unwillingness to house imperfect children. Alexei had thought he would never see his Lilas again.

The pair both wept openly, crying tears of joy and sublime happiness as Alexei ran just out of reach of the confused chasing minders, towards his long lost love. The burly men knew instinctively that he posed Lottie no danger and had stood aside as he ran forward onto the rocks. Lottie stood naked above Alexei, but then covered herself slowly and modestly as she suddenly remembered Lilas. She was once again the innocent Russian girl who had changed her name and moved abroad, heartbroken and unable to find any trace of Alexei, to lose herself in work and to forget her identity in the Danish porn industry.

She moved towards Alexei, searching the rocky outcrop for a quick way down after realising Alexei was having difficulty climbing with such small arms. Lilas picked her way slowly downwards towards Alexei, craving her return into that small hug of her life's destiny. As she descended down to a ledge above the road, Lilas looked for a safe point to jump down in order to reach her lost childhood soul mate. Alexei could take her away from this squalid life of baby oil and exposed genitalia, return her back to a deeper happiness and more innocent times. As she edged along closer to his position she suddenly noticed the smooth black mass of a large rock just below her, easily within jumping distance. Her heart sang as she launched herself downwards towards her lost love.

At least it sang for a second or two until she hit the glossy black surface of the rock. Or what she had assumed to be a rock. The hefty black outcrop below her had turned out to be the decomposed carcass of a huge black sea lion, washed ashore in recent storms, the bloated dark cadaver having lain for days fermenting in the sun.

As she hit it, the force of her impact caused her naked body to detonate the swollen mass with a dull thump, putrid seal flesh burying her up to her knees. Alexei was beside her in moments, jumping forward excitedly to gather her with his outstretched miniature embrace covered in rotting flesh. He landed in the putrid carcass with a loud sucking sound, feet sinking easily into the rotten flesh alongside his long lost companion as he attempted to partially gather her in his arms.

The distraught magazine editor had later been incapable of persuading Lottie to continue in the industry, but after some negotiations she had agreed happily to recount the entire details of the day as a serious story, with an extensive final farewell shoot of tastefully posed photographs, included one poignant shot of the reunited couple hugging while partially buried inside the remnants of the exploded seal carcass.

Once reunited with Alexei, Lilas had officially made a statement to announce her decision to retire with immediate effect and to spend her remaining days with the short armed Russian postman. Lottie was never to appear again in these sordid descriptions of depravity and those final photos of her naked body, knee deep in sea lion carcass and being hugged tenderly by a disabled postman, were to remain forever her last published work.

In a tragic footnote to this epic tale of romance, Alexei and Lilas decided not to hang around the town to wait on a passing Russian ship to carry them safely home across the sea. Alexei decided to hire a small boat in order to return homeward immediately, both desperate and impatient to begin their new life.

It was aboard this small vessel that the two are thought to have perished, drowned by a titanic storm which blew up the night they departed. It is thought that Alexei's small arms were not wide enough to fight the massive ocean swell and row them both to safety.

Weeks later, pieces of the smashed boat wreckage shattered and broken by massive waves were found floating in the sea off the jagged rocks at the entrance to the town's hidden approach channel. Theirs was a terrible tale of true but tragic love and no bodies were ever recovered. They lie together forever at sea, somewhere off the secret town of Strathcarnage.

Alexei Burchovsky 1957-1978
Lilas Dontrevski (aka Lottie) 1958-1978

## CHAPTER 5

## Day Three – Yoyo

Hubris Moss tipped the glass upside down over his mouth and drained the very last drops from his third cloudy Pernod, whisky and lime, the intense burning deep in his chest contorting his face into the glassy eyed expression of pain that gave his drink its name: The Stroke Victim.

Recovering, he ordered another from the blind barman Sean, loudly guiding him along the array of bottles behind the bar until he again laid his grasping sightless hands on the correct ingredients.

Ever prone to invention, Sean's blindness had been cunningly incorporated by the bar owner into a daily happy hour, an event where more adventurous customers paid a flat rate and Sean staggered around behind the bar pouring a random mixture of spirits. You got four measures in your glass from different optics of, quite literally, blind choice. Even with the other marginally more predictable options available to Strathcarnage drinkers, this remained the best pub in town.

The village, in common with many coastal towns, was well blessed with pubs. In addition to the local hotel's bar, there were five other dedicated drinking establishments; The Lech, an underground Albanian theme pub hidden in one of the caves in the town's walls, where the food, drink staff and décor were uniformly grey and utterly disheartening; The Ruptured Horse, high on the cliff road and frequented mostly by locals with strong horses and good hiking boots wanting to gaze down over the village; The Zoo, near the village green, which doubled as a "nightclub" and was named after both the behaviour of the customers at the evening's end and the local's habit of closing the steel barred gate to keep them inside and off the streets; The Rosebush, a harbour side bar so called because it always had a distinctive aroma together with a customer base of dangerous pricks. That left one more pub in the town, the one sat among the village's twisting lanes and where Hubris Moss sat right now. It was called simply The Harse.

Aldo DeLauro, a shady second cousin of Giuseppe the local garage owner, owned the Harse. He was presumed to be Italian, but locals remained uncertain, since Aldo was a difficult man to locate let alone to ask. Even Harse regulars had only ever spotted the dark haired man on the premises once, on the fateful night when he had accidentally blinded Sean during the insanity of a "free pints of gin with every packet of squirrel eye snacks" promotional night.

The bar's name had proved popular around the village, pronounced as it was with a dropped 'h'. It didn't help that the H from the word Harse had long since fallen off the sign, leaving the locals to fully justify their comedy dropped consonant. Blind Sean the barman had once tried to fix the sign, but in the failure to calculate the correct ladder height, he had first nailed the pub doors shut, and then proceeded to energetically hammer the newly acquired gold 'H' to the back of a passing teacher.

Partially to recover customer confidence after the incident, the bar had embarked on an aggressive press and radio advertising campaign. The chosen advertising slogans of "Wedding? Christening? Take your entire family up The Harse!" and the even more memorable "On Valentines Day, be sure and make the effort to take your girlfriend up The Harse. You know she wants to..." had all contributed to making the pub the busiest in the town. In fact, at weekends it was nigh impossible to manoeuvre yourself down the narrow lane where it lay and into the entrance. Of course local legend had it that once you managed to eventually squeeze yourself inside, you were certain to become a devotee of the sensation of tightly packed familiarity and enjoy the warm greeting.

Hubris Moss, currently sitting inside The Harse draining his next freshly mixed cocktail, worked as a gardener for Lord Strathcarnage at his sprawling home of Haversack Hall perched on the cliff side at the far end of the town.

Or at least he had until this afternoon.

The great sandstone house had burst into a flurry of commotion around midday, when a sea of local law men and journalists from the local Porcupine newspaper had suddenly descended onto the Hall grounds. Staff were told to gather immediately in the lawns below the house where acting head manservant Kwai forlornly told the small crowd the news of an incident in Rome, where the Lord had been killed in a freak explosion in his suite.

On hearing the news, Hubris had glanced worriedly at the oriental manservant, Kwai, still swathed in bandages and unsteady on his feet after an unfortunate motor accident earlier in the week. All the Hall staff had gathered here, Hubris presumed, to be told of their redundancies. Without any readily evident heir, the sprawling hall would remain empty until the family line could be determined and the title of Lord Strathcarnage passed on to a new Lord who would assume responsibility for the entire operation. This clause was a stipulation of the only known existing will, tattooed on the back of a small Spanish child with a lazy eye found wandering the stables in chains. Save for a skeleton staff, it was announced that the hall would close for the time being and the entire workforce were to be released with immediate effect.

Hubris Moss was devastated. He had worked at Haversack Hall ever since Lord Strathcarnage had hired him, a sympathetic gesture announced in the week after the Lord himself had ran over and crippled Hubris' father during a tractor accident on the harbour side. Since then, Hubris' entire working life had been spent as a gardener in the Hall and now, made redundant, the young man had little idea what to do with his life.

There was very little work in the town available to use the services of a decorative hedge trimmer specialising in phallic symbolism. What now for a young man whose only other vaguely notable talent was that he enjoyed it up The Harse. It was here the despondent young man had gone to seek cold comfort in a few 'Stroke Victims', having immediately headed into town seeking the comfortable familiarity the bar offered after the bleak news of joblessness was broken to him.

As Hubris drained his fourth Stroke Victim of its remaining power, his unfocused eye had been drawn to a bright new orange poster pinned above the end of the bar. Lost in his misery he hadn't noticed it before, but as he tried to focus just enough to read he found his dark mood lifted slightly at the prospect of an evening of his favourite music.

The poster announced an upcoming weekend concert certain to draw a big Strathcarnage crowd; the recently reformed local punk band "The Ruptured Spleens". As if the prospect of seeing his childhood heroes wasn't enough to raise his spirits, the upcoming show announced the return of Quentin Smithee as compere for the evening.

Quentin was a local Strathcarnage child prodigy who had the unusual gift of being somehow able to recite, when asked, the date and manner of any relative's death, the precise location of the fatality, and many other strange details involved, such as the identification of the first two courses of the victim's final meal.

Rumours in the village suggested that the young boy was now working on extending his act further to add impersonations of the final sounds made by the failing victim. Nothing was yet been confirmed on that score but the poster promised a luminous evening's entertainment.

Hubris sat lost in thought, absentmindedly running the remaining drops around the thick base of his empty glass and deciding what to do next. He had asked about a redundancy package earlier, after hearing the news at Haversack Hall, however he had been informed that the current executors of Lord Strathcarnage's estate only held legal powers to dispose of his stable of show children.

Indeed, under the terms of the recently deceased Lord's will it was dictated that the only prospect of redundant workers receiving any severance payment in the present circumstances lay in them challenging the heavily tattooed Haversack Hall book-keeper Miss Scrimshaw to a battle to the death with samurai swords in the Hall parlour.

Hubris had politely declined his own option to battle for payment after watching the heavily muscled woman swiftly dispatch both Alan and John Butters, the Hall's twin 75-year-old gardeners, with flashing sweeps of her expertly wielded blades.

Indeed Alan Butters almost looked to be on the verge of winning his modest award of redundancy cash at one point, but had caught his foot in the empty neck of his now dead brother's decapitated body. Seeing the slight pause Miss Scrimshaw had taken her chance and sliced the elderly man clean in half, receiving as she did a large round of applause from the assembled spectators.

Hubris had little money remaining from his final wage packet, but decided he desperately needed cheering up. Finishing the last drops of his Stroke Victim, the young topiarist was sure an evening's welcome distraction fighting and being spat on to the music of Ruptured Spleen was too alluring a prospect to miss.

He also calculated that it may be possible to make up the monetary shortfall brought on by events by offering his gardening services and hedge trimming skills around the village. After all, the young man was forever being asked to do odd jobs by those locals lucky enough have gardens, often being stopped in the street and called upon at home for help and advice in gardening matters. With some hard work he hoped he might just be able to earn enough money to survive on.

The Reverend Whisp was one example. This mad churchman was constantly trying to persuade the gardening man to complete work on the sprawling bush at the door of his church just off the village green, frequently asking the young gardener to fashion the vast growth into the shape of a multi-bodied orgy.

Hubris decided he would splash out on a ticket for the forthcoming concert, confident his finances would quickly pick up. He rose shakily from his stool, steadied himself against the gyrating room and headed off outside into the lane, staggering northwards towards the Strathcarnage Holliday Inn to buy tickets for the concert. He was grinning at the prospect out of just one side of his mouth, his partially paralysed face a mark of his recent drink's potency.

The Strathcarnage Holliday Inn was a strange place, even for this village. It had been established for over 60 years and was named in honour of the original founder, Tommy Holliday. Although a long established historical landmark carved into the town caves, it was an old dark cramped building with odd shaped damp rooms and few customers. Indeed the opening of a newer Strathcarnage hotel of the very same name in the elevated town streets beneath Haversack Hall had caused Tommy great frustration at the sheer cheek of the new building's owner, Jack Holliday. Jack was Tommy's younger brother.

The older hotel owner had objected to the new identically named competition and had sent over a small party of Strathcarnage lawyers to persuade Jack to change his establishment's name to something less likely to affect his business. Jack had quickly found negotiations extremely tiresome and soon exhibited the violent streak habitually brought on by his notorious short attention span. The younger Holliday brother had chosen to conclude proceedings by excusing himself during the middle of the meeting, changing into a green Lycra wrestling leotard and decorated mask, and then slamming two of the eminent lawyers through an outsized mahogany boardroom table.

The lawyers returned to their client unsatisfied, one in traction.

Tommy was a bitter man and soon took it upon himself to close his hotel in the caves near the harbour and relocate his business. Tommy's decision was to build an exact replica of his brother's hotel, right next door to his sibling's new building. It was an initiative designed, he declared in the press release, "purely to get right on my brother's tits".

Tommy Holliday had exhibited considerable foresight in later adding a large conference hall behind his own new version of the Holliday Inn, inside which he planned to use a section to house his extensive collection of prosthetic limbs and orthopaedic memorabilia from his time as a war surgeon.

Indeed Tommy had gathered the money to pay for the new hotel's construction by selling looted Nazi war memorabilia from this era of his life, paying tribute to his greatest obsession by continually flying a large stolen swastika flag above the hotel. In addition Tommy's large new conference hall now served as the only event venue in the town, ever since a suspicious fire had completely destroyed the town Fisherman's Mission. Until the inferno had taken hold, the building was the only other space in Strathcarnage capable of housing any large group of people.

As Hubris eventually climbed through the maze of twisting lanes and alleys and arrived on the long arched road at the top of the town, he walked toward the bizarre sight of the two identical hotels, turning into the car park of the building with the vast swastika flag rippling in the breeze high above the fresh tarmac. As he stood and gazed upward, the faint sound of a pitched battle had floated toward him across the car park, emanating from the open lobby doors. The young man had glanced in the direction of the hotel but saw no visible sign of any excitement and had returned his attention to the flag and the large rotating sign.

Tommy Holliday had erected a large Las Vegas type neon display, to exactly match that of his brother next door. It rotated slowly on a massive steel pole above the car park, a blinking monument to Tommy Holliday's ongoing ambition and determination to annoy his sibling.

Under Tommy's sign was a large lettered panel, announcing forthcoming attractions to both his brother and to the only two other nearby hillside residents who occasionally used the road to drive their sheep to grazing. Hubris had climbed to the isolated hotels looking over the village solely to buy tickets for the forthcoming concert, but soon found his attention diverted by the large red announcement hanging on the slowly turning sign.

While he waited on the sign to revolve to a better angle to read the message, he listened to the flapping swastika above and the fresh clamour of raised voices and screams emanating again from the open hotel doors. As the sign turned to angle where Hubris could read the message, he noticed with some confusion that it announced this version of the Holliday Inn was currently hosting the annual World Freestyle Yo-Yo Championships.

In his capacity as an Army surgeon Tommy Holliday had accidentally sawn both legs off an unfortunate American serviceman during the war and in the years following the surgical gaffe the two men had kept in touch. The limbless soldier, one Ryan Kolowski from Buckwash, Idaho, had gone on to father a child, one Ryan Jnr, who had gone on to exhibit the skills and talent needed to become the World Freestyle Yo-Yo Champion of 1974 and 75. In a show of great personal appreciation at Tommy Holliday having saved his father's life, Ryan Jnr had secretly brought an unofficial version of the World Freestyle Championships to the new hotel in Strathcarnage, together with a small boatful of contestants from abroad who had been sworn to secrecy and smuggled there from the mainland.

Thankfully, given the men's lifelong friendship and the effort he had made in secretly organising the competition, both Ryan Kolowski's Jnr and Senior remained blissfully unaware that Tommy Holliday had been roaring drunk on the evening of the surgical procedure which linked the two men, and that he had actually sawn off the older man's legs purely by mistake. On the evening in question over 30 years ago now, the young American soldier had been admitted the field hospital suffering only with a suspected concussion.

As Hubris crossed the busy car park and entered the bright Holliday Inn foyer to buy tickets for the show, he found the hotel's front desk empty and a full-scale riot underway. It transpired the small Israeli yo-yo team had taken offence to the swastika flying above the hotel, and on marching to the reception desk to complain, had come across the German team presenting their extended right arms toward the glowering face of team manager Herr Fischer. Unfortunately, dressed in his team's khaki uniform and red manager's armband, the man bore an uncanny resemblance to a certain dictator with black hair and a penchant for invading Poland.

Unfortunately for the stern German team manager, and for the sensibilities of the Israeli party, today was Herr Fischer's birthday. Some immature members of the young German team had decided to play a practical joke on the perpetually miserable man by offering him an explosive trick cigar. The cigar had subsequently detonated while Herr Fischer sat relaxing and reading a newspaper in the hotel foyer, leaving a thick black scorch mark directly under his nose, and causing his heavily gelled black hair to fall over his eyes on one side. This detonation caused the German Team great amusement and the group had collectively begun mimicking Herr Fisher's attempts to waft the smoke away with a stiff extended arm, just as the Israeli party had arrived en masse from the upper floors of the hotel.

Greeted by the sight of the collected German party surrounding their manager and waving stiff arms in salute, the Israelis had failed to appreciate the larger context of the joke, immediately wading into the German Yo-yo team with a viciousness unseen since the last Strathcarnage Women's Guild coffee morning. On that occasion the brutal incident involved a sherry fuelled rampage of anger and recrimination after an elderly Mrs McSween had violently disputed low marks given to her handmade crack pipes by three heavily built elderly judges.

Unfortunately the town press and TV had been already gathered at the hotel to interview the first Israeli team to visit the town, the unusual event given blanket local coverage in the village media. The assembled news gatherers couldn't believe their luck.

The local TV Company had heavily sponsored the event, hoping to force repeated highlights on a largely uninterested local audience, but had quickly realised that footage of this riot would help promote keen interest in the event, especially in a community obsessed by any outbreak of violence and disorder.

The village lay tucked inside a massive cavern under vast sea cliffs, the collection of buildings making up the town and harbour nestled deep inside colossal walls of stone. This geographical location, as well as serving to contain the locals in this vast rock womb, also had the unfortunate effect of keeping any national TV or radio signals out. Therefore the sole source of TV entertainment for the village was the Strathcarnage Community Associated Broadcasting Services.

Run by an American Acid casualty originally from San Francisco and known simply as "The Ox", the local company provided an obscure mix of hardcore pornography from visiting ship crews, grainy 8mm home movie footage of The Ox at Woodstock and a quantity of rubber fetish porn films from The Ox's personal collection. This output was supplemented with any local programmes the company could make cheaply about town life, or any films produced by the residents themselves.

No event of any note ever passed within Strathcarnage without the appearance of the small blue van with the broadcast company's logo on the side. Under a cartoon representation of a TV camera, the logo read simply, "Pick SCABS".

The Ox was a huge bearded man, who had chosen his current title since forgetting his real name after dropping a complete sheet of Blue Flash Acid in the late sixties during a free love sit in in San Francisco. The Ox had subsequently adopted this new name on the basis it was easy both to remember and to write when gripped by one of his more aggressive flashbacks. He had managed to keep the company running continuously for 30 years by rotating this collection of material and the occasional self made fetish video featuring him and his long time girlfriend Big Nancy. The station costs were paid for by dealing home produced drugs both in the community and with visiting sailors, and some blackmail, both activities greatly helped by his unfettered access to free advertising.

However as an experienced television executive, he knew this current riot in the Holliday Inn foyer was an unmissable opportunity to make fresh and cheap programming for the townsfolk of Strathcarnage. He knew instinctively that the more people watched, the more his locally made drug and fetish video adverts would encourage locals to buy his products.

As a result, when the fight started, The Ox had quickly and instinctively ripped off Big Nancy's clothing and thrust her into the thick of the riot, her massive breasts swinging unfettered in the melée. The Ox knew his market and was keen to enhance the potential appeal of the footage. It was this high level executive directing decision that was to impact profoundly on the remainder of Hubris' night.

Hubris had been watching the fight progress from the relative safety of the open foyer doors, only to suddenly find himself broadsided by a huge pair of swinging, naked breasts, knocking him forward, off balance into the battling crowd of bodies.

As the fight progressed, the whole pack of combatants crashed repeatedly to and fro across the foyer, and, just as suddenly as he had been dragged into the melee, Hubris found himself ejected out of the other side of the melee through the double doors leading to the World Freestyle Yo-Yo Championships arena. As the sprung doors closed behind him with a whoosh, the shocked young man looked up and found himself in what seemed like a whole other world.

The Yo-Yo crowd, both competitors and audience alike, were a sight to behold, flamboyantly milling around to noisy music, utterly oblivious to the riot outside. As another condition of his local TV Company sponsoring the Freestyle Championships, The Ox had insisted on a number of local novelty acts being introduced to the event to help viewing figures. As a direct result Hubris found himself inside the main hall inspecting the extraordinary sight of a crowd of youthful men in baseball hats and black rock band t-shirts whooping enthusiastic support at a man entirely covered in thick body hair and deftly swinging a pair of flashing yo-yo's around his monkey-like body.

The new 'Hirsute Flyers' category was a hugely popular, and one of the few chances for folically challenged Yo-yo obsessives to showcase their talents. The display drew an enthusiastic crowd, drawn there by the fascination of watching had freakish natural talents of excessive body hair growth combine with the comedy potential for yo-yo string getting caught in thick shaggy pelt. The complexity of the more showy tricks led to a number of hairy competitors being halted by tangles and snagged string, sudden piercing screams of pain bringing about the attendance of onrushing stewards with sharp silver scissors.

Hubris watched for a time as a panel of tattooed judges, identified by name racks on the desk before them, marked the hairy contenders on their expertise. The romance of their glamorous names entranced Hubris; "Spinner Mackay", "LeRoy Lasso", and his new personal favourite, "The Whip". Hubris had never seen such an exciting show.

Around the hall there were stalls to buy memorabilia; personalised Yo-Yo's, posters of the greats, signing sessions from past champions. There was colour, excitement and a huge sense of occasion, all helped by the constant background mixture of cheering, pockets of applause weaving through the ever present sound of loud pounding music.

Each competitor on the main stage had his or her routine accompanied by an energetic soundtrack as they were introduced enthusiastically onstage by Clint, a mulleted, leather faced man in a rhinestone encrusted white suit. It appeared to be Clint's sole task to whip the crowd as quickly as possible into a frenzy of whooping encouragement for whatever act was due to arrive onstage next. Hubris raised an eyebrow as he noticed the presence in the hall of the Strathcarnage Mayor, Alice Noyce, concluding to himself that this event must surely be of greater local importance than he had first imagined. Hubris found himself rapidly becoming converted to the ways of the Yo-yo.

Hubris was unaware that Alice Noyce had attended the Championships for two main reasons. Firstly, she was astute enough to realise she would be guaranteed TV exposure as a figure of importance in Strathcarnage, and she knew this exposure negated any further need to crawl slowly around the narrow warren of lanes in the town going through the torture of meeting and greeting the local people. These were people that she both loathed and was intimidated by.

Regardless of her distaste Alice knew that she still required these townspeople's votes to retain her position as town Mayor. She retained a standing majority of only three, two of whom, she had learned earlier, had been cut to pieces earlier today during redundancy negotiations at Haversack Hall.

Alice calculated that presenting prizes at such a fashionable event might help promote her image with the town's younger voters, without any need for her to directly interact with these most fearsome residents.

Her secondary reason for being here was to secretly meet her father, Aldo, the owner of the town's favourite pub, The Harse.

Following her election as town mayor, she had encouraged her father to spend very little time in his pub for the good of her political career, fearful of the press uncovering the secret family connection between the pair and of them bringing up the incident where her father had blinded Sean Driscoll, the pub barman. Alice Noyce had been the reason her father had been distracted that evening, and thus the indirect cause of Sean's blindness. It would ruin her career. However the arrangement had worked so far and no-one in the village had yet linked the two. So far, so good.

Meanwhile Hubris had begun chatting to a small group of older men all wearing t-shirts with the slogan "Yo-Yo fans like swinging every which way!" They had travelled from the mainland in the darkness, signing legally binding declarations of secrecy in the hold of the special boat laid on to ferry the small number of contestants and fans from the outside to this strange hidden village. The group were keen fans from America, only present at the championship to support the appearance of their hero "Loopy Maria", an entrant from their hometown in Skeem, Nebraska.

Maria, the group had excitedly revealed to Hubris, was a strong second favourite to win the Nude Female Freestyle category. Hubris had been chatting to the men for some time when conversation had moved on to the topic of his day's bad luck. Hearing the recent story of his redundancy, a few members of the group stopped and stared between each other, then back at him, mouths agape.

"What did you just say there, boy?" asked one of the men.

"That I lost my job," Hubris said confused.

"No, no boy, just before that," the American man asked eagerly.

"That I was an ornamental hedge trimmer?" Hubris asked, now even more confused.

The group huddled together and whispered amongst themselves excitedly. After some unheard discussion and gesturing, the group began cheering and hugging Hubris warmly.

"My boy, you come with me. You just done gone and made our day."

The largest of the men slipped an enormous arm around Hubris at the shoulder and steered him quickly through the crowd toward the backstage area, men at the front clearing a path while appreciative hands from the rest of the following group patted him on his back. Hubris soon found himself in an unfamiliar area beyond the edges of his already blurred mental map of the gathering.

After a winding journey through a further maze of busy corridors backstage, Hubris soon found thrust through an unmarked red door. Staring back at the confused young man was the unclothed form of Loopy Maria, Nebraska's premier naked Yo-Yo proponent. The dark haired girl looked to Hubris as if she had been crying heavily. She sat alone with her head in her hands, a look of profound sadness in her eyes as she glanced up from under her long brown fringe at the faces of the small crowd now packed into her changing room.

The man who had initially seemed most excited by the news of his occupation was now whispering animatedly into the naked athlete's ear. Maria suddenly began to smile before gazing with blue eyes in the direction of the younger visitor. Hubris was at a loss to work out precisely what was happening. The whispering man walked over and shook his hand before collecting the others and leaving the room. Each of the men had again patted him on the back and shook his hand warmly, smiling broadly as they left. The final member of the group told him to 'do his best for our girl son, y'hear' before closing the door behind him, gently. Suddenly he was alone with the naked female Yo-yo maestro.

Loopy Maria walked slowly across the room and shook Hubris by the hand with a friendly smile. The young man blushed faintly at the nakedness of the woman, noticing her beauty of the woman's young face, trying desperately to fight the natural inclination of his eyes to fall downwards over the curved lines of her stunning body.

"Don't blush, Hubris baby, it's just what we were all born with. Anyways, I think that maybe you can help me," she said recognising his discomfort and dismissing his shyness with a wink.

Hubris blushed again, this time at the realisation of how quickly his feelings for his new naked friend were spreading through him.

Outside in the hotel lobby, The Ox had checked he had all of the fight footage he required before stepping in and trying to restore calm. As the two sides gradually parted and retreated back to take positions on opposite sides of the lobby, The Ox had ensured his crew got fresh images of the badly injured German team leader lying unconscious in the centre of the room.

Big Nancy, it was quickly decided, was to remain at the hotel fully topless, to walk round the Yo-Yo competition hall and hopefully draw a substantial appreciative crowd. The Ox left the hotel foyer with a satisfied smile, moving both himself and his camera crew into the main arena to film the highlights of the sporting side of the night. As the doors swung closed behind him, he heard the fighting begin afresh in the lobby.

Already convinced the captured fight footage alone would ensure one of his ratings highlights of the year, The Ox happily arranged his camera crew around the main stage to capture another sure-fire ratings winner for his station, the Woman's Naked Freestyle Finals.

No sooner had he finished setting up his broadcast equipment than a noisy buzz of expectation grew in the hall. Clint, the mulleted announcer, strode across the stage, winked directly into the camera, and declared start of the event was a matter of minutes away. Before exiting the stage he returned back to the spot lit microphone to announce the attendance of Town Mayor Alice Noyce as a special guest to present the trophies and the winner's cheques.

Alice had worked with The Ox on many occasions and had agreed with the local television mogul that she should only be filmed after the event had completed and once the naked competitors had fully covered up. She hoped the verbal agreement would save her from any potential embarrassment and any chance of losing vital votes. The Ox was happy to oblige the mayor, delighted with capturing the riot footage which he was sure would be the night's highlight. No one paid much attention to the office of town Mayor anyway, and The Ox figured people would have wiped themselves down and turned off long before the frankly boring coverage of prize presentation and shaking hands began.

Meanwhile, Tommy Holliday, the hotel owner, had been rushing anxiously around backstage with his ear glued to a phone. Tommy had been badly let down by his usual trophy designer. A talented local model maker, Crosby Stanton had been designing a unique selection of tournament trophies, but had been killed after a fire the night before at his home workshop and now Tommy had been forced into making an emergency change of plan. His last minute decision was to prove not only a highlight of the evening, but to also provide the town with a glorious shock.

On the other side of the arena, Hubris was busy backstage, putting the finishing touches to the job in hand. Redundant a few hours ago, he could never have dreamed he was to be back in demand so quickly.

Maria had been distant second best in the championships for a number of years, repeatedly beaten to the title by her main rival, a Dutch Yo-Yo artist called Ulle from Utrecht. The young Strathcarnage man had initially found Maria so upset because she was convinced there was little hope of beating her fiercest rival at yet another meeting. The Dutch girl was almost identical in technical ability to Maria, but had continually won enthusiastic crowd support and extra judging points by cleverly utilising a range of quirky gimmicks.

Ulle had won in Norway due to painting her breasts in the colours of the Norwegian Flag, and recently, at an event in Australia, because her sudden appearance with a hand painted kangaroo across her long Dutch back combined with a pierced nipple with an attached a small Australian flag. Maria had seen Ulle enter the hall smiling broadly earlier in the day, her entire body covered tightly by a robe and a woollen hat. Maria despaired at the use of another novelty, desolate that any chance of Championship victory had gone again.

At least so she had thought, until her little band of loyal supporters had brought her the news of Hubris' previous occupation.

Her chairman of travelling supporters, Hank, had whispered his news of Hubris and details of his idea. As his plan was explained, Maria grew less forlorn and began smile, confident she might at last have some small chance at beating the showy Ulle at her own game.

When Maria eventually hit the stage later in the evening, the audience had erupted. The previous competitor and Maria's competitive nemesis, Ulle, had revealed to the crowd her head dyed in the colours of the Scottish flag and paintings of a Scottish Lion down both thighs. The patriotic crowd had cheered noisily at the sight and enthusiastically clapped the Dutchwoman in time to her music throughout her routine.

But this time, for once, Maria had not watched in despair. She was smiling broadly, content that she might this once manage to beat her nemesis at her own game.

With Hubris Moss's artistry and skill at foliage design, and nearly an hour cutting feverishly with a borrowed pair of sharp nail scissors, the young man had fashioned Maria's unruly pubic hair into a silhouette of the town skyline, managing even to skilfully arch the name Strathcarnage above the scene across her lower abdomen.

The local crowd went absolutely berserk at the sight, chanting Maria's name repeatedly throughout her routine. As she landed her finish with perfect timing, the entire hall had erupted in a deafening roar. Ulle watched from the edge of the stage, her face pale and expressionless. It was the look of a beaten woman.

On finishing the competition to her thunderous ovation, the judges had then gathered Maria and the other competitors together on stage to reveal their marks. Maria received easily the best scores of her career, soundly beating the now weeping Dutch girl into second place. The winner's trophy was to be hers at long last.

Maria wept openly with delight. Her chance meeting with a shy and attractive local boy had made the difference and ended her long, lonely wait for victory. Indeed such was the quality of the artistic workmanship on show that the local TV network had asked afterwards to take close up shots of her exquisitely crafted pubic hair for use in links between programmes. The Ox had even suggested slowly opening her legs to give greater illustration of the town's deep valley location, a request that was denied with a well placed slap.

Yet Maria was ecstatic at the victory and nothing was going to spoil her celebration of this euphoric moment of victory, fighting her way through the large crowd of new fans and well-wishers after her performance to find Hubris and offer him her deepest thanks.

Back onstage, Tommy Holliday was preparing for the prize giving and had pulled back a white sheet to unveil the trophies. Owing to the fire at the trophy designer Crosby Stanton's home, the original awards had been ruined, melted by the ferocious heat into unrecognisable blobs of metal. Tommy had been distraught.

However, right at the last minute, an unlikely solution had presented itself. The local town blacksmith had been told of the crisis and let Holliday know of the sudden cancellation to the annual Strathcarnage Horse Breeders Awards as a mark of respect to the recent death of Lord Strathcarnage. These bronzes intended for the horse show were the only remaining trophies available at such short notice. Tommy had accepted the offer graciously.

The uncovering of the replacement trophies explained the shock gasp of reaction from the crowd, the look of horror from Mayor Alice Noyce and the sudden heightened joy of The Ox. All parties immediately realised the implications involved with the handling and subsequent presentation of these emergency stand in awards. Before them on the table lay three twelve inch high, anatomically perfect, bronze sculptures of horse penises, the substitute tokens for the winners.

Even with the hurried painting of the attached bronze testicles to better resemble yo-yos, Alice was stunned at the prospect of appearing on local TV clutching a twelve inch bronze erect horse's phallus. It was even worse than even Mayor Noyce had anticipated. Once The Ox had seen the trophies unveiled, he had whispered immediate instructions to his team to cut into the station signal and beam the event live throughout the town. He knew potential television gold when he saw it.

Bad news indeed for the Mayor, but even worse was yet to come.

Alice sat stunned, staring like a zombie at the glinting trophies on the judge's table. She was transfixed, barely noticing the participants taking the stage for the closing ceremony before the final presentation. With the main events already over and the winners decided, all that remained was for the evening's event to be formally closed by one final display of yo-yo skill.

Enid 'Wheels' Brownlee was a popular wheelchair enthusiast from the village, and although she had only given jaw dropping demonstrations of her talents in local pubs, she had been invited by Tommy Holliday to perform an exhibition routine to close the show.

The Strathcarnage crowd knew the local woman and admired her spirit, clapping noisily in appreciation at her appearance. Yet while some of the gathering were clapping in open recognition of her courage in the face of adversity, the vast majority were applauding the sight of her huge vast unencumbered upper torso. Enid performed naked.

The Strathcarnage woman had been performing her routine magnificently, smiling broadly from under her tight blonde perm, her chair specially adapted to be thrown fully through 360 degrees at great pace. The special design allowed both her yo-yo acrobatics and her pendulous breasts to whirl freely. All was going well for Enid and her gravity-defying display was mesmerizing. Right up until her fatal attempt to complete the final show-closing move.

Enid had decided on the innovation of using two yo-yos for her final flourish. It was a new adaptation to her act designed to please the crowd and show a new technical proficiency. As she brought the second yo-yo into the act swinging wildly in time to the music, the crowd chanted their approval.

However, as the wheelchair spun around the stage at greater and greater velocity, one of her undulating breasts had swung free and caught in the tread of her special competition wheelchair tyres. The sudden meeting of breast and rubber caused the tyre to come to a sudden halt and the chair to violently jack-knife, throwing a naked Enid, and her chair, over the stage edge. Her trajectory was propelling her fatally in an arc towards the judging table.

Alice Noyce returned her attention back to the show on hearing the crowd's sudden gasps of horror. Catching the faint odour of burning rubber in the air, she turned just in time to watch the naked mass of Enid hit the table, breasts first, with a deafening bang.

The force of the impact on the table's edge was so great as to cause the complete flat surface to pivot and act like a huge catapult. In seconds, the three heavy brass horse's penises were propelled aloft, rising upward and soaring through the air like rockets.

The Mayor followed the upward path of the objects, but lost the trophy in flight, its path masked by the glare of the spotlights. The largest and heaviest of the collection of bronze horse penises spun in mid air and shot back to earth, hitting Alice Noyce heavily on the side of her head, knocking her instantly unconscious.

Alice fell heavily to the carpeted floor, her final position leaving her lying right next to the offending brass phallus. She lay positioned in such a way that the unfortunate sight being broadcast live to the town was that of the Town Mayor with her limp hand on a huge erect horse member pointing straight to her gaping open mouth.

Even at this point, all remained potentially manageable for Alice, an inopportune accident captured in full and soon forgotten. It was an unfortunate mishap that may even promote sympathy amongst some.

However, any potential salvaging of the situation soon collapsed as her worried father had pushed his way through the crowd to his daughter's aid. Aldo didn't reach his daughter until she was just regaining consciousness; his arrival coinciding perfectly with close ups from an onrushing TV camera crew. As the unit editor switched to live transmission from these cameras, her entire political career was to about to end.

Strathcarnage mayor Alice Noyce appeared on the TV screens of the whole town, captured in glorious colour, turning to her father while still clutching and waving around an erect bronze penis, before loudly announcing "Daddy, Daddy, can we go home? Please daddy, take me up The Harse. Take me up The Harse like you used to do when I was small, don't tell them our secret. " Alice smiled sweetly at her father, looked round bewildered at the cameras, rolled her eyes and suddenly slumped to the floor again, quite dead.

Hubris had missed all of the excitement and these subsequent events brought about by Enid's accidental tumble. Maria had found him. The naked girl had pushed her way through the anonymous faces of the crowd until she found her young pubic topiarist, embracing him warmly before slowly leaning in and planting a lingering and passionate kiss firmly on his lips, to loud cheering from the surrounding crowd.

Hubris had been initially shocked, but kissed the woman back, his hands sliding little by little across her naked back before gently pulling her closer. It had been a sudden accidental romance fuelled by fate and a demand for pubic hair manipulation, but there was a deep glow of emotion felt keenly by both parties.

As they pulled apart from the kiss, one of her group of fans draped a silk dressing gown over Maria's naked frame and winked knowingly at the young man. Hubris grabbed her hand in his and wound them together. Smiling knowingly at each other, the young man led her quietly out the hall, through the foyer littered with unconscious bodies and out into the still Strathcarnage evening.

Maria stood admiring her erect bronze penis prize, the phallic shape recovered in the melee by fans and presented to her quietly as she left the building. Maria now held it high above her head in a victory salute, the phallus glinting in the bright hotel lights. Hubris met Maria's proud gaze as she turned her toward him and couldn't believe his luck. He was here, outside the hotel high above the twinkling lights of his home town, falling deeply in love with the first Strathcarnage Freestyle Yo-Yo Champion.

The swastika fluttered on high above the pair as he pulled her in close and kissed her tenderly.

Hubris drew back and gazed into the eyes of his beautiful naked new saviour.

"Maria? There's something I really want to do to celebrate this moment, something special I want to show you. My dear sweet Maria, I'd really like to have the honour of taking you up The Harse."

"Why, sure honey pie, I'd really like that…"

She paused thoughtfully.

"...but I could do with a drink, can't we go to the pub first?"

Enid 'Wheels' Brownlee (Wheelchair Yo-yo genius and trailblazer) 1958–1978

Mayor Alice Noyce 1939–1978

## CHAPTER 6

## Day Four – Christmas Tales

A white Christmas in Strathcarnage was a rare event indeed given the town's location within a huge cave. In fact the last recorded incidence had occurred late in the December of 1968, when the town had awoken on Christmas morning to see fat white flakes falling gently from the sky and the whole town carpeted in a soft white layer. Children had rushed to windows inside homes, breathless with anticipation, their excitement steaming up the glass. They had snatched at their winter play clothes, anxious not to miss the fun. Before long before the streets and gardens of Strathcarnage were echoing with childhood noise. The whole town seemed alive.

Unfortunately this reckless fun wasn't to last long, as Strathcarnage TV broke into programming to announce that the local Asbestos Factory had caught fire, raining its contents over the whole town. In the years to come the excited children of 1968 would relive the breathlessness of that morning every day, in a rather literal manner.

Standing in the pulpit high above his flock, the Rev. Aubrey Whisp looked out over the assembled congregation. As his thin angular face and sunken eyes scanned the assemblage, the memory of that fateful day had came back to him, brought suddenly to life as those once excited children of 1968 came wheezing through the front doors of the church, roped together to stop them wandering, and the line had gradually snaked through the dark pews of the church and inside the oxygen tent beside the choir.

The clear plastic tent had been decorated in a Christmas theme, with each of the wheezing occupants encouraged to dress like a character from the nativity. The tall churchman smiled as he signalled with a thin nicotine stained thumb that the tinsel covered oxygen tanks were turned on. Gradually the assorted noise from a variety of gasping wise men, Virgin Mary's and one solitary donkey quietened.

Reverend Whisp took the moment to reflect on those sad events three months ago when Old Jack McShane had decided to steal a clandestine cigarette at the rear of the tent, during a sermon on the Christian values of wealth. The resultant fireball had arrived, quite fortuitously the Rev Whisp now mused, as the sermon had turned to the subject of the fiery gates of damnation. As if in an act of oxygen fuelled religious symbolism, the flashing detonation had instantly robbed those twelve adjacent rows of worshippers sitting nearest the point of ignition of eyebrows and facial hair. The Reverend Whisp reflected on the massive impact he might have as a churchman if only all his sermons were as well illustrated.

The psychotic churchman was growing old. The young Aubrey Whisp had arrived at Strathcarnage hospital in late 1945, after serving as a World War Two army chaplain alongside the town's hotelier Tommy Holliday. It came as a relief to be free from the pressures of bearing witness to Tommy's hugely unpredictable career as an Army surgeon, the religious man offering post-operative succour to his friends newly limbless patients. His 1944 occasions of administering Last rites to those worst affected by Tommy Holliday's erratic surgical career remained to this day an Army record unlikely to be beaten.

Regardless of the difficulties of his posting as chaplain to the haphazard surgeon, Reverend Whisp was pleased to have been invited to the town by Tommy at the war's end. The surgeon had watched the churchman keenly and thought the young man an ideal choice to provide solace to the godless parishioners of Strathcarnage. Whisp arrived in Strathcarnage, was both welcomed into the community and kept extremely busy. It was fortunate the position had become available in the town for the churchman, since Whisp's own church hierarchy had shown no interest in employing a newly qualified minister with such pronounced Tourettes.

The Reverend Whisp had at first found his raging Tourettes Syndrome to be a handicap to his church work, but as his congregation had grown to understand his distinctive personal difficulties; the sudden outbursts of foul language and the violent twitching gradually becoming less of an issue.

The Reverend had been much comforted by the manner his congregation often overcame their obvious embarrassment with noisy laughter in a heroic attempt to make the new churchman feel less self-conscious of his disability. Before long his services were packed to the rafters, the local TV network forced by pubic request to cover them live every Sunday morning, to fulfil the demand from those disappointed crowds of parishioners commonly locked out of the packed services.

Aubrey Whisp had now found his true calling and was grateful God had found it in his heart to allow him to bring the good word of the Lord to the hidden town of Strathcarnage.

The Reverend Whisp shuffled in his pulpit ready to begin his service, waiting for the hand signal from the TV crew to inform him the commercials had finished. As he checked his handwritten notes, Reverend Whisp jerked violently to one side, displacing some greasy strands of grey hair and cleared his throat, ready to begin. The assembled crowd in the hall suddenly fell deathly silent in keen anticipation. Whisp began to speak.

"Jesus, Son of God. Born unto us here on earth, to show us how best to treat others and to do God's will."

The reverend paused dramatically to slowly look around the packed hall. The congregation were hanging on the edge of their seats, the mass of faces and bodies leaning forward as one in wide eyed anticipation. They didn't have long to wait. As the Reverend Whisp turned the page of his sermon he gave sudden violent lurch forward, gripping the front of the pulpit, his head suddenly jerking aggressively to one side as he bellowed a serious, ear-splitting "FUCK".

This first sudden explosion would have been regretful enough. The newer members of the congregation began to shake uncontrollably with laughter, but more seasoned regulars who had secured the best tickets from the touts that gathered around the streets around the village green leading to the church knew what was coming next, and remained open mouthed in expectation.

Adding to the Reverend's troubles was the fact that when the Tourettes seized him, the churchman both increased greatly his volume and then generally threw his tall thin frame around violently on every curse, battling with himself in a brave but futile attempt to fight his impulses. In addition to the verbal outbursts, the church man was also afflicted with sudden involuntary hand movements, making his every sermon an unmissable event.

Reverend Whisp struggled on, knowing that regardless of the fight with his disability he was performing his chosen task and bringing God's word to the previously pagan community. He was here to deliver his important Christmas Eve sermon to the packed congregation, just as he had done every year on the 7$^{th}$ of January.

The Reverend Whisp's complaint didn't just cause explosions of colourful swear words and violent shuddering. At times the religious man prayed that his misfortune was indeed limited to that. Alas, his complaint meant that once locked on a particular subject, his brain had enormous difficulty pulling away onto another matter.

He continued, "And it is at this time of the year we turn our thoughts to the baby Jesus."

As he fought to contain his latest mental outburst, strands of dirty grey hair were flicking from side to side as his arms took it in turns to punch the air while his body began again to jolt aggressively as he fought to suppress the fresh thoughts welling up inside his brain. He risked another line.

"We are gathered here to...to..to..FUCK! BIG COCKS !! And at this most holy time, let us sing about ARSE...."

The entire congregation were now rocking in silent hysterics at the whirligig in the pulpit, the wall of muffled swearing and flailing arms now peppered only occasionally with any recognisable religious reference.

The Christmas Eve sermon continued in this manner, as on every Sunday previously, to a packed church with the congregation crammed into pews, helpless with silent laughter and now a mass of shuddering shoulders. Indeed the most audible noise in the hall was the loud wheezing and rasping emanating from the oxygen tent, as the occupants housed within found strange comfort in drawn out attempts at laughter through ravaged lungs.

Strathcarnage had come to celebrate Christmas on the 8$^{th}$ January every year due to a single event destined to remain hugely significant, even in the town's long mottled history of catastrophe.

Owing to a series of regrettable events, Christmas Day in Strathcarnage itself had become dislodged in time and had floated adrift from the traditional date used by the rest of the modern world. However the change wasn't due to any change in the Gregorian or Roman calendar. Instead the story behind the move was an altogether more intriguing matter, and one which was only fully resolved by the delivery of a badly translated Thai calendar entitled "Shaven Leather Big Jug Ladies Look Sex".

Ever since the town's foundation by a wrecked ship of mental patients, Strathcarnage had, until recently, adopted the democratic practice of allowing every resident to be Town Mayor for a period of a few days wherever possible. The situation promoted a healthy sense of democracy in the town and many felt the sporadic pandemonium which had followed various Mayoral changeovers was an acceptable price to pay to instil a feeling of community to the town residents.

Alteration of the date of the Strathcarnage Xmas had arrived during the reign of Burton Harris as Town Mayor. Burton, a local garage worker, well known in the village for his prodigious capacity for masturbation, had taken office just before Christmas. By tradition handed down from generation to generation, it was the task of the reigning Mayor to sound the Town Hall bell to signal the official beginning of Christmas day.

However a combination of unfortunate events in the lead up to this very event had proved the cause of Christmas Day in the town to become altered and then set adrift altogether.

Burton had been appointed to the post of town mayor by surprise, late on Christmas Eve. The abruptness of the title transfer occurred because the current Strathcarnage Mayor of five hours, Willie Masson, had abdicated. Due to his rampant Alzheimer's, Willie had forgotten a previous engagement playing in a festive Russian roulette dominoes match in The Ruptured Horse Hotel that would make his ringing of the bell impossible. Willie had no choice but to hurriedly hand the mantle over in order to make his appointment. However after successfully locating an heir, the confused man had later forgotten completely not only about his brief period as mayor but the domino match too, and had just gone home to bed.

Burton, although essentially an educationally subnormal man, was still intensely proud to be chosen as the new mayor. This excitement and pride was greatly increased since the new position came with the distinct honour of sounding the town hall bell later in the evening to signal the beginning of Xmas festivities in the town, one of his favourite times of the year. Since the official Town clock showed a number of hours remaining before his proud duty, Burton decided to take advantage of the trappings of his new office and drained a huge glass of whisky or two from the Mayoral crystal decanter on his desk, before retiring to the private executive lavatory in the corner of the office to pass time engaged in his much loved solo pursuit of the lower body flesh.

Burton was legendary around the town for his hobby of passing both large amounts of free time and bodily fluids in the grimy outdoor location of the local garage lavatory, often at full mercy of the winter elements. He was unused to the comfort afforded by the cleanliness and warmth of the new Mayoral lavatory.

The uncharacteristic heat soon caused a roaring drunk Burton to grow drowsy after completing a sustained period engaged in his chosen hobby, soon falling deeply asleep still clutching his fleshy apparatus of choice. All would have remained well had there not have been a severe onset of bitter frost in Strathcarnage that night, an extreme drop in temperature causing a burst pipe in the Town Hall Fetish Room, located directly above the Mayoral bathroom where Burton lay contentedly dozing.

Burton awoke feeling suddenly cold; only to find that as a direct result of the burst pipe in the Town Hall heating above, the whole central heating system had ground to a juddering halt. Attempting to move, his attention was rapidly drawn to a weird sensation below.

Staring downward, he noticed his hand frozen solidly to his now flaccid apparatus, iced up by his final emission before sleep. Looking up from his genital misfortune, the garage man noticed a solid wall of ice right across the room, caused by the flow of water from the burst pipe above. The thick opaque wall covered his legs and now trapped him where he sat on the toilet.

Burton realised that his trapped hand made little difference, the now solid wall of dripping water having anchored him firmly on the cold porcelain pan, bare buttocks frozen solid to the toilet seat. He twisted his head round to look at the watch still attached to his trapped wrist. Less than three hours remained until he was due to ring the bell to signal Christmas Day.

The intense cold weather lasted 12 days. Burton was stuck in position for the entire period.

The imprisoned man had managed a short period of optimism on the third day when he had managed to reach a copy of a women's magazine with the toes of an outstretched frozen foot, hoping to turn a few pages and receive enough visual inspiration to raise some heat and life into his frozen flaccid member. However as his appendage began to twitch to life, Burton discovered it sat bent horribly under his hand, the soft skin attached to the cold steel of his watch strap and frozen solid in the extreme cold. The pain was too distracting. He drooped back in sagging disappointment. He would have to sit tight and wait for rescue.

On the twelfth night of his ordeal, the short armed Strathcarnage postman, Alexei, had noticed that a recent delivery of obscene publications to Burton's home remained untouched behind the door of his home. Seeing the pile, Alexei knew instantly something was wrong, since Burton rarely left any fresh delivery pushed through by his tiny arms for longer than a period of a few seconds. Alexei had pulled his gloves up over his shoulders and fought through the icy road to the garage to check the cubicle for any sign of Burton. Finding the grubby and soiled latrine empty, the postman set off anxiously to search for his friend.

Alexei had found Burton around 11:30pm that same night. After being informed by locals in The Ruptured Horse that Willie Masson was the last man known to have been asking after Burton, and being told by the blissfully unaware man's much put upon wife of the change in mayoral circumstances, Alexei had realised where Burton was likely to be and had headed for the town hall lavatory. After a noble but hopeless attempt to barge through the frozen door with his curtailed upper body, Alexei started to chip at the sheet ice holding the door shut with a spoon, managing after a long hour's work to open the tiniest of gaps into the lavatorial ice cavern. Burton mused later that he had never been so glad to see stumpy arms waving a spoon through an iced shut bathroom door.

Alexei had only eventually managed to free Burton from his icy hell with the inspired application of a badly translated Thai "Shaven Leather Big Jug Ladies Look

Sex" calendar, the one he had been attempting to deliver to the man earlier in the day, and which fortunately he still had in his post bag. Alexei slid the calendar through the rough icy hole with his diminutive arms and opened the publication out, displaying each of the sordid pictures to the trapped man a month at a time.

Soon, Burton could stand the revelations of hugely endowed hairless oriental temptresses no longer and had produced enough warm body fluid to free both his trapped hand and manhood. It flew free and grew again rigid just as "Big Girl Sexy Whopper Udder Show" Miss June was withdrawn through the hole to be refreshed to "Shave Secret Place Smooth Dirty Dog" Miss July.

As Burton gradually freed himself by means of his sticky web of self produce, he remembered his Xmas duty. Glancing at his watch and wiping the sweat of effort from his brow, he knew he had failed to ring the town bell at midnight to allow the official beginning of Christmas, and to prove to everyone that he was an able mayor to his town.

As Burton gradually thawed more and more from the icy prison of the toilet seat, he managed to slide sideways off the wet porcelain onto the slush covered floor, his legs paralysed and unable to hold his weight after such a prolonged period sitting frozen in the same position. Hearing the crash behind the door, Alexei had realised the situation remained dangerous for his friend and showed the clarity of thought to remain calm and to continue thrusting the obscene calendar pictures through the small hole dug in the ice.

Burton had been trapped and unable to engage in his favourite pastime for a long period of days and the voluminous build up of internal fluids were considerable. As he lay on the floor, the acting Mayor gazed at Miss October "Bendy Lady Consume Man Meat Gift" and began expelling delightful salvos of warm ropey fluid clear across the room in the general direction of the thick wall of ice. In less than an hour, and two further passes through the obscene months of the calendar, the ice wall had been thawed thin enough for Alexei to barge his way into the room.

In a truly heart-warming Christmas display of man's love for his fellow man, Alexei had gathered Burton from the floor and supported the sodden exhausted figure on his journey up the steep steps to the Strathcarnage town hall bell tower. On reaching the bell room the mayor had found he was so weakened through his exertions that he was still quite unable to stand. Falling heavily to the wooden floor, Burton shouted at Alexei to stand on his body, a measure designed to give the postman the extra height needed to allow his miniature arms to grasp the thick knotted end of the bell rope and pull hard, to begin Christmas for the whole town right on the stroke of midnight. On the 8th of January.

Such were the events as they had occurred a couple of years ago, but even with the subsequent passing of time the heroic exploits of the duo were never to be forgotten.

On relief of being finally able to begin celebrating a delayed Strathcarnage Xmas, the town population had embarked upon a competition to write a Xmas hymn in commemoration of the event: man helping fellow man with a simple kindness of spirit and deep humanity to save a whole town's festivities. The competition was won by a local schoolchild Euphemia Crawshaw and her hymn was a simple yet moving celebration of compassion and the triumph of man's will.

The Rev Aubrey Whisp shook violently once more and instructed the gathered congregation to be upstanding for its recital. It was called, simply and touchingly, "Raise Thine Stumpy Arms And Pull At Thine Bell End".

The hymn suited Reverend Whisp well, since the details of the story in every verse enabled him to legitimately scream "WANK!" at the top of his voice at least once, and as he lurched forward in time to the tune he did so without fear or embarrassment. The congregation soon began to follow his lead, and soon the throng was entering into the Christmas spirit, single voices echoing the churchman's loud random screams of "Wank" during the hymn's choral tribute to the kindness of man.

The Rev. Whisp grew emotional watching the scene unfold, watching even the oxygen tent get into the spirit of the moment and lurch forward as the occupants let out enthusiastic wheezes in time to the moving music. Christmas brought special moments like this to the town, even though the occupants of the clear plastic marquee had less reason than most to celebrate the festive period.

As the service ended, the townspeople filed out the church doors past the Reverend, each person sent home with a warm greeting and a shake of his bony cold hand. Reverend Whisp had suffered a minor attack of his Tourettes during this personal salutation to local parishioners, unleashing a volley of sexually explicit abuse at wheelchair bound Old Mrs Reedy, only managing to regain his full composure after overturning her and her wheelchair into an open grave just outside the church door. The hospital had phoned later to let him know that it was a clean break, she was out the coma and she'd be off the oxygen before Easter.

After the service had finished, another strange Strathcarnage Christmas tradition was permitted to take place.

The giving of gifts had been banned in 1857 in the town after the then 10th Lord Strathcarnage had found himself infected with a hideous bout of gonorrhoea after overindulging with a dwarf Portuguese prostitute received as a festive offering from a grateful passing Dutch merchant ship. In his anger, the Lord had written into Strathcarnage law that townsfolk should be permitted to neither give nor receive presents. The law remained, but the locals had found a loophole to circumvent the ancient ruling, and a way to continue to enjoy the traditional receipt of Christmas gifts.

At the stroke of eleven on Christmas Eve, all Strathcarnage residents left their homes and performed the ancient rite of robbery of the neighbours. It was the tradition at this hour for each person to walk quietly to the house directly to the left of their own, whereupon the strongest member of the family would perform the annual Christmas "Breaking down the doors" ritual. Tradition dictated then that each person claim five items of choice from the neighbouring house and then carry them home to their own property as Christmas gifts. Since no one in the village had willingly offered anything as a gift, the ancient law of 1857 remained unbroken.

Most families in the town purchased special gifts for the occasion, placing them

in easily visible locations near the door of the home, to better allow for nuisance-free robbing. Often a more adventurous neighbour would pay no heed to this tradition, ignore these goods and go on a search for other valuables concealed around the home, turning the whole ritual into a parlour game as well as a ritual housebreaking. Residents laughed and sung merrily as they passed each other in the street weighed down with huge armfuls of each other's possessions, happily wishing each other a Merry Christmas.

This system was not without minor faults though. Owing to the high number of surrounding properties, and the building's location within a circle of adjoining houses, the orphanage was always particularly badly hit. On more than one Christmas the place had been stripped of clean of beds, carpets and, on one particularly busy year, a quantity of children. They had been later been returned after a successful television appeal offering a portable black and white television and a steel drum of home brewed town vodka for each child returned.

Another habitual Christmas casualty of the ceremony was local elder Tobias Sheefer, a farmer whose home on the high ground at the edge of the village unfortunately had no adjacent house in the traditional left hand position for him to rob. Tobias had gradually watched his house being stripped bare by enthusiastic neighbours over a period of 30 years, eventually losing both his front and back doors and a quantity of floorboards last Christmas. He often mused about moving to a better location as he sat swathed in blankets with the bitter sea wind roaring over the town from the waterfall and into his empty shell of a home, but he had never quite got round to it. After all, he dearly loved Christmas in Strathcarnage.

Indeed Tobias loved the Xmas celebrations in the town so much he had nominated himself to stand in the last four Santa elections in the town. He enjoyed taking part in the ritual of the ceremony but had lost each time, although not caring too deeply about each loss as it got him out of his freezing barren shell of a home.

The people of Strathcarnage had the chance to vote for their town Santa following the unfortunate recent death of Alice Noyce. The position of town Mayor had been changed to a permanent two yearly post following the unfortunate events with Burton, and the holder of that office traditionally served as the town Santa. However since the latest mayor, Alice Noyce was killed during the Yo-Yo championship, the position had remained vacant, and Strathcarnage residents had been forced to quickly organise a vote to ensure they had an official Town Santa for this year's festivities.

Lord Strathcarnage had previously filled in, playing the part of Santa at various times of need in the years before Alice Noyce's election. However while the plump Lord had made a jovial enough Santa when required, on his most recent outing he had taken to measuring and thoroughly examining each of the children, placing the most agreeable specimens in a tinsel decorated cage hidden in the corner of the grotto. The Lord had taken the youngsters with the intention of exhibiting them at a forthcoming Child show.

Parents become unhappy at the indiscriminate kidnapping and the Lord had to be politely asked to stand down from the trusted position with immediate effect, a decision taken only a few short weeks ago. The local nobleman had taken the judgment hard, leaving the town disgusted to travel to Rome on business. It was around the same point that Alice Noyce had died and locals had undertaken to hold the election to find a Strathcarnage Santa by more democratic means.

The Reverend Whisp won the election by a landslide. However he had been forced to resign within days when a parent had taken offence to a Santa screaming "Fuck!" repeatedly in their child's face while handing him a present of a small quantity of L.S.D. wrapped in Christmas paper, the year's gifts having been donated by The Ox, the slightly deranged head of the local TV Station.

Town residents had wondered the reason for the hysterical objection of the parent concerned, confused by the sudden outburst in the town of such unusual sensitivity. Drinkers debated in the town's pubs whether the reaction had perhaps been as a result of the woman involved having being forced to enter Santa's Grotto fully naked, a simple new local precaution introduced to the town following a spate of recent Christmas shoplifting.

After Whisp's dismissal, the search for a replacement Santa was a straight fight between legendary onanist Burton Glass and Alexei the short armed postman. Alexei had eventually won the votes of many townspeople in a close run race. His was a last minute victory, winning only after Burton had noticeably soiled his Santa suit while shaking hands too enthusiastically with a local fishmonger's wife while out canvassing votes in the town centre. However Alexei vacated the position shortly afterwards after a chance encounter with an old flame had seen him hurriedly leaving the town by boat to return home to his Russian homeland. Burton, hit hard by his defeat, had refused to stand in the quickly reorganised new election.

The next replacement Santa, a fat spectacled local doctor called Herman Glossop, had imbibed all the drugs intended for the children's presents within an hour of beginning his first shift in the town grotto. Running from his false cave in the grip of vivid hallucinations, the new Santa was electrocuted while climbing a huge lighting show mounted above his festive base on the town green. It was a source of some amusement in the town that as he remained fused to the display and burning fiercely, a huge neon arrow pointed to the rapidly blackening corpse while the lights flashed "Look Kids! It's Santa."

And so to the town's newest and most current Santa, the imposing figure of Big Nancy the engine lifter. She had easily won the latest town vote and had proved a popular Santa with both the town's male children and their fathers. Owing to the loss of the only Santa costume in the previously mentioned fire incident, the large woman had been forced to strip to the waist and paint each naked breast merrily with the face of a reindeer. Half naked and decorated, Nancy threw herself into the role with gusto. The town had eventually found the Santa it deserved.

So it came to pass, that Strathcarnage celebrated another Christmas. Children gazed on with wide eyed innocence as their fathers kicked neighbour's doors off their hinges, a new buxom Santa swung her painted reindeer breasts in circles to amuse the little ones and their parents, and the Town Hall bell rang once more at the precise time, to signal the magic had begun again.

In the distance you could hear the sound of carol singers wafting across the cave's night air, merrily signing the first few verses of that traditional paean to the Strathcarnage spirit of Christmas, "Raise Thine Stumpy Arms..."

If you really listened, occasionally, somewhere in the distance, the Reverend Whisp was celebrating the season in his own inimitable random way, joining in with a loud delighted cry of "Fuckers!"

The strange magic of another Strathcarnage Christmas.

Herman Glossop (Town Santa) 1943-1978

# CHAPTER 7

## Day Five – The Pubic Modeller

Crosby Stanton pushed his black-rimmed modelling glasses onto the top of his head, relaxing back into his chair with a scarcely perceptible sigh. Spread before him, on the vast flat wooden surface of his desk, was a jumbled pile of books and drawings. The mound consisted of technical information, plans, photographs and naval architecture blueprints of one of the most majestic crafts ever to have sailed the high seas, the famous German battleship Bismarck. This was Crosby's newest modelling project; a perfect scale replica of the renowned and feared German wartime naval giant.

Recreating the legend was proving hard work, principally because he was building the vast scale model of the ship entirely from pubic hair.

Crosby gazed intently at his latest masterpiece, slowly and meticulously coming together atop the desk before him. After three months of work, the outline of the great craft was beginning to take shape, and the twelve foot long hull was more or less complete. He carefully studied the reproduction from both ends, allowing himself a faint smile as he stooped slightly to check the perfection of the model's fine details. The practised sculptor was convinced that this construction would easily be recognised as his finest pubic creation to date.

Crosby Stanton had begun using pubic hair as the medium for his creations around twenty years ago. The keen model maker had experimented and persevered with human hair for a number of years, but had eventually grown increasingly frustrated with the thin strands, concluding them too tricky to handle and work with.

Human hair lacked strength for the bigger constructions, a key consideration since Crosby was resolute in his ambition to build big. The continued failure of materials disappointed him greatly, since his current job as town hairdresser provided him with a dependable source of raw materials to supply the delicate work. The admission that head hair was of little practical use in pursuing his dream threw the forlorn modelmaker into deep depression for a number of weeks. However, just when he had fallen to his lowest ebb, a chance encounter with his wife in the bathroom suddenly opened up a whole new aspect of modelling possibilities.

Crosby had courted and married a sallow skinned local girl called Agnes Bury who worked in the cliff side workshop of her father's local Undertaker firm of "Bury and Burns". The two had met by chance on a misty August morning when Crosby had been called in to the head office to provide a tight perm to one of the corpses on the eve of one of the company's trademark themed 70's funerals.

Agnes was the gifted costumes designer for the 'event funeral' wing of the company and her expertise with needle and thread allowed Bury and Burns to offer a huge range of event funerals to compete with the town's more popular undertakers, "Hitchcock and Chalmers". Crosby remembered that first meeting still, and those unusual events that had brought them together.

The company had begun to use Crosby as the firm's corpse hairstylist many years ago, providing his services to corpses ever since the untoward incident when a previous stylist had accidentally ruined the set-piece funeral of a local transvestite truck driver Billy "Stocking Tops" Marshall.

Billy Marshall had left instructions in his will instructing that his final wish was to be buried in the style of Marilyn Monroe, a figure whom he had long worshipped. The deceased driver had specifically requested a final ceremony held in a stylish tribute to the iconic white dress scene from his favourite movie, "The Seven Year Itch".

The plan detailed in his will included instructions to dye and style Billy's own long dark hair into a frightening platinum blonde cascade of curls, dress him a specially made white dress, and then to mount his decorated corpse upright over an industrial air conditioning unit. The arrangement detailed that the dress be blown around his bare shaved muscular legs in a tribute to the film, with the unit beneath circulating warm air around at full power. Billy had requested to be driven around the town on the back of his own lorry one last time, skirt flying around his gold drop earrings, before arriving to be interred at the local Strathcarnage Cemetery on the edge of town in a sunset ceremony accompanied by a disco soundtrack played by local amputee DJ, Stumps La Salle.

The local hairdresser at the time, Ian "Knickers" Differ, had worked vigilantly and expertly, and on the morning of the funeral Billy had looked a vision, his face fully made up and shaved, his hair cut, dyed and styled in an exact replica of Marilyn's.

Agnes Bury had carefully dressed the corpse in the handmade white satin gown after shaving the well-muscled corpse arms and legs and covering the mass of tattoos with heavy foundation. Billy was then hoisted atop the truck and mounted on the air blower using a carefully fixed metal pole and a special harness hidden under the silk dress.

As a final touch, the broad-shouldered corpse had his newly manicured lorry driving hand positioned with a single false red nail just touching his sparkling shining cherry lipstick and a coy look on his face. Everything was perfect, and just as Billy had requested. However the perfect vision of his final request was not destined to last.

As the corpse was driven through the town's narrow streets, no one had noticed that the air blower chosen for Billy to stand over was a heated industrial model, specifically designed to run at great warmth to speed dry plaster on large building jobs. The simple but significant error wouldn't become obvious until it was too late.

Billy had planned his final journey carefully, weaving through the narrow town streets past his favourite Strathcarnage sights, the decorated corpse fully displayed atop the lorry. What Billy had omitted to tell the funeral director was that he had never openly revealed to those significant others in his life that he had enjoyed a secret life as a closet transvestite. It was just as his decorated corpse arrived at his local pub, The Harse that the double disaster struck.

Billy had been forced to acquire copies of Marilyn's shoes from a specialist transgender clothing dealer in Latvia who could cater for a white stiletto in a broad fitting size eleven and a half. Unfortunately the supplier could only source such a large version of the shoe as a white PVC copy, not in the requested natural leather.

The melting PVC stiletto was now slowly dissolving in the heat, molten plastic dripping slowly onto the red hot heating elements of the industrial blower just as the flat bed truck slowly pulled up in front of the small crowd of mourning friends and regulars gathered outside the local pub to toast and pay their final respects to their old drinking partner.

The white silk of the dress billowed merrily around the solid muscular legs of his corpse as the assembly of friends looked quizzically at each other, trying to work out why their previously pony tailed, lorry-driving drinking companion was now displayed atop his own truck wearing heavy eye shadow and a full set of false nails.

The school opposite had also allowed pupils to gather and pay their respects to a man they had known only as Billy the tattooed weightlifting coach. The children murmured to each other in some confusion as the funeral lorry passed before them carrying their heavily decorated trainer. Ironically it had been one of the distraught, heavily muscled eleven-year-old girls who had noticed the first indication of flame.

As the melting PVC dripping from the stilettos had ignited, the assembled children gasped at the sudden appearance of the small darting red flames. Some powerfully built children cheered loudly, thinking the fire was just another pre-arranged part of the bizarre show. Indeed all may have remained well had glowing sparks from the burning debris not been blown upward by the powerful fan, straight into the peroxide nest of his newly styled hair.

"Knickers" Differ, the local hairdresser, had spent a large portion of the morning spraying the hair lustily with lacquer in order that it would retain a firm shape in the powerful blast from the blower below. It was this highly flammable cocktail that had ignited instantly.

Billy "Stocking Tops" Marshall passed the stunned crowd of mourners outside the pub and school with his hair completely ablaze, specially mounted loudspeakers on the truck roof blasting out a scratchy recording of Marilyn singing "I Wanna Be Loved By You" as the procession moved slowly past.

The situation could still perhaps have been rescued at this point; however Gus Ebersole, the unkempt and partially deaf driver of the truck was oblivious to events, listening to pipe band music at full volume in the cab to drown out the repetitive drone of blaring show tunes coming from the huge speakers above him. So the decorated lorry continued on its winding journey around the town, unmindful to the shouts and waves from gatherings of stunned locals, the lorry in due course turning into the curved road around the village green with Billy now fully ablaze on the rear.

Billy's wife had been waiting for her husband's final journey to pass the family home on the green with a sense of pride. She wanted Billy's four children to see how striking their father looked in full drag, hoping the beautiful sight would better facilitate her final revelation to the children of this important part of their father's life. It was something which had, until now, been Billy and his wife's 'little secret'.

It was time now to finally share the news amongst the whole family, and his wife hoped the promised impact of the sight would help her explain events to the children as they followed the truck to the town cemetery.

As the tiny family group stood and watched the source of the curious moving plume of smoke turn into the curved road that passed their home, Billy's wife had let out a scream, sprinting toward the truck as she realised exactly what was happening.

Neighbours suggested later that the whole sorry tragedy that then unfolded may have been due, at least in part, to the sudden swerve the driver had been forced to undertake to avoid Billy's hysterical wife.

Billy Marshall had lived a rough, hedonistic lifestyle as a ship's cook before meeting his wife, smuggling cargo to the village before subsequently falling in love and remaining in the secret town to settle down. As a direct result of these many previous naval adventures Billy, had a glass eye fitted to replace the original, lost during a vicious fight while working in Thailand.

Crew members later reported that the ferocious fight had started over Billy's desire to obtain the mystical Thai knowledge of carving decorative flowers out of root vegetables, but it was only ever a rumour.

In his later years Billy had also been fitted with a pacemaker at the local hospital, to fix damage thought by doctors to be a direct result of years of tremendous stress from the pressure of his hiding of his cross dressing from friends and family. Those two operations to replace parts of Billy Marshall's body were to have solemn consequences, from far beyond the grave.

The heavily flaming body had remained upright throughout the journey due to the heavy steel pole and harness on which Billy was mounted. As his wife ran towards the truck and it had swerved to avoid hitting her, the body had suddenly fallen over to one side as the flaming shoe's weakened heels buckled in the intense heat. Then it happened.

The treated hair had been burning like a furnace for three or four minutes, and the concentrated heat had caused intense pressure to build inside Billy's lifeless and heavily made up skull.

Just as his wife had reached the stationary truck and ran alongside attempting to clamber on the back to reach her blazing husband, Billy's glass eye had exploded out of his socket with a massive wet thud of detonation. The eye had blown out of the blazing skull at pace, hitting his wife flush on the middle of her forehead, embedding itself with huge force into her skull and killing her instantly.

Just as the children had run forward toward the truck holding their burning transvestite father, and now dragging their three-eyed mother's corpse, the pacemaker had gone too.

The sheer power with which the glass eye had been propelled outward had pushed Billy's flaming corpse backwards, and the shift in position seemed to dislodge his pacemaker somewhere in the billowing inferno of his flaming silk dress. Heated beyond any possible hope of survival, the device had detonated inside his chest with a deafening thump, the force of the massive internal blast showering all four children, and a passing couple on a tandem, with small frayed pieces of their father's internal contents.

One other mourner at the scene was knocked unconscious with a false silicon breast implant, fired at ferocious pace and still contained inside the scorched bloody FF cup of a white silk bra.

The deeply distraught and newly orphaned children stood motionless at the roadside, dripping heavily with the remains of a partially cooked transvestite parent while the truck continued on its way, the booming voice of Marilyn roared from the back of the lorry singing an ironic and heavily distorted version of "My Heart Belongs To Daddy". The children's hearts may have belonged to daddy, but daddy's heart was now lying in fragments on the road, and as such, was legally public property.

In a final ironic twist, Billy's dog, a large German shepherd called Sabre, had been attracted by the commotion, and had hopped over the garden wall and onto the back of the lorry, lovingly attempting to gnaw off the bottom half of the cooked leg from his master's detonated remains.

Authorities had declared the day's events an unfortunate accident during the inquest held the next day, although explicit mention was made of the colossal amounts of hairspray having contributing heavily to the rapid spread of the initial fire. The final report recommended that the town undertaker immediately and permanently suspend use of the hairdresser responsible.

Sabre the Alsatian had to be heavily tranquillised with drugged darts fired by a police dog handler before he would surrender the best bone he had been given in years, a heavily gnawed red fillet with a melted size eleven stiletto still hanging scorched and limp on the end.

Crosby Stanton had been immediately appointed as the replacement corpse hairdresser after the inquiry. As a new employee of the undertakers helping with themed funerals, it was only a matter of time before he and Agnes were thrown together by circumstance.

On the day they first met, Agnes had been struggling with the heavy corpse of a fat local farmer called Poker Hodges, wrestling the fat cadaver around the yard in a sort of comic tango, lurching to and fro while trying to dress his bloated cadaver in the jumpsuit for the requested Elvis Funeral.

Crosby had just been inside finishing another perm and dye job on a corpse for a 70's disco funeral that evening, and had been delivering the freshly Afro'd body to the yard when he noticed the sleight frame of Agnes through an open door, trying to wrestle the fat agricultural Elvis into his sequined white burial attire.

Agnes was unaware that Farmer Hodges death had been the result of a combine harvester accident, and as she wrestled the considerable weight of the corpse to one side to try and tease the man's thick arms into the white satin sleeves, his legs had fallen off. This unexpected turn of events had caused Hodges upper half to suddenly fall over on to Agnes, trapping her under almost 23 stones of rural mortality.

As Crosby dragged the enormous weight off a trapped and now distressed Agnes, her pale beauty had appeared around the farmer's heavily scarred face and dyed black hair. Their eyes met over the glittering sequins and the rest was romantic history.

Many happy years had passed from that initial meeting until now, the morning of the bathroom revelation incident with Agnes, and Crosby stood lazily brushing his teeth before leaving for the salon.

The frustrated model maker had been in a foul mood for weeks because of his crushing disappointment at the unsuitability of human hair for modelling purposes. However, as he rinsed his mouth and turned to leave the bathroom, the modeller suddenly glimpsed something that was to change his life.

Agnes was perched on the edge of the bath, casually trimming her unruly pubic hair with a set of Crosby's hairdressing clippers. He stood transfixed for a moment, before a thin smile played on his lips and the inspiration hit him like a thunderbolt.

The head hair had failed as it was too soft and supple. It was too difficult to gather, bind and maintain in strong shapes when constructing a larger model. The sight before him had given him an idea he hadn't even occurred to him until this moment. How on earth could he not have thought of it before? As he gazed at the pile of ginger pubic hair gathering in the white enamel bath below, he laughed loudly, proud of his brilliant idea. Crosby knew instantly he had come up with an inspired solution, and that his modelling troubles were potentially solved.

He dropped to the floor before Agnes. Agnes, ever quick to take the initiative and misinterpreting both the situation and the look of unbridled excitement on her husbands face, clamped her legs firmly round Crosby's neck.

Crosby was so excited by his new spark of model making brilliance that he scarcely noticed the naked matrimonial thigh lock. He had looked up holding a handful of pubic hair and gabbling excitedly, only to be confronted by an onrushing expanse of pink fleshy wife. Only then did he try to move his wife's limbs into a position where his muffled voice could again be heard. Agnes looked down in confusion at her struggling husband, his voice mumbling incoherently from just below her waist. Only once Crosby had wriggled himself free and returned her legs to their original position on the floor did he begin to jabber at Agnes about his brilliant plan.

"Pubes!" he exclaimed excitedly.

Agnes looked down, confused at the statement of the obvious.

"The models! I've got it! I need to use pubes! And I know how to get them!"

Crosby rose, still excitedly waving the handful of pubic hair around the room as he set off and disappeared into his study. He remained there a few minutes before returning to a now fully dressed and thoroughly perplexed Agnes sitting silently on the edge of the bed, thoroughly unsure of the implications of her husband's recent outburst and subsequent strange behaviour.

Yet she hadn't seen him this happy in weeks she had decided that whatever the reason for the abrupt upturn of spirits, it must be worthy of listening to. Crosby sat next to his wife and began a full explanation his master plan.

He had bound together the pubic hair collected from his wife, and after some swift tests to confirm his initial suspicions, had found the organic below waist material to be both strong enough and pliable enough to be ideal for his large scale modelling dreams. Collected together and bound, then treated with hairspray, the pubic hair bonded together with the strength of a matchstick, yet with the crucial ability of also being pliable enough to be moulded easily into complex shapes with no loss of strength: it was the modeller's nirvana.

Agnes knitted her brow and enquired how Crosby would be able to harvest sufficient quantities of pubic hair for his idea to be viable, but Crosby had just smiled distractedly while staring into the distance before winking at his wife and running off in the town lanes in the direction his barber's shop.

The hastily written sign had gone up in the hairdresser's window almost immediately. It read simply, "Free Pubic Trim with Every Haircut". Crosby was by now desperate to embark on a career as the town's first pubic modeller and couldn't wait to harvest raw materials.

He set off around the town advertising the new service he was offering, and encouraged interest amongst locals with fantastical tales of the medical and hygienic benefits of shorn genitals. Uptake was sluggish to begin with, but as the idea had begun to slowly catch on and the wiry piles began to form around the shop floor, Crosby soon began to dream of what his first construction would be.

In a tribute to the wispy red inspiration for the idea, Crosby had decided his first creation would be a carefully constructed, highly detailed scale model of the Forth Rail Bridge.

This decision in itself, however, created a fundamental problem for the excited model maker. In order to replicate the structure faithfully, it quickly became clear to Crosby that he would be dependant on a steady supply of red pubic hair.

He had a ready source at home in Agnes, but rapidly began to get frustrated at the time it took her flimsy pubic covering to regrow heavily enough for fresh wide-eyed harvesting with nail scissors. Crosby had managed to secure the further services of a couple of red haired customers in the shop, but to build a model of such epic scale he needed more, were his new obsession to continue at a sustainable pace. As his exasperation steadily grew at the slowness of the subterranean auburn growth around him, the modeller began to rack his brain for fresh ideas to increase his stock of reddish raw materials.

Crosby took to sitting in his car at the supermarket, the school and other busy places in the town, and he had began following local redheads home before sliding a leaflet through their door advertising his curious free new hairdressing services. These actions provided a modest increase in stock, but still it wasn't anywhere near enough.

He needed more raw materials.

Crosby began to buy the local paper and scan the death notices for red haired fatalities. He persuaded a hesitant Agnes to permit him access to any auburn corpses passing through her father's business. As the oldest funeral firm in the town, this was an inevitable destination most of the elderly deceased of the town, not purely the ginger hued unfortunates. It had been the younger townsfolk that had responded most positively to the recent new trimming service Crosby had offered, this way he had most of the town's genitals covered.

Crosby had celebrated wildly too on the occasion of hearing news of a local car crash, recognising a customer's breathy account of having just witnessed an accident involving three members of the same red haired family. The modeller was on the scene swiftly, excitedly fingering the clippers in his pocket and setting to work on the unconscious bodies before emergency services had arrived to cut the family from the wreckage.

The obsession grew. Even with all his assortment of hair collecting schemes and the harvesting of corpses, Crosby was finding it difficult to amass the quantities of wiry red pube he needed to continue construction of his bridge model at the hoped for pace. A chance dinner invitation was to provide him with an unexpected windfall.

Agnes's father had asked Crosby and his wife to his home for a lavish dinner party to celebrate the centenary of his company operating in the town. Crosby had turned down the invitation at first, preferring instead to remain in his workshop and continue his obsessional work on his model. However, after Agnes had gently reminded him of how useful it would be to maintain good relations with her father, and how useful his current job at the firm would prove as a continued source of raw pubic materials, he grudgingly decided to go. It was a decision that was to change not only his modelling career, but his life.

As the family sat talking around the immense flat mahogany plateau of the dining table, Crosby heard a knock on the door. Mr Bury's manservant Ignatious appeared in the dining room and announced the arrival of his funereal business partner Mr Burns and his family.

Crosby had never met Mr Burns since his partnership in the company was mostly in the role of hands off partner and the model maker was unsure what to expect. As Mr Burns entered the room followed by his wife, Crosby shifted in his chair, barely able to contain his excitement when the woman had removed a large black hat to reveal flowing locks of rich auburn hair.

Crosby grew wide-eyed at the sight, but he was set to almost detonate with delight when the unsightly faces of the couple's twin daughters entered the room.

They were overwhelmingly ugly offspring, but both girls were visions in ginger, long thick curls cascading down over gruesome features, down past bony pale shoulders. As Crosby bound up and approached the twins to greet them, he noticed both girls sported quite severe shadows of unmanaged facial hair beneath their twisted noses. He was besotted.

Over dinner, Crosby had taken every opportunity to carefully scrutinize the twins directly opposite him. He smiled thinly as he ran his eyes over their slender but heavily haired forearms. From his experience in the hairdressing trade Crosby knew that heavy facial and arm hair pointed, most likely, to a spread of pubic hair as lavish and heavy as an expensive Russian travel rug.

He knew immediately what he had to do, even before the specially decorated coffin shape celebration cake had arrived. The modelling obsessive spent the remainder of the night deep in conversation with both girls in turn and had soon found out from subtle but meticulous questioning that both girls were single and lived and worked apart in separate parts of town. Crosby mentally noted every tiny detail and beamed sweetly at the pair. With a deal of charm and a great amount of grubby wickedness, he would soon have his bridge.

Over the next few months and with great cunning and ingenuity, Crosby embarked on torrid affairs with both twins. His initial suspicions over the quantity of raw genital materials on offer had been fully confirmed, and soon enough both twins were generously providing the model maker with as much raw material as he could handle.

Although both the twins were initially suspicious of his obsessively kinky behaviour concerning his repeated shaving of their nether regions, Crosby soon had them both working unconsciously alongside his wife in a carefully calculated secret production line. The new arrangement was soon supplying him with sufficient raw material to ensure the bridge began to take shape at a cracking pace.

Although both twins were unsightly almost to the point medical freakery, this ugliness ensured that both women were both deeply flattered at the sudden abundant attentions of the handsome man, and Crosby easily managed to persuade the duo of the need to conduct their illicit affairs secretly, all the while ensuring the triumvirate of lovers all shaved themselves in carefully calculated rotation to ensure he was never short of material to work with. Soon the model was progressing at great pace.

In around six months the bridge was almost complete. Crosby had also forced himself to embark upon a passionate homosexual affair with a Spanish vet called Carlos, since he needed a ready jet-black supply to finish off the support structure detail at the bridge's base. Within weeks of his arriving home in the dead of night clutching handfuls of raven black pubic hair and sitting with an extra cushion beneath him as he worked, the meticulous model was complete.

With the finished product looking glorious, Crosby informed his now redundant pubic harvesting workers that their various affairs were over.

He informed one twin that their relationship was leaving him emotionally unfulfilled, while he told the other that he had developed an unsightly case of genital herpes, picked up from dirty lavatory seat in the town public toilets. The Spanish vet was gently let down with a yarn of a suspicious wife and having to stop such improper behaviour before he hurt her.

All parties seemed to accept the news with first-rate grace and a small number of tears and Crosby had returned home triumphant to relax and admire one of the finest models he had ever seen. The modeller smiled conceitedly that it had all been so easy. Or so he had thought.

With his masterpiece complete, Crosby was anxious to show off his work of art. The six foot long model was perfect in every detail. Every last girder and support was the perfect shade of deep red of the original, and yet poker straight and in exactly the right place. The modeller was thoroughly elated with this visual representation of both his talent and modelling skill.

After a few weeks secretly admiring the model while alone in the seclusion of his modelling room, Crosby decided to let a close artist friend of his, Twitch Trelander, see the creation and give Crosby the keen eyed judgment of a fellow creator. Twitch was the well respected Chairman of the town modelling club and an ideal opinion to seek.

After some mystery about the purpose of his visit to the house, his friend arrived at the agreed time and was admitted quietly through the thick wooden back door. Crosby had tempted his friend under the ruse of needing general creative advice in producing anatomically perfect polystyrene sculptures of male genitals; the guest's chosen area of expertise.

Crosby was unsure of what his friend's reaction would be to his model. He would be the first person other than Crosby to see it, since the model maker wanted to keep the entire creation totally secret from his wife, given she was bound to ask difficult questions about the quantity of raw materials used. Twitch Trelander watched curiously as Crosby turned the key in the heavy lock and motioned into the doorway, sweeping his hand regally to signal admission to his most secretive inner sanctum.

Twitch entered the modelling room to find the large outline of an illuminated object atop a table, covered its whole length with a white sheet. Twitch Trelander initially misread the situation and thought Crosby had fashioned a six-foot long polystyrene phallus, a logical assumption given the initial premise of the cover story which Crosby had used to lure his friend there.

"Jesus H Christ, Crosby buddy, that's one helluva monster cock!" Twitch had blurted out on seeing the size of the covered object on the desk before him. Crosby had suddenly been confused at the outburst and had begun checking his flies to see if the buttons had suddenly come undone at the front of his tweed slacks. Twitch Trelander laughed heartily on realising the misunderstanding.

"No, no, my friend, your creation on the table. And just for the record I've witnessed your tackle before, and if you don't mind me saying, there is little chance that I could possibly mistake it, even illuminated and covered in a sheet, for anything close to huge."

Crosby looked at his friend for a second then began laughing. The humour had broken the tension in the room, and he was suddenly glad of his friend's innocence at what really lay under the blanket. He smiled knowingly to himself as he wrapped his hand around the edge of the white sheet.

"It's not a cock, but it is something with its roots in the same rough area," Crosby announced as he winked conspiratorially at his ever more mystified friend.

Crosby carefully drew away the silk sheet covering his masterwork and took a few steps back to allow his friend to better examine and fully take in what lay before him. He turned off the main lamp and flicked on a number of carefully positioned display lamps beside the model to allow the full splendour and fine detail to be revealed.

Trelander was amazed. He stared intently at the perfect model as he moved slowly around the table, eyes darting between the bridge and his friends face.

Twitch Trelander was suitably stunned by the creation. He had known Crosby for a number of years, but had always thought of the man as some enthusiastic amateur whose preceding attempts at fashioning models from human hair had always led to brittle deformed models of planes, and on one particularly disastrous occasion, a violently unbalanced model of the Eiffel Tower. The latter model had caused the local model club to suspend activity for a month due to an infestation of head lice, thought to be breeding on the observation platform.

But this creation was totally flawless in both scale and intricacy. Twitch recognised it instantly as a model of breathtaking quality and great beauty.

Crosby left the room in silence to prepare a stiff whisky for them both, his friend's shocked face relaying the strong likelihood of needing one. He returned to the desk with ice clinking loudly in the crystal glasses. Crosby offered his open mouthed guest a chair and animatedly began to relate his entire tale of the planning and constructing of the most realistic model Twitch had seen in his thirty years on the circuit. As Crosby recounted his whole story his friend's eyes never left the model for more than a second, and only then during the story's juicier episodes.

After he had finished recounting his story Crosby watched his friend rise and walk slowly across the room to again admire the model, this time even more closely and with a continued look of awe. The whisky had dulled his initial shock, but it was obvious his friend still felt supreme wonder at the pubic creation in front of him.

"Crosby, my friend, you really have got to let the world see this baby. It's....it's...just..... utter perfection."

Trelander turned and looked at his friend with a look of profound seriousness Crosby had only ever seen him use once before.

That occasion had been at a model show in the town, where an American genital modelling expert called Jack Blunt had confided to Trelander details of his newly discovered ability to perfect an anatomically perfect brown polystyrene model of a gentleman's tumescent phallus.

Crosby felt intensely proud that his bridge was worthy of such high regard by his friend as the veined, erect dark masterpiece of polystyrene modelling folklore.

Twitch Trelander sat Crosby down and pleaded with him to allow the Strathcarnage Modelling Club to use his pubic engineering jewel to represent them in the next open model show. The modeller was impressed by the intensity of his friend's plea and his opinion that his Forth Bridge was of sufficient quality to officially represent the club in such a high profile event.

Flattered, he had instantly agreed to the request. Little did Crosby know that this agreement to show the model in public was to begin a chain of events that would lead to both fame and fortune and then ultimately to tragedy.

Crosby Stanton's masterpiece had won the main prize in the 34$^{th}$ Annual Modelling Awards Show in Strathcarnage. The model had been the talk of the weekend, drawing large crowds to its glass display case from the moment the doors opened on the first day. A number of creators of nearby displays had asked to be moved; such was the obsessive and excitable mood of the crowd swarming around the glass case, all transfixed by the pubic masterpiece.

Indeed Crosby's bridge had even overshadowed what had been previously billed as the highlight of the weekend, a display of motorised penises from a modern avant-garde artist calling himself simply 263.

263 had travelled secretly from his studio in Chicago for the show, and his

motorised creations performed a complicated choreographed formation dance in the floor of the main arena. The act had a spectacular finale in which the motorised penises had mechanically risen one at a time from flaccid to tumescent in a huge choreographed line only then to twitch and arc thin gossamer streams of carefully pre-loaded face cream across the arena floor.

Yet even this spectacular showpiece finale didn't manage to draw a significant number of the crowd away from around the glass case containing the bridge. In the period of only one quick weekend, Crosby was the new enfant terrible of the modelling world.

On his triumphant return to his studio all was well for a few days. However in his anxiousness to promote the surprise success of his friend, Trelander had phoned The Porcupine, the local Strathcarnage newspaper, and had informed them in great detail of the model's quality, providing his own pictures of both the model and the trophy presentations at the gala ceremony.

Trelander had mistakenly assumed that the story would be an enormous uplifting surprise for his friend, as well as a boost for his club's standing in the modelling world.

Crosby had been in his hairdressing shop trimming the unruly moustache of Artemus Glance the local slaughter man when the first person had entered the shop to congratulate him. Initially confused as to exactly what the well-wisher had been referring to, the congratulatory person had slid a rolled up copy of the local newspaper from his jacket pocket and showed Crosby the large front page headline.

"Victory for Bridge of Pubes"

Crosby just stood and stared, his clippers sliding out of his hand and falling buzzing onto the dunes of hair on the floor.

Below the headline was the colour picture of him accepting his award and an artist's impression of a hand shaving an untidy auburn muff for illustration. Crosby was aghast. Turning off his clippers, he quickly closed up the shop and sprinted home to explain to Agnes. It was already much too late.

Agnes had bought the local paper on the way to the funeral parlour. She hadn't even glanced at the headline as she lifted the paper from Benny Chan's counter and placed it inside her bag.

She had been dressing a corpse for a war themed funeral later in the week, a spectacular affair that involved the corpse being burned inside a mock Spitfire cockpit in full pilot's attire, to a taped soundtrack of authentic German gunfire. Subsequently Agnes had thought nothing of the shouted inquiry as to whether her copy of the local newspaper could be borrowed, a request which had emanated from the embalmers canteen.

Unfortunately the enquiring party turned out to be one of the Auburn twin daughters of Mr Burns, visiting the workshop to drop off a prosthetic limb she had been soaking in tea at home to match the rest of the body for an upcoming Bob Marley burial.

The twin was about to relax with a cup of tea and have a glance at the local news before returning home. It was the shrill scream that had alerted Agnes to the headline, and that began the process of detection that was ultimately would cost Crosby his marriage.

The first twin had been hysterical and had phoned the second twin for advice. The second twin, equally distraught on being told the headline, blurted out the secret of her affair with Crosby to the first. After the two had realised how they had been so callously and indifferently used purely for their genital merchandise, they both agreed to convene back at the undertakers and reveal the whole sordid story to a deeply distressed Agnes.

Crosby arrived at the undertaker's yard to find three red-headed women staring angrily back at him from the doors of the workshop, flanked by a corpse dressed as fighter pilot ace and a Rastafarian cadaver with one leg and a guitar.

Crosby realised instantly what had happened and turned on his heels to run for home.

On arriving, Crosby found himself having to sneak through the garden at the rear to avoid a weeping vet Carlos, sat on the front step of his house still in blood stained surgical scrubs clutching a balled copy of the newspaper, having driven there at speed from a hastily aborted horse castration. The Spanish vet had clearly read the headlines thought Crosby, and had discovered his own hurtful part in the entire episode.

The modelling guerrilla had waited until the weeping figure of Carlos had eventually left and had then hastily loaded the pubic bridge creation into his van. Crosby realised his marriage was most likely over, but he had no intention of surrendering his newfound pubic modelling career without more of a fight.

Crosby drove over to Twitch Trelander's studio in the shadowy outskirts of the town, and his friend, taken aback and remorseful at this course of events he had inadvertently set in motion, instantly offered a home to both his friend and his wiry auburn construction.

The next few months were hard for Crosby. His hairdressing salon was forced to close after vandals had covered the entire front of the shop with glue and tufts of red hair. Someone had painted "Pube Thief" in huge bright red letters across the whole sad scene.

Police also reported another bizarre incident to Crosby weeks later, where the salon windows were mysteriously smashed by what were later discovered to be a pair of horse testicles wrapped in a copy of The Seville Times, with a simple note proclaiming angrily "Bastardo!"

The local press tried to gain interviews with Crosby for a time, but the modeller locked himself away silently in his new home, resolving to remain in hiding until the town lost interest in the matter.

With no fresh news of sightings of the man, the local press soon switched their attentions to a bizarre story involving the sudden recent disappearance of Crosby's wife Agnes with a local Spanish vet, together with a large quantity of cash and surgical instruments.

Six months after the incident, once interest in the matter had died down, Crosby had left the sanctuary afforded by his friend and returned through the winding lanes of the town in the dead of night to his empty home, to contemplate his future and his ruined career as a hairdresser and a modeller. What he found there astonished him.

As he forced open his front door with his shoulder, he found behind it a huge pile of letters. Crosby had expected some mail backlog; after all it had been almost four months since his wife had disappeared with the vet. What he hadn't expected was the quantity and content of the letters.

After opening those few letters that were obviously bills, Crosby turned his attention to the huge pile of other mail. Crosby had opened the first letter fully expecting to be met with hate filled abuse, detailing ways in which angry locals wanted him dead or, at the very least, ruined. He couldn't have been more wrong.

As Crosby opened the first letter, he jumped back as he felt something brush against his hand. He panicked, dropping the envelope, imagining some nasty contents as a revenge for his behaviour. As he carefully approached the discarded wrapper to see what had fallen onto his hand, he was astonished to see what lay on the floor. It was a large unkempt bunch of what appeared to be brunette pubic hair, carefully tied in a tiny pink ribbon.

As Crosby sat on the empty hall floor and began to examine other envelopes, he discovered that at least eighty per cent of those he opened contained carefully shaved bundles of pubic hair, together with letters of support from fans far and near.

Word of his modelling brilliance had somehow spread around the town during his self imposed exile, and Crosby soon realised that he had somehow become a cult figure, not just in genital related modelling, but also in the wider modelling community. Crosby sank back against the wall in the hall of the empty house and, as the realisation of his new status began to sink in, smiled for the first time in months.

As the weeks wore on letters continued to arrive and he grew heartened by the support, Crosby again started building models in his huge bay windowed modelling room at the front of the house. Strathcarnage residents gradually began to wave and shout greetings at the man as he ventured around the town stockpiling his supplies of hairspray.

People began to chat, to ask after his health. He was being forgiven his previous errors and gradually becoming a welcomed face again. The model maker was happy, and recovering his confidence, beginning to work at a furious rate.

Over the next few years, Crosby had built pubic model after pubic model: the Taj Mahal, the Golden Gate Bridge, tanks, cars, and even a huge 15 foot model of a Lancaster Bomber, complete with miniature pubic crew and moving nipple hair guns, a creation he suspended proudly from the workshop ceiling.

His models won both praise and prizes, and since the show where he had premiered his bridge model, Crosby had never won less than first prize in any competition he had entered either in the village or on his occasional travels abroad in the last seven years.

However the success and trophies weren't enough for the proud modelling perfectionist.

Crosby wanted to build something that he could never be forgotten for, an epic model so perfect that it would stand alone above all his previous creations and whose very presence would cause the any viewer to gasp in sheer awe at its ingenuity, perfection and scale.

After much contemplation Crosby had decided to embark upon a twenty-three foot fully operational and floating model of the German Battleship Bismarck. It would be, he was determined, his finest hour and his defining moment.

The project obsessed Crosby. He required his creation to be absolutely perfect. He laboured for hours on end, poring over the designs and carefully examining envelopes of grey pubic hair he now received daily since making a televised appeal on the local station. But none were that exact shade he required. He needed it to be just right, to be perfect. None of the generously offered samples seemed to match his ideal.

Then, while out collecting his stockpiles of hairspray from a newly docked boat in the harbour, out of the corner of his eye Crosby noticed a small woman browsing through the sunglasses stand in the local chemist shop.

Crosby knew instantly the hair was the perfect shade of grey, glinting and teasing him as individual strands caught in the sunlight pouring in through the shop's windows. He had waited almost nine months for this moment, and he wasn't going to let it pass now.

Crosby studied the woman from a distance, pretending to finger various tubes of haemorrhoid cream that sat jammed into the crevice of the plastic display arse on the counter. After a while Crosby walked over to the lady and pretending to examine pairs of sunglasses right next to her, secretly drawing from his pocket a small photograph of the German battleship he kept about his person for such an occasion.

He held it up furtively next to the woman's hair as she distractedly turned to leave. It was the exact match for the hull of the Bismarck. Crosby had to act quickly.

Crosby began chatting charmingly with the woman, just as he had done all those years ago at the dinner party with the twin bridge suppliers. However this wasn't to be so easy, as the woman was of an age many years past thinking herself capable of attracting a man as young as Crosby.

When she revealed to Crosby that she was an elderly historian called Florence D'Arbo researching ancient shipwrecked pirate ships in the area, and had bribed a visiting French trawler to drop her secretly in the town harbour, the resourceful man saw his chance.

Crosby had charmed the lady into believing he held a collection of ancient town documents and shipping charts back at his house and invited the woman to tea the next day in order she might examine them, explain them to Crosby, and see if any might be of help to her studies. The lady agreed gladly, flattered by the appeal to her expert knowledge. It was just as Crosby had planned.

Crosby's scheme was in full swing, and the next day, just after finishing her second cup of heavily drugged tea, 78-year-old Florence D'Arbo found herself sleepily press-ganged in her new role as the unwilling supplier of the raw materials for the hull of the biggest German battleship ever constructed.

Crosby thought it only fair that since Florence was providing the raw materials for the model, she should be offered the opportunity to watch as it was built. This state of affairs also allowed Crosby to keep his eye on his captive during long hours spent at work. He even bought a selection of old records from the charity shop so the elderly woman could perhaps relax a little and hum along to the melodies from behind her gag.

He was a modeller after all, not a monster. That was a fact that Crosby used to remind the woman of as he removed her underwear for shaving in the dead of night, so no-one would hear her weak squeals of protest.

Months later Crosby sat down and relaxed back in his chair, happy with the steadily growing line of the hull. He slid the thick modelling glasses off the top of his head, placed them back on, and gazed out his window at the view over the town.

The last six months had seen the model come on well, and Florence had grown to almost enjoy the casual atmosphere of the situation and the routine genital shavings. In time Crosby hoped to be able to remove her gag completely and chat to the woman as they both watched the ship finally come together. That was his dream.

Occasionally, as Crosby sat at his desk at the first floor window, he would notice small horse drawn carts of obsessive Japanese fans disembark and stand staring up at the window.

He had discovered that interest in his models in the Far East was enormous, since they saw all forms of miniaturisation as an exquisite art form and yet also held a deep fascination with all things pubic. As a result small knots of secretly travelled Orientals would often appear behind the wall at the bottom of his garden waving excitedly and taking photographs of him working away at the window.

When not engrossed in his work, he would take a moment to casually stand and slowly nod back, careful to keep the bound and gagged Florence well out of view at the back of the room.

However today, as Crosby sat back in his chair surveying the town below, he noticed one of the younger Orientals had become overly enthusiastic and had climbed atop his garden wall in order to perhaps get a better photograph deep inside the workspace of his modelling hero.

Crosby suddenly panicked that from his heightened position, the young fan might see something of the bound and gagged Florence and had hurriedly thrown his glasses onto the desk before rushing downstairs to berate the youth for this gross invasion of privacy. Crosby knew that he wouldn't be quite so popular if his fans discovered exactly how he currently sourced his raw materials.

The little group of enthusiasts went wild at the sight of Crosby running from his front door to pull the youth from the wall. The wider group began snatching adoringly at Crosby's sleeves, trying to get a stroke of the famous craftsman's hands they so faithfully worshipped.

It was just then that the youth still perched high on the wall suddenly unleashed a chilling scream. It was a horrible sound louder than anything Crosby had heard in his entire life.

The whole group, including Crosby, turned as one in the direction the youth was now pointing, in order to see the reason for the commotion. Crosby, fearing the unexpected discovery of his 78-year-old shaven secret captive, shaded his eyes from the strong sunlight to see exactly what had prompted the piercing oriental scream.

The sight that greeted him was much worse than the discovery of the captive Florence. As Crosby followed the pointing sallow fingers, he suddenly realised why the youth had screamed at such ferocity and volume. Framed by the wide window, the Bismarck was on fire.

The discarded glasses had fallen on the desk into direct sunlight, and the thick magnified lenses had concentrated the sun's rays on one single bright point on the side of the model. Within seconds, the hairspray binding the wiry hairs together had begun smoking in the intense heat and had ignited.

The model had begun to burn and sizzle like a firework, setting off other models in the room as the stray wisps of partially aflame and red glowing pube embers were carried round the room by the light breeze from the open window. By the time Crosby reached the room, the whole place was ablaze and the acrid smell of burning pubic hair filled the air. After dragging Florence to safety, Crosby returned into the inferno in an attempt to salvage whatever he could of his burning creations.

The later inquest heard that the group of fans had watched from the garden as a bewildered half naked elderly lady had suddenly appeared from the front door and weaved around on the lawn in front of the house. They said she moved with tiny steps, face black with soot, shaven, gagged and still tied to a chair.

She had motioned with her head towards the blazing room, and the group turned just in time to see the burning hulk of the ceiling mounted pubic Lancaster Bomber collapse. As the model fell in a huge yellow fireball, it brought to a hideous end the life of the world's most gifted and twisted modelling genius. The gathered fans in the garden heard only a single short scream of surprise as the blazing 23 foot frame of the bomber collapsed down, directly on top of an oblivious Crosby Stanton.

Crosby Stanton 1945-1978

# CHAPTER 8

# Day Six – The Clairvoyant

A small queue had formed outside the tent, the bitter sea wind causing the filthy canvas to snap and thud as it was buffeted in the icy blast. Those standing patiently in line moved repeatedly from foot to foot, blowing into their cupped hands trying to keep themselves warm in the cutting coastal gusts. This was July in Strathcarnage.

As the tent flap at the head of the queue was abruptly thrown open, the line craned their heads to see what the source of the fresh movement was. Those at the head of the queue close enough to witness the sudden ejaculation from the tent had watched as a thin man with a look of terror drawn over his pale face had emerged from inside, shaking his head in bewilderment.

As the next closest in the long thin line was beckoned to enter through the open canvas flaps by the curled, ring laden finger of an outstretched female hand, the queue silently shuffled forward. As the person disappeared through the tent entrance into the darkness within, a momentary gap in the shuffling line had revealed an ornate hand painted sign announcing the reason for the small group doggedly suffering the worst effects of the bitter wind. It read "Madame Lantana: Faecal Fortunes".

The latest customer gazed around the tent interior nervously, squinting in the flickering candlelight to take in his surroundings. As he turned himself fully around in the garishly decorated space, suddenly the man found himself staring at the veiled face of Madame Lantana, and he sprung back across the tent in shock.

"Hello, my friend. Please, do not be nervous. I am not to be feared. Come, follow me and let us prepare for your reading."

Madame Lantana raised a hand and motioned towards a curtained entrance leading to a smaller area in the darkness of the rear of the tent. The small man entered and waited.

"Please drop your lower clothing for me, loosen these trappings of your outside life. You will need them not here. Please remove and discard them and then we can prepare for your reading."

The man unfastened and dropped his trousers, nervously covering his underwear with cupped hands to preserve modesty. Madame Lantana smiled and shook her head, the small gold discs hanging from her lilac headdress tinkling gently in the silence.

"You are clearly new to my methods, aren't you my modest friend? To proceed with the reading I must ask you to become as the animal in the wild, free and unfettered. I must have you pure and naked as the day you were born, unencumbered by both clothing or fear, else we shall not be able to reveal to you anything."

The visitor stood looking bemused in his underwear.

"Drop them," Madame Lantana abruptly added, sensing the confusion.

The middle aged man looked at her perplexed, but then slowly and self consciously removed his underwear, returning his hands instantly to his body to cup and hide his naked genitals.

"And the socks."

He stared down at his feet, again totally bewildered at the request.

"Possible splashback" replied the clairvoyant helpfully as she continued to fold the man's recently vacated and still warm trousers.

After hopping around in unbalanced circles while endeavouring to remove his socks, almost twice crashing naked through the canvas wall and back out into the field beyond, the man stood completely naked, waiting with his head bowed before the figure of the old woman in flowing robes. The man stood self consciously waiting for the next turn of events.

She presented him with an ornate silver platter, removed from somewhere between folds of her clothing and now held at arms length. The plate glistened in the candlelight and looked to be silver, ornately decorated with the carvings of the zodiac signs around the rim.

The visitor accepted the object with a nervous smile and a nod of thanks. Madame Lantana stood and stared at him, waiting patiently with her arms folded. After a short uncomfortable silence, the man gestured with a shrug of his shoulders that he was unaware of the next turn of events. Madame Lantana looked skyward and shook her head in frustration, returning her stare to his.

"I need you to evacuate your inner soul, by way of your bowels. Aim as close to the centre of the plate as you can control and try to produce as close to a single movement as your exertions can manage. Right here, right now and witnessed by me. Then we may give you a reading."

He stared at his warped reflection in the silver plate, his shock at the directions causing his mouth to unconsciously fall open. Looking over the rim of the plate, he saw Madame Lantana snap on a latex glove and beam a gold toothed smile back at him.

This was his first visit to a fortune teller of any kind and he had already made a mental note not to make it a habit.

Outside the tent loud straining noises were readily audible to the chilled shuffling queue, even in the strong wind. The waiting locals threw their eyes up to heaven on hearing the noise, for they knew fully what it signified; a long wait. A regular Madame Lantana customer in the queue, frustrated at having to shuffle from foot to foot to stave off both cold and a looming bowel eviction, cursed loudly at no one in particular, frustrated at the potential wait.

"Fucking tourists", she mumbled loudly, unleashing a shrill discharge of wind from her effort, a sombre expression instantly appearing on her face. It was the well-known panic of unintended follow through, clearly visible in her widening eyes.

The woman's facial expression relaxed and she sighed with relief, signalling a false alarm as she returned to carefully shifting from foot to foot, thankful that her seal remained unbroken.

Madame Lantana had been operating from these new tented premises ever since the recent opening of the themed holiday camp in Strathcarnage in the driving hail of the previous summer. The camp was intended to offer a new amenity for Strathcarnage locals and for visiting crews from the clandestine ships constantly arriving at the local harbour.

The park had been designed around a consistent historical theme and was located on a recently cleared section of land against one of the massive cave walls which enclosed the town. The new facility was packed with accommodation and facilities themed in the same subject in both style and décor. It was the first, and to date only, family holiday camp anywhere in the world with a Mass Murderer theme.

Each chalet in the small park had been carved in a long line into the cliff walls, designed and named to reflect a notorious mass murderer from the town. There were a good number to choose from. Each lodge was then subsequently decorated to reflect the style and methods of the individual murderer, with modest thoughtful touches to ensure a wide appeal to all the family.

The "Frank Whipple Axe Murderer" chalet, for example, featured a wooden front door heavily spattered with blood and pock marked with deep axe blows, with a nature trail winding from the front of the chalet through the entire park and marked with the sign of the axe in tribute to the final route of the dragged dismembered bodies Whipple had made his trademark.

Above the fireplace was a fibreglass model of the head of his sixteenth victim, attached to the stone wall with a huge fireman's axe. A spring loaded dismembered corpse was designed to fall repeatedly on every opening of one of the kitchen cupboards, spraying the room with blood and a deafening taped scream as it fell apart before your eyes into pieces on the floor.

Any children staying at the property could amuse themselves trying to reassemble the internal organs of a full-scale corpse in real-feel rubber, thoughtfully located in their bedroom. If successfully assembled in the right order, the electronic model would all of a sudden sit bold upright and utter a series of chilling threats of revenge until it was subdued with blows from the plastic axe hidden under the bedding. Children loved the challenge.

The attention to detail was the main attraction, and visitors leaving messages in the skin covered chalets visitors book with the dismembered finger pen, had commented that such attentive touches had made their stay a more memorable experience.

Of the other five carved chalets, the Wilson Fenton "Gas Chamber" room was the most popular, but bookings were brisk at the "Strathcarnage Scarf Strangler" lodge and the "Orphanage Arsonist" villa. In addition, there was a small on-site bar simply called "The Filleter", which as well as serving themed pub meals, offered a nightly costumed re-enactment of each of the murderer's crimes. These events were performed lustily and with full bloody special effects by children from the local primary school.

Madame Lantana had moved to her tented base in the "Victims Final Rest" mock graveyard section of the camp after being hired as a key attraction by the new park owners. She was sad to leave her previous base in the lounge bar of The Harse public house, although the pub owners were delighted at the move.

Although they fully acknowledged and appreciated Madame Lantana's unique gift, the nightly spectacle of her encouraging customers to defecate on her silver plate during meal servings was a bit much for some diners to stomach. Indeed the customary sight of the woman manipulating the fresh movement with latex gloved hands while in lost a trance had been seriously affecting the establishment's catering takings.

Lantana had initially been sceptical that her mystical gift would remain popular in its new surroundings at the edge of town, but on nervously folding back her striped canvas flaps on that opening day, she had found a long queue of Strathcarnage locals shifting from foot to foot outside wearing strained expressions and cautiously awaiting an opportunity to partake of her unique gift.

The entire park had proved hugely popular with locals. The experience was designed to provide a quality day out for visitors of any age, packed as it was with attractions to suit all tastes. Adults could laugh as they found themselves under surprise "attack" by any number of the hired performers, wielding mock chainsaws and spraying mock blood as they dug their specially designed harmless props into surprised screaming bodies. For the children there were similar delights as actors made up to resemble heavily scarred gangsters suddenly surprised them and "cut" their throats with prop open razors.

In addition to Madame Lantana and her unique fortune telling abilities, there were a number of other thrilling attractions on offer in the park.

A 'Cadaver' food stall served a range of snacks from a themed menu. A local slaughterhouse owner, Artemus Glance, had supplied kebab meat in the shape of body parts, and a cackling one eyed assistant with a blood soaked apron could offer customers a choice of succulent cuts from the slowly rotating virgin's leg, child's torso or sailor's arm range. They were all served in warm pitta bread, and presented wrapped in a facsimile of a newspaper front page from the day of an important local crime, all the while dripping blood red chilli sauce through the newsprint.

There was a tent run by the local handicapped school, where every half an hour the children would be led out into a fully operational kitchen set and invited to prepare a four course meal. The loud barking and screaming noises of the children, combined with the ensuing carnage of dropped knives, naked flames and red hot pans always drew a large appreciative crowd. This was especially so on a Monday afternoon, which traditionally saw the unmissable show featuring the eternally promising combination of both the school's blind pupils and the large mechanical bacon slicer.

The amusement arcade in the park gave blindfolded locals a chance to win prizes by their placing of the correct mummified severed head from a bloody sack onto the appropriate decapitated torso. This all occurred in numerous reconstructions of rooms decorated faithfully from local victim's crime scene photographs.

Older patrons looking for more traditional amusement could try their hand at the Broken Neck Bingo, where a costumed bingo caller in a cage barked out numbers which players had then to mark off on a mock crime report. The system of numbers was also unique, and true to the theme.

The caller used local knowledge to spice up his calling of the numbers, such as "Blows of the axe – sixty six" and "Two bloated corpses – eighty eight". The first person to cross out all the numbers was required to scream "To the gallows!" before being led to the front of the stage to drag a rusty lever down to open the wooden trapdoor next to the caller and watch a local actor dressed as a criminal twitch and struggle for breath as they swung, eyes bulging, on the end of a rope.

Since the town had recently adopted a compulsory euthanasia policy, the Black Bingo exhibit owners had been able to dispense with the costumed actors on certain occasions, which only served to add to the thrill of the players.

Child visitors could have their photograph taken as a victim in the 'Savage Murder House', with an actor dressed as one of a number of local killers standing in a mocked up crime scene liberally decorated with real offal and blood from the local butcher, Alan Savage, who had sponsored the exhibit.

Madame Lantana was pleased at her new location since the park atmosphere complimented her unique but eccentric talent for telling fortunes using the unusual medium of bowel expulsion.

Madame Lantana had stumbled upon her faecal reading gift while still a child. As a little girl she had regularly entered the family toilet only to happen upon an unflushed movement. The young girl found herself both fascinated and strangely drawn by the floating log. She had later discovered from ancient manuscripts that her profound fascination for stools was considered by experts on the supernatural to be a once common power we all possessed, but one which had gradually regressed over the years through adoption of more acceptable social behaviour.

Young Lantana, however, was still an innocent child acting instinctively, and had reached down and grabbed at the floating stool, lifting it dripping out of the white porcelain bowl.

As Lantana grasped the movement, she felt a strange sensation instantly course through her entire being, her mind at once receiving a clear image of her father having an energetic sexual liaison with Lena the family babysitter, a petite blonde Transylvanian girl with the habit of screaming dialogue from Doris Day films at the point of climax.

When she confronted her father with details of those scenes she had witnessed in her mind, he had told the child her vision was merely the product of a vivid imagination, but yet had made the child promise to keep her visions secret, especially from her mother. On hearing of the vivid truth of his daughter's visions Lantana's father had grown disturbed by the accuracy of her powers and then confused at just how his daughter had discovered his secret.

The young Lantana had been bemused by her strange powers, and was soon drawn to repeat her actions, a decision helped greatly by the fact her father was an

old fashioned Strathcarnage man who saw it as his marital right to leave his wife to flush away his expulsions. Lantana continued to use her powers in secret, receiving fresh visions of her father's insatiable sexual appetite but now only observing without making any further comment. Sadly Lantana was soon to discover the darker potential of the visions her powers afforded her

While experimenting with her excremental gift one morning, Lantana had again witnessed brand new visions of her father pursuing his carnal pastime. The young girl watched helplessly with soiled hands in the family bathroom as she felt her consciousness pulled out her body and transported across the village.

Suddenly Lantana found herself flying high above the houses before suddenly swooping and travelling along the familiar dark passages she knew led to the baker's workshop. Lantana watched on as the husband of his father's newest lover had arrived home unexpectedly to discover her father engaging pornographically in energetic acts of copulation with his wife.

Lantana watched over the scene, weeping as her father's crimson, heavily sweating features were about to magically metamorphose into the grotesque mask of climax. Just then the door of the baker's workshop had flown open.

The baker's wife had been first to notice the appearance of her husband and had attempted to warn Lantana's father, but it had been far too late to avoid the approaching blow from an angrily swung rolling pin, the attack upsetting a tray of fruit scones in the process.

In a freak synchronicity, the fatal blow had landed precisely at the point of no carnal return, and Lantana's father had fallen back dead out of the warm embrace of the baker's wife while giving a final twitch and arcing a stream of liquid sex all over the baker, his wife and a tray of Danish pastries waiting, ironically, to be iced. Then after watching more unspeakable horrors of the attack, the vision had suddenly darkened and the young girl saw the vision reverse, carrying her high above the down and suddenly snapping her back to reality in the bathroom.

Lantana fell to her knees, exhausted. She had watched the entire episode as it happened, the scene channelled to her through her powers of stool reading. The young girl stood in the family bathroom dazed, her fingers tightly closed around what was to be her father's final brown swansong, remembering what she had witnessed.

The traumatized young girl had watched as the wronged baker fed her father's doubly limp body into the stainless steel industrial mincing machine in the corner of the workshop, pressing the switch marked "on" with a thin smile. She heard the cackling laugh of the baker grow as the body disappeared gradually into the grinding metallic jaws of the machine, listening while weeping to the gurgling sound of her father gradually becoming pie filling. The mad eyed baker had then fed his fully conscious cheating wife into the machine, but only after holding her head up and forcing her to watch Lantana's father meet his fate first.

The baker was a ruthless, wronged man, but his actions were not purely those of cold revenge. The baker knew the machine had a habit of jamming on bigger carcasses, so he had heartlessly waited until her partner was fully minced before feeding his struggling wife into the snapping jaws, the ferocious noise of the machine masking her last desperate screams. The two secret lovers would enjoy the closeness afforded by entangled flesh one last time.

Lantana was to be destined to be reminded of those horrific screams in her new home in the park, since the town baker's horrific crime was one of those daily re-enacted by a small deaf theatre company who had dramatised the story in the 'True Crimes' tent next to hers.

Although most of the dialogue consisted of dull roars and random barking noises, the hideous finale of screaming from the deaf and dumb actress playing the bakers wife was uncannily accurate. The group even sold pies to the audience at the end of the performance, accurately shadowing the reality of the culinary horror in the real event.

Indeed, only the discovery of one of his wife's earrings in a pie, still attached to an earlobe, had led to the police arrest of the baker and the eventual discovery of the crime.

None of the carelessly decorated Danish pastries were ever recovered from the scene, and only a small number of pies were ever traced even after discovery of the ear.

Lantana had gone into shock immediately after witnessing those murderous events which had unfolded in the bakery, her mother discovering the young girl curled on the floor of the bathroom, weeping and with a heavily kneaded doing still clutched in her tiny brown stained hand.

Lantana had been washed and put to bed where she remained in a silent trance for a number of days, stirring only to scream horribly when presented with a warm pie for her evening meal. Lantana's mother had herself been eating the refused pie when news had broken of the local baker's arrest for double murder and contravention of Strathcarnage food laws.

As the newsreader was detailing the facts of the crime, and the baker's immediate expulsion from the Pie Makers' Guild, Lantana's mother had asphyxiated on a large unshredded piece of her father's white silk underwear. Some romantically inclined people maintain she died of a broken heart, but the frayed square of white fabric recovered from her windpipe proved otherwise and the evidence had later been returned to Lantana by thoughtful local police, together with a replacement pie.

Lantana was now orphaned and alone in the world and the young girl soon found herself both penniless and destitute, owing to her father's cavalier attitude toward providing for his numerous unsupported children in the town. The persistant claims on the meagre resources from those siblings still owed money from her father's estate had quickly left the young girl bankrupt. Lantana now was faced with the prospect of both homelessness and starvation. Knowing she had to support herself, the young girl turned to the only talent she knew she had, faecal readings.

The orphaned girl used the last of her spare cash to take out a small advert in the local Strathcarnage paper. It read "Madame Lantana: Faecal Forecasts and Stool Readings". Her phone never rang once during the week long period which the advert ran, and she decided any career as a mystic was over before it had even begun.

Desolate, the young girl began work in the only place that she could find to employ her, the sympathetic baker's son offering her a position at the very site of her own father's death. Lantana put the events of the past few weeks behind her and began serving in the bakers shop. She was not to be labouring with lightly floured hands for long though, as only the next week she received a surprise phone call that was to change her life.

The young American wife of the local TV station owner had noticed the small advert in an old copy of the local paper she was using to line a squirrel cage, and had shown it to her husband, knowing he had been desperately searching for a final novelty act for a themed "Anal Evening" on the channel. The bulky station head known affectionately as The Ox had contacted Lantana immediately.

She had been grateful of the offer, but remained unsure of how best to choreograph her first public appearance, having at this stage only ever worked among small groups of friends as an enthusiastic amateur. After visiting the local library and consulting the well-thumbed volumes on spiritualism, Lantana opted for the clichéd mystic's costume, complete with gold earrings, mysterious veil, floating silk sari, and headdress. That is how she was dressed as she walked out onto the set for her television debut, smiling nervously and fingering her newly bought silver zodiac platter, an extra prop designed to give her the appearance of a professional.

Lantana was to appear between two other local bowel based performers on the specially themed edition of the show. The preceding act, a camp stool modeller called Stefan Effen, had finished his presentation by transforming a number of dried animal droppings into a reasonable facsimile of the comic Charlie Chaplin. Stefan had built the model quickly, bringing the house down as he finished by smearing a brown finger across his top lip and waddling off set swinging a cane.

As the applause had died down and the channel had gone to an advertising break, it was Lantana's big chance. As she strode out onto the set, she found herself fingering the small white square of parental silk undergarment retrieved from her dead mother's throat for comfort.

Lantana had wasted no time in beginning her act, having previously been made fully aware of the tight time constraints imposed by television. The young girl had asked softly from beneath her veil for a volunteer from the audience. With the minimum of instruction, the gentleman answering the request had rapidly found himself squatting over her silver zodiac plate and unleashing a steaming brown trout onto the polished surface. After snapping on her rubber gloves with a dramatic flourish, Lantana had begun the reading. Appearing to lapse into a deep trance, another tip learned from the books on her library trip, the young debutante began to give a free rein to her powers.

Within seconds of fingering the fresh expulsion, Lantana had informed the gathered audience that the gentleman was named Jorge, was a visitor on a fishing boat from Portugal, and more specifically, had been born on a small farm just outside Lisbon.

She carefully informed Jorge of the details of his family, his job and his house, and with a final flourish, recounted that he had also enjoyed dining on a small well-done steak with French fries within the last few hours. Jorge had looked taken aback at the accuracy of the reading, his thin tanned face falling immediately into an honest expression of amazement that the TV cameras had cut to in glorious close up.

Lantana's phone had begun ringing even before she had returned backstage to her dressing room.

The local head of the Strathcarnage Law Homicide Unit had been watching the impressive display and it was his voice Lantana heard on the crackling phone line as she answered that first call in the dressing room.

The next day, Lantana found herself sitting waiting outside the office of Inspector Claude Grayling, having been asked to attend urgently for a meeting of some importance. After a short wait a slight, bespeckled secretary informed the young girl that Inspector Grayling was ready to see her, and Lantana pushed open the door into the senior law man's innermost sanctum.

Having shaken hands with the gigantic imposing figure of the town's most senior law officer, she was offered a chair, which she shyly accepted. Grayling had asked her to recount the brief history of her unique gift, and while the story of her father's death was told again, the man relaxed back in his padded chair, nodding silently. After hearing the whole tale, Grayling leaned forward and pressed a finger onto his desk intercom, asking his secretary to send in a man called Beeman.

Beeman announced his arrival seconds later with a sharp knock. Grayling had barked a loud "Come" at the door and the small man had entered, carrying a covered silver tureen, which he placed on the desk in front of Lantana before retreating to sit out of sight behind her.

Grayling looked up at Lantana from his seat with a narrowing gaze of concentration, and still maintaining eye contact, lifted the domed silver lid on the dark desk before her. Lantana was met with the sight of a large freshly harvested brown log. From the condensation forming around the object's edges on the metal plate, Lantana safely assumed the object had been freshly laid for her visit.

"You understand that as a town law man, I am almost duty bound to be a natural sceptic," said Grayling, his eyes searching Lantana's face for a response.

Lantana understood the nature of this test and returned the man's gaze while reaching into her bag and removing a fresh set of latex gloves.

"What do you need to know?" she asked, expressionless.

"Tell me everything you can, " replied Grayling.

Lantana began to carefully examine the lukewarm mahogany test sitting in front of her, deciding to close her eyes as she had done on television. This time it was not for show, but to block out any outside distraction and to better concentrate. She squeezed, prodded and allowed herself to engage with the object, steadily becoming more and more annoyed as she did so.

"Well?" questioned an impatient Grayling.

Lantana opened her eyes and stared blankly at the law man, sat opposite her and smiling knowingly as he waited for her findings.

"It appears, Inspector Grayling, that you have asked me here purely in order to mock me, to belittle my powers. I feel hurt and somewhat humiliated that you have wasted both your time and my own."

Lantana stood up to leave the room, noticing as she turned the expression of scarcely hidden smugness on the face of Beeman sitting behind her. The angry woman was annoyed by the knowing grin and suddenly turned back to face Grayling. She walked back to the desk and leaned forward. She plunged a single gloved finger into the middle of the cooling brown mass.

"This, Inspector, is the product of Sabre, a dog of your acquaintance. Sabre has four legs, a soft coat and lives in a kennel that is kept in a draughty place. Although cold at night, Sabre is happy, fit and eats well. From the evidence before me, I would hazard a guess at tinned rabbit substitute and water as the main constituents of her diet.

She also has a bone that she has hidden from you, and on which she likes to gnaw after dinner. Oh, and one final thing, she hates Beeman and longs to bite him again in the groin, much like she did a number of weeks ago only harder. On a purely personal note, I do very much hope that you let her."

Lantana again rose, this time watching the slack mouthed look of incredulity before her. She shook hands in silence with the Inspector before walking towards the door, pausing in front of an equally stunned Beeman to shake his hand also, taking the opportunity to press the quantity of warm dog mess into his outstretched palm.

"I believe this is yours, Beeman. Inspector, you already know how to contact me should you need me for something more than mere parlour games."

Lantana walked out the office leaving the two men standing aghast, staring at each other in a state of silent shock. The dawning realisation that Lantana had not removed her gloves before shaking hands began to bring both men back to overpowering reality.

Later the same day Inspector Grayling had phoned again to ask if Lantana would accept his personal apology on the manner and enquired whether she would be prepared to assist them on a particularly complex case his men were working on.

The woman agreed, in turn offering an apology for letting her anger result in the soiling of hands. They both decided the meeting had contained mistaken behaviour on both sides and arranged to meet again at the crime scene the next morning.

Lantana had arrived at the address in the dark part of town very early, but to her surprise as she turned to knock at the house door on the winding lane, it swung open and Grayling was already standing there. He greeted her with a smile and a warm handshake. It transpired there had been a murder in the house, and a whole family had been wiped out horribly; attacked with knives, tied to chairs and forced to watch re-runs of Strathcarnage daytime TV movies as they bled to death. They were clearly hunting a callous monster.

Grayling had informed Lantana that a team had searched the house from top to bottom, but had been unable to find any clues whatsoever. There were no fingerprints, no forensic evidence and no witnesses. All that remained to indicate the visit of an outside assailant was a large floating calling card left in the house's upstairs guest lavatory. Since the murdered family were all wheelchair bound and attached to lavatorial bags, it was a safe assumption the torpedo shaped russet clue did not belong to them.

Grayling told Lantana that they would probably have lost this evidence too, however the house had been experiencing plumbing problems which had stopped the perpetrator from flushing, thus retaining the important evidence. Lantana was asked to employ her unique talents to examine the icy floater to see if she could establish any leads for the law men to work with. Lantana had agreed to give it a try, but warned Grayling that her understanding of cold anal matter was untried.

Lantana pulled on her gloves and had asked to be left alone in the room with the object. Once extracted it from the cold water, she set in motion her reading.

Images flashed and sparked through her head immediately. Although fainter than usual due to the coldness of her subject matter, she still witnessed sights clearly enough to pass them on to Grayling after a short recovery period to collect her thoughts.

Lantana explained to the burly head law man that she was unable to clearly see her subjects face, since the sample had gone cold and consequently her usual clarity had suffered. In cold material, she explained, visions sometimes narrowed in scope and were visible only through the eyes of the stool maker, but she had still managed to give a detailed description of the house where he lived and other elaborate particulars concerning the crime. She had also watched chilled as the murderer sat laughing, taking great pleasure in watching television surrounded by seriously bleeding wounded victims. This illustration of the killer's derangement had caused Lantana severe pain to witness.

Lantana had answered the phone days later to be informed by Grayling that they had caught the killer, directly due to those facts she had provided. Her evidence was inadmissible in court owing to her methods being somewhat untried by law, but luckily the murderer had pleaded guilty when confronted by law men and as a result, a full trial had been unnecessary.

The man, whose unflushed evidence had been his undoing, was a gentleman called Elmer Skeet and the local court sentenced him to a double term of life imprisonment two weeks later. Lantana had allowed herself a huge smile after reading of her part in the success as detailed in the local paper, and happily returned her attentions to the more mundane task of building her career as a more traditional faecal fortune-teller.

Word of Lantana's powers had spread through the town after her local television appearance, and now the details of her police approval had been released, she soon began to find herself in great demand in the local area. Her career had taken off with daily readings in the pub nearest her home, but since her move the new base in the theme park, she was seeing more customers than ever.

Lantana sat patiently waiting for her latest customer to unleash a sample onto the lucky silver zodiac plate now shaking in a tremulous hand under his perched exit. The fortune teller was used to a regular clientele when she worked out of The Harse and her customers were usually locals familiar with her methods. People always arrived fully prepared for the expected request: with one already in the barrel if you will.

This new customer was ill prepared for the reading, and the stress of the heavy straining was showing on his contorted reddening face. He let out another deep grunting noise as his body went rigid with effort, followed immediately with a small squealer of a fart, whistled out under the pressure of the effort. Thankfully, Lantana heard her phone ring in the outer room of the tent, and had excused herself from the squatting man, instructing him to continue to push on in her absence.

The phone call wasn't as she expected. Lantana had lifted the phone expecting an enquiry from another customer phoning to ask her to clarify some detail of her services. Instead it was the deep voice of Inspector Grayling.

The convicted murderer, Elmer Skeet, he informed her, had escaped from prison that morning, and was last spotted heading in the direction of the holiday village.

Grayling advised that for her own safety, Lantana would be best heading home immediately, where she would be met with two law officers he had specially assigned to protect her. Lantana replaced the receiver to end the call, and stood alone in the silence. As she contemplated what to do next, another pained moan of effort escaped from next door, closely followed by the piercing noise of another squealing fart.

Lantana decided to close up for the day and to head home immediately after this final customer, phoning on site security to come and meet her at the tent. She informed the still pacing queue that she would be shutting early today, prompting a chorus of disappointed voices, a sprint for the camp toilets and one mortified man to lose his will to clench and soil himself where he stood.

She returned inside the tent, set on informing her straining visitor that he should get dressed and return on another occasion. However on entering to notify him of her decision, the now smiling face had triumphantly offered her the silver plate, a fresh motion lying coiled in the very centre. Lantana decided to obtain this final reading quickly so then she could return to the relative safety of her home.

As her fingers hurriedly sank into the fresh sample in front of her and closed around the warm softness, Lantana suddenly stopped dead.

She could see the inside of the house she had visited all those months ago, the dead wheelchair family watching the sickening images of cheap thoughtless drama flicker lifelessly across the television screen. She saw the inside of a courtroom and a judge passing sentence, the harsh grey interior of a prison cell and finally, the overpowering of guards and a subsequent escape. She slowly pulled her fingers out of the brown mass in front of her and looked up.

Grinning back at her was the contorted face of Elmer Skeet. He had come to get revenge.

Events happened so quickly that they were a blur to Lantana. Elmer had lurched towards the faecal clairvoyant, the feral look of a madman in his eyes. He had grabbed her powerfully by the arm, but Lantana had thought quickly, utilising the only possible weapons at her disposal. She stamped on his foot with the pointed heel and, as he recoiled, forced her still gloved and heavily soiled fingers into his open mouth.

Elmer, shocked and now gagging heavily, fell backwards away from Lantana, against the canvas wall. Elmer's face now grew as crimson with rage as when he had been while recently bent over and straining. Gathering himself he again lurched towards Lantana. As he did so, she spun, and with all the power she could muster, launched the spinning zodiac plate straight at the onrushing murderer's head.

The plate was only in the air for a fraction of a second, and, before Elmer Skeet could react, he found himself standing immobile and silent, the heavy silver zodiac plate firmly embedded straight through the front of his forehead, deep into his skull and through his brain. The signs of Taurus through to Leo were now invisible behind the entry wound, and Elmer dropped to his knees then slumped forward onto the damp grass, quite dead.

Lantana was hailed as a hero by the local press, and her debut performance reading the Portuguese man's stool was rerun on television as accompaniment to the news story all week. Inspector Grayling recommended her for a town bravery award and commended her personally for her quick thinking and bravery, even agreeing to a private reading sometime in the near future.

The Mass Murderer Holiday Village also honoured their new resident heroine and new star attraction. The "Victims Final Rest" amusement park opened a new attraction, the Skeet Shoot where for a small fee patrons could buy three sharpened replicas of zodiac plates to throw at specially mounted model heads of Elmer Skeet, with the winner the one who took the top clean off exposing the fake grey jelly brain inside.

However the camp saved Lantana's greatest honour for a surprise ceremony later in the year. With a great deal of pomp and circumstance, they renamed one of the newly built chalets "The Elmer Skeet Head Slicer" in her honour.

Two months later, and now a local celebrity, Lantana married the baker's son in a lavish ceremony in the chalet, and was given away by Police Chief Grayling. A massive crowd from the village witnessed the ceremony and celebrated with huge party, presenting the happy couple with a specially decorated chocolate Wedding cake in the shape of a huge sweetcorn encrusted bowel motion, in appreciation of her art.

Elmer Skeet 1955 -1978

# CHAPTER 9

## Day Seven – Country & Western

The opening fatality of the day had occurred before the town had even woken from its night time winter slumber. Benny Chan the one armed local newsagent had been dragging out the day's bright newspaper board when tragedy struck.

Across the street, one of the local abattoir staff was returning home from a night shift spent liquidating a portion of the town pig population and had caught sight of the fresh headline from across the narrow cobbled street. As Gus Ebersole strained his gaze in the misty half-light of the Strathcarnage morning, the short-sighted man narrowed his eyes to better read the blur of letters opposite, while blowing into his hands for warmth.

As his bloody work boots left a trail of crimson footprints on the frosty white cobbles behind him, the exhausted slaughterhouse worker had moved close enough to read the headline from across the street, deciding to treat himself to a copy of the Strathcarnage Porcupine to enjoy the gruesome details.

The local paper, after all, did gruesome details brilliantly.

Gus stepped distractedly off the pavement onto the road to cross, searching among a pocketful of warm pig's trotters for change, the bloodied feet a stolen windfall from his job in the factory.

Unfortunately for Gus, years of operating the thundering steel jaws of the factory's mincing mechanism had left his sense of hearing badly spoilt. Stuffed under his thick woollen winter hat, his damaged ears had caught the thundering approach of the onrushing vehicle far too late. The workman had spun around to locate the strange rumble growing beneath his feet only to see the vast carved wooden snout and hooves on the front of the six horse "Mr Bacon Corpse Express" wagon bearing down on him at great speed round a curve in the road in the thick fog.

The speeding black horses and wooden wagon roared through the stationary man before he could react, exploding his tattered remains across the street where he had stood whole just moments ago. Owing to the velocity of truck, the tired driver taking full advantage of the empty dawn streets, Gus was trampled first by the flashing hooves of the galloping horses, his broken body thrown up and impacted by the sneering wooden pig head bolted on to the closed wagon front. The massive collision left a scarlet ribbon of human remains along the street's shop fronts, beginning on the windows of the local shoe shop and ending at the end of the row at the open door of the newsagent. One-Armed Benny stood dazed, frozen to the spot in shock and covered in the slowly dripping remains of his first missed sale of the morning.

The collision had caused bewilderment amongst emergency services as they arrived at the scene, although confirmation that Benny's arm was already missing had allowed some of the earlier confusion to settle down. Local medical recovery personnel had found themselves further troubled on discovering the exploded streak of remains partially consisted of both human remains and a quantity of still warm pig trotters.

Once this mystery too had been solved, and no evidence was discovered of any treatable casualty at the scene (other than the pale, silent and deeply shocked Benny), all that remained was for officers to clean up while casually speculating over the karmic irony of Gus being despatched by a cargo of two hundred pigs he himself had dispatched and then minced into fragments less than an hour previously.

It was to be that news headline which had initially caused Gus to fatefully cross the road, however, that would provide Strathcarnage with the greatest shock of the day.

The news had appeared on the doorsteps and breakfast tables of the town, the headline screaming "Burnt Out", complete with flaming red letters for extra effect. Under the headline was a picture of local councillor "Grubby" Hans Nash, grinning, his arms outstretched over an architectural model of the planned redevelopment of the local Strathcarnage Special Needs School. The plan was for the school's closure and for replacement by a newly built combination old folk's home and drive-thru crematorium.

The details behind the headline were the talk of Strathcarnage. Crowds gathered on the main shopping street to gossip about the proposal whilst distractedly pointing out those pieces of Gus remaining on the higher points of the collection of shop frontages and buildings. Stronger stomached parents pointed out the larger chunks of residue to curious children, jabbing walking sticks and fingers in the direction of the remains and occasionally attempting an educational recognition of their original biological location.

Local dog owners began to gather in numbers too, viewing the free bounty of edible titbits as an opportunity too good to waste. However among the parental identification of shredded organs and the sound of greedy dog teeth crunching on human remains, the gathered townsfolk soon found themselves deep in conversation about the newspaper headline.

Curiously enough, the majority of the dialogue was indifferent to the proposed new united crematorium and old folk's home venture. That idea seemed, to many, a clever initiative. An incredibly blunt local businessman called Al Frank was responsible for developing the idea of the new experimental building. "Frank by name, Frank by nature", was his company motto, an attitude recently displayed to the full on the previous night's local television documentary about the man.

During the show the ex-Australian had been interviewed at length about his rumoured new proposal for housing the town's old folks and their means of burial under the same roof. When asked to sum up his radical new idea to the town, Al Frank had slowly straightened his tie, looked straight into the camera, and said, "It's all time and motion people. Just wipe their dead wrinkly arses, toss them into a chute to the basement, and fire 'em up. Everybody home in time for tea."

The residents of Strathcarnage had historically admired any man who called a spade a spade, or in this case, a burnt corpse a burnt corpse. The innovative new idea met with approval from many in the small community, a site historically limited in both space and methods to dispose of their dead.

So it was that the burning topic of conversation on the narrow winding Strathcarnage streets that morning was focused not on the actual creation of the new Frank Industries Care and Flare Facility, but the proposed closure of the only local site for the mentally unbalanced members of the community. It was to be demolished in order to provide a suitable building plot for this innovation.

Locals were adamant that the John Cavendish Home for the Mentally Unsound and Feeble Minded must not be allowed to close, no matter how ingenious and welcome the new replacement. The overall idea for the crematorium was accepted and admired, but only if it could be built on a site which didn't involve closing the home.

The John Cavendish home for the mentally unsound had cared for the town's unfortunates for over a century and was the only resource in the town willing to take responsibility for those residents that local schools and hospitals were incapable of managing. The home had opened in 1878, in the cliff side residence of John Cavendish, a kind hearted man with a hideous squint who had bequeathed his property to the town in order to ensure continual compassion was provided to those most unfortunate children of the community.

Cavendish had left the large property to the care of the town in his will, a gesture of kindness to those townspeople who had themselves suffered through the rich man's own numerous bouts of mental instability. Soon after his death, the result of a mistimed overhead shot while floating high over the town shooting seagulls in a homemade balloon, the new facility had opened and begun to care for the more unfortunate elements in the community. In appreciation of the generous Cavendish gift, townspeople had lovingly adopted the name "Squinty Johnnies Strange Kids" for the residents.

Strathcarnage had a long history of mentally unstable residents. Indeed the town had itself been founded following a shipwreck of the mentally disturbed, the smashed hulk of the S.S. Cloven Hoof driven upon the rocks while carrying a cargo of adults and children from older prisons and asylums around the area to a new facility on the mainland. The boat had lost its bearings in a storm and had run aground while making for the shelter of the shore.

With the vessel completely wrecked and the collective minds aboard too feeble to attempt any escape, the town had slowly grown inside the vast hidden cave behind the waterfall on the massive sea cliffs. The majority of those living in Strathcarnage today were direct descendants of those mentally unsound founding fathers and the town still felt a close bond to the hereditarily unstable. The town had embraced the way of the unhinged, albeit grudgingly and purely through necessity.

The John Cavendish home was run by untrained volunteers without qualifications, with the exception of a single nurse called Liz, who held a forged correspondence certificate in Cake Decorating. As a result, the school was less of a sanctuary for professional treatment and care, and more of a heavily fortified holding area.

Behind high walls built to keep the three hundred residents inside the cliff top site, the children remained until they turned eighteen. After this age of consent were reached they were then traditionally tied together and driven down the long cliff road to the harbour, to be sent off to sea with bribed crews to seek their fortune. The pandemonium witnessed daily in the home made it certain that any proposed closure guaranteed prolonged mayhem for Strathcarnage residents in the town's mess of homes and twisting streets. Townsfolk knew that the home must stay open, for the well being of the town residents and property as much as for any desire to treat the town's children.

However the hundred year lease on the land was due to run out, and because of a recently discovered loophole in the original John Cavendish will, the entire site was destined for sale to the highest bidder.

The town residents needed to immediately organise and plan protests against the moves. Strathcarnage needed to find some way of ensuring the twisted faces remained safely behind the iron bars and barbed wire, staring outwards over the town, not cavorting frantically around in the middle of it. The solution was straightforward. The town population had to raise funds to secure the site lease before Al Frank managed to acquire it for his new facility. And the concerned townsfolk knew just who to turn to for help.

The home lay at the very summit of the steep road that ran upwards in a long curve around the black wall of the ragged cave. Directly across the road from the striking main gate and heavily armed watchtower of the facility, perched on the very edge of the massive drop beyond, lay the town's busiest pub, The Ruptured Horse.

The pub had acquired its name due to its location at the crest of the town's lengthiest and steepest hill, a frightening incline which ended directly outside the door of the property. Such was the punishing gradient of the road that drivers and passengers of stagecoaches and horse drawn carriages coming from the main town below would often take refuge inside the pub to await veterinary help for prolapsed beasts attempting the climb to bring visitors to the pub to take in the view over the town. As the popularity of the spectacular panorama grew, the pub grew ever more crowded, as did both the horse graveyard in the cliff face across the road next to the home and the hastily opened vet's surgery next door. This final new building sat perched on the massive rock fall that marked the very end of the hideously steep highway.

However, as smuggled and invented variations on the powered motorcar had begun to become ever more popular in the town, the numbers of ruptured beasts requiring emergency treatment fell. Yet it still remained common on summer days for pub patrons to rush outside onto the cliff road to marvel at the occasional uninitiated visitor on horseback who had attempted the climb only to have their beast collapse in the car park, laid out on its side in the gravel, foaming at the nostrils and twitching its last.

As time passed and news spread of the road's power to serve as a regular gateway to horse heaven, the incidences of fresh tombstones in the animal graveyard hewn into the sheer cliff face began to lessen.

Indeed the pub patron's main source of amusement in modern times was the recurrent cycling casualties often seen staggering into the car park, broken men either collapsing utterly exhausted into the gravel next to the flower beds or gasping for breath limp against the decorative cast iron fountain of the small boy in a wheelchair. Next to the first aid heart defibrillator that was kept underneath the pub's commemorative robbed horse brasses, a small scoreboard was nailed to the wall in order to keep a running tally of the heart attacks. The impressive total reached in the baking hot summer of 1965 was proving a hard target to beat.

However recent events had witnessed the pub's history take a strangely prophetic turn, one which would see it pitched into very centre of the battle between residents and those keenest to close the home.

The faction most vehemently advocating the closure of the home to enable the building of the new crematorium was led by local councillor, "Grubby" Hans Nash. The opposing campaign fighting for it to remain open was led by each and every sane resident of sound mind in the town, all of whom wished to continue to sleep easy in their beds.

Councillor "Grubby" Hans Nash was the driving force behind the whole closure initiative, and his presence on the project committee was another reason for the deep mistrust of the locals. Nash had enjoyed his much deserved nickname of "Grubby" for many years. Surprisingly, given the man's reputation for corrupt business deals and having a greedy grasping hand in every source of illicit income presented to him, his nickname actually owed more to his perpetually dishevelled appearance. "Grubby" Hans was indeed in truth grubby. In fact he was absolutely filthy, carrying the wearing of excess dirt to an Olympic standard.

Rumour had it that the local politician had not once changed out of his tattered navy blue wedding suit since the night of the fateful reception. It was an event which had finished, give or take a few hours, around 10 years ago. The occasion had ended abruptly, much to the stunned surprise of all attending, with the new bride giving birth during the first dance. She continued to dance on in shock, trailing the newborn around the polished floor by the glistening umbilical cord. Luckily it had been a slow waltz, since the spinning velocity of a foxtrot or salsa could have been catastrophic to the newborn child's health.

"Grubby" Hans and his new wife had parted even before the cake was cut. Hans had wed his sweetheart blissfully unaware of both her pregnancy and her legendary reputation as a recipient of sailor's swollen goods in the lanes and boarding houses clustered around the local docks. His new wife had walked weeping from the dance floor and had never been seen since.

Indeed such was her reputation that rumour in the town suggested a travelling Lithuanian marine engineer of her "acquaintance" had paid tribute to her god given capacity by naming a new style of vast hydraulic ferry doors in her honour. Whatever the truth of the rumour, it certainly would not have been the first incidence of Russian seamen passing through the welcoming entrance of Susan Finter to unload a heavy cargo deep within.

"Grubby" Hans never again spoke of his wedding night ordeal after the event, instead embarking upon a continuous wearing of his suit as a silent badge of his personal remembrance. No one ever discovered the fate of the wife and child last seen sweeping past shocked guests across the polished mahogany to the gentle sounds of Strauss. "Grubby" was a man who said very little, except when he could be was sure his eternally soiled hands were about to come into money; money commonly as dirty as he was. His natural talent to become deeply involved in shady business dealings was the stuff of town legend.

It was no accident, for example, that the small group of engineering "experts" who had appeared at a meeting to 'advise' town elders prior to the secret vote on the closure of the home, consisted entirely of heavily made up females many suspected of being council hired prostitutes. The women were last spotted through the town hall windows sharing their technical opinions with the gathering, resplendent in latex crotchless clothing, before leading away individual members for secret 'engineering consultations'. The motion was passed unanimously, but only after some problems reading voting papers heavily stained with baby oil and unidentifiable secretions.

So it was that residents were unsurprised to see "Grubby" Hans driving around the town recently in a new car with a large yellow and black painted sign on the side supporting Al Frank Industries, mirroring the large badge pinned to his stained lapel, reading simply, "Free the kids! Let's roast the pensioners!"

In response to the proposed closure, local residents had begun to organise their concerted plan of action, quickly establishing the "Ruptured Horse" pub as their campaign centre owing to its location directly across from the home itself.

The pub had long enjoyed a close association with the John Cavendish home, the main door of the bar situated directly across from the home's heavily fortified entrance. For many years now pub patrons gathered in the car park of the pub to enjoy free entertainment provided by the more determined inmates of the home.

The facility rewarded the keener patrons of the Ruptured Horse with three potential escapees a week, the piercing echo of the alarms enough to guarantee a frenzied dash of pub patrons to the large bay windows overlooking the gates. Now that the entertaining line of prolapsed horses and cyclists were diminishing in regularity, watching the escapees had become the pub regular's primary source of entertainment.

When the alarms sounded, whoever was serving behind the bar rang a painted crimson escape bell to inform the pub that the game was afoot. This ringing led to an untidy scrum of drinkers clambering over each other to get a space at the windows, hoping to catch the full glory of proceedings. Speed was of the essence though, not only because the alarm from opposite was a clear signal that final lines of defence had already been breached, but also because failure to reach a good viewing space at one of the packed windows meant watching the unfolding escapee entertainment from outside the pub doors. While this outdoor option afforded better views, it also carried the risk of lockout should the escapee head in the wrong direction and view the nearby open doors of the pub as a potential means of escape.

Pub policy was firm on the matter, with a well rehearsed plan in place to close and bolt the outer storm door should any escapee look likely to cross the car-park and reach the cheering sea of bobbing pink faces in the pub windows. This was a conscious decision based on health and safety, since the last escapee to gain entry to the pub interior had taken almost a day to capture, leading to twenty-five broken chairs, over two hundred broken glasses, an overturned fruit machine and a severed ear.

The ear was kept as a souvenir in a glass case behind the bar, next to the cyclist scoreboard, the horse brasses and the cardiac equipment. As a result of this particular incident, anyone now finding themselves locked outside the bolted front doors also ran the risk of being caught up in the chaotic and frequently violent throes of escapee desperation.

Pub regulars each had their favourite runners, and seasoned watchers would often bellow advice and tactics to wide eyed children emerging from the gates and bolting for freedom onto the main road. Generally the major excitement was to be had from watching the children negotiating their way between frequent and fast moving traffic heading up the hill to take in the view over the town. However, over the years regulars had also witnessed various shrewd techniques to avoid capture, including one notable attempt to climb a lamppost in hope of reaching safety on the pub roof.

That particular attempt had initially looked promising, only for the heavily salivating ill-fated youngster to be electrocuted and welded securely to the metal construction by the sudden surge of voltage provoked by saliva meeting live electricity.

Those breaking for freedom often lacked rational thought or preparation and were normally captured extremely quickly, unless mown down by passing traffic or having run straight over the nearby cliff edge. Some luckier and slightly more coherent escapees had avoided capture by taking a lucky turn down the long cliff side road, absconding into the town's warren of dark twisting cave streets and tunnels. The younger, fitter maniacs were driven by fear and quickly outran the overweight and unfit guards who were driven after them only by the unappealing prospect of minimum wage and a free lunch.

One notable hero of the pub regulars was serial escapee 'Balloon Face' Mercer, who after dozens of unsuccessful escape attempts had eventually managed to avoid capture by taking the correct turn down the hill and reaching the maze of the town. Unfortunately, having successfully escaped, it was then that Mercer had made the catastrophic decision to hide in Benny Chan's ice cream freezer for a number of weeks.

His corpse was only found when the summer arrived, his fragile icy hand being snapped off by a distracted local mother buying her son an ice cream. The child had begun crying at the unusually sour taste of the icy dead fingers in his mouth, drawing his mother's attention to the episode. Only then was Mercer's body discovered, thawed and taken for burial.

Over the years, the pub had also attracted large numbers of former residents of the home. Many previously incarcerated residents returned to the town after long periods at sea, their ability to trace the route home allowing them to be pronounced 'cured' and given their papers permitting full release back into the community.

Many of these ex inmates chose to return to the pub, sitting at the window gazing across the road at their previous home. To many former inmates the pub stood as a symbol of the outside world and many had recollections of gazing longingly across at the building from the home's barred windows, staring at a place they recognised as a visible symbol of the free world. Now they were free, many sat and gazed back across at the home overcome by the memories of old friends and a life safer and filled with less uncertainty.

Well, most of them did. The remainder who had relapsed and just barked, dribbled and pointed whilst howling were often assumed to have made comments along those lines, but no one was ever quite sure.

The home also had a number of borderline inmates attending on a day release programme. Those parents with problem children intent on smashing objects around the home and displaying extremes of behaviour were allowed to bring their offspring to the home in the morning to enjoy the respite of a daytime lockdown.

It was to be one of these part time inmates, "Crazy" Alex Hopkins, whose circumstances were to further involve the Ruptured Horse at the very heart of our story.

"Crazy" Alex was brought to the home on a daily basis from an early age. From the very first occasion of his arrival at the home's fortified stone entrance, the child would struggle free from his harness, darting across the road to stand in front of the Ruptured Horse and stare longingly through the windows. Evading all attempts at capture, the child's pink face would be pressed against the glass, watching the flashing lights of the pinball machine inside. He would stare silently at the illuminated display for a while before shaking violently, throwing his head back and uttering a loud guttural roar before throwing his vacuum flask heavily onto the concrete outside.

This performance continued daily for a number of years, and a behavioural expert contacted with details of the case had speculated that the boy had formed some sort of rudimentary bond of attachment to the gaming machine inside. The specialist had recommended letting the wild haired child continue this expression of his behaviour, theorizing wildly that it was allowing him to fleetingly view the pinball machine as a real friend, the sound of his smashing flask becoming a recognised indicator of his need to return to school.

The expert had grown so fascinated by the behaviour that he had planned to visit the school to do a more detailed academic study on "Crazy" Alex. Sadly the planned trip had to be indefinitely postponed after the man received a lengthy conviction for sexual molestation of farm stock in the town square on market day.

As the years passed, the sound of screaming followed by shattering glass became a familiar one outside the Ruptured Horse. However as the town shops begin to run dry of supplies of imported flasks, and the costs to his single mother mounted, Alex was gradually weaned onto less fragile cartons of fruit juice and placed in a stronger more secure harness to allow his mother easier control.

The young wild haired boy still looked longingly towards the pub frontage every morning, but could only manage to gaze across from afar as he was physically manhandled from the car, straining against his leather harness as he was wrestled into the school grounds.

"Crazy" Alex remained a pupil at the school for many years and over time he was trained to overcome his urge to throw fragile drinks storage containers on unforgiving concrete. Staff at the home were delighted at Alex's newfound behavioural control and reinforced the point by praising him constantly. At least they did until the young boy developed a new and most unfortunate habit of driving his small container of fruity liquid into the random heads of those other children standing nearest when his internal urges struck.

It was the same pattern every time with the boy. Alex would silently reach for his small carton of chosen drink of the day, leisurely detach the straw from the side of the package, make sure it was safely inside, then smile as he summoned every ounce of energy he had to drive the soft carton at speed into the side of his chosen victim's head. His mission complete he would grin back knowingly at the dripping face, seemingly delighted and calm after unleashing his act of juice based terror.

Thankfully, the cartons were generally soft and flexible, and, since Alex always placed the straw in the carton prior to impact, any physical damage to the victim was minimal.

Given the mentally unhinged state of most of those children around him in the home, however, the sight of the wild haired boy sidling up to them, smiling trustingly and then unleashing his detonation of juice based terror on their muddled heads, often provoked an prolonged and violent episode of hysterics.

Especially if Alex's chosen refreshment of the day were in any way scarlet coloured. The bang and accompanying fountain of crimson liquid was the cause of many a heavily sedated visit to the padded recovery room for Alex's fellow inmates.

However this strange behaviour was to be the catalyst that would allow the townsfolk to rescue the home itself from closure.

Alex's mother, Gina occasionally helped out at the home on her days off from her job at the make up concession in "Barfack and Barfack", a small local department store where she had recently begun working to pay off the family's massive flask debt.

Gina had thrown herself in her new job with gusto, combining her hobbies of make up and Country and Western music to take her mind off the ongoing problems of both her finances and her son. Gina always seemed to have a lot preying on her mind, but found that throwing herself into her twin passions of country music and industrial quantities of cosmetics helped her cope.

The dumpy woman distractedly applying huge quantities of make up to her face while humming Country and Western tunes was a nightmarish sight to behold in the store, but staff and customers were sympathetic to her domestic problems and thought it unfair to pass unpleasant remarks on these small things that seemed to cheer her unhappy and haunted soul.

So it was that young Alex would see his mother each evening when she collected him, her face a thick mask of the latest make up trend of the day, her rotund frame clad head to toe in tasselled leather and denim. When false tan had become popular,

Gina would emerge from the car to collect her son wearing a deep mahogany face, similar in colour to a restored Victorian dining table. When bright eye make up was the latest fashion, the young mother would arrive at the home with the latest shimmering colours plastered above and beyond the natural hairy barrier of her eyebrows, escaping round nearly to her ears like a pair of comedy glasses.

On the day in question, marking the launch of a new foundation powder and mascara range, her sad face took on the appearance of a large basin of flour with two spiders trapped in the curves of powdery white. The look, although ghostly and frankly hideous, was fully complimented by her white rhinestone-covered jumpsuit. Gina looked like a country and western ghost.

Gina had arrived to collect her son, who had spent a productive day with the rest of his fellow pupils attempting to electrocute one of the volunteer teachers, and he had seemed calm and stable. However, as she sat waiting for the latest dose of his medication to kick in and to settle him enough to be strapped safely into his harness, Alex decided he had one final act to perform. Sitting at the small art and craft table provided for the children, Alex silently withdrew the small carton of blackcurrant juice from his coat pocket and smiled sweetly at Carrie, the girl drawing quietly in the seat next to him.

It was the shrill bang and subsequent scream from the terrified Carrie that had caused Gina to suddenly look up from her lottery entry, another favourite pastime. Gina looked up just in time to be showered in the oncoming explosion of dark sticky liquid.

As Gina had wiped herself down, carefully avoiding smearing her white powdered face, she noticed that the purple spray from her son's sudden cordial assault had spattered in a dark stain across her white lottery entry. Gina thought little of the tarnished ticket at the time, quickly stuffing it back into her handbag while attempting to subdue the now hysterical blackcurrant saturated figure of Carrie.

Later in the week however, as Gina entered Benny Chan's to put on her latest lottery entry, her numbers chosen from her carefully recorded measurements of the length in minutes that it had taken her latest sexual partners to reach climax, she again found the blackcurrant spattered lottery ticket at the bottom of her handbag and had decided to take a chance and enter it also.

Of course it lost.

But the ticket containing those numbers determined by coital ejaculation time had won the unclaimed Strathcarnage rollover jackpot, a substantial amount which had been unclaimed for nigh on five years.

As the local press arrived at her small home for publicity photos, Gina made the shrewd decision to tell the journalists of the partially true story of the accidental spilt blackcurrant juice having been the chance method used to choose the numbers. After all, with all six of the winning numbers under ten on her winning ticket, Gina was mindful of not risking prolonged examination of her eerie and ongoing ability to date men whose post coital cigarette often lasted longer than the actual act itself.

And so it was that the press gathered to see a woman wearing a thick mask of white powder under a pale cowhide stetson, standing proudly holding hands with a small boy with mad hair who stood at her side beaming sweetly and clutching a carton of orange juice. Gina was there to collect an oversized cheque for just over a million pounds.

During the presentation in front of the black iron gates of the children's home, Gina repeated a well rehearsed recital of her heart-warming story of how her winning numbers were chosen by chance by her "troubled" child. One of the assembled pressmen had even asked young Alex what he wanted to buy with the winnings. The crowd fell silent to hear his answer.

Young Alex looked up shyly, gazing silently around the sea of faces before raising a thin arm and a small outstretched finger. The crowd followed the finger, and turned as one to look at what he was pointing at. The digit was aimed straight out across the road, directly at the distant shape of the Ruptured Horse Bar.

Alex took the opportunity to tighten his grip on the small carton of orange juice in his pocket, a thin smile appearing on his face. The sound of the impact, and that of the subsequent reporter's scream, could be heard clearly on the report on the main Strathcarnage TV news bulletin that evening.

The proud powdery-faced mother purchased the Ruptured Horse pub from the grateful almost bankrupt current owners within days.

Gina saw the purchase as a sound business investment and a place to indulge not only her son's strange and as yet unexplained attachment to pinball machines, but also her own love of Country and Western music. As a tribute to her life and experiences, she renamed the pub in honour of "Crazy" Alex. As the shock haired child snatched at the gold rope to release the folded purple velvet covering the new name, it fell away to reveal new gold letters announcing the opening of Strathcarnage's latest pub.

"The Smashed Flask" was open for business.

Gina immediately set about refitting the pub interior to better suit both herself and her son. She employed local coffin maker Hitchcock and Chalmers to build her a stage at the far end of the room together with a totally enclosed new play area for both Alex and other visiting children from the home opposite. Gina was determined not to forget her own struggles with her difficult son and intended to offer whatever help she could to other struggling parents. Gina hoped that by mixing a relaxed atmosphere with specially built amenities within The Smashed Flask, children from the home might better learn how to integrate themselves into Strathcarnage society.

This was a noble ideal, but almost as soon as the freshly built play area was declared open, young Alex had taken the decision to take to the shelter of the brightly coloured ball pool. He had remained there ever since, resolutely refusing to let other children enter through the single narrow tunnel, guarding it ferociously with a combination of violence and shrill screaming.

Gina had decided that since her son was happy in his new spherical laden environment it might be best to leave him there, waving at him whenever his face appeared periodically from beneath the mass of multi coloured balls. Her only interaction with Alex now was to leave food at the tunnel entrance and to then collect the empty dishes he returned to the entrance once finished.

Occasionally new and inexperienced children would arrive in the building and attempt to play in the tempting collection of bright balls. This decision would invariably lead to the unwise explorers returning to their parents in hysterics, dripping in fruit juice and with a square red impact mark on the side of their faces.

Now her son was settled and happy Gina found herself with other bigger things on her mind. She was determined that her new bar would be a cowhide covered epicentre for all things Country and Western in the town and had set about building her dream.

Turning the bar into her personal vision was a struggle. However after a few months labouring over the redecoration and the organising of events, Gina had launched her new dream with a charity gala opening concert. In keeping with the theme, Gina had decided to celebrate her new Country and Western passion by embarking on a full staging of Calamity Jane, cast entirely from the various child inmates in the John Cavendish home directly across from the pub.

As an occasion to draw publicity and funds for the home, and to make a declaration of her intent for the bar, the show was a great success. However as a work of theatrical merit the show was an unmitigated disaster, albeit a highly comic one.

Even allowing for the surprise casting of a profoundly deaf child as Calamity Jane, the show had become "difficult" early on in the first performance.

As the show's lead had begun incomprehensibly screaming the first musical number, one of the children in the chorus had taken it upon himself to draw and repeatedly fire his replica gun at the round face of a fat guard from the Home sat in the front row of the audience. Although only firing blanks, the deafening noise sent a section of the mentally unstable cast immediately into a state of high terror which included a number of unleashed bladders.

The deaf Calamity "sang" on regardless, unconscious of the unfolding panic behind her.

As the cast had began to stampede, a number of children had slipped and fallen in the unleashed bladder contents of the more affected performers, sliding around on the stage with a series of wet slaps just as the donkey intended for the later scenes suddenly appeared from the side of the stage. The wide eyed animal bolted at the sight of the numerous collapsing children and stampeded out through the gathering, knocking over most of the set and launching itself, braying loudly, off the stage edge and into the crowd.

The watching audience also contained a high proportion of ex-home pupils and it wasn't long before the unexpected gunshot and astonishing donkey gymnastics had provoked a panicked audience riot among those unable to reach the crowded doors.

As the donkey had bolted out of the wings and set off across the urine soaked stage, those cast members assembled in the wings at the other side of the stage awaiting the next number had taken this as their cue and had emerged onstage to enact their roles. This premature entry to proceedings provoked some fierce hair pulling and flailing of limp limbs from those struggling bravely to continue the ongoing first act.

The deaf figure of Calamity continued 'singing' on at the front of the stage, eyes closed in oblivious concentration as the carnage erupted behind her.

The performance was cut short as the children's carers clambered onstage to calm the most hysterical performers down, only for fights between jealous parents to begin to break out all over the stage. Swinging parental combatants wrestled with each other violently in a mixture of urine and donkey droppings as the continuing screeching soundtrack of the deaf soloist grew ever louder as she mistook the commotion and gesticulating of the crowd as proof of their appreciation of her singing ability. The now anxious donkey continued stampeding around the audience, braying loudly and unloading its bowels with stinking regularity in a clear sign of fear.

Alex watched on from the ball pool with his smiling face pressed against the clear Perspex front amidst the balls. Gina began emitting small clouds of white dust as she surveyed the scene laughing at the mayhem. This was just like the Old West she had read about in her overdue make-up stained library books.

Although challenging, reports of the staging of Calamity Jane ensured the pub immediately gained a reputation as the place to visit for entertainment in the strange town of Strathcarnage, and the pub sitting high above the town became the first stop for the visiting sailors and townsfolk looking for a first-rate and authentic Strathcarnage night out. As a result of the huge influx of local customers, and because of its location, the pub became the obvious choice for a base to focus attempts to save the nearby children's home from demolition.

It quickly became clear to campaigners that the best way to ensure the continued survival of the home was to concentrate efforts firmly on the one thing that "Grubby" Hans could not resist: money. Any appeal to his non-existent better nature or any thin remaining strand of conscience was time wasted, since the councillor had time and again proved he had an unemotional heart of stone.

Indeed the numerous television appeals fronted by the local man regarding the matter had themselves been sponsored by a local crematorium. The only possibility of reversing the decision was to offer Hans a vast quantity of the one thing he loved most, to buy the lease for the town's people. The town had to somehow make him an offer he couldn't refuse.

During the meeting to discuss the raising a sufficient amount to purchase the lease and satisfy the intense greed of "Grubby" Hans, it had become obvious that the sum expected to be raised by the campaigning group's various sources and events would fall far short of that likely to satisfy the local councillor's huge expectations.

He was, after all, already likely to be receiving a huge amount of cash from Frank Industries, the chosen crematorium project developer. They needed a massive amount to dangle in front of the fat, dirt engrained hands of the councillor in order for him to relent, sign the lease over and call off the bulldozers.

The meeting quickly turned to the subject of Gina and her recent lotteries win. Locals knew of her intense love for the unfortunate children of the home and some hoped she might be the rich patron who had the funds to come to the town's rescue. Locals had already approached child adoring Lord Strathcarnage about funds, but while awaiting his final decision the Lord had left the town to travel to Italy on business. Locals hoped Gina could use her recent windfall to help.

However Gina had spent almost all of her win in refurbishing The Smashed Flask before events had been announced. She would have happily helped but had simply nothing left to give. This should have been the end of the fight, the final blow of misfortune's hammer driving the rusty nail of fate into the coffin of despair.

Yet Gina suddenly began to smile broadly from under her mask of heavy foundation, grinning at those arguing around her as a fresh idea took hold.

The assembled throng noticed the woman's broad smile and one by one stopped shouting and fell silent, asking why she seemed so happy with only days to go until the home met its fate. Gina beamed even wider on being confronted, rising quietly from her seat and announcing to the gathering that she had a plan.

If her idea came off, Gina claimed, the plan would raise more than enough money to save the home. She needed some time to sort out fine details, but asked the group to be patient and to wait for a call to return again to the pub in a few days with the press for an official announcement. An uncertain but optimistic ripple of applause went round the small group. They knew they had little time left in which to save the home and that this was destined to be their final drink in the last chance saloon.

Or in The Smashed Flask, to be more accurate.

Three days later, Gina phoned around and told people simply, "It's sorted, bring the press tonight."

That night, The Smashed Flask bar was jam-packed with townsfolk and local journalists and cameramen, anxious to hear how the heavily made up woman in white leather chaps, with a damaged son silently gazing out from his ball pool home, hoped to save the town from the onslaught of violently disturbed children. Gina took to the stage, asked the crowd for quiet and began to announce her plan.

"Over the last few days, I have been busy. Busy phoning, organising, persuading and planning. And now, I have the matter sorted and the details are in place. My finalised plan will raise enough money to buy back the home into Strathcarnage hands and also to pay the consultation "fee" I have agreed with Councillor Nash's lawyers. We may even have enough extra money for a celebration party."

Gina paused and looked around the quietly murmuring crowd. She cleared her throat and began to outline her plan.

"On the night of Sunday week, in this bar, there will be held a Gala Country and Western Fund Raising concert. Tickets will be on sale immediately after this conference from the bar, and I have also arranged a substantial and most generous fee from The Ox, the owner of the local television station, who feels he may have interested contacts in America who will buy footage of the highlights.

You may ask why there might be such interest in just a local show, especially after the recent 'eventful' production of 'Calamity Jane'. Well, it is with great pleasure that I wish to announce today that a world famous and highly respected recording star of the real outside world of Country Music has been contacted and will be taking to this very stage for the concert, performing live in the Smashed Flask in order to help save our home and keep our poor children safe. All hail the power of Country and Western!"

As Gina hollered, she slapped her hand on her thigh before turning and bowing low to the audience to reveal her bare cheeks through the split in her trousers. The entire hall erupted. They respected Gina's encyclopaedic knowledge of country music, and when she made the claim that the visiting artist would be 'world famous', they knew she meant it. Strathcarnage was going to be welcoming a real star from the outside world.

Gina steadfastly refused to reveal the star's identity, but was adamant it was a name everyone would know, regardless of their opinion of Country and Western music. She also apologised for the timing of the show, but insisted that because of the last minute organisation involved in securing this stellar name the only date possible for the show was on the very night that the bulldozers were poised to begin demolition of the home on the stroke of midnight.

The scene was set for a memorable night, one which even the incident strewn history of Strathcarnage would regard as legendary. Consequently, as the days passed, the town began to buzz with anticipation, the concert drawing ever nearer in a blur of excitement and organisational frenzy. Almost before anyone could quite believe it, the night of the concert arrived.

The town was awash with local media, attracted by the unusually positive human-interest story of a concerned mother who had single-handedly arrived at a way of saving her community. Most were also gathered to see who the mystery star would be, and to make sure that they caught the celebrity on camera and in print. They arrived in keen expectation, since everyone knew that nothing ever happened in Strathcarnage without at least one major hitch.

The entire concert line up was kept a mystery, but the highly priced tickets had sold out within minutes. Gina had planned to have the crowd gather in the car park and then enter The Smashed Flask by red carpet while the media beamed live pictures.

What Gina had not taken account of while planning this spectacular and media friendly entrance was the appearance at the event of an opposing demonstration made up of large and noisy numbers. The large group of protesting pensioners began to gather across the street from the Smashed Flask from around midday, and planned to make their feelings known about any potential delay in building their dream of a dual purpose home and crematorium facility.

The pensioners had banners, slogan t-shirts and loudhailers, and, in one case, a large industrial burner from the inside of a hot air balloon, complete with basket, for illustrative effect. The wrinkled mob began chanting almost immediately the first of the ticket holders had arrived on the specially decorated horses and carts Gina had organised to carry them up the steep hill. The drivers were under strict orders to take the steep hill very slowly.

In the centre of the steadily growing numbers of the opposition group, encouraging the crowd and leading the chants, was "Grubby" Hans. He was guaranteed a pay day whatever happened and had decided to amuse himself by protesting for a time before crossing the open ground and attending the concert.

As a result it was he who began the wrinkled protest group's chanting of slogans.

"What do we want?", "Cremation", "When do we want it?" "Nowww". A number of the group wore t-shirts with lurid slogans including "My Turn to Burn" and "Why deny my right to fry".

Some even had waved pictures of random crematoria above their heads. At the rear of the crowd, the man in the balloon basket would occasionally unleash a huge fountain of orange flame from his burner above the gathering to loud cheers.

As if this display wasn't already enough to disrupt the evening ambience, the crowd of chanting pensioners had burst into loud applause as the bulldozers began to arrive up the cliff side road, rumbling noisily towards the entire gathering only to stop at the gates of the home to wait for the very stroke of midnight when the lease lapsed and they could legally begin demolition.

However such events were all a distraction to the main event of the evening. The crowd steadily packed inside the hall of the pub, and to the dull background noise of the protesters still chanting outside, the Gala concert to save the home and the fates of the children began.

The entire event was to be hosted by a Tex Wong, the renowned oriental local Country music DJ, substituted at short notice after The Ox, the local TV head, had watched rehearsal tapes and then vetoed the townsfolk's choice of compere; the tourettes riddled local churchman, Reverend Aubrey Whisp.

The Ox had taken the decision after having concerns at the Reverend Whisp lurching to one side during rehearsals of his first link, the elderly churchman suddenly shuddering before leaning to one side, going rigid and then screaming "fucking cowboy shit" repeatedly instead of the planned script. As the local TV executive had correctly presumed, such outbursts, although familiar and much loved by locals, would compromise his idea to smuggle highlights tapes of the show to sell to American stations interested by the family appeal of the event. He was also a hard man to keep framed in the cameras. Tex was phoned and had taken over duties immediately.

And so it began.

Tex Wong announced the first act. He was a local favourite, a tribute to Kenny Rodgers from a hideously deformed and brain damaged local man called Rodger Kenny. The resemblance, barring his broad moon face, scarring and metal callipers, was astonishing.

Appearing onstage resplendent in white beard , suit and cowboy hat, the crowd had rippled with applause and then cheered in recognition as the opening chords of "The Gambler" filled the hall. However as the music played, it soon became obvious that Strathcarnage man lacked a great deal of the showmanship of the real thing. Dropping his guitar midway through the opening verse, Rodger stood for a moment staring out at the audience, shrugged, fished around inside his pocket and began to silently unwrap and eat a small cake.

This distraction continued until the cake was finished, then Rodger shuffled forward pointing towards the lights and emitting a low moaning noise as his tongue lolled wetly at the corner of his mouth. The TV networks cut to adverts and Rodger was led off the stage looking somewhat startled.

Regardless of technical flaws, the act still drew generous sympathetic applause from the large crowd. Loud enough appreciation indeed to cover the screaming of the number of pensioners flailing around wildly outside, a few members accidentally set alight by a recently unbalanced and toppled balloon burner.

Then it was time for the second act of the evening, a display from the local line dancing troupe, led by their instructor, a club footed man known simply as The Hawk.

As the music started, the entire troupe began to lurch violently from one side to the other in time to the music, throwing in the odd series of random claps for effect. While the line dancing was in the same general style of those familiar to the more recognisable version of the discipline, the surgical shoe of The Hawk had ensured that the entire ensemble had been taught over time to follow his movements exactly, leading to the sight of the entire troupe lurching violently in perfect time to one side on every second step.

This too had encouraged the crowd to give its applause generously, for effort if not for technical proficiency, and those sweat soaked dancers still standing upright at the finale had left the stage limping heavily after their teacher, still waving and smiling at the appreciative crowd.

Then it was time for the benefit show's next act. As the lights in the packed hall faded, a single white spotlight lit up the centre of the stage. The crowd gasped. In the central circle of light, with her back to the audience, was the sequin-covered figure of Marie and Coco Rosencrutch. It was technically accurate to refer to the next act as 'figure' in the singular sense, since this was the twin legged, double backed, two headed Siamese country star, consisting of one set of legs, but two sweet voices. The hall erupted.

The huge expanse of the single heavily sequined jacket back read "Sisters Co-joined in Country", picked out in ruby sequins against the silver, and Marie's head had turned inward to mouth "Hi" to the cheering audience, followed in the same manner by Coco, before the jacket slid from the pair's shoulders to reveal an separate pair of upper torsos, each covered by a richly embroidered cowboy shirt, spread tightly across a collection of four ample breasts all belonging, theoretically at least, to the same woman.

The Rosencrutch Sisters let the cheering die down a fraction and then launched straight into their signature tune, a bluegrass reworking of Roxy Music's "Let's Stick Together". The sister's set was genius, and as they played through "Dancing Cheek To Cheek " and " Stuck On You", the crowd clapped and cheered wildly at the collective multi-breasted, dual-headed country frontage. By the time the final rendition of their local radio hit "Two Heads, Mississippi Bound" arrived, the crowd were on their feet long before the last echoing banjo note was picked. The performance was a triumph.

Excitement in the hall had barely died down before the next local highlight took to the stage, Voice Box Willie Nelson, a local man who had overcome a gruesome episode of throat cancer to pay tribute to his hero.

As he eased himself onto his stool and struck up his guitar, the crowd again fell silent. Breaking into his first number with a tinny click and the hiss of interference, the metallic buzz of his voice box caused glasses in the entire bar to rattle and vibrate along with the opening number. Voice Box Willie had been on the circuit many years, and his unique ability to utilise feedback from his throat based vocal apparatus like a mournful train whistle was his trademark.

The clicking and buzzing from the newest act also served to cover the sound of the ornate carriage with blacked out windows arriving in the car park outside, carrying the star of the show direct from the harbour. The night's star turn was in the building.

Voice Box Willie halted his set after receiving a signal from the side of the stage and through a screaming wail of feedback welcomed onto the stage the lady who had made the evening possible. Gina walked across the worn boards to the loudest ovation of the night, the packed hall rising as one to hail the woman who had raised the money to save the home opposite and thus enabling the community of Strathcarnage to remain safe. Gina stood in the spotlight halo, all in white, including her face, and motioned for the crowd to quieten.

"Thank you all so very much, and thank you for taking the time to attend our show tonight. Without any further delay, I'd like to dedicate this next song to all of you here, to the townsfolk watching on T.V., and to the children of the home opposite. Everyone, you know, you truly were 'Always On My Mind'."

The hall gasped as, from the side of the stage, the pigtailed figure of Willie Nelson himself appeared, strumming the first few chords of his most popular hit, and now the anthem for tonight's event, "Always On My Mind".

As he wandered to the centre of the stage, towards Voice Box Willie, the two began to sing a duet, the metallic robotic tones of the local man's Voice box perfectly complimenting the longingly fragile tones of the country legend. Many in the hall were in tears, the simple power and raw emotion of the duet even attracting "Crazy" Alex to show his face from inside his wall of balls.

As the song finished, the crescendo of applause threatened to take the roof of the hall. Willie Nelson smiled and graciously waited for silence before looking to the side of the stage and announcing the re-emergence of Gina onto the stage, this time appearing carrying a huge oversized cheque.

As the hall erupted and eventually fell silent again after some considerable period, Gina moved towards the microphone. She mopped sweat from her brow, leaving a pink streak in the white mask of her face, cleared her throat and addressed the hall.

"Would you please put your hands together and welcome Councillor Hans Nash, who I believe is now amongst us and about to join us."

From the far end of the hall, the filthy figure of "Grubby" Hans Nash appeared from the back of the crowded hall, propelled towards the stage by two sets of heavily muscled arms hired by Gina for this very purpose. The crowd turned to watch the Councillor, his eyes narrowed, blinded by the single spotlight that followed his journey to the stage. Many people hissed and booed the man's path, one helpful soul even taking advantage of the blinding glare of the spotlight and tripping him up to a huge round of applause.

As he was almost at the stairs leading up to the stage, Gina returned to the microphone once more. Her face was now wiped totally free of the heavy make up by a towel she had been rubbing aggressively over her head while Hans had made his journey through the hall. .

"C'mon Hans, come up and get your dirty money, honey."

On the last word Hans froze, rooted to the spot. He raised his hands to shield his eyes from the glare of the spotlight, his face a pale mask of shock.

"But.. but.. I.. it can't be...it...it can't be...."

The crowd turned to each other in confusion as a murmur ran round the hall. Gina silenced the gathering as she spoke up.

"Yes, Hans. That's right. It's me. It's your darling wife, Susan Finter. The woman who left this hall 10 years ago this very night. It's me."

Hans stood still, mouth gaping, as the crowd around him gasped and murmured anew amongst themselves at this new and shocking news.

"Hans, I left you that wedding night and swore never to return. I left the town on an Egyptian Potato ship and sailed to Cairo, where an American freighter then took me to New York, from where I began to travel America.

I said I would never return here, but I just couldn't leave this weird little place, even with you in it, so I changed my name to Gina, put on weight and returned. I always took great care to keep out of your way, hidden behind the heaviest quantities of make-up I could find."

Gina moved fully into the light and removed her cowboy hat.

Hans gasped in shock as he recognised the face of the bride he had last saw escaping into the night a decade previously. It was his first sight of the woman since she had run off into the darkness dragging their baby. Then, all at once, Hans' face seemed to soften. He gazed at his once beloved bride and began to fight back the welling tears.

"But what... what about my baby? What happened to *our* baby?"

Gina decided that this might not be the most opportune point of proceedings to share the knowledge she had no idea who the child's father had actually been.

As far she could calculate Little Alex could have been any of a huge number of marine based personnel; from the Lithuanian engineer she had grown fond of, the crew of a Russian fishing boat, or a number of the engineers of a Polish Oil supply ship who had come ashore at around the same time. Even Lord Strathcarnage could have been in the frame.

She had often thought back to the events of that hectic month and was unable to settle the identity of the father of her child, working through the dates with the aid of her diary and paper receipts. She had concluded uncertainly that the father had been Gus Ebersole, the recent victim of the "Mr Porky Bacon Corpse Express" wagon.

However sure she was, keeping all this information to herself seemed to be the correct course of action, especially under then gaze of the entire village watching on TV. It was also information vital to her plan.

"Hans," Gina announced from the stage, "your son is here, in this very building, right now."

Hans's mouth fell open. The shocked man looked around, searching the faces of the crowd for some sign. He looked back at Susan, pleading silently to be told where his only offspring was sitting. Susan showed no reaction, only to smile and then hold out the lease for the man to sign in a cold act of moral blackmail Hans himself was impressed with.

Once he had dashed off his signature and the hall had exploded into thunderous cheers of victory, Susan pointed off stage into the darkness. Hans followed her outstretched finger, his gaze moving slowly towards the huge pit of balls in the children's play area. Just as Hans stared at the colourful mass of featureless spheres, a pink face appeared and smiled. Susan began to speak from the stage again.

"Hans. Before you go and join your son, I think the time has come to remove the past."

Hans nodded slowly his understanding, walking toward the smiling face in the balls while item by item discarding he suit he had worn daily for the last decade. Gina turned her attention back to the audience.

"Ladies and gentlemen, I apologise for the personal drama you have had to witness tonight. When I was in America, I visited Nashville, to see the home of the music I love so dearly. While I was there, I met a man who introduced me to our guest of honour tonight, Mr Willie Nelson.

Well, Willie took me under his wing and gave me and Alex a home while I was in America, and was very kind to me. I hadn't seen him now for almost ten years, but when I phoned him and told him why we were having this concert, he agreed instantly to do it for me, and for Alex.

So, to finish the concert, I would like to have Willie Nelson play the song we wrote together in his bedroom all those years ago. It's an appropriate finale for both tonight and for all the events surrounding it. Ladies and Gentlemen, please put your hands together for Willie Nelson singing the song we wrote together for Alex, "Smashed Flask Blues".

As the first chords of the song rang though the hall, Willie gave Susan a kiss on the cheek, and Susan watched Hans clamber into the ball pool to meet his son. It was a beautiful and fitting end to the evening.

The children's home was still demolished though.

The domestic drama of the show finale had meant that proceedings had overrun, and everyone had forgotten in the excitement to send someone outside to inform the bulldozer drivers that they were no longer required. As a result the home was partially flattened by the time anyone noticed the noise of collapsing masonry above the excited cheering. Only as the first of the crowd had rushed outside to celebrate with the signed lease were they met by rumbling bulldozers crawling slowly over a growing pile of smashed rubble.

However, in the end it didn't matter. The crematorium and old folks' home was built on the site, and since Hans had signed the lease for free before midnight in front of a televised audience, Susan now officially owned the site and all rights to any building thereon. After weeks of angry negotiations, the smiling Strathcarnage woman subsequently sold on the lease at almost double the market value to a most upset Frank Industries. This amount was added to the proceeds from the concert to build a new, bigger and even more secure home on a new site at the other side of the town. There was even enough money to train qualified staff.

Alex remained firmly hidden in his ball pool, where a much changed and kinder Hans would join him for long periods of the day. Susan retired her alter ego Gina and her thick make up, and returned to making the Smashed Flask the best venue for live Country and Western in the town. On returning home Willie Nelson went on to top the Billboard country charts for ten weeks with "Smashed Flask Blues" and subsequently won awards for the song in fifteen countries.

Everything in the town slowly returned to as close as the place ever came to normal behaviour. And that included Susan, who, now freed from the duties of constantly caring for her son, quickly realised that there would always be unfortunate sailors with heavy wallets standing looking forlorn and unloved in the pubs by the docks. With Alex being looked after by his father, Susan found herself with the free time to return her most charitable and freely given talents back to another type of needy cause that she was only to happy to help. Smiling broadly, she once more made her way toward the town docks.

Gus Ebersole (Pig Slaughterman and Unconscious Potential Father) 1949-1978

# CHAPTER 10

# Day Eight – The Defective Detective

The twin doors of the lounge bar at The Zoo crashed open with a loud bang. The entire room fell silent in a heartbeat, all except for old Quinton Gunn, whose deafness as the result of the misfired shotgun accident that had killed his wife saw him continue to bellow his new favourite story to a nearby friend.

Quinton's current tale was based largely on his recent discovery of two elderly female charity shop helpers in the town engaged in a lesbian liaison. It was a sordid but amusing revelation, happened upon quite by chance whilst returning to the shop a set of false teeth found in the pocket of a newly purchased cardigan. On realising neither cardigan nor teeth fitted, Quinton had returned both items to the musty store, and on entry to the premises, the older gentleman been met with the sight of Moira and Morag lying half naked and engaged in frantic lovemaking amongst a number of scattered jigsaws.

Quinton continued to describe the scene in vivid detail to his friend in the now silent pub, bellowing a meticulous description of the sight of vast pants draped precariously from puffy elderly ankles.

Quinton was getting to his favourite descriptive part of the story, which required removal of his discoloured false teeth, waggling of his tongue and a full catalogue of loud slurping noises, when he suddenly noticed his listener had lost interest and was staring open mouthed over his shoulder. The old storyteller halted and followed his friend's gaze towards the open doors of the bar. With the man now silent, the only sound in the room was the high-pitched howl of his hearing aid feedback.

A car was parked directly outside the hotel, facing the open doors with the headlights full on, silhouetting a large figure in the opening. The shape stood dark and motionless. The bar clientele stood squinting against the searing brightness of the lights, tying to identify the figure's silhouette. Quinton's hearing aid carried on whistling.

As the figure moved inside the bar, customers began to glance around the room at each other in complete confusion, making silent enquiries to fellow patrons to see whether anyone could identify this tall stranger. Each questioning glance was met by a similar look of confusion and a slight shrug of the shoulders. No one seemed to know. As if reading their minds, the man looked slowly around the faces in room.

The visitor thought them an extraordinary looking lot, the gathering giving off an aura of being both a bit backward and very, very strange.

The man wandered across the polished wooden floor towards the bar, stopping just in front of Old Quinton. The tall figure raised his hand slowly to the cowering old man's face and then suddenly flicked a long thin finger at his hearing aid, making contact with the plastic shell and producing an audible hollow crack. The high-pitched whine stopped instantly.

This lot looked like a bizarre shower of inbreeds and he instantly took a fierce dislike to the locals.

The strange visitor took a final long draw from his cigarette, and flicked the glowing stub to the floor. As he turned away to face the rest of the room the hanging strap from the stranger's backpack caught Old Quinton's double brandy, knocking the glass off the wooden bar and to the floor.

As the dark amber liquid flowed across the dirty floorboards and hit the smouldering cigarette, the mixture ignited, blue flames catching the frayed brandy soaked trouser hem of the man standing behind Quinton. The elderly companion burst into flames with a loud whoosh.

Quinton remained oblivious to events, still staring intently at strange package strapped across the stranger's back as his drinking partner stood behind him, partially alight and screaming loudly whilst beating at the flames.

Those others surrounding the burning man did their best to help him, quickly realising that throwing numerous cheap town brewed whiskeys into the inferno seemed not to be aiding the attempt to extinguish the flames. Someone then attempted to quell the blaze with a nearby jacket, only realising as it began to quickly shrink and melted that the garment was made from nylon and quite likely another bad move.

The smell of burning flesh in the air provoked distinct pangs of appetite in the oblivious Quinton, prompting him to turn his head slightly away to the other side of the inferno and bellow an order for some well done steak from the bar menu.

The stranger watched impassively as a small knot of drinkers kicked and prodded the smouldering man out of the main bar and into the pub toilets in a fresh attempt to extinguish his flaming body using a selection of French dry white wines.

Quinton licked his lips and looked forward to his steak, glancing around and noticing his devious drinking partner had slipped away quietly after obviously stealing his double brandy from the bar. Quinton shook his head in disgust at such deceit and returned his gaze back to watch the stranger now move slowly to the middle of the bar-room floor before clearing his throat. The growing murmur of bar customers fell instantly to silence, save for some muffled screaming and distant thumping noises coming from the toilets.

"Listen to me," the stranger began in a rough, gravely voice, "I'm the new law man in this godforsaken shithole of a place. You might not like me. I don't really care. I'm not here to be liked. I'm here to do my job. Yes?" The stranger looked round the room for some sign of a response.

"This steak's shite," bellowed a deaf Quinton as he fought to force a blunt knife through the thick slab of heavily browned meat on the plate now sat in front of him, next to his removed false teeth.

What a bunch of losers, we'll soon sort this shower out, thought Detective Kerr.

Someone from the anonymity of the crowd at the rear of the bar shouted a question.

"So where is your partner, tough guy? Strathcarnage lawmen always work better in pairs," the unseen voice asked.

"Yeah, like breasts," added an anonymous voice from the other side of the pub, as everyone laughed heartily.

"Comedians, eh? Well, wake up people, we're both already here", shouted the stranger.

The patrons of the bar looked again from face to face, but all present in the pub were local, except the newly arrived figure of the stranger. There were no new faces in the room to identify as a new partner. The Strathcarnage locals were confused.

"Fucking hell, these chips are crap too. Burnt to a crisp," hollered Quinton again, utterly oblivious to events as he stood stooped over his plate, chewing the tough meat with his wet gums while chasing a selection of peas around with his knife.

The stranger ignored the old man and gazed slowly and menacingly around the room while sliding off his black rucksack and dropping it to the floor at his feet, thinking.

'Yeah, you just stare away bozos. You probably can't even spell policeman. I'll enjoy turning this town upside down and then inside out.'

"My partner is here," he shouted.

The crowd again studied the room; faces searching the gathering for a new arrival, checking the exits to see if someone else had perhaps entered the room or had given an indication of who this partner may be. The stranger leant forward and untied the top of his rucksack.

As the lid flopped open, a small angry face pushed itself out from under the wrinkled flap of nylon.

"As I said before," said the freshly unconfined head, "stare away bozos, you don't half look like a bunch of losers."

The stranger rummaged around inside the backpack, fully opening the top now and lifting out the torso attached to the angry face within. He placed the legless, armless trunk on the bar floor. The face glared up angrily at the surrounding silent crowd.

"What's up people? Have you never seen a limbless detective inspector before? I'm Detective Kerr, and this here is my brother, Constable Clint Kerr. Welcome to law and order people."

The room remained deathly silent in both surprise and shocked amazement.

"What the *bloody* hell is that?" shouted an amazed Old Quinton, spraying fragments of chips and partially masticated steak around him as he had suddenly glanced up from his meal and noticed the small red-faced torso now sitting in the middle of the floor. He pointed an extended fork towards the middle of the floor, a lump of gristle impaled and swinging from the end, dripping gravy on the scorched floor.

"Can we keep it?"

Moira Gray and Morag Leech had worked together in the Strathcarnage Charity Shop at the rear of the town hall for a long number of years without notable incident or excitement. However when the wife of the local TV executive known as "The Ox" had donated some secretly imported American books to the shop, that leisurely existence had quickly changed.

One of the titles, "Heading South: The Taste of a Real Woman", had intrigued the two women, who had mistaken the bright cover and the title of book as a culinary guide. It soon became clear as the two women leafed through the liberally illustrated book that the guide was closer to pornographic than it was to gastronomic. As the two elderly women sat together behind the counter and read in more detail, Moira felt Morag's warm wrinkled hand slowly sliding across the nylon covered blue ridges of her varicose veins, travelling north.

At 70, Moira felt herself a little old to be engaging in a practices she had previously only read about in a few of the more sordid and heavily thumbed donated paperbacks handed into the shop. However Morag's enthusiasm had been infectious and Moira soon found the second hand books were soon destined to not remain the sole well-fingered items in the shop. The two lonely seventy-year-old women had quickly embarked on mutual adventures of the flesh, at first with caution, but gradually becoming more open and brazen as both discovered their long repressed passions.

As time had passed the pair had grown ever more flagrant with their trysts, eventually throwing caution fully to the wind after being discovered by deaf old Quinton in mid-session, overcome by lust while attempting to fix the shop's jigsaws. Morag had gone home that night worried if she was doing the right thing, but while relaxing in her evening bath she found herself crying with happiness at discovering a piece of a giraffe's face and a random corner of sky fused by lusty sweat to her most delicate extremities. There was no denying the fact she was in love with Moira.

Relations between the two women had then grown steadily more uninhibited, leading the pair to a fateful sexual crescendo one afternoon some weeks later.

Moira, whilst grasping Morag's blue rinse with her arthritic fingers during a particularly enthusiastic episode, had caught her foot on a box of second hand glass eyes, and the two women had lost their footing on the sightless orbs and fallen backwards through a curtain and into the shops window display, where they carried on their explicit mode of loving in full sight of a gathering crowd.

The party of passing school children had been particularly affected when Moira had briefly stopped progress of her public demonstration of carnal love to carefully remove both her false teeth and Morag's vast incontinence pants.

Even at this point, things may not have been quite so bad had there not been a large handwritten notice directly above the naked elderly coupling in the rapidly steaming window reading "Closed To Let the Girls Eat."

The window based exhibition was bad enough; however offering a running commentary to events and utilising a rolled newspaper as a pointer was the ever informative children's science teacher, Cassandra Leech, sometime daughter of Morag.

As Cassandra had pointed out the various anatomical features visible through the window to the excited clapping children, Moira had forced a naked Morag against the shop window whilst in the heady throes of passion. It was then Cassandra had fallen silent and dropped her rudimentary newsprint pointer to the pavement as the slow realisation hit her that she was watching her mother's tattoo, rhythmically sliding backwards and forwards through the grey condensation on the window.

Cassandra remembered clearly taking her mother to the local Tattoo Parlour to receive her Sixtieth birthday present, recalling how she had watched Twitchy John the tattooist complete the chosen design. Using three-inch black letters, Cassandra watched on as John had tattooed "Morag!" across her bottom, omitting the middle "O". Cassandra had wondered aloud if John had made some rudimentary spelling mistake. She had only wondered about the omission for as long as it took for Morag to position herself in front of the mirror, the smiling elderly lady bending over with a soft laugh to reveal the natural russet of the puckered "O" as she parted her cheeks.

Cassandra stood aghast in the street surrounded by giggling pupils, as her mother's tattoo began another journey up and down the steamy glass, pressed against the window complete with visible O. She had tried to guard the young eyes from the worst of the scene by standing in front of the offending sight and opening her jacket, but Moira was too lost in enjoyment to notice spectators.

Her enthusiasm, combined with the steamed lubrication of the window, meant Cassandra was left outside shuffling continually to and fro across the window in a vain attempt to hide her mother's artwork from the gathered crowd. It was only when Moira had spun a gasping Morag around to fully re-enact page 68 of the manual that Cassandra had found herself face to face with her mother, her elderly wrinkled features a sweating mask of intense pleasure.

Constable Clint Kerr had been dispatched to reports of the disturbance and had rushed to the scene with his limbless brother bouncing around on his front in a black leather harness. The two brothers had been forced to abandon the rucksack arrangement after a foot chase with a couple of local vandals, when the bottom had been torn out of the bag whilst climbing over a barbed wire fence. The unfortunate event led to the limbless Detective Inspector falling from the hole, before rolling into the road and under a parked invalid car on the high street.

The Strathcarnage Porcupine had recognised the comedic irony of the situation, and to the embarrassment of the pair, the local newspaper had printed a large photograph of the limbless law enforcer trapped powerless under the car, with the memorable headline "Crippled Kerr kept captive under Cripple Car!"

D.I. Kerr had barked instructions for his brother to strap him securely into his new harness as the charity shop incident had been reported anonymously to the Strathcarnage station. The limbless senior officer had thought the incident might perhaps be related to the recent spate of charity collection box thefts that had plagued the town. He was anxious to break that particular case, since in the six months since he and his brother Clint had been sworn in as law men to keep an eye on events in the town, these charity robberies had been the first major crime which resembled what they had regarded as actual real police work. The ex mainland policeman had embraced a case not involving the freakish population of the town behaving in a manner they regarded as perfectly normal.

D.I. Kerr had been born in the town but had left Strathcarnage by fishing boat with his brother Clint many years before to find work, and both men had eventually become highly regarded and regular limbed policemen in a big city in the south for a number of years. The men joined the force at the lowest level, but had quickly risen through the ranks to become a thorn in the side of many of the city's professional career criminals.

The Kerr brothers had been a uniformed annoyance to those tougher hoodlums that no other policeman had dared confront. Ironically, it was this very willingness to confront only the hardest criminals which had led to both Kerr's having to return home, and to seeing them back walking the winding streets of their home village with the older brother strapped to his brother's chest in an adapted "Naughty Boy" S&M harness.

Kerr had been investigating a drug dealing operation in the city and had been close to cracking the case and putting some of the country's biggest criminals behind bars for a very long time. However he was too close to disrupting the steady stream of dishonest income some senior city policemen had enjoyed from organised crime kickbacks. Some very powerful men had decided to close Kerr's persistant drug investigations permanently.

One evening Kerr was phoned and advised that a respected informant had some vital intelligence to pass on. The policeman had been told this new information would finally break the case, and was asked to meet the informer at a local biscuit factory. His deep craving to finally bring the group to justice led the policeman to fatally underestimate the possibility of a trap.

Soon after arriving at the abandoned factory alone in the middle of the night, Kerr was kidnapped by masked men and held hostage for a number of days. The single condition of release stated clearly that Kerr and his brother were to be immediately removed from the case and both men transferred from the area to somewhere far away, to some distant location where they were of no trouble to the city's powerful drug gangs.

On receiving notification of the kidnapping and the subsequent ransom demand, senior police had demanded evidence the criminals actually had Kerr. As proof the gang had begun sending the hierarchy severed limbs, one at a time.

The force was left appalled at the criminal's violence. However, what senior officers were unaware of at the time was that Kerr had already fallen into the jaws of a large caramel wafer machine during an earlier struggle, and as a result, the policeman's limbs had already been severed by the massive blades of the machinery, coated in chocolate, and packaged as 'best before' August. Kerr would have bled to death from his severe injuries, had he not found all his wounds coated generously in a thick quick setting caramel filling.

After receiving a different limb on four consecutive days, the police force had caved in and agreed to the gang's demands. Shortly afterwards Kerr was released, his ravaged torso found wrapped in brown paper and stuffed inside the tip of a metal rocket in a children's playground in a remote city park. Kerr was de-caramelised at a local hospital and, once recovered, immediately invalided out the force.

Both men decided to return home to the hidden village of Strathcarnage. The limbless man had protested his release from the force, but all his pleas had been met with reference to the police handbook, specifically the subsection of chapter eight relating to the absence of a continued ability to serve in any useful capacity while in a limbless state. The brothers had been unable to force a change of rules or to gain any other employment and both men soon found themselves under a tarpaulin on a fishing boat, huddled together against the weather, sailing slowly back home to the harbour at Strathcarnage.

On arriving home, the two brothers had visited the local council and announced they wanted to apply for the long vacant and unwanted post of local law man. The council agreed unanimously and promptly sent the men the same night to the local bar to announce themselves to the townsfolk.

The two Kerr brothers had arrived at the charity shop and quickly cleared the crowds from the scene. After happily allowing the elderly women to get dressed, the officers listened with interest as the two amorous seventy year olds linked hands and attempted to distract the men from worst of the day's events with their tale of a recent attempted robbery of the charity box from outside the premises.

D.I. Kerr couldn't help but notice the two ladies caressing each other from behind, out of view of his brother taking the statement. The younger Kerr brother took notes on the incident, resting the open book on his brother's head whilst writing and sniffing distractedly, absentmindedly wondering where the sudden strange aroma of lavender and lubricant had emanated from.

Kerr was determined to solve this case of disappearing Strathcarnage Children's Home charity boxes. After his recovery from the kidnap gang, the limbless man had received enormous support from charity organisations in coping with the terrible effect of his injuries. He now viewed robberies from any charity institution as the most heinous of crimes. But his determination to solve the case came from a deeper and much more personal motivation.

The limbless officer of the law wanted to prove to himself that he could still solve crime in his current condition, dreaming that someday he might travel back to the mainland with a proven reputation to show his superiors that they might allow him back to take up some position within the city force. He was bitterly determined and defiant that no one would stand in his way. He saw the charity box robberies as a path to the vital final chapter in his recovery.

Cassandra had remained deeply shocked at finding her mother naked pressed against the charity shop window, and had vowed to stop the woman seeing Moira. Cassandra had phoned the shop to inform the organisation that her mother would not be returning to work there, hoping her action would prevent the relationship from blossoming any further.

She forbade her mother to see or contact Moira, and grounded the elderly woman in her room for indeterminate period. Cassandra had also secretly gone about ensuring that the head of the charity organisation try and relocate Moira to another position on the other side of the town, well away from her mother. The chairman relented and agreed to Cassandra's request. The love affair was over and Morag was distraught.

One afternoon, some weeks later, once Cassandra was confident enough to be back at school teaching, there had been a knock at the door of her mother's home. Morag, still deeply distraught at losing her lover, had answered, only to find a hideously disfigured man.

"I can help you," the man had said in a strained voice, as the words escaped slowly from his hideously malformed mouth.

Morag was unsure whether or not he was winking at her, since the whole left side of his face seemed to ripple and convulse when he spoke. She had no idea who this man was, or indeed what he was offering help with. She prayed that she may have had some idea.

"Help me in what way?" Morag enquired hopefully.

The man looked left and right, and motioned with a burgundy stump of a limb for her to come closer.

"Moira. I can help you with Moira." The man looked around again nervously.

Morag gasped and held her hand to her mouth. It had been weeks since she had last seen Moira, and had given up hope of ever getting close to her again. The long days saw Morag often drift away to heavenly daydreams of those soft wispy curls of blue rinsed pubic hair and to wrapping her arthritic fingers round those tightly permed locks on the head she remembered working so energetically and passionately away below her on the vacant changing room floor. The disfigured man's whimper of pain brought her back to reality.

"But how? What can you do? Please, please, help me." Morag pleaded with the man.

The man smiled, or at least Morag thought he smiled, again confused in her attempts to read the expression as his charred mouth somehow moved his disfigured eyebrows into a scowl and caused his left eye to suddenly widen involuntarily.

"I will. But you must also help me." The burnt man tapped at the empty space where his nose used to be with his fingerless stump in a much devalued sign of secrecy, before turning to walk away.

Morag was sure he had tried repeatedly to wink knowingly, but this time he had begun salivating heavily during the attempt, and had abandoned it with a loud sigh of frustration.

"What have I to do? Please, tell me. I'll do anything you want, don't go," shouted Morag after the shuffling figure.

The figure stopped. He shuffled back to Morag, again looked around furtively and then reached his stump into his jacket, dragging free an envelope, which he then attempted at length to hand her before eventually dropping it on the path.

The strange man attempted a final smile, the charred stumps of his ears wiggled, and he shuffled away muttering to himself in annoyance.

Morag instantly recognised the handwriting on the envelope as that of Moira. She looked up to question the man, but as she searched both ways along the curved street to follow his path she noticed Cassandra appear out of a distant lane as she returned home from school.

Morag quickly returned to the house and closed the door, hiding the illicit letter in her room amongst her extensive collection of vibrators. She knew her daughter would never lower herself to look there and vowed to read the note later, as soon as Cassandra had gone to bed.

The note was from Moira and full of gentle affectionate words. She told Morag how deeply she missed her and proposed they elope secretly from the town by boat to a German Lesbian commune just outside Hanover she had read of called "Die Flapenschmackers". The letter also gave full and detailed instructions of a plan that would allow them to achieve their escape to the enticing vision of a single sex utopia, and as Morag digested the details of the proposal she smiled to herself and nodded her approval.

D.I. Kerr had grabbed the note from the shocked secretary with his teeth. The paper he had between his lips gave details of a reported phone call in which law men had been asked to visit a local address to discuss some new information in the case of charity box thefts. As he was carried up the path to the house in his harness, Kerr felt confident this new promised information would lead to his finally solving the case and starting on the path to a triumphant return of the Kerr brothers to the big city force.

As he pressed the doorbell with his nose, Kerr looked up to his brother and winked knowingly.

As the door opened, D.I. Kerr immediately recognised Morag as one of the two ladies who had been interviewed in the local charity shop. Leaning out into the street and nervously looking around Morag ushered the men inside, closed the door behind them, and led the visitors into the lounge.

Once seated, she began to tell the D.I. exactly what he had hoped to hear, watching him wriggle impatiently within the leather straps of the harness with excitement. Morag grew increasingly confident while watching the policeman's obvious enthusiasm that she had made the right decision to put Moira's whole plan into operation.

Morag informed the pair that she had remembered some further small details which she thought may perhaps be of importance in solving the case. She told the policemen that there had previously been an unreported attempted theft of another Strathcarnage Children's home charity box a few months before, long before the two men had arrived in the town. The elderly woman had since checked back her diary and had discovered that the timing of the previous attempted robbery had coincided with the date for the collection and emptying of the full boxes in return for new ones.

Morag had guessed, she told the two policemen, that the criminals somehow knew when the box would be at its fullest, perhaps, she mused dramatically, an inside job. The successful attempt to steal the box had occurred in the same manner, again just a day before it was due for collection. The new outdoor charity box had filled quickly after sympathetic people heard of the robbery and this freshly full box was due to be exchanged again in the next few days.

Morag thought she might have a cunning idea to snare the thieves. Kerr nodded and leaned forward in anticipation, the leather straps creaking at his keenness.

Morag's suggested plan was guaranteed to capture the criminals, she said, if it met with the Kerr brother's approval. It was quickly agreed the proposal would be put into full operation with the policemen's help. The older woman smiled sweetly as she realised the men had approved every single important facet of her lover's plan and that it would lead her to Moira, escape, and their elopement away from Strathcarnage into a life of Germanic lesbian bliss.

She grinned and trembled with anticipation at the thought.

The next evening, just as Morag's careful plan had suggested, the Kerr brothers had acquired an empty freestanding charity box from the charity organistion, ready to begin the operation.

The large plastic charity boxes used by the local home were shaped like wide eyed mentally disturbed children, freestanding and with an outstretched mechanised hand pleading for help. Once any kindly resident placed coins on the hand, the arm suddenly shot backwards and threw the coins at great pace into the gaping artificial mouth. The whole collection of these charity boxes were moulded from plastic, and, crucially to the plan's success, almost life sized.

D.I. Kerr was to be placed inside one of the boxes. Due to his surfeit of limbs he fitted inside the empty internal cavity perfectly, and the man sat inside the plastic child ready to be placed on the pavement outside the local Charity Shop on the eve of collection. He would watch from two holes drilled in the models own plastic head, waiting for anyone arriving to steal the box. When the robbers appeared Kerr would raise the alarm on his carefully positioned radio, allowing his brother to swoop and catch the thieves red handed. The plan was an ingenious one and couldn't fail.

Or so he thought.

It was a long and boring wait but D.I. Kerr sat patiently enclosed inside the charity box, daydreaming about his return to the city and his revenge on those who had wronged him. He had watched occasional locals wander past the box oblivious of his presence, and relaxed inside his trap, waiting with anticipation for the robbery.

Morag had locked up the shop as planned, leaving the charity box sitting alone in the darkness outside. D.I. Kerr knew that there would be action soon and as darkness fell he readied himself, growing more aware of the sights and sounds around him. It wouldn't be long now.

Around ten p.m. things began to happen.

Constable Clint Kerr sat in an unmarked van, just around the corner from where his limbless brother sat entombed in the street, waiting patiently for radio communication. The carefully mounted radio would allow the older Kerr brother press the alarm button with his nose and to bark the prearranged signal from inside the plastic head for the pair to then pounce and catch the charity box robbers.

D.I. Kerr's brother sat in the van absent-mindedly fingering his brother's empty harness, his thoughts drifting to his own dream of staying here in Strathcarnage, alone and free from his ever ambitious brother and his unappealing wish to rush back to being a policeman with all the city pressures.

The younger Kerr brother had hated being a policeman, staying in the job only to win his brother's love and admiration. While sitting thinking over his decisions and dreams, the deep in thought younger Kerr had only given a passing glance to the two elderly women strolling past the van, arm in arm.

D.I. Kerr sat inside the plastic child, watching the street silently from the narrow eyeholes as old deaf Quinton Gunn ambled along the street towards the box. Kerr watched on, and as Quinton passed he relaxed, waiting patiently for sign of the robbers.

Suddenly the limbless policeman saw the wrinkled eyes of Old Quinton staring back at him through the drilled holes in the plastic head. He was smiling. Kerr reached for the button of his radio with his nose, to signal his brother in the support vehicle.

However he was too slow, and as he looked out his eyeholes, he watched Old Quinton begin to mound huge piles of coins into the automated hands, watching helpless as the motorised arm shot back to shovel pocketfuls of loose change through the open hole of the plastic boy's mouth, driving the handfuls of bitter copper into the mouth of D.I. Kerr. Quinton was laughing to himself as he piled more money onto the hand and watched the arm spring back and disappear into the welcoming hole again, steadily filling the helpless policeman's mouth.

Now quite unable to speak, D.I. Kerr caught sight of the two lesbian shop assistants, laughing as they helped Old Quinton pile more loose change into the arm and watch it disappear through the hole. Morag stooped down to pluck out the radio connection from the hole drilled in the plastic boy's backside and the limbless policeman found himself silently entombed in the plastic child, his mouth full of metal and rendered mute. His orifice jammed full with coins and without hands of his own to remove them, he was unable to even scream for help.

Old Quinton had stood on the narrow pavement honking with laughter as Kerr watched Moira signal to something off to her side, invisible from his eyeholes. He watched on helpless as a horse drawn wagon had pulled up in the street and the twisted driver had shuffled off his seat to open the back wooden doors. As the doors swung wide open with a creak, they revealed inside a cargo of twenty identical small plastic boys.

Kerr had tried repeatedly to press his nose against the red button on his radio and mumble for his brother's help, but the walkie-talkie was dead and all he could manage was a quiet burble of a scream, a quiet echo inside his hot plastic tomb. No one else could hear.

As the driver shuffled over to the child shaped box, he too leant forward to peer inside through the staring eyes. He seemed to be laughing too, but it was difficult to work out the expression on the disfigured burnt face.

Suddenly D.I. Kerr felt himself lifted and carried towards the back doors of the wagon, where he watched silently as another identical plastic figure was taken out to replace him in the street. He was spun around and dropped heavily now inside the coach. Old Quinton appeared before him again, now laughing so loudly that the top plate of his false teeth slid forward to reveal a line of slavering pink gums, stringy

threads of saliva visible as his hearing aid began to whistle. This was the last view Kerr got of the town as his plastic prison was thumped down onto the wagon floor and the doors slammed shut.

D.I. Kerr felt himself being pulled around inside the now moving wagon. Jolted suddenly to a standstill, he found he was facing the back of the hideously burned driver and the grinning faces of both Moira and Morag. Moira smiled at him and began to speak.

"Hello D.I. Kerr. I believe you've already met my partner Morag. Let me introduce also my brother Dan. You've met before I believe, in the lounge bar of The Zoo Horse? You gifted him a double brandy, a cigarette end and third degree burns if I recall. He wasn't best pleased.

Anyway, we can't sit here all night gossiping. Dan is going to drop us at the harbour where a fishing boat is waiting to take me and Morag directly to Germany. I told Dan he didn't have to, but he wouldn't hear of it. He insisted on taking us there because it's on his way. You see, he's going to the local plastics recycling plant.

Seems all these charity boxes here are due to be destroyed. Change of image I think. Melted down and reformed into strange new shapes. Just like Dan's face was that night in the bar. Anyway, just to show you we're not totally heartless, we've decided to let you watch me and Morag get reacquainted in the back of the van on the way to the harbour, just as way of a final little send-off. We so hope you enjoy the show."

Moira winked as the whole wagon shook with laughter.

D.I. Kerr tried to scream again, but no sound came out. Just the tinkling of escaping coins from the piles of small change crammed into his mouth, the coins tumbling from his mouth as his jaws widened in shock at the sight before him.

The last thing the entombed limbless policeman ever saw was a pair of seventy-year-old women slowly begin to kiss and undress in front of him, huge pants slowly sliding downwards off wrinkled blue veined hips right in front of his eyeholes.

Before he managed to close his eyes, one of the aged pairs of buttocks bent forward to reveal a final message.

It read simply "Morag!"

Detective Inspector Charles Kerr (Quadriplegic Policeman) 1930–1978

## CHAPTER 11

## Day Nine – Pensioner's Brothel

The Strathcarnage Home for the Terminally Bewildered had opened in 1953, the product of a complex tax dodge of local entrepreneur Ulysses Frisk. Frisk had accumulated a huge sum from illegally importing bootleg pornographic magazines to the town and had been anxious to find a legitimate method of laundering his income.

The result was his purchase of the long derelict Rollins Hall, and the appointment of his mistress, Anna Phillip, as the home's trustee. Anna would be in charge of the neglected properties conversion into a retirement home for the care of the town's considerable older population.

The scheme had initially gone well, with the Hall in the dark quarter of the town doubling as a legitimate front for laundering the considerable amounts of illicit cash Frisk was now accumulating, and then later serving as a convenient base to store his growing collection of exotic prostitutes imported from numerous business travels abroad, currently housed in various locations around the town. The steady stream of sailors and smugglers constantly visiting from the town harbour often paid well for a bit of variety.

While they were 'calling' upon his ladies, sea bound customers often took the opportunity to stock up on fresh reading material in the Hall's shop, choosing from a selection cleverly featuring the girls engaged in their work. The local man had enjoyed a most lucrative market. Indeed everything about the arrangement was working well for Frisk and his business investment was both profitable and legal, at least according to the somewhat strange and unusual local laws.

However his luck was soon to desert him on a trip to Bombay while on a secret excursion to evaluate a substantial quantity of cheap Indian pornography offered to him by a dealer in Asia.

Ulysses Frisk had examined the consignment in the dusty corner of a shadowy Indian warehouse, and although concerned about the properties of the substandard paper for the "messier" reader, he had shaken hands with his cross dressing Indian contact and agreed to buy the entire batch, including some particularly colourful elephant related material. He had made arrangements with the turbaned man for the goods to be packed in crates and despatched back to Strathcarnage by boat, and had returned to the bar of a local hotel to celebrate the closure of the deal with a cold beer and a warm ladyboy.

As he drained his glass in anticipation of an evening of athletic exertions behind the lithe dark skinned body of his new friend, Ulysses had heard the first sign of commotion. Wandering across the hotel bar toward the crowd gathering at the open doors to investigate the disturbance, he had watched a large mob of locals milling around in the dust thrown up from the dirt road outside the hotel. The colourful gathering seemed to be excited, cheering loudly at something hidden by the mass of bodies and the clouds of dust.

Being an inquisitive man, Ulysses elbowed his way through the bodies at the door and walked down the creaking hotel steps to join the local crowd. Pushing his way to the front of the melee, the Strathcarnage entrepreneur found himself suddenly face to face with the bloodshot eyes of an angry bull elephant called Winston, the main attraction of the town's annual Rubba Rubba festival. Ulysses, although only an inquisitive transitory businessman, was soon to enter into town legend forever.

The Rubba Rubba festival was a celebration of the town's heavy reliance on the elephant for transport and industry. On this date every year, the largest bull elephant in the surrounding area was brought to the nearby town square, painted with tribal symbols, serenaded by local musicians and allowed to feast on a specially prepared banquet provided by grateful locals. After such pampering and the fine feast, a local mahout gently and lovingly aroused and then masturbated the huge beast to a glorious noisy climax as a local offering of thanks to the Elephant god.

The day's celebrations had gone well, up until the point where the local mahout had assumed he was bringing the enormous beast to closure. He had watched the elephant's round bloodshot eyes begin to roll and the huge hind legs of the beast begin to vibrate and then slowly stiffen, the point when the mahout traditionally adjusted his dusty goggles and yellow oilskin raincoat in anticipation.

However, just at that crucial moment near the point of elephantine release, a local builder's van had backfired loudly on the opposite side of the packed town square.

The elephant had suddenly shuddered in distraction and had reared up and spun suddenly towards the source of the noise, knocking the small mahout over a vegetable stall with his gargantuan twitching phallus. Unfinished and angrily frustrated, the animal had then begun a journey of rampage across the town square, his massive feet kicking up clouds of dust as he angrily thundered around.

This path of trumpeting destruction had led the huge beast to his current location, where it had suddenly stopped. The great beast stood in front of the local hotel, swinging its trunk to and fro, shifting from foot to foot with his swollen undercarriage twitching as his great bloodshot eye stared into the face of Ulysses Frisk.

Investigation of the incident by the British Embassy coroner flown in from Delhi had determined that the catalyst for the horrific events that followed may have been as simple a factor as Ulysses Frisk's choice of aftershave.

The elephant had stopped dead when confronted by the white suited figure of Frisk, and the huge crowd had fallen silent. The Strathcarnage gentleman, in anticipation of his evening of passion with his ladyboy, had doused himself liberally with one of the popular new colognes for men, a particularly pungent brand called "Gash !" purchased from his hairdresser before he left the town.

Frisk was aware of the notoriously unscrupulous hygiene of the area's ladyboys and had decided to mask the heady aroma of musty tool with copious amounts of his new fragrance. What he had failed to take into account was the extraordinarily sensitive sense of smell enjoyed by the aroused bull elephant.

The huge leathery animal, used to a life spent toiling trunk deep in mud and filth, had caught the fragrant smell of Ulysses Frisk on the night air, and on turning, had found himself assailed by a full waft of "Gash !". Those to the rear of the beast report seeing the huge pink phallus instantly stiffen as the aroused beast had pulled in repeated samples of the night air with his swinging trunk.

The British Embassy Coroner had determined that Ulysses Frisk might yet have escaped the situation had he not tripped and fallen as he turned to run across the uneven dusty ground to escape from the advancing beast. The elephant, driven to new heights of arousal by the sweet smell, had taken the odour as a signal to mate, and seeing the pale cotton rear bent over in the dirt before him, had attempted sexual congress forthwith.

The fatal accident enquiry later ruled that it was not the forced entry of thrusting elephant appendage that had killed Frisk straight away. Local witnesses gave evidence at the hearing of witnessing his pale western face widen in shock as he was impaled on the beast's member and seeing the man carried some way round the square back towards the hotel. Other witnesses recalled terrible pained moans and the Strathcarnage man's horrifically contorted face bounce past them as he was carried, still skewered, across the uneven local road.

What had eventually killed international pornographer Ulysses Frisk was the force exerted when the elephant eventually reached the very apex of sexual nirvana. With a roll of his watery eye and sudden stiffening of the rear legs, the enormous beast quickly reached a trumpeting climax of delight.

Onrushing local policemen had drawn revolvers and fired at the great quivering beast in an attempt to halt the hideous drama, but the animal retained just enough sexual vigour to conclude his task before finally expiring in the hail of bullets.

The force of the enormous flood of bestial expulsion had been too great for Frisk's human anatomy to cope with. In a stream of misplaced elephant love and with a fiendish scream, Frisk had been launched upward in a long arc at great pace, his broken body propelled over the packed town square and through one of the vast plate glass windows of the hotel bar. Ironically the ravaged body had eventually come to rest in the shocked arms of his ladyboy date for the evening. It was in those carefully shaved arms where he had expired, quite dead. The elephant too had died soon after, a thin smile of satisfaction on his face as he was comforted in his final moments by the loving caress of a weeping mahout in full ceremonial make-up.

The verdict of the British Embassy Coroner remains the only recorded verdict of death by propulsion of elephant semen.

The body of Ulysses Frisk had been returned home to Strathcarnage for burial, packed in a crate of recently acquired Indian pornographic magazines featuring badly focused shots of Indian women in various states of undress, some posed in grainy images alongside tumescent local elephants. The close presence of such images of elephantine arousal was a final strange irony of the local pornographer's career.

After extensive enquiries by Frisk's chosen firm of lawyers, Phister, Pleb and Billycock, it was discovered the entrepreneur had left no legal will. Since the firm could find no trace of any recorded next of kin, it had been decided after some discussion to award his entire estate to Anna Phillip, the caretaker of Rollins Hall and named trustee of his only legitimate company. The ownership papers for the huge property, five crates of Indian pornography and a small roll of sticky fifty rupee notes were turned over to Anna Phillip. The kindness of the bittersweet award had shocked the enthusiastic prostitute Frisk had met in Strathcarnage as a younger man.

Anna Phillip's real name had been Rita Gobbles, a name quickly changed on advice offered from one of her fellow ladies of the night, Anita Fuchs. The young woman had drifted into a lifestyle dictated largely by imaginative bedroom gymnastics in order to support her extended family of twenty four. It was a huge number of dependents, even for Strathcarnage, but owing to television still not having reached the town at this point, and her father the disgraced town gynaecologist, it was a wholly understandable total.

Anna had used her prodigious talents for rutting to feed and clothe the entire clan, often laughing and reciting to the gathered family her motto for life: "Just using my clever mouth to feed The Gobbles." Her statement was always met with firm pats of appreciation from her father, together with wild wails and muffled sobbing from her churchgoing mother. The remaining siblings were just glad to eat.

Anna had first met Ulysses Frisk after being employed as VIP backstage 'complimentary entertainment' at an early child show in Haversack Hall, where Frisk was due to be judging with his friend Lord Strathcarnage. Now her siblings had mostly grown into adults and left the family home to live around the town, Anna had made the decision that night to abandon the ongoing pressures of supporting the large clan for a less tiring life of her own, an opportunity suggested to the beautiful blonde woman as she knelt in front of the swiftly besotted and grinning Frisk.

Anna Phillip mused over these events of almost twenty years ago as she gazed over the dark winding Strathcarnage streets, wiping away her tears as she drank another toast to her lost love in The Ruptured Horse bar high above the town.

The small print of Strathcarnage business law had awarded Anna the entire estate of a kind man who was not only her lover, but her escape from her life on the streets. The huge house she could see far below in the middle of the dark quarter of strange town she had grown up in, this was all hers now, but only thanks to the unfortunate death of her dear Ulysses.

She was determined to finish the renovations and to somehow make the building a permanent monument to the memory of Ulysses Frisk. Such an act was the only way to fully show her appreciation for her lost love, and for the way of life that had brought them so much happiness and riches. She smiled as the idea came to her through the tears. She could make it work. It would work. And so it came to pass that the world's first sexually liberated home for the aged came to be based in Strathcarnage.

Anna worked alone for a number of months on renovating the home. She paid for the work with the small amount of money left to her by Frisk, but that particular pot had soon run dry after all the secretive payments were made to return her lover's body home from India.

Anna had ensured work continued on the home by performing sexual services with local contractors in the town, in return for both materials and labour. It was with great pride that Anna had calculated the lavish entrance hall and reception had cost her only a tiny splash under 500 oral encounters.

Ever resourceful, Anna had used those final few crates of Indian pornography to wallpaper a number of the upstairs rooms, finding the dusky shades of Eastern private parts offered the rooms certain warmth unmatched by even the more physically bartered for emulsions.

Ever pragmatic and keen to utilise every resource open to her, Anna had reduced costs further in the renovations by persuading workmen, post coitus, to deposit their collective seed in a large steel bucket placed in each room. It was these biological and ecologically friendly expulsions which she subsequently utilised to hang the wallpaper on the entire upper floor. The rest of the house had slowly come together too, with Anna blowing and thrusting her way to a completely finished and freshly refurbished home within a year.

On the week before the official opening of the building, an exhausted and limping Anna had been surprised by a group of visitors whilst in the middle of the act of "paying" for the home's paintwork.

Anna's eyes widened at the sudden re-appearance of a group of ex-prostitutes who had quickly fled the town, moving abroad on the news of Frisk's death, fearful of losing both his protection and the profitable patronage of work in the Hall. They had returned, Anna was told, after hearing rumours from passing sailors of this proposed memorial of remembrance to the man who had so kindly taken them all so warmly to his heart.

Anna had welcomed the returning woman back to their rightful home town and after hugging them and renewing old friendships, she had immediately put them to work "settling the bill" with the remaining workmen, now queued down the stairs and along the winding street running past the front door of the new home. The home was fully decorated, all outstanding building invoices had been settled and Anna now had a full compliment of staff to run her new idea for the home. All that remained was the name.

Two weeks later Anna unscrewed the old battered brass Rollins Hall sign and replaced it with the sparkling new replacement. "The Strathcarnage Frisk and Gobbles Home for the Elderly" was ready to open for business.

Anna decided that all prospective new residents wishing to stay at the new home had to go through the process of rigorous interview with her and the newly returned 'staff', and it was with some excitement she welcomed the first batch of hopeful townswomen.

Anna had decided to make the facility single sex, since Ulysses Frisk had always had an eye principally for the ladies. There had been some strong rumours to the contrary, but the only hard evidence of Frisk's "wider" interests lay in an out of focus reel of film posted anonymously from Bombay featuring grainy Indian newsreel footage of a young Lady boy covered liberally in elephant semen claiming to have engaged in "jaunty jaunty" with Frisk around the time of his death. The poor creature had been clearly distraught, begging directly to the camera for compensation from the British Embassy and Frisk's estate, but a disgusted Anna dismissed the request as that of an opportunistic local and had immediately destroyed the footage.

It was to prove an important decision in the history of both Anna and the home.

That first interview session had yielded only two prospective residents from the assembled group of more than two dozen applicants. A preliminary meeting and tour of the home had put a few ladies off, the more sensitive elderly women claiming that the Indian porn décor and selection of sex toys displayed in each room had proved a bit much, even for lifelong Strathcarnage residents.

A few others had decided to withdraw their applications during the specially choreographed three hour lesbian staff floorshow. The final seven had remained for the more rigorous interview process with Anna in the sauna, a welcome chance for the women to sit and recover after participating liberally in the introductory "therapy session", where they were paired off to be entertained by a group of those more perverse workmen who had cheerfully agreed to act as voluntary experts in this application stage.

During interviews Anna had explained the home's new ideology of sexual freedom, assessing the suitability of the candidates to ensure only those liable to receive maximum personal benefit would welcome. After extensive discussion the first pair of successful applicants were formally invited to become residents.

The whole process was not without trouble, since that first session of welcoming prospective residents had brought the home's first fatality. It had been ruled an accidental death, 83 year old Alice Mares finding herself struck down by a severe asthma attack thought to be accentuated by blocked airways during a visit from three male "therapists".

Although the incident had been unfortunate, it was not wholly unexpected, and once the set of false teeth had been chiselled off the man's phallus at the local hospital, the home returned to a more normal schedule. Anna had used experience of the incident to alter the institution rules to ensure no more than two males at a time were allowed in the therapy rooms with residents over 80, and only then when dentures and plates had been removed.

The home's quota of residents grew steadily over the next year, and by the time of the home's first anniversary the vast whitewashed building had become a popular part of the community. After an initial settling in period, the new residents had thrown themselves into the home's routine with gusto.

On Mondays and Thursdays, the home offered residents a visit from local male "occupational therapists", gentleman who would cater for any of the ladies needs and demands. Some of the older, more infirm ladies often chose just to watch proceedings, another taste that was catered for by a row of especially padded commodes. The home had fitted the strengthened yet comfortable waterproof seating facilities to allow it to cater for whatever combination of activity was preferred by residents.

Tuesdays and Fridays were Cinema days, where selections of hardcore pornography were shown to the residents in a specially built cinema within the building's basement. There would always be a towel boy on hand during performances to help with retrieval of the women's sex toys, since arthritic hands often found gripping the moist plastic and rubber a difficulty. During intervals he also stood in as a naked usherette, his small lit serving tray thrown around his broad shoulders and offering fresh lubricant, batteries and a selection of confectionary.

Wednesdays were given over to a lecture from one of the numerous local experts in a particular field of depraved sexual behaviour, often with demonstrations. These were increasingly popular with the residents, in one incidence causing the home to run out completely of their stock of anal lubricant within a twenty-four hour period following that particular week's graphically illustrated finale.

Weekends in the home were a free for all, with residents allowed to partake in whatever chosen activity pleased them most, just so long as they convened for the twice-daily set mealtimes. Family and visitors of the residents were allowed access to the home at weekends and permitted to use the various equipment and facilities, so long as it was by personal invitation of their nominated resident. It was not unusual for small queues of curious relatives to gather at the more popular features such as the love swing and the S&M dungeon. Weekends were busy times in the home, but all in all, things went well.

However this carefree and sunny outlook remained only for a relatively short time. After three years in operation, the home eventually began to run at a steadily growing loss.

The liberated home's overheads had begun to rise as the cost of smuggled batteries, lubricant and the expenditure of replacing worn out equipment began to creep slowly upward. Anna had partially foreseen this possible increase in running costs of the home; realising residents would gradually begin to use facilities more as their inhibitions loosened.

However the sexual ferocity and wantonness of her troupe of rampant pensioners had surprised even her. This increase in running expenses had coincided with a total withdrawal of funding by the town council, following an incident where a member of the local inspection team had found himself "surprised" by an unlubricted "Big John" vibrator, the whole episode an unfortunate misunderstanding while carrying out an inspection of one of the darkrooms.

The home faced an uncertain future as Anna called an emergency meeting to explain the funding situation to increasingly worried staff and residents. The population of the home had already suspected something was wrong. The Wednesday lecture had been moved to a fortnightly slot, and the quality of the "therapists" invited to the home had declined.

Indeed the whispered gossip around the home involved the re-introduction of carnal self sufficiency via the use of the home's well worn strap-on collection and whispered rumours in the home's corridors suggested that a rationing of the daily lubricant provision was only days away. Residents grew increasingly worried about the potential friction caused by these changes to both their lifestyles and genitals. Many residents predicted rough rides ahead.

Anna had addressed the meeting honestly, outlining her numerous concerns frankly and openly, informing the gathering in great details of the problems they faced. Finances were in a precarious state and Anna had broken down in tears under the pressure of describing the real possibility of root vegetables being employed until a cheaper battery supplier was sourced. It was a dark day indeed.

However, in the midst of the homes troubles a possible intriguing solution had emerged.

87-year-old Nan "Fister" Brinksworth had wheeled herself to the front of the assembled party and had quietly announced she had an idea for getting the home out of their current predicament.

Nan had manoeuvred her chair to the front of the podium, wolf whistled for silence, wiped the resulting saliva off her hand and arm and began to outline her proposition.

"What do we all own, ladies? The one possession which we all enjoy using and that we can employ to save not only our home, but our very lifestyle from ruin?"

Residents had looked from wrinkled face to wrinkled face, brows furrowed and lined not only in age but also now in a mixture of bemusement and confusion.

Nan laughed, moving her weight slightly to one side in her chair in order to hitch up her pinafore dress and give a depraved wink. The room remained silent as Nan laughed again, this time louder and with her skirt completely over her head.

"This!" she said prodding at her exposed lap with her swollen arthritic fingers, "This is our way out. We use it daily for pleasure, why don't we use it for business too?"

The room began to murmur slowly at first and then, as the penny dropped, with increased volume.

"That's right!" screamed Nan her arms held aloft, shaking above her head with enthusiasm, although now in quite the wrong direction owing to a struggle to maintain her bearings with her skirt covering her head, still half naked and exposed in her chair.

"Let's all use our natural equipment to pay the bills!" she screamed at the blank wall.

At this Nan pushed her whole body up proudly, standing unsteadily for a second and pointed in quite the wrong direction, before her skirt slid from her face. Confused at the sudden disappearance of the crowd, her arms began to buckle and she thudded back into her chair exhausted at the exertion.

Those present that were able had risen to their feet at varying speeds, and as a mark of unity, exposed themselves in a show of solidarity. Soon the whole room was full of unsteady elderly women and rocking wheelchairs chanting "Pay the Bills! Pay the Bills!" whilst prodding at the exposed flesh of their newfound pink empowerment.

Anna soon found the tears welling in her eyes, the younger woman overtaken by proud sobs as she prodded along in a show of solidarity with the women, unable to chant as she fought back the emotion.

So it came to pass that after the briefest of discussions the local "Frisk and Gobbles Home for the Elderly" became the first over 60's brothel and porn film studio anywhere in the Western Hemisphere.

It was not long before both customers and money began to mount. Anna had invited a local TV executive, The Ox, to the re-opening, and while in the process of road testing the merchandise on offer, Anna persuaded the man to sign a contract to show films shot in the home on the local network, in return for free advertising. The home could hopefully become self sufficient and if the plan worked they would never look back.

The first advert for the home had aired on the Friday night, during the local Strathcarnage channel's Danish Hardcore Hour. The home had voted unanimously that Nan should lead the campaign and appear in the first commercial. After all, it had been her idea.

The ad had featured a naked Nan giving a guided tour of the various facilities of the home in her wheelchair. She displayed the large Jacuzzi bath and mechanical lift, the nude stair-lift lapdancing, and the outdoor naked electric wheelchair displays, weather permitting.

The home was, Nan recommended with a wink, a virtual oasis of depravity and filth for all ages. The ad ended with a background shot of 67-year-old Ida being 'entertained' by a couple of masked local men on the love swing, all to an easy listening soundtrack.

Within seconds of the carefully placed contact number being displayed on screen, in a position to obscure the worst details of the ongoing depravity, the phones begin to ring incessantly. The first step was a success. The gamble had worked.

As the weeks passed, it became clearer than ever that the home was not only going to survive, but prosper. Customers had begun rolling in almost as fast as the pensioner residents could service them, and funds for the home were again beginning to look healthy. In an unpredicted fringe benefit, there was a huge response from the town's elderly female population now increasingly anxious to become residents. Anna found herself turning away scores of daily enquiries, some women even taking to hanging around in the street outside the home in varying states of undress and disability, hoping to catch the owner's eye. Indeed Anna was helping unload forty gallon drums of lubricant from a horse drawn wagon when her own mother had suddenly appeared at her side, fully made up, winking and displaying her heavily wrinkled wares in a fishnet body stocking.

As the money continued to pour in and the home's bank balance grew to unprecedented levels, Anna decided to use the massive cash surplus to relocate the more worn out residents to a luxurious new location acquired in Bermuda.

Anna shipped these exhausted, smiling women out of the town harbour three times a year, under cover of darkness. They left Strathcarnage on specially chartered boats, travelling from the town to see out their final days in peaceful sunshine, free now from the continued sexual demands on their already well worn parts.

However it wasn't an easy task to retire many of the women and some had point blank refused to leave their hectic life in the home. Indeed such was the fervent dedication exhibited by many of the women that a number had died while happily engaged on the job.

One of those whose decision not to retire would prove fatal was Nan, the star of the original advert. She had proved a huge attraction well into her 70's, the advancing years never dulling her prodigious appetite, eventually passing on exactly as she would have wished, impaled happily on a well-muscled young German fisherman in the Jacuzzi. Nan had expired on the very point of his climax, trapping him internally with a sudden muscular stricture during violent death throes which the Hamburg trawler man had mistaken for screams of enjoyment.

The highly traumatised trawlerman had quickly grown hysterical as the situation became more obvious, and the conjoined couple had to be lifted out the still bubbling bath using the mechanical wheelchair crane. The distraught German had eventually calmed only on the offer of a compensation package comprising free priority passes to the love swing with a pair of residents of choice.

Anna had grown fully aware of the aged bodies' fragility and any sudden expiration on the job was fully covered by a section the homes rules and regulations detailing compensation. People rarely complained for too long, since priority passes to the love swing were an incredibly popular reward, especially as that particular facility was both expensive and heavily booked out months in advance.

While organising a theme day for the home, to celebrate the tenth anniversary as a working brothel, Anna had received a phone call in her office informing her to come down to reception urgently. She had imagined the request was for the planned update on the problems with the new equipment in the futuristic themed room and had headed off down the vast staircase to solve the latest in a long line of technical hitches.

The new attraction was based on the newest fad, "Alien Orgasm: Shooting into Your Own Inner Space". The attraction was fully booked weeks in advance and any operational problems at this late stage might prove costly. Anna had rushed along the deep pile carpet from her office corridor at speed. What confronted her had halted her swift progress as she looked down the large carpeted staircase.

Anna stood motionless on the stairs with her mouth swinging silently open, quite unable to speak. Standing in the hall's reception area, partially clothed in PVC, was a sight that had brought the entire home to a standstill.

"Hello. I believe you are Anna."

The soft voice drifted to Anna up the stairs, complete with the polite offer of a well-manicured hand.

Anna stood frozen to the spot, her mouth still silent and agape.

"I believe it's you I have to speak to, as regards entry to your establishment ?"

Anna was unable to find the words, her brain still partially frozen in shock. It was not, after all, everyday that one saw a co-joined Siamese twin prostitute.

The two heads of Coco and Marie Rosencrutch, the world's only Siamese twinned working girl, turned toward each other, smiled, and then turned slowly back towards Anna.

Anna had silently recovered her composure and had ushered Coco and Marie to her office, away from the staring eyes of the considerable audience gathering in the reception. The fascination was understandable, for the woman was a truly bizarre yet beautiful sight.

She had a stunning single set of legs, which looked shapely, exquisite and totally normal, at least until your eyes followed them upwards to the inevitable conclusion. Then, just above the waist, the thin body began to widen and separate, until, had your gaze managed to make it past the collection of four impressive breasts on the two separate torsos, you would have found yourself staring at two quite separate yet beautiful heads.

Anna sat in total silence, staring at the striking figure before her. The twins thought it best that they do the talking, now well used to the initial level of shock they provoked in even the most confident of people. Coco and Marie made herself comfortable in the chair, and proceeded to tell her story.

It turned out she had been quiet housewives in Strathcarnage, smuggled there from Northern Thailand many years previously by a local man known as The Major. The girls had ended up living in his cramped village home in complete seclusion, too afraid to disobey their obscenely jealous husband and leave the marital home on any occasion since the day of their secretive arrival.

Her husband had recently been killed during a fight, and the event had forced the women outdoors, the twins vowing to make up for the lost years she had spent hidden away inside the prison of their house. Her husband was a kind man who had loved them both dearly, but had found himself quite unable to engage in sex with his co-joined wives as both the women's unusual bodily configuration and the man's own hideous war injuries had ruined him to well past the point of impotence.

Coco and Marie had read of the unique brothel home combination in an old copy of the local paper found when clearing their husband's bedroom of possessions after receiving news of his death. The women had decided Rollins Hall might be just the place to not only fulfil long suppressed dreams and desires, but to also help the home's struggling finances with her unique talents.

As it turned out the co-joined twins possessed only a single set of normal functioning genitalia, but the woman could also offer two pairs of breasts and a pair of independently working heads as compensation.

Coco and Marie pointed out to a still silent Anna that she could administer oral sex and still hold a coherent conversation with a client at the same time, as well as offering a self contained partial lesbian experience while being engaged normally on the job at the lower business end. They suggested it may be a popular selling point were they lucky enough to be accepted as employees.

The twins had offered to provide demonstration of their unique capabilities, but Anna had stopped her before that particular highlights package was unveiled. As this point was made the sound of disappointed hissing and sighing from just behind the office door was clearly audible, forcing the home director to shout to the unseen gathering to get back to work.

The twins were willing to work without payment in the home, purely to compensate for those long years of unfulfilled and barren sexual experiences. Anna had smiled, wiped away the tears she had shed on hearing their sad tale and had shaken hands, immediately offering the co-joined women a place in the home. With this new decision, the home instantly became an even greater magnet for the local media.

Coco and Marie, after years of life isolated and shut away from any human contact in the dark depths of the rural village, were understandably shy of the media and had refused all interviews. They wanted only to be allowed the privacy and freedom to catch up all those many lost years of sexual unfulfillment. Anna felt protective of her new charge, but even without media attention word of mouth had soon spread, and within days the delighted Siamese twin found herself fully booked almost a year in advance.

The home was running smoothly again, but new events were soon to be the catalyst for more major upheaval in the organisations day-to-day running.

Later that year, The Ox had negotiated with Anna to bring the day to day workings of the home to the Strathcarnage Community Associated Broadcast channel in the form of a nightly fly-on-the-wall documentary programme, "Plastic Hips and Wrinkled Nips".

Coco and Marie had agreed to appear after some persuasion, having grown increasingly comfortable around people. The show was filmed over a period of months and had gone to air on the local network, instantly proving a fantastic success. Now their talents and beauty had been exposed to the town's greater population, the twin's personal video sales had soon begun to overtake all the other titles in the home's extensive range. Her "Two Heads Give Better than One" title broke all previous local records for an adult title, with the church shop selling out on the day of release.

However all in the home was not well and this unease would lead to further tragedy.

The other residents grew to resent the home's new girl. They had watched as their own bookings and video sales had begun to drop significantly, suffering at the popularity of the dual headed, multi breasted new resident. Professional jealousy among prostitutes is a vicious thing, leading to a fierce desire for revenge, and for the first time in the history of the building's sordid operations, a bad atmosphere began to develop.

The other contributing factor to the home's problems lay in the unheralded success of the fly-on-the-wall TV series. As a result of the show's unfortunate tea-time scheduling, many local men had discovered that watching television over dinner with their families had now become an uncomfortable and often dangerous experience.

It was unusual, even in Strathcarnage, to be forced to attempt explanations to younger children of the sudden appearance of fathers on television straining away behind a moaning, sweating pensioner on a love swing. While such scenes were visible in the background of the town's living rooms, it became an almost impossible task to maintain enough parental authority to encourage wide eyed viewing children to maintain a healthy intake of green vegetables.

Increased incidences of local marriage breakdown soon began to occur; divorces and separations often hastened by extensive and detailed video evidence of carnal occurrences with wrinkled love parts. The documentary series had quickly caused the town's goodwill towards the home to turn nasty. Taking care for the town's female elderly population was one thing, but their steady drain on the income of male family members, and the televised evidence of exactly where the money had gone, was quite another.

A protest march had been organised to rally local female opinion against the pensioner's brothel. The gathering was to be fronted by angry and upset townswomen and the group planned to converge on the town market square for a rally, before a moving on to protest outside the home itself. However the home's residents, themselves long standing residents of Strathcarnage, had heard rumours of the action. They organised themselves a counter demonstration, their clear intention to confront the mob of local protestors.

Anna decided it best to stay away from the march. She had no wish to become involved in any trouble, viewing her role at the home as purely a charitable attempt at honouring the memory of her Ulysses. Anna had stood on the broad white arc of the home's marble front steps and waved off the first wave of wheelchair bound prostitutes, resplendent in lingerie, make-up and best wigs, rumbling off in formation towards the market square slowly in buzzing electric chairs.

The next wave had set off using Zimmer walking frames, this group clad in S&M gear. Finally the more able bodied women set off, walking proudly behind a gigantic model of a huge male phallus, built and mounted on the rear of the lorry belonging to the shabby local man Gus Ebersole and straddled by a naked dual headed Coco and Marie.

The giant model had been devised and built by Crosby Stanton, the local model maker, to create a visual focus of attention for the women, and the construction had been designed to provide an unforgettable finale to the march as it mock ejaculated a huge number of leaflets over the opposing demonstration. It was destined to be a colourful event.

Back at the deserted home, Anna had used the solitude to relax, choosing the warmth and bubbling water of the sunken Jacuzzi to wind down. It was an easy choice of location, since all of the home's beds remained unchanged because of the march and sheets still lay caked liberally in the previous day's unleashed cargo of gentlemen's relish and various lubricants. Anna soon found herself unwinding and had quickly dozed off in the warm spiralling currents of the water.

If she had remained awake a few minutes longer, she may have noticed the arrival of a large rusty tank mounted atop a small horse drawn wagon outside, the driver dismounting warily from the cab with his wide brimmed hat pulled down to disguise his face.

The two groups of protestors made their way to the town square from opposite sides of the town, chanting filled the narrow winding Strathcarnage streets.

Disgruntled local women were marching towards the market square chanting lustily, "Grey Hair Out! Grey Hair Out!" together with other far more depraved and

unkind abuse detailing the unsuitability of elderly ladies engaging in acts of sexual congress.

From the warren of streets on the opposite side of the square came the opposing chants of "What Do We Want? MEN. When Do We Want Them? NOW" and "Get Our Teeth Out For the Lads". The scene was set for a nasty confrontation.

Back at the home Anna was sleeping soundly in the warm gently bubbling water as the mysterious overall clad tanker driver quietly opened the garden door and entered the room.

He had already searched the empty home for Anna, unable to believe his luck on finding her totally alone and unconscious in a deep slumber. As he slowly undid the buttons and discarded his disguise of dirty overalls, he slid off his hat, checking his make up carefully in one of the mirrored panels of the room before smiled to himself as fresh red lipstick was applied.

The two demonstrations were about to come together in the market square when as the heavens opened, rain pouring down on the assembly from the vast open hole high above in the roof of the cave. As the torrential rain began to soak both sets of protesters, the two groups came face to face across the wide expanse of cobbles as they entered from opposite sides.

Normally the rain would have dampened the anger of the two groups and caused feelings to cool. Indeed that may very well have been the course of the afternoon's events, had it not been for two chance occurrences.

The rain was falling very heavily, and due to the purely indoor design of the gathered electric wheelchairs, this onset of moisture proved fatal. Several of the leading women's chairs short-circuited, leading to total steerage failure, charred faces and slumped bodies now lurching forward at full speed straight toward the centre of the opposition demonstration.

A pair from the first wave of uncontrollable chairs had jack-knifed on the uneven cobbles and thrown the occupants from their onrushing path, the sudden twist of the chair throwing wrinkly lace and silk clad bodies heavily onto the unforgiving stone surface.

The Zimmer frames fared no better. The cobbles were made treacherously slippery by the downpour, and the full PVC S&M costumes made gripping the wet frames almost impossible for weak arthritic hands. The second wave of ladies of the night had gone down in a blur of black fetish clothing near the centre of the square, falling like dominoes once the first lady had fatally overbalanced.

The opposition group of local women from the town had become incensed as the remaining short-circuited electric wheelchairs had proceeded apace like mounted cavalry through the front lines of their oncoming march. Immediately angry and injured members of this group counter charged and sporadic hand-to-hand fighting broke out amongst the two groups, with the pensioners battling lustily using the handheld array of walking sticks and sex aid weaponry they had carried to wave in a show of peaceful defiance. Worse was yet to come in the sexual battlefield.

Back at the home the mystery tanker driver had now slipped fully out of his uniform, emerging like a butterfly from a stained blue cotton chrysalis to reveal a magnificent silk ball-gown and matching diamante earrings. He had waited a long time for this moment, and after studying himself again at length in the mirror he returned to the tanker and flicked a small iron lever to start the low hum of the specially mounted pump.

In the town square, the scene was now one of utter mayhem. After the initial setback the pensioners had regrouped and managed to drive the protesting town's women back from the square into narrow side streets with the expertly wielded sex toys, leaving the cobbled market square littered with casualties of the fighting.

In one particularly nasty incident, a photograph of which made the cover of the Strathcarnage Porcupine and soon to become a defining image of the day, a local housewife had found herself heavily gored at both ends by a particularly fierce pensioner onslaught, the woman photographed in all fours, dually impaled in an astonishingly compromising position.

As the fighting continued, both sides seemed oblivious to the appearance of Coco and Maria astride the monster model phallus as the truck had ominously rolled into the market square from a surrounding street. On witnessing the ongoing carnage before him, Gus Ebersole laughed heartily and turned up his bagpipe music in his cab to better soundtrack his view of the free show.

Anna had woken with a start in her Jacuzzi, stirred by the noise of the squeaking patio doors closing behind her. She had attempted to turn to look, but had found herself handcuffed securely to the underwater infirmity rails on the side of the bath.

As Anna craned her head around as far as possible, she could see a heavily made-up dark skinned man grinning at her as he dragged a huge hose through the open doors into the Jacuzzi room. He had smiled manically at Anna with uneven lipstick covered teeth as he had pulled the fat hose to the very edge of the bath.

Leaning down, he pushed his dark manicured hands through the bubbles and unplugged the bath, standing with arms crossed while patiently watching the water drain away with a loud slurping sound. He sat silently on the floor at the side of the bath grinning broadly at the naked handcuffed body of Anna before replacing the plug in the now empty jacuzzi.

The town square was a scene of almost medieval chaos. The local women had now rallied, counter charged the older women and now violent fights were in full swing all over the square, the cobbles now a mass of torn off wigs, discarded sex toys and ripped girdles and support stockings.

Suddenly a loud and hideous mechanical groaning sound focussed the attention of the gathering, leading the entire battlefield to halt their ongoing combat and look around in an attempt to locate the monstrous grinding source of the noise. What they saw was to silence them for many years.

In the corner of the market square the huge truck-mounted phallus was squealing horribly while undergoing some kind of catastrophic mechanical failure. Due to the torrential rain running down and inside the upward angled oversized construction, pools of water were collecting in the large synthetic gonads at the base containing the leaflets. The contraption had been designed specifically by Crosby Stanton to explode flimsy paper leaflets outward with massive blasts of compressed air, firing them upward across the square and over the anticipated protesters. However the model maker hadn't designed the contraption for operation in the rainy weather and the powerful internal mechanism was now blocked, wet and short-circuiting, just as it had reached the moment of intended release.

Coco and Marie had presumed an obstruction at the tip of the device and had worked themselves slowly upwards along the shaft, planning to reach the tip to unblock the obstruction and allow any remaining leaflets to be distributed. What the Siamese sex worker could not have anticipated was that the remaining leaflets far below had now been turned to paper pulp by the steady stream of rain, and that a series of moisture induced electrical faults had caused the explosive firing device to short circuit and become live.

As she pushed her thin arm around inside the massive opening to clear the blockage, the twins had leant over the device to see if the two heads could spot the cause of the problem. As the pair gazed downwards into the darkness of the barrel, there had come from below an ominous rumble. Before they could locate the source of the noise far below, there had been a sucking noise and the wet leaflets causing the blockage at the tip had suddenly cleared.

The strangely configured body of Coco and Marie was hit by the full impact of the sudden onrush and found herselves propelled clear across the square as the internal pressure finally gave way.

Amazed onlookers watched on in shock as the twinned headed, quadruple breasted figure was blasted off the end of the device, propelled upwards, spinning across the town square carried by a massive arc of paper pulp fired from the end of the monster machine. Her short unexpected flight ended with the Siamese twin stuck fifty feet up the town hall front; her thin underwear clad body unconscious but held firmly in place on the wall by huge quantities of the thick white paper pulp mixture.

The entire square had fallen silent to watch the long arc of her journey and eventual sticky landing. The women stood open mouthed at the sight before turning to look back at the phallic truck mounted construction, their attention drawn by fresh groaning noises. The huge machine vibrated and fell silent, before suddenly twitching and firing again, indiscriminately covering the entire crowd with the remainder of the leaflets, now warm, liquid and fired at huge velocity.

Gus Ebersole sat in the safety of his cab, helpless with hysterical laughter as he was thrown around inside his lorry by each subsequent launch from the model phallus overhead. As the gathering was in the square was soaked by the massive gouts of white fluid, Gus turned up his swirling bagpipe soundtrack put his feet up and laughed harder and harder as he pressed controls manoeuvring the massive construction behind him from side to side.

Anna lay shackled in the bath, deep in shock and utterly lost as to who this dark stranger was, and to his strange plan. It was only when he spoke in broken English that the realisation began to dawn on her.

She had seen this same distraught face many years before, a hysterical image on that grainy footage posted from India containing news reports of her beloved Ulysses' unfortunate elephant related death.

The moisture streaked face of the distressed man who had watched his beloved die in his arms had stared at her then down the camera lens, demanding compensation. It was the same face now staring back at her across the Jacuzzi room, older but much clearer and better made up than in the grainy image.

"I come avenge my wrong." The man had said as he lowered the end of the wide hose into the empty bath.

"You owe."

Anna now knew exactly who this was.

The thin Indian man spoke no more, sobbing deeply at the memory of his lost love as he turned the handle on the end of the hose to begin filling the Jacuzzi with the contents of his horse drawn tanker, contents shipped all the way from India and from years of careful collections at his town's Rubba Rubba festival.

Anna lay helplessly shackled to the bath, the handcuffs digging into her wrists as she struggled against the thick liquid pouring over her. She screamed and pleaded, desperately begging the ladyboy for mercy. Anna fought hard to keep her head above the rising fluid, gradually losing her strength and growing silent before slipping just beneath the milky surface.

Finally, as she began to lose consciousness for the final time, she thought of the face of her beloved Ulysses Frisk and slid silently beneath the rising white liquid. She had finally joined her dear lost love, together forever as the only cases in that slim coroner's file marked "Death by Elephant Semen".

Anna Phillip (Pensioner Madame and Brothel Proprietor) 1925-1978

## CHAPTER 12

## Day Ten – Roadkill

The Ox slammed his huge fist into the boardroom door with a ferocity and impact which silenced the arguing figures seated around the large oval table. This would have been classed a stormy meeting in any boardroom, anywhere in the world, however this was Strathcarnage and there was bound to be at least one extra bizarre aspect involved. On this occasion the extraordinary feature was the centrepiece of the huge boardroom desk. Rising out the dark wood at its centre, glinting in the overhead lights and fully encased in Perspex, was the body of the Ox's first wife, a stripper called Xantia.

Xantia had expired while attempting to beat the World pole dancing endurance record at a special televised event in The Lech bar. The Ox had persuaded his wife to attempt the challenge, arguing that the high profile event would help both promote both Xantia's dream of securing a lead role in the hugely popular films featuring the local brothel while also raising the profile of the Ox's own role as a local TV network owner.

All was going well in the event until the fifty fourth hour, when Xantia had accidentally trodden on a greased and discarded cucumber she had previously been making most liberal use of during her act.

As the dancer had put her full weight on the well-lubricated vegetable, her flat soled white stiletto had suddenly shot backwards, causing a fatal overbalance. Xantia had partaken in numerous surgical alterations, and as she slid, the unwieldy mass of her size 48 FF breasts had suddenly shifted above her centre of gravity, propelling her violently and fatally backwards.

The Ox had framed the incident through the camera viewfinder, watching helplessly as Xantia Sparks had slid and lost her grip on the pole, her body tumbling backwards before impaling itself fatally on the six-inch stiletto heels now pointing upward at the ends of her twisted legs. She had jerked violently as the sharp heels entered her body; her massive breasts slowly obscuring her face as gravity had drawn the unrestrained fleshy orbs slowly downward over her sloping naked body.

The Ox had fought his way through the audience, tears in his eyes as he pushed past the crush of guilty erections and shocked faces to his wife's naked body. As he scooped and dragged the massive breasts from her face, he saw he was too late. Xantia had suffocated.

Footage of the lap dancing death had proved popular, but the Ox had been initially reluctant to broadcast the incident. However as rumours of the footage spread, the amount bid by old friends in stations outside the town topped one hundred thousand dollars and he suddenly realised that Xantia had indeed provided the means not only to achieve her own immortality, but to fully realise his Strathcarnage TV executive dream from beyond the grave.

The Ox had vowed, as he signed the contract to release the footage, to remember Xantia's sacrifice. As a result, the huge grief stricken man used part of the money to have the still naked and baby oil soaked body encased in Perspex and then mounted right at the centre of the huge boardroom table. It remains there to this day, staring out at those executives meeting in the boardroom of Strathcarnage Community Associated Broadcasting.

Xantia had been encased by Mad Larry Gross, a local man specialising in Perspex corpse preservation and display. However, the Ox had decided on one last change to the local madman's suggested design. Rather than have her mounted standing at a pole as Mad Larry had originally planned, displaying her impressive portfolio of breast gains, the huge television executive had decided on an alternative arrangement to better display his wife's own favourite asset. After some hard but largely enjoyable effort involving Larry and the overcoming of rigor mortis, Xantia was mounted at the very centre of the specially built mahogany table. There the naked frame lay for eternity, encased in clear plastic and positioned kneeling in the middle of the design.

The feature was much admired as a beautiful natural centrepiece, with a daily floral tribute of fresh white petals being sprinkled over and around her perfectly curved bottom as a sign of his undying love. The Ox knew that this was the way she would have wanted to be remembered.

The Ox's hammering fists had caused white rose petals to dance around the encased plastic rear as the table vibrated, the sudden outburst of anger at the meeting prompted by news of the previous month's disappointing viewing figures. The station had enjoyed a long monopoly over the townsfolk's leisure time, but as other pastimes had grown more popular around the town, the local captive population audience share watching the only TV channel in the town was beginning to fall steadily for the first time since he had moved to Strathcarnage three decades earlier. The Ox needed to encourage people to remain loyal to his company. He needed fresh ideas.

The station had initially broadcast material The Ox and Xantia had smuggled into the town on their journey from San Francisco. The pair had studied the legend of Strathcarnage for many years, drawn to the place after finding a single mention of hidden town in a dusty and partially burnt ancient book, discovered in a second hand store by a perpetually stoned hippy guru of their acquaintance. After parting with massive bribes and sailing secretly for a number of days in the darkness of a ship's hold, they had arrived in the cave where the town lay. The perpetually stoned pair had fallen in love with the town, immediately deciding to stay and become residents, which would enable them to set up a local TV station broadcasting only to the strange but welcoming locals. As a result Strathcarnage townspeople had developed a sudden taste for moving pictures, becoming addicted en masse to the mixed diet of fetish pornography and local news that was the station's sole output over the initial years of operation.

The Ox had carried with him from San Francisco an extensive range of banned underground pornographic material, and over the years many residents in the town had been raised on the graphic imagery of leather clad perversions and grainy plot less rubber fetish movies.

However, given the limited stock in The Ox's personal collection, the audience had recently begun to tire of watching reruns of the same old titles and familiar lubricated genitals. The channel had been forced to diversify to maintain interest, and found the only plausible method of doing this on a budget was to smuggle cameras into the town and start making cheap local interest programmes.

The channel had begun the new programming with a local strand called "Fight Night", placing camera crews outside the town's five pubs and around the town harbour on weekend evenings, to catch drunken local townsfolk's repeated and continual attempts to murder both visitors and each other after consuming industrial amounts of alcohol. It was violent stuff, all set to a jaunty sixties soundtrack the Ox had found on a tape of in the pocket of an old kaftan. This footage had proved popular for a while with the bloodthirsty local audience, but again the novelty soon began to wear off and ratings began to fall.

After Xantia's death had provided a few weeks of steady ratings as her footage was repeated, The Ox had taken the executive decision to supplement the station's programmes with a nightly interactive sexual advice show featuring his buxom new girlfriend, Big Nancy. Nancy presented the show topless, illustrating sexual problems suggested by the locals with the help of a masked and smilingly obedient Ox.

The shows had been well received, most notably the weekly "Ass Hour", but Nancy had struggled to find the dedication, enthusiasm and stamina needed to continually host such a 'hands-on' programme in its nightly four hour slot. Citing painful chafing, muscle strains and friction burns, Nancy had demanded reducing the show's frequency to a single weekly episode. Grudgingly The Ox obeyed, broadcasting the show for only an hour, the new format featuring Nancy sitting mostly in a leather swivel chair wincing as she carefully crossed her fishnet covered legs, occasionally flashing her crotch while rearranging her mini-skirt and taking viewer calls.

In addition to this new programming, the station also began for the first time to carry local adverts. Since the channel's signal could only be received by those people who lived inside the massive cave that housed Strathcarnage, there was no need for either censorship or any great expense involved in production. This led to a number of astonishing local broadcasts, items screened completely uncut for a small fee of ten pounds, should anyone had desire to have thirty seconds to express themselves to the rest of the town through the medium of television.

People still talked fondly in the village's streets and pubs about the more extreme examples, a particular favourite being the surprise announcement of a local husband's affair.

That particular item came live from a suite in a the local Holliday Inn, where the fornicating man in question had delivered a personal news bulletin live to his wife, speaking straight to camera as he continued being 'worked upon' somewhere under a mass of his mistresse's bobbing blonde hair.

The activity continued throughout the message, the gent pausing only at the end of the message to blow his freshly informed wife a kiss while grinning and waving. The lady below had continued working silently throughout the broadcast, only turning to the camera at the end, wiping her mouth with the back of her manicured hand while holding up a final selection of signs written in scarlet lipstick reading "Agnes, It Appears You're Dumped!" and "Tommy Wants A Divorce!"

The Ox had then announced his famous fly-on –the wall documentary strand, featuring the everyday experiences of the local pensioner's brothel.

"Plastic Hips and Erect Nips" had made a few OAP's local celebrities, in addition to being cited in just over half of all local divorce proceedings. The programme had continued to air at present, but owing to the potential for personal embarrassment amongst townsfolk, the audience share had begun to drop as the popularity of the establishment grew. This law of inverse proportionality was now proving a real problem with ratings, since the more coverage the programme created, the more the establishment became a massive hit with locals and those numbers actually watching the show fell. They were too busy queuing to partake in the reality than to watch second hand coverage at home. Audiences were at an all time low.

For that reason the board of the television company had called the current meeting to think up much needed new ideas, to raise both the company's flagging profile and audience share.

The only continued ratings successes enjoyed by the local station were from the weekly broadcasts beamed live from the local church and featuring the astonishing sermons of local churchman Aubrey Whisp. The station needed more unmissable local programmes to pull in regular high numbers of viewers. The Ox needed fresh inspiration.

The gathered board members, perhaps petrified by the Ox's show of anger, had presented a few good ideas to the meeting that had shown potential.

One board member had suggested a series of programmes under the title "Knockout Suicide Dominoes", where each week two local competitors would play each other, until the eventual loser ritually disembowelled himself live on TV at the game's climax. The eventual series winner would receive the grand prize of a modest static caravan on the harbour road, a reward already negotiated for free in return for the fatal blade used in the show carrying company sponsorship. The idea sounded promising, but The Ox had reservations about the popularity of dominoes on the small screen.

Another proposal had been suggested by one of the board's church elders, who had the idea of a new show called "On The Balls" where four local women would be asked, blindfolded and dressed in football kit, to identify ex lovers using only their sense of touch and the aforementioned genital parts of the title.

The executives had hoped to expand eventually to a same sex version, to cater for the town's large and highly active bisexual audience. The Ox was forced to admit that the idea was a good one and likely to gain a high audience, but had decided not to proceed further when it was pointed out to him the obvious similarities of a previous show called, "Moist Finger". The Ox was prone to acid flashbacks from his student days in San Francisco and his tendency to be forgetful was legendary.

The Ox listened patiently to the remainder of those less original ideas presented to him, sitting through suggestions ranging from Wheelchair Boxing to Blind Children's Saturday Night Knife Fighting Party.

Nothing seemed to have the broad appeal and longevity he was looking for. Nothing that is, until he was presented with one final idea from the group.

The last idea raised for discussion was one The Ox he knew immediately had potential to be solid gold television. It was called "Roadkill !" and once the small executive gathering had heard the basic format explained, the group had mumbled amongst themselves agreeably, convinced the TV station was on to a sure-fire winner.

The idea had been raised by the local hospital doctor sitting on the board, an elderly heavily squinting and confused man called Captain Fulbright. It was he who had come up with the seed of the idea, months previously, during a sex change operation on a local rugby coach, Joe Anders.

Captain Fulbright had paused during the operation to make detailed notes as the idea had occurred to him, his observations only partial after losing his fountain pen in an open wound. Joe had since made good recovery and changed his name to Persephone, and although disappointed with his new vaginal depth, had returned to playing the sport he loved, tearing lustily through the Strathcarnage mud in a selection of silk trouser suits and, on big games, a magnificent scarlet velvet ball gown. Persephone had also enjoyed additional fame as a direct result of a strange and newfound ability to sign autographs naked, in a squatting position.

Captain Fulbright had risen slowly from the table at the board meeting and, eyes transfixed on the curves of the naked Perspex table decoration, laid out to the meeting his detailed ideas for "Roadkill!"

The gathered executives looked from face to face as the plan slowly unfolded, realising this was the very programme to revive the stations fortunes. At the end of the presentation, a loud cheer had gone up from the men, and The Ox had thrown his arms around the Captain in appreciation. The Ox wept lightly as he clutched the Captain, stealing a smile over his shoulder toward the centre of the table and the plastic curves encased within, knowing Xantia would have been delighted at this turn around in fortunes.

The idea for "Roadkill !" was like all truly great ideas, simple yet distinctive. The program would follow the general format of a traditional yet bizarre quiz-show, however the real magnificence and individuality of the show lay in the fact it had no predictable start or finish time. The show could be an hour long, or a day long, the broadcast beginning at any time. In order to better explain the genius of the idea, and the innovation involved, we are best placed examining the whole concept detailed in the boardroom by Captain Fulbright in the meeting.

"Roadkill !" would be a television event. An ongoing set-piece show allowing anyone in the village to receive a huge cash prize at a moment's notice, simply by using their local knowledge of both families and friends and of the numerous dangerous roads surrounding the village.

Two local camera crews would be on call twenty-four hours a day, and at any given point, when circumstances permitted, they would leap into action and the programme would begin. All they needed was a massive incident of road based carnage.

On the local lawmen receiving a call informing them of any fatal traffic accident in the town, the officers would immediately phone and inform the station. The camera crew would then race to the scene along with a specially created team from the local council, their task to reach and secure the crash site in order to film the accident from every angle possible.

Meanwhile, at the same time, a second production team would then grab three local families from their homes and transport them immediately to the specially built Roadkill set, a soundstage built in the corner of the town abattoir utilising old car wrecks, offal and hospital equipment. The presenter, as yet undecided, would dress as a traffic policeman, or a fireman, or a surgeon, depending on the programme's numerous rounds.

One of the three families present would be the next of kin to the person involved in the crash, but none of the three would have any idea whether their group was attending the studio as the family of the bereaved, or merely a family of panicking red herrings. By using their knowledge of the town, the three families were to guess if they were the soon to be grieving relations of the victim or merely random players in the spectacle.

Tension was to be achieved by clever emotional manipulation over a number of different rounds, with a final revelation of the covered corpse at the end of proceedings to see who had guessed correctly.

The genius of the programme was founded in the tension of the contestant's ongoing anxiety, combined with the fact all of the participating families had the potential to secure prizes if they guessed the corpse identity correctly at the show's climax. They could win whether the deceased victim belonged to them or not.

Given that most people in the small isolated town knew everyone else intimately, it was a genius idea guaranteed to keep the entire population on the edge of their seats.

The local press were told of the idea at a hastily convened press conference and had met news of the idea with as much enthusiasm as The Ox.

The local paper, The Strathcarnage Porcupine, had devoted the new show an entire week of front pages leading up to the launch date, and townsfolk had soon been caught up in the huge excitement of the event. After weeks of publicity and innovative advertising using car wrecks littering the town, Strathcarnage was buzzing with anticipation by the time of the launch night.

There had been a few sceptical voices in the town from some of the older residents, many of whom bemoaned the way things were changing in Strathcarnage. They were used to the old ways; the bondage and S&M films, the foreign pornography. In a last minute genius decision, The Ox was destined to silence even these critics and increase the programmes profile yet further.

The local clergyman, the Reverend Aubrey Whisp, was contracted to be the presenter. His rampant Tourettes and universal local appeal would ensure a huge audience and make the programme unmissable, even to the more traditional crowd.

Then there followed almost three weeks of massive anticipation following the launch night, the town's inhabitants watching in huge numbers until eventually circumstances had permitted the first edition of "Roadkill!" to be aired.

The town had been foggy all day, and as night had fallen, black ice had begun to form on the town's roads. The local paper had publicised the change of conditions, and the town was poised. Hopefully tonight would be the night for the inaugural show. And so it was to prove.

Not long after eight in the evening, a phone call was placed to the show hotline notifying them of a massive fatal crash on the steep cliff road. The caller had won himself a thousand pounds, providing he signed a contract ensuring complete silence and agreeing to sit in a soundproof booth within the town hall until the end of the ongoing "Roadkill!" episode. For the show, total surprise was integral to success.

The film crew were there in minutes, the crash scene cordoned off and hidden completely from view by large metal fencing covered with sponsor's logos. Unfortunately the first show sponsor was badly thought out, with the initial site emblazoned with the logo of the Strathcarnage Abattoir where the show studio was based.

The red tarpaulins covering the crash site read simply, "Is Roadkill *Dead* Good !! Or Is It Just Offal?"

The three families of contestants had been dragged from homes around the town and rushed to the studio immediately. The parties found themselves dressed in black mourning clothing within minutes and led on set for the programme to begin. The backroom team on the show could perceive the excitement in the family's faces at the prospect of being the first town residents to have a chance at winning the big prize. All of the families taking part had every transport owning relation immediately taken off the local streets and transported in secrecy to a safe house. The only other family member with access to transport, the person actually involved in the accident, remained pretty much static where they were at the scene. No one in the gathering knew who was safe and who perhaps lay fatally injured. The tension among the group was unbearable; after all, the prize was worth a lot of money.

Pre-recorded adverts had been flashed immediately onto all radio and television channels throughout the town and word spread instantly that the inaugural episode of "Roadkill!" was about to begin.

The show music had begun after an advertising break, with a specially commissioned theme song from a local death metal reggae fusion band "Slaughtered Rasta Kindergarten", entitled 'Roadkill: Dat Street Meat Ting'. Then as the distorted steel drums and grinding guitars died down, a selection of blue flashing lights and sirens signalled the beginning of the show, broadcasting to the biggest audience in Strathcarnage TV history.

The Rev. Whisp bounded onto stage and introduced the three families before moving immediately into the shows first round, entitled "Bits and Pieces".

The gathered families each had one minute to examine some wreckage brought directly from the crash site to the studio, to determine if they recognised any of the twisted car parts. This round was carefully designed to reveal nothing obvious and The Ox had planned this section merely as a cynical addition to fill airtime, build tension and make the show running time a little longer.

In actuality the plan almost backfired as one of the families noticed some blood and hair mixed through the windscreen fragments displayed on black velvet trays. Reverend Whisp had quickly informed the families, after hurried instruction in his earpiece, that not all this evidence may be from tonight's crash scene and that some items may be accidental red herrings from previous crashes.

Thankfully the moment passed and none of the families had identified any family members potentially having been in the crash at this early stage. The Rev. Whisp had brought the round to a close with a sudden unprovoked scream of "Fuck!" and a violent jerk of his head to one side, the outbursts both unfortunate yet crowd pleasing symptoms of his disease. The packed studio audience applauded loudly in appreciation.

The next round was entitled "Are They Out Yet?" where a large clock in the studio informed the families of the time from the crash discovery. It read approximately 23 minutes, and it was the task of the families to determine whether the crash victim remained in the car wreckage or whether they had been extracted by rescue crews. They were given an audio link from the scene to help them determine, played in conjunction with an extra soundtrack from a scrap metal yard to make their task a little harder.

Midway through this round Reverend Whisp had taken a particularly violent turn, swearing repeatedly and jerking violently across the stage to further applause from the enthusiastic studio audience. The Ox grinned from his position in the gantry, since the display had worked the crowd up to even further displays of excitement, while the loud swearing had served to further complicate any possible identification of the noises from the crash location.

The following round was more interactive. Each of the three families had to nominate a single family member to move to the front of the studio, where they were met with a spot lit chalk body outline. Each member then had the chance to mark the outline with a chalked white cross, whereupon a smiling Captain Fulbright would drive a sharp needle into the real body at the accident scene at the same point and write down the response on a card in black marker. The round was called "Surprised or Paralysed."

Remaining family members would write their guess at the bodie's reaction, and if correct and the two cards matched, they were met with a loud cheer from the audience and awarded the spot prize of a chainsaw. The Rev Whisp had injected some excitement into the round with his repeated loud cries of "Done For!!" at various points of high tension.

Events at the show now began to heat up. The programme had reached the first point of possible elimination, "Gash Dash". Three screens were revealed, and each showed a still photograph of a gruesome open wound. The family members had to move forward and stand directly in front of the screens one at a time, with only a correct true or false identification of an actual wound from tonight's accident allowing each member to proceed through to the next round.

The audience had begun to chant "Gash! Gash!" repeatedly during this process as the gruesome wounds would appear, the Rev Whisp rocking and muttering with his stiff arms clamped on the coffin shaped podium sides, fighting back his urges to unleash fresh tirades of swearing. All three families had a number of members eliminated from the game during this identification process, but fortunately each family retained enough numbers to remain active in the game and to stay in the hunt for the cash jackpot.

The show had continued in a similar manner for a number of hours, through round after round, until the programme reached its glorious climax.

Those remaining family members still in the game had to confer and nominate a single representative from within their number to play in the spectacular final round of the programme. The final chosen three were to stand individually spot lit on the stage while live pictures from the Tommy Holliday Memorial operating theatre at the small local hospital were beamed to the studio. Each contestant would be asked if they could identify from three grisly close up images of the procedure which of them featured live footage of one of their family, and which were merely old footage of another operation from the files. This final round was called "I'd Know Them Inside Out".

The three representatives were then asked to announce their final decision on which bloody clip they thought was the actual post mortem of the road accident victim and then were taken away to the side of the stage for the show's final reveal.

If accurate in identifying the correct body they received the cash prize, together with a small trophy model of a crashed car with the "Roadkill!" logo arched above it in brushed aluminium. The tension was almost unbearable in the studio as the families made their final choices. A heavily sweating Reverend Whisp was even reduced to stifled cries of obscene swearing from behind a shaking fist as the tense process was played out.

As the families returned back to centre stage to join their representative and watch the final reveal, they stood together in small groups with their arms linked, silently waiting. The studio was plunged into darkness and the whole studio, barring Reverend Whisp, stood silently as a blood spattered Captain Fulbright came onto the screen live from the operating theatre.

The Captain paused for effect, his elderly hand resting on the bloodied sheet hiding the cadaver on the operating table. He offered the families one last "Good Luck", and with a final smile and a wink to camera with his heavy squint, quickly pulled the sheet away to reveal the identity and subsequent success or failure of the participating families.

There was a mixture of cheers and howls of disappointment from family supporters in the studio as the sheet fell.

The first family, who had been convinced that the body was that of their youngest son Tony, were utterly devastated to find it was not him. They began to wail and grab onto each other in tears, shaking their heads in angry disappointment at missing out on the prize.

In the post show interview the family team leader had still been too distraught to speak, angrily cursing himself for incorrectly identifying what he was convinced was his son's ruptured spleen. Reminded by Whisp that it hadn't been an altogether wasted night, the man lifted up his small runner-up trophy, kissed it half heartedly and waved it to the cameras with a forced smile.

The second family had correctly guessed that the victim had not been their daughter Elisa, and had leaped about ecstatically as the revelation of the corpse had proved them both correct and thus winners of a smaller cash consolation prize. They also received a surreal dinner set made by a one armed local potter and badly fired complete with the programme logo. This was presented to the unlucky family onstage by the potter, who dropped the misshapen soup bowls as he attempted to hand over a modest cheque.

The third family, the actual family of the victim, had also guessed correctly and when they realised they had recognised the ravaged body of their son Ignatius Blart correctly, had exploded with joy and ran around the studio cheering wildly and hugging.

The boy's father had run to the audience where other family members were in the audience and began high-fiving the celebrating gathering. The winning family were ecstatic. An emotional celebration followed, with explosions of glitter and coloured paper falling from above as the family opened bottles of champagne and the audience applauded their approval.

The huge screen in the background continued to broadcast the ongoing scenes from the post mortem as the family danced around celebrating their success.

The Ox presented the delighted Blart family with their oversized prize check onstage. The presentation was due to have been made by a local sporting personality, the rugby player Persephone Anders, but she had been forced to cancel the appearance after being rushed into the local hospital to have a new ink refill installed, the ravaged genitals having run out of ink at a book signing in the town the previous day.

The presentation part of the show almost had to be cancelled, with the pictures on the studios big screen showing the victim partially regaining consciousness just before the handover of the cheque.

Luckily the director of the feed had managed to cut all potentially distracting live sound from the scene before the panic, switching to an uplifting classical feed to accompany the pictures of the jolting body arching and spurting blood during futile attempts to get his heart restarted on the large screen behind the still celebrating family.

News of the huge audience share for "Roadkill!" had arrived, as fate would have it, on the morning of the first programme victim's funeral. The TV channel had arranged to show the whole service live, not least because the Reverend Whisp had insisted in performing the service himself.

In a final ultimate irony, the hearse had itself crashed on the way to the service, with waving mourners fighting to get on television while trying to retrieve the coffin from the window of the local Butcher's shop. The scene became further confused when the whole group was suddenly surrounded by a confused "Roadkill!" camera team trying to build a fence around the scene after receiving a call informing them of another potentially fatal crash in the town.

The mourners had eventually managed to transport the offal draped coffin the remainder of the journey to the church without further incident, owing to a kind emergency loan of the local Butcher's horse drawn open cart.

The irony of the situation had escaped the majority of locals as the blood soaked cart was manhandled into the churchyard and the coffin was unloaded. Only then was the butcher's logo on the cart painted side clearly visible. It read "Dead Meat – Pre Packed."

Luckily close family members had missed all of the excitement. They had been at home, awaiting the delivery of a whirlpool spa bath, one of the numerous products purchased with their recent windfall.

Other minor relatives had arrived at the church clad in newly acquired black designer clothing, and driving sparkling new cars. They had emerged, smiling to the cameras and waving, before entering the church to the theme from "Roadkill!" sung lustily on the lawn beside the front doors by the all girl church choir.

The group moved through the packed church to the empty front pews, pausing only to sign a number of autographs and have souvenir photos taken with occasional members of the appreciative congregation. The family then took their places in the front row and gazed at the coffin, a grand mahogany casket provided personally by The Ox himself from Hitchcock and Chalmers coffin builders, tastefully emblazoned on both sides and the lid with carved representations of both the programme and TV station logos.

The service had been a quick one, hastened by the Reverend Whisp bawling "stiff" repeatedly whilst repeatedly gripped by a particularly vicious episode of his illness during the reading. This unfortunate incident was followed by the churchman pulling the wooden front off his altar and collapsing through the open hole into the aisle, before eventually being led away by a number of concerned choir members.

The father of the deceased had said a few words via a video link from a Spanish seaside beach, before movingly displaying the items of jewellery he had recently bought with the winnings from the show. The man had then fallen silent, sipped from a cocktail and lowered his head toward the coffin while a Blart family member present at the service produced, from a small velvet bag on his person, the "Roadkill!" winner's trophy, which was placed lovingly on top of the coffin.

It was a moving moment, enhanced for the audience at home by a spectacular laser lighting show inside the church that The Ox had arranged for the occasion, planned when suggesting this televised finale to the family.

The Ox smiled in the studio at the effect of the lights shimmering off the brass name plate, content that the exhaustively rehearsed family member had managed to place the trophy exactly on the chalk X marked on the lid of the coffin. It was vital that it were placed there correctly to enable a good clear shot of the award, providing a contrast of glittering gold against the wide tracking shot filmed through the black clad mourners.

The funeral then moved outside to the churchyard where the coffin had been lowered slowly into the plot specially provided by the television company.

The family had chosen burial only at the last minute, deciding not to avail themselves of the generous offer from The Ox of a heavily discounted mahogany dining room table with their son's remains encased in the middle in Perspex. The internment of the coffin had gone well and was almost a perfect end to the live broadcast.

Almost, since Reverend Whisp had freed himself from that group of choir members subduing him and had sprinted across the churchyard screaming loud car noises and shouting obscenities at considerable volume, before reaching the burial party and launching himself sideways down the hole meant for the coffin. After he was extracted, the service continued without incident.

So ended the first ever episode of "Roadkill!" The programme had been as popular as anticipated, proving the salvation of Strathcarnage Community Associated Broadcasting Station.

The winning family had soon spent all the money from the winner's cheque and their lives had slowly returned to normality. For a time they occasionally met around the grave marked by the huge black marble and gold "Roadkill!" logo headstone provided by the television station, for ever less frequent publicity shots.

The Blart family had eventually been forced from the town, exiled forever soon after it was discovered by a local investigative TV crew that they had tried to engineer another crash using their remaining children, in a desperate attempt to relive the notoriety and excitement of that appearance on the first show and to regain their wealth and local fame.

The family couldn't live without the publicity, or without the prospect of a new whirlpool spa bath.

Ignatius Blart (Crash Victim and TV Star Corpse) 1958-1978

## CHAPTER 13

## Day Eleven – School Days

For as long as any local could remember, the old Strathcarnage Grammar School had stood on the same site right in the centre of town. The imposing gothic edifice had stood as a town landmark amongst the crowded mess of other smaller structures, stubbornly resisting the architectural chaos on all sides. Yet while the school organisation remained, the old building had now sadly gone. On an isolated site beside the steep cliff walls that marked the very edge of the town, a newly built replacement stood waiting.

The school's fresh relocation on this "reclaimed" site had been prompted by a massive inferno, one which had decimated both the original site and a number of surrounding properties near the town green. The day after the disaster, Strathcarnage town elders had held an emergency meeting and ruled that a new site be found immediately. Council funds were to be used to purchase and drain marshland on the furthest edge of town and to relocate any nearby residents to other locations for their own safety. The decision was deemed a sensible precaution, the committee voting unanimously to locate the new site deep within a safe boundary of open ground. It seemed a prudent move for other town residents, especially given the spectacular manner in which the previous school building had exploded.

Indeed the huge black crater remained, a dark hole still piled full of charred broken masonry and smoking building debris, the site left as a monument to remind locals of the ingenuity and potential of a chemistry class full of thirteen year old Strathcarnage children. The deep hollow stood near the centre of the town, occasionally still smouldering and cordoned off by a huge electrified fence nearly a year after the detonation.

The town planned to reclaim the void once council officials had passed the site safe for human habitation and free from radiation. Once this restoration work was complete there were plans for a permanent monument to be sited at the epicentre. In a contentious decision by a panel of surviving teachers, the winning design for the memorial had been that submitted by a local artist, Ian Combs, a former classmate of the lost chemistry class children.

Ian had been absent on the day of the inferno. He had been elsewhere, lying enveloped in bandages and screaming in intense deep while being treated within in the local hospital intensive care unit, having sustained heavy acid burns from ongoing class experiments into the mechanics of chemical warfare.

The judging panel of charred survivors later decided that his carefully worked design of twelve children's blackened and limbless bodies, piled high and cast in bronze, added a certain haunting poignancy the other submitted designs lacked. Ian's proposal also planned for the entire memorial to be ringed by an eternal flame, designed to lick up the side of the bronze cadavers for added effect.

Work on the new school site for the town had begun almost immediately the flames had been brought under control at the decimated site of the initial accident. The prospect of a town swarming with delinquent Strathcarnage children ensured a new school was viewed by most as a matter of some urgency. A television fund raising drive to aid construction costs had immediately been organised by the local Strathcarnage TV station, the ensuing blind panic raising almost half the funds required for school rebuilding in a single night. The highlight of the special fund raising night programming was a drama documentary made by the pupils themselves about the incident, entitled "The Burning Flesh of Class 2D".

The pupils involved in the programme claimed that the concept had been intended as a loving tribute to those lost in the blast, the victims all openly declaring an enormous love of extreme horror cinema carefully nurtured by the school's weekly snuff film club. In an ironic twist, four more pupils had been killed during filming of the tribute, having fatally miscalculated the quantities of petrol and homemade explosive required for the spectacular special effects involved in the movies realistic finale.

The additional funds required for completion of the rebuilding work arrived in a bizarre manner few days later. The money was delivered to the town mayor's office in cash, wrapped in brown parcels and smuggled there secretly by the crew of a small rusting Bolivian steamer. Contained in the bulging packages was a massive donation from a gifted chemistry student who had left the town many years previously to become a big player in the South American cocaine trade.

The Strathcarnage Grammar School ex pupil had quickly changed his name from the original Nicholas Wasson, adopting the more apt moniker of "The Hawk". This information was only discovered at a later date from the armed Bolivian customs unit who had lost the former pupil's trail after a fierce gun battle near the same Ecuadorian port where the young Hawk had arranged delivery of the parcel. The Hawk had escaped back into the local jungle after evading capture. It turned out the small arms training received as part of his unique Strathcarnage education hadn't been such a waste after all.

Once the parcel of cash was counted and the location decided for the new school, the marshland was secured. The land was 'purchased' from a stubborn but slow-witted local farmer called Bryson, in a fixed poker evening in The Harse bar. The farmer had looked at one point to be sure of winning the game, but the hasty introduction at the side of the gaming table of a well endowed female councillor in a low-cut, see-through lace top feigning continually dropped keys had proved enough distraction to the salivating framer. His eyes were drawn to the massive fleshy orbs of the head of the planning committee just long enough for a fresh deck of marked cards to be brought into play to ensure the win.

As a result the new Grammar School had opened its gates in time for the first anniversary of the original firestorm. A poll of pupils taken by the Strathcarnage

Porcupine newspaper had decided that the new site should be opened by a young maverick Strathcarnage horror movie director called Ivan "Gorefest" Andreshevitch. The director's work had been extremely popular with many Strathcarnage children following the decision by the head of programming at the local TV station, The Ox, to keep station production costs low through a policy of giving local talent a chance. His new idea provided any locals with promising and interesting ideas both a small budget and the basic equipment to produce their own movies.

Andreshevitch's locally made films had been shown in the TV channel's "Children's Slot", which specialised in broadcasting those hardcore horror titles thought unsuitably light for evening viewing by the town's adult population. Andreshevitch's classic "100 Flashing Scalpels of Dr Chang" had been a particular favourite, narrowly beating the eternally popular "Shaven Strathcarnage Farmers Wives" series as the highest rated programme ever broadcast during the children's hour. The local bloodthirsty film-making genius was a natural choice among the local children to open their new school.

The young director had opened the school with a flourish typical of his clever eye for publicity, cutting the official scarlet ribbon with a large blood soaked sabre while dressed in full costume and make-up as a character from his new movie "Diced Flesh". As he raised the sword, screamed and then slashed through the ribbon, a number of stunt players hidden throughout the crowd began to ritually "disembowel" themselves, lumbering forward and moaning while spraying onlookers with fake blood as they staggered around screaming and dragging mock offal behind them.

The whole crowd cheered as Alexei leapt into the gathering and hacked false prosthetic limbs from the numerous stunt players with his shining sword, blood fountaining from wounds over the official opening party. The whole assemblage of Ivan and his limbless zombies had then gathered themselves, turned and marched forward down the small avenue toward the iron school gates trailing a red carpet of gore. Ivan and his extras lined up along the gates, pushing the black iron entrance open and declaring the school ready for business. Gangs of excited child film fans fought amongst themselves in the sticky blood to recover a souvenir of a severed rubber arm or handfuls of the pig offal used in the ceremony.

The ceremony had been a memorable successful, but not one totally without incident. During Ivan's pre-planned assault on the costumed zombies secreted around the crowd, he had lost his bearings and managed to accidentally sever the arm of a Senior council elder's wife, a wide hipped woman arriving late for the ceremony due to a furtive sexual liaison with the Head of Town Planning. Among the whole bloody spectacle no one paid much attention to another severed limb and had imagined it all part of the carefully choreographed part of the show. Only the quick thinking of the Head of Planning had saved his bleeding lover's life, the unkempt man managing to staunch the real blood spurting in long crimson arcs from the freshly opened wound with a pair of expensive silk crotchless French knickers pocketed after earlier events as a carnal souvenir.

Doctors later speculated that they might have been able to save the arm had it been retrieved quickly enough. Alas one of the town's strange collection of pets had already retrieved the limb and taken it home as a memento after winning a bloody and extensive tug of war with a local pupil. The arm was only retrieved weeks later, after complaints about a strange smell led local lawmen back to the town square home of recently deceased transvestite truck driver Billy Marshall, to prise the rotting gnawed artefact away from an irate dog with a strange taste for human flesh. Upon losing his battle, the dog had returned to his scorched kennel whining loudly, distraught at the loss of a second tasty memento.

The school opened its gates for official educational business the very next day, to loud protests from the building's cleaning staff. It had rained overnight and for the first few hours the entire building had been steadily covered in hundreds of small bloody footprints, trailing material left at the school entrance from the previous day's opening ceremony. Contrasting strikingly against the fresh white walls of the new corridors, the winding trails of small scarlet footprints would have made film-maker Ivan Andreshevitch a very proud and inspired man. Unfortunately the sight would remain unseen, his dead body found later in the day lying on the school rugby pitch, frozen solid and still hugging his sword and a celebratory bottle of Vodka.

The entire school intake met in the new assembly hall that first day to take part in a small service of thanksgiving to bless the opening of the new site. It was with great shock, and some amusement, that the assembled throng of pupils and teachers realised they had inherited the same wild eyed school chaplain as had plied his holy business in their previous school.

Reverend Bentley Lyons was a small wiry man, partially bald with an intense heavily squinting stare and the bizarre appearance of constantly chewing when he wasn't speaking. The churchman had the habit of fixing his extraordinary and unreadable gaze on pupils throughout his sermon, disconnected eyes gazing down at the gathering from over wire rimmed glasses and focusing on pairs of separate confused faces on different sides of the hall. The wild eyed man's other notable trademark was his original and highly amusing method of getting the message of God over to his highly apathetic flock.

Bentley Lyons unique style of religious engagement involved actual live demonstrations and reconstructions of stories from the bible. As if this were not entertainment enough, Reverend Lyons also had adopted the highly unusual method of springing these unpredictable re-enactments on his congregation when they least expected it.

"Sin will creep up on the weak, the faithful must be prepared", was the churchman's preferred mantra, and his oft quoted reasoning for launching sudden allegorical bible attacks on unsuspecting members of the school community.

In keeping with this style of surprise re-enactment Reverend Lyons had began his new reign at the new school with an ill judged attempt at bringing the story of David and Goliath directly to the children.

During the first morning break on the new school premises, the Reverend Lyons had suddenly appeared through a side door and strode into the crowded playground, loudly reciting the relevant bible passage concerning David encountering the colossus of Goliath. He was dressed, comically for a man approaching his sixtieth birthday, like a peasant boy, carrying a rudimentary loaded leather sling in his free unbibled hand.

The Reverend closed the good book, laid it down on the grey concrete before him and preached the remainder of the passage loudly from memory while swinging his sling above his head. His swivelling eyes darted about the gathering crowd before singling out the largest child. With a colossal grunt of effort, the churchman proceeded to launch a stone at the oblivious victim's forehead.

The stone hit the unfortunate chosen victim hard, impacting with a horrible hollow thud. The Reverend looked pleased with his demonstration of the Lord's message and reached down to pick up his leather bound bible to continue his impromptu sermon. Bent over, he had missed the livid onrushing figure of the child with a stone sized swelling on his forehead.

The "child" hit with the allegorical stone was none other than Big Jerry Bletzkoff, an enormous muscular pupil with an unrivalled capacity for wanton violence only just matched by his substantial strength. Jerry was the captain of the school weightlifting and boxing teams and current under eighteen Strathcarnage bench press record holder.

Witnesses reported later that the impact of Jerry's first kick had lifted the ageing churchman completely off the ground, his thin hands still clutched tightly around his bible. All but the strongest stomached turned away before the next barrage of punches landed from the boy's enormous fists, so reliable eyewitness accounts of the subsequent beating were thin on the ground. Many present commented on the hideous sounds of breaking bones and screaming at the height of the attack, and the noises alone were enough to cause a number of the younger children to seek heavy sedation from the school nurse and miss afternoon classes.

By the time the Reverend Lyons' broken body was recovered by the collection of teachers required to pull Big Jerry off his prey and adequately restrain his frame, the churchman was clearly incoherent, mumbling hymns through broken spectacles and his swollen bloody mask of a face. The ambulance men who had attended the scene noted that the injuries to the church man seemed commensurate with textbook examples of a large plane crash or an attack by a stampeding bull elephant. Teachers had taken the opportunity to point out to the confused gathering of emergency services personnel the massive, barely restrained frame of Jerry, only just trapped under a mound of anxious looking staff and pupils.

Jerry was suspended and expelled from the school for his part in the incident, but not before he had been carried shoulder high around the building by a crowd of cheering pupils. The celebratory gathering was joined by a significant number of badly disguised teachers whose opinion of Reverend Lyons was somewhat less than positive.

Rumour around the school claimed later that Jerry Bletzkoff, had gone on to become a particularly vicious bare-knuckle fighter called "The Lyon Tamer" after being expelled , but none of the rumours of his subversive late night bare knuckle bouts for money with sailors around the harbour were ever proved. The Reverend Lyons spent a considerable time in plaster and bandages and being fed through a tube at the local hospital following the incident, but the churchman had soon recovered and found himself drawn back to the school to spread the Lord's word in his own inimitable fashion.

The headmaster of the old school was a nervous, decrepit old gentleman called Charles Charles. Although surviving the massive fire at the old school, the incident had provoked in the man a nervous breakdown of some significance and had retired. The broken man left Strathcarnage immediately on a boat heading to the Spanish Riviera, undertaking the journey once released from the local hospital under industrial quantities of sedation.

This act of medically induced emigration had allowed his deputy the luxury of promotion, and it was with a broad smile and a spring in his step that the rebuilt school's new headmaster Cornelius Templeton had entered his new post. In truth his almost constant smile owed more to a heavy drugs habit than any love of his job, since he hated children with a passion. The pronounced spring in his step, however, was the result of an altogether different matter.

Cornelius Templeton had lost both his lower limbs during prolonged sampling of new drugs perfected by fourth year chemistry students. The strength of the pupils' initial crop was a great success, but when fire had engulfed the first school during an ongoing programme of testing, Cornelius had found he was quite unable to walk and had been crushed by a falling statue as the wrecked building crumbled around him. The statue was that of another of the school's former pupils, a tall granite effigy of an enormously endowed go-go dancer called Zita who had recently left the school to become quite a star in the local porn industry.

Cornelius Templeton's lower limbs were lost during attempts to free the man from the fallen effigy using cutting equipment, as he lay almost catatonically doped and pinned firmly to the ground by a pair of 46 EE granite breasts. The cutting equipment had been snagged on one of the statue's gargantuan nipples and as a result the metal teeth had suddenly sprung free and closed on Cornelius's soft trapped legs instead of the intended hard granite. In a final blitzkrieg of irony, it was later discovered that the gentleman operating the cutting equipment was Zita's father Tommy. The local fireman had been quite unaware of his daughter's choice of career, mistakenly believing his daughter was earning her money as a trainee mucus collector in the respiratory ward of the local hospital.

A later inquest into the accidental removal of legs had totally exonerated a distraught Tommy from any blame, instead citing the stone nipple as the sole reason for the accidental divestment of lower limbs. The statue's proud nipples had been an important school tradition, with superstitious children entering the adjacent exam hall having a quick providential rub of Zita's exposed left breast. As a result of the perpetual contact of small nervous hands, the nipple nearest the hall doors had taken on an unnatural polish and had reduced significantly in size after a number of years of nervous pre exam interaction.

If only a single positive result had resulted from the entire unfortunate inquest, it was the revelation that the woman known to the gaggle of local fetish enthusiasts as the exotic and mysterious "Dirty Zita" was in fact a local girl, born with the much less exotic name of Agnes McKinstry. Zita had arrived in the local courtroom in a raincoat, travelling straight from the set of "Floods of Passion 6" to support her father during proceedings. Indeed the local paper, The Strathcarnage Porcupine, reporting on news of her father Tommy being found blameless in the loss of Cornelius's legs because of the excessive wear to a granite nipple, ran with the headline "Dirty Zita Nip Slip Trial: Small Rubbers Blamed".

In the weeks following the incident, Cornelius Templeton had begun to walk with both a real and a metaphorical spring in his step. The headmaster bounded happily around the new school grounds not only through pride and happiness at his new position of authority, but because Alex Glass the head of the school metalwork department had engineered the man two false replacement limbs. These carefully engineered legs were constructed around huge shock absorbers salvaged from the suspension of a wrecked car on the coast road donated to the school by the local TV station after appearing in a new game show. Ironically Cornelius had originally secretly imported the car from the mainland himself, using the money from his huge compensation award, but had quickly been forced to sell it on to a local family to pay off his massive drug debts after a threatening visit from the town's new debt collector, Big Jerry Bletzkoff.

Although the head of metalwork, Mr Glass had faced some initial design problems building the innovative new legs, with only Cornelius' threat to expose the teacher's hobby of hanging around lavatories in the High Street seeming to focus his brilliant engineering mind. Within a week of being threatened with Polaroid evidence of his nightly local toilet trading, Mr Glass presented the new legs to the headmaster in his office, the new headmaster sharing a celebratory drink and a cigar with the relieved teacher as a series of lurid photographs burned in his ashtray.

Cornelius had grown quickly accustomed to his new legs and was soon observed bounding around the school playground sneaking glances through first floor windows. The surprise of seeing a grinning headmaster appear behind a first floor window twenty feet above the ground was a great shock to everyone concerned, but pupils had soon grown used to the sight of the new headmaster bounding round the building, black cape flailing behind him. After years of hard drug use during which he had been convinced he could fly, Cornelius was now partially capable of the feat and enjoyed it immensely.

The Reverend Lyons had returned to the school unannounced a few months later. During a long period of recuperation following the attack, he had planned another surprise encounter to educate the heathen school pupils with his holy message. On the day he returned, sporting a long grey beard grown while in traction, Lyons had suddenly burst in to a class of third year children studying Basic Street Arithmetic. The teacher had been explaining a particularly complex problem of how to best cut drugs into concealable weights when the door had flown open to reveal the swivel eyed churchman dressed in a long red robe. He was carrying two large granite gravestones, specially carved with the Ten Commandments by local undertakers Hitchcock and Chalmers.

"I am Moses..." he had exclaimed bravely, failing to complete even the first sentence as the spring-loaded classroom door had flown straight back into his face with considerable force.

The orthopaedic specialist in the hospital said he had never witnessed a patient presenting with the number of broken bones in both feet that Reverend Lyons had enjoyed that day. Indeed the school had been forced to take an early lunch due to the inconvenience of the prolonged screaming drifting from the Arithmetic corridor, and the next morning the school's cleaning ladies bemoaned the appearance of yet more trails of bloody footprints on their clean scholastic floors.

The Strathcarnage Grammar School had begun life as a traditional education system teaching traditional subjects, the details of which were smuggled from the mainland's national curriculum. However, a number of years ago Strathcarnage town council had sent an inspector to officiate over the town's exams, but the man had never returned to the office. Law men had found the burnt out shell of the man's wagon on a quiet street in the town's shadowy quarter, but a thorough search of the surrounding area and the school itself produced no positive findings of the whereabouts of either of the official or his horses. As a result of the disappearance, and the later delivery of various body parts arriving wrapped in threatening letters, the school was now largely abandoned by the attentions of local officialdom. Free from the strictures of authority the school had taken the opportunity to embark on a new curriculum more in keeping with subjects useful to pupil's practical life in the town.

The school administration had settled upon this policy after asking children for input over their own curriculum, a decision agreed upon after some particularly nasty incidents while trying to enforce the more traditional subjects. This new negotiated course of pupil consultation had been embarked upon soon after the firebombing of the Latin teacher Mrs Stokes' house and subsequent kidnap of one Geometry and three Physics teachers and their families. Things soon settled down after successful negotiations had released the educationalists largely unharmed and the school had begun to teach again, albeit in a manner uniquely suited to Strathcarnage and its residents.

The Biology lessons were altered to incorporate some basic knowledge, with the "How to Cripple any Assailant with One Blow" and "The Naked Human Body: A Hands on Guide" classes proving extremely popular. Sex Education lessons were now taken by an assortment of the town's sexual experts, in addition to some informative and highly practical displays and exhibitions presented by the ladies of the local Pensioner's Brothel. The final examinations in the subject brought together the male and female classes to demonstrate collective practical knowledge and were carried out and marked over a period of nights in bedrooms at both the local Holliday Inn hotels. Pupils were graded on performance, presentation and technique, then passed or failed accordingly by marks submitted by both teachers and their randomly chosen partners.

English lessons dispensed with the dated prose of Shakespeare and Chaucer, instead concentrating equally on the modern prose of those writers found in the pornographic publications of which the town was awash, and the odd bestselling pulp novel left by visiting seamen. Indeed the Jackie Collins Practical exam remains one of the main core English courses still taught at the school to this day.

Arithmetic was changed to allow practical and accurate guides to debt collection and exorbitant interest calculations, drug weighing and measuring, and practical guides to betting, while history was taught solely by watching costume drama productions performed by local theatre groups and a boxed set of war movies starring Audey Murphy stolen from the below deck TV room of a visiting Danish trawler.

The chemistry curriculum was adapted to offer pupils reward in showing aptitude in the manufacturing of potent pharmaceuticals, with twenty five per cent of net sales being filtered back to the pupils through an unnumbered Swiss Bank account set up for the purpose by Lord Strathcarnage while at a child show in Geneva. Indeed the school further encouraged the career path of those keener pupils showing an aptitude for dealing through additional night classes, ensuring the entire trade was kept "in house". This themed policy continued through into the special Enforcer classes run by the Physical Recreation department, and the class had groomed a number of violent debt collectors before the whole scheme was halted after local raids investigating a number of unusual local deaths.

Geography was altered to concentrate solely on the town of Strathcarnage itself, with groups of children led around the village to examine local sights of interest. These trips often proved eventful in a town like Strathcarnage, and only recently a class of First year pupils had been fortunate enough to witness the onset of an episode of same sex pensioner erotica in a charity shop window near the town hall. Those in the geography class who graduated with high marks were keenly sought as taxi drivers in the town, providing they could recite stories and local gossip without pause for breath and owned at least one hideously patterned pullover with unidentifiable stains.

In addition to these core classes, numerous other subjects provided for pupils with special aptitudes. Metalwork pupils were put to use building S & M equipment for sale via a showroom in the local pensioner brothel, and the dark basement computer labs were home to a shadowy team of child hackers who were continually attempting to circumvent bank security codes far away on the mainland and thus increase the frequency of cash deposits in their teacher's accounts. Strathcarnage children might not have left the school with any recognised qualifications, but they were trained to be well honed criminal minds capable of outfoxing the limited local Strathcarnage detection techniques.

The school teaching staff too overflowed with characters, ensuring the establishment provided a lively entertaining atmosphere for education which virtually eliminated truancy, although the low incidence suggested by this statistic may have a root in either the woeful maths skills used to calculate numbers or in the decision to train pupils as members of special Truancy Enforcer classes. These classes would often send well trained squads of masked children to retrieve any fellow pupils missing from the day's school roll, their success rate marked routinely as part of the course. Small groups of children dressed completely in black were often seen dragging absent colleagues back to school using a combination of physical force, specially tipped sedative blow darts and threats made with savage weaponry carefully manufactured in the schools metalwork workshops.

Reverend Lyons returned once more to the school, shortly after the plaster and a number of metal pins were removed from his decimated feet. This time more careful planning had gone into his next biblical raid. The churchman had chosen a small party of third year girls to bear witness to the next unexpected biblical enactment, this time as they engaged in a swimming lesson.

Still sporting the long white beard from his now frequent stays in hospital, Lyons had burst into a swimming lesson dragging behind him a large wooden ark on wheels specially constructed for the occasion by a first year woodwork class. As he launched himself into the pool atop his wooden construction, he had began to read feverishly from the story of Noah, the churchman's bulging off centred eyes darting round the assembled girls as he preached. The demonstration was entrancing, silence falling over the group as the girls watched the churchman atop the craft bob at the edge of the pool's clear blue water.

The biblical demonstration continued without incident, until the churchman had begun to introduce the beasts he had intended to store inside his Ark to aid his sermon. The supplier of the animals for the latest re-enactment was the town pet store owner, Crazy George Ellis.

George was a good man, but had a reputation for being a little slow mentally and with a tendency towards bad planning. As it turned out, the Reverend's request for a random selection of paired beasts had provided George with a humane way to get rid of two massive and specially bred Japanese Akita fighting dogs, returned to the shop by their angry owners after they decimated and ate both a large quantity of the family home and a slow moving grandmother. Unfortunately, the canine duet was the final pair of animals that the Reverend had loaded onto the small Ark in front of the gathered pupils, having already symbolically loaded the craft with two cats, two chickens, two rats, two small sheep, two gerbils and a pair of African grey parrots.

As the Reverend had loaded the pair of canine beats and pushed his small ark away from the pool edge, all hell broke loose inside. Both dogs began decimating all other living beasts aboard the small craft, and the audience of young girls watched dumbstruck as the vessel lurched violently from side to side, the sound of grisly slaughter emanating from within its wooden bowels. As the boat rocked slowly outwards toward the pool centre, the churchman's legs had suddenly disappeared through the badly constructed ark roof. As the ark swayed onward, the captivated audience listened to the Reverend screaming as the only two surviving animals aboard continued their fatal bloodlust. Now all other bestial travelling companions were dead the trapped dogs below deck were focusing their growing terror and significant bestial violence on the soft pink flesh of Reverend's juicy legs

Just to add to the visual impact, the boat was now leaking heavily and beginning to sink.

This steady slide under the blue pool water would have been bad enough, but the blood inside the boat now began seeping through the hull, turning the pool a steadily deepening shade of pink as the gore escaped through holes in the hull to make room for the rapidly onrushing water. The unfortunate spectacle continued to the soundtrack of barking, frenzied chewing and increasingly frantic screaming. The ark now began to list heavily to one side and occasional glimpses of a bobbing head were visible to the crowd as the churchman attempted to kick at attacking jaws with whatever free leg the rabid canines weren't chewing on at the time.

Having caught one of the dogs with a lucky kick to the side of its massive head, the subsequent shift of weight had caused the construction to suddenly capsize and roll upside down. The carnage inside the boat, with a wiry drowning Noah and two frenzied fighting dogs drowning within, could only be imagined at by those unlucky enough not to have witnessed the scene firsthand. Indeed all the watching crowd of schoolgirls could now hear was the sound of loud panicked thumping on the wooden hull now mixing with continued screams, the holy man's squint eyed face only occasionally breaking the reddening water's surface.

The ambulance arrived to find a pool full of ravaged animal corpses, red water and the broken flotsam of a partially submerged wooden boat. Strathcarnage ambulance men were well accustomed to such religious episodes at the school by now, and had just looked at each other, shrugged, and dragged the small man covered in savage bite marks from the water, onto a stretcher and into the ambulance. The cleaners had gathered at the pool entrance on hearing the sirens, expecting the worst. As the Reverend was carried to the rescue vehicle, the women checked along the route. On noticing a lack of bloody footprints, they began cheerfully celebrating, dancing jigs by the poolside as the horse drawn ambulance disappeared along the coast road en route to the hospital.

Cornelius Templeton, the new headmaster, bounded past the windows of the pool on his false legs, smiling and waving at the gathering inside, stoned and quite oblivious to the latest events.

Although the specialist classes at the school were taught by local experts, new staff members were often shocked at some of the children's names. Indeed it was rare to find a class without a child called either 'Balls', 'Cock' or something infinitely worse. Indeed one form in the third year had an entire basketball team worth of children with the Christian name 'Arse'. The blame for this unusual turn of events could be laid squarely at the door of the only other local churchman in the town, Reverend Aubrey Whisp, a man whose rampant and unabashed Tourettes syndrome had ensured Strathcarnage children suffered a higher than average chance of being christened with a swear word somewhere in their name. If nothing else it ensured that the morning checking of the register was something of a comic delight.

In addition to this comedy, and the ongoing tragic-comic drama produced by the antics of the Reverend Lyons, there was another ongoing saga at the school guaranteed to cause much amusement. One of the school's Physics lecturers lay at the centre of an enduring affair causing much staff and pupil hilarity.

Owen Strain had been one of those teachers kidnapped by a hit squad of children before consultations on the new change of curriculum were forced on the school. He had suffered terribly during the ordeal, the direct result of being an

extremely boring man teaching an extremely boring subject, and had been top of the kidnapping mob's list when revolution came. Owen and his attractive wife Susan had been taken hostage by a small group of younger kidnappers and had been taken to an unknown location where the pair were due to be held until the education board agreed to demands for an overhaul of the school timetable.

In Owen Strain's case this kidnap snatch squad had turned out to be little more than a splinter group of the larger cause, demanding written confirmation from the authorities that all pupils could both smoke and do light recreational drugs in an attempt to stay awake during the man's frequently tedious science lessons. During their lengthy kidnap, events were to unfold which were destined to create a great deal of amusement for school staff and pupils for years to come.

During the three-week ordeal, a bound Mrs Susan Strain had grown emotionally attached to one of the kidnappers, an athletic fifteen-year-old called Alan Grindall. Later, in counselling, Owen had been assured his wife's behaviour was perfectly natural behaviour for captives, but experts had later confessed to the distraught teacher that even allowing for such an attachment to form during the ordeal itself, it was unusual for the kidnapper to move into the victim's house and co-habit with his wife while her husband and his possessions were thrown out on the streets. The seeds had been sown for an ongoing series of highly entertaining incidents in the school's daily activities.

When Owen Strain returned to the school, the sight of his wife's grinning new live-in partner was too much for the teacher to bear. During the first assembly at the school after the incident, Owen had snapped during the daily rendition of the school hymn. To the organ accompaniment of Old Mrs Browning, the entire hall were singing "Pretty Vacant" by The Sex Pistols, just at the point Owen caught sight of his wife's new boyfriend. Alan was walking into the hall dressed in one of his old favourite suits and sporting a neck ringed in love bites.

Owen had launched himself off the stage at the sight, throwing himself through the parting mass of children towards Alan, who was making his way towards a group of friends in the very middle of the hall. After chasing the boy through the crowds, a violent brawl ensued, pupils cheering Alan quite vocally as a few teachers on the stage shouted support for their colleague. The two were eventually pulled apart by the huge frame of Mr Grimes the gamesmaster and led away to different parts of the school to be questioned about their behaviour. Both were reprimanded and asked to pledge to no more fighting on school premises. A truce seemed to have been agreed and there were no more incidents between the pair. Not, at least, for a while.

During a music lesson some weeks later, Owen Strain had found himself called upon at short notice to cover a class since the regular teacher, a Miss Clancy, was on a considerable run of winners at the local betting shop and still at home waiting on some results from the afternoon card. Owen filled in and, in an almost inevitable twist of fate, again found himself thrown face to face with Alan.

The teacher at first seemed to be manfully ignoring the presence of his young nemesis and had carried on the lesson with a broad carefree smile. He even asked Alan to hand out some sheet music to the rest of the class with a grin. A relieved Alan took the large sheaf of papers and began to distribute them amongst fellow pupils. The pupil was glad that Owen seemed to be dealing the disappointment of the whole affair and the young pupil looked forward a return to quiet normality living with the teacher's young wife.

It was his 'looking forward' that proved to be the younger man's problem, since he didn't see the figure of Owen Strain barrelling toward him from behind, an acoustic guitar raised high above his head.

The initial blow had been a huge surprise to Alan, however the acoustic guitar had been flimsy and injury had been minimal. With the smashed remains of the guitar still hanging from round his neck, and surrounded in a halo of plywood, another violent wrestling match had commenced between the men.

This time, Alan was coming off best as it was broken up; having subdued his older assailant with blows from a set of African maracas grabbed as the teacher had repeatedly tried to jam the younger man's fingers under the snapping piano lid. The incident led to Owen Strain receiving another verbal warning from the headmaster. However given the school head's well documented hatred for children and the lingering effects of a strong cannabis resin presented to him by the first year chemistry class prior to the meeting, this latest incident was quickly forgotten.

The battles between the pair continued unabated, and for a number of months it remained a strong possibility that any lunch break or lesson might be interrupted at any moment by a wild-eyed teacher launching an attack on the unsuspecting pupil. It also should be noted however that Alan was not entirely an innocent party in events, having entered particularly graphic naked photographs of the Owen Strain's wife to the school magazine before proceeding to have them printed onto a series of tee-shirts by a third year art class and subsequently sold around the school. The popularity of the shirt was such that it was now rare for Owen Strain to attend a lesson without having to stare at his exposed naked wife emblazoned on the chest of the children in front of him.

Life at Strathcarnage Grammar school continued in this familiar pattern for a number of months, with the school's daily routine only broken by a couple of police raids: one to break up a prostitution ring being run by second year pimps in the playground during lunchtimes, and one to recover a large cache of explosives manufactured by a group of more liberated girls operating in the school chemistry labs, ironically planning a revenge attack on the first group. This period of calm was not to last however, as Reverend Lyons was once again released from hospital to continue the Lord's good work.

The churchman's next major incident of note began during a school assembly. There had been strong rumour of a fresh encounter between Owen and Alan during a specially planned welcome assembly for the proposed intake of some troubled children to the school, an interim measure after their own special school was recently demolished to make way for a new old folks home crematorium hybrid. However the gathering was almost over and had passed totally without incident, the only event of note having occurred during one of the wheelchair races organised by the current pupils to welcome the new intake.

The woodwork department had organised a large wheelchair racetrack running round the entire hall. The measure was intended as a spectacular greeting for the new pupils, the track banked steeply around the hall sides very much like a bobsleigh run. The sharp incline of the hall meant the visitor's wheelchairs had been reaching great speeds on the corner sections, nicknamed somewhat unkindly Intensive Care Bend. This steep plywood corner of track was to be the catalyst for the further events of the day.

During one of the semi final heats, one of the wheelchairs had misjudged its entry to Intensive Care Bend and both chair and passenger had left the track, turned through three hundred and sixty degrees midair and had smashed through one of the large glass windows of the assembly hall.

As the pupils ran to the windows to survey the anticipated damage, the crowd noticed the unmistakable returning figure of Reverend Lyons at the far end of the school football pitch, just inside the bared wire perimeter fence. The churchman was moving slowly across the muddy field far in the distance, dressed in white loin cloth and dragging a huge twenty-foot high wooden cross towards a post hole dug he had specially prepared earlier that morning.

The religious educator was planning his most powerful and symbolic act yet. With the help of some grinning cleaning ladies, he was about to crucify himself in full view of the school.

As the pupils slowly filed out the hall towards the scene, barely noticing the twisted wreckage of a quickly forgotten wheelchair and still unconscious occupant, a crowd soon grew around the loin-clothed figure of Reverend Lyons. The man of cloth smiled as he saw the multitude moving towards him, content in the knowledge that he really would get his message across to the maximum audience. It was, he mused, a piece of tactical religious brilliance.

As the cleaning ladies had begun hammering the nails into his hands, the Reverend had reminded the beaming women through screams that they had earlier agreed to symbolically tie him to the cross, but the cheerful smiles of the well-muscled and grinning group swinging hammers told him his protests were in vain.

Unable to see what exactly was causing this fresh commotion in his school, Cornelius Templeton the school headmaster was unable to find sufficient open ground in the gathering on which to work up enough momentum to best utilise his spring-loaded false limbs. He had been forced to take a longer route around the side of the school to reach the cause of the sudden crowd, pausing momentarily to watch as an irate Owen Strain attempted to take advantage of the lack of witnesses to wrap the wreckage of the crashed racing wheelchair round his nemesis Alan Grindall's head, the young boy dancing around the flailing man and keeping just out of range while pointing repeatedly to the front of his tee-shirt and goading the teaching man further.

When Cornelius Templeton realised the subject of interest on in the school playing fields, he decided he must put a stop to the religious re-enactment. He could hear loud screaming from the far end of the field, the result of the cleaning women continuing to hammer multiple nails into the outstretched hands, having quietly decided amongst themselves that it was best to ensure the churchman was unable to trail dirt through the school after this particular enactment. As the women began to raise the cross holding Reverend Lyons into the muddy post hole, Cornelius made the unfortunate decision to bounce down the field past the cheering children to put a stop to this sick spectacle.

The headmaster was travelling at pace, with his legs carrying him rapidly around the edges of the crowd as he bounded along. Then he hit the thick clinging mud of the field drain.

Cornelius Templeton found himself embedded in the mud, quite unable to move. His attempts to force himself out of the mud had the comical effect of making him lurch back and forth on the flexible axis of his sprung legs like a huge child's newly released Jack in The Box figure. It was a comedic sight and one not lost on the assembled crowd, who stopped watching the ongoing crucifixion to admire the headmaster swinging violently to and fro in the filth, his black cape flapping around his vacillating body.

Cornelius knew he somehow had to free himself and stop this religious madness, and after steadying himself in an upright position, began to try and pull his legs free from the mire. The headmaster decided the best way to achieve release was to repeatedly push his body weight up and down on the false legs until the momentum of the springs built up enough power to lift his whole frame out of the thick mud and toward the crucified man of the cloth.

As Cornelius rebounded his weight with repeated ferocity, the headmaster felt the pressure in the springs build under him. He began to throw himself even more violently onto the metal coils, like a human jackhammer building up energy to pull himself free. His attempt might have worked, had the couplings holding the springs not given way, the metal weakened by the huge heat generated by the headmaster's actions.

With a loud bang, both couplings snapped and the springs exploded loose from the fragile plastic of the buckled false legs, the lower limbs too made pliable by the heat produced by the continual friction. As the devices gave way, a loud gasp ran through the crowd as Cornelius Templeton was propelled skywards, thrown upward with enormous force by the large springs. From his elevated position on the cross Reverend Lyons watched silently as the headmaster flew upwards in a wide arc across his line of vision, launched like a rocket from his sprung base.

With a whole open field to use for landing, it was only the sickest of ironies that saw the black caped headmaster falling inexorably toward the new school's own electric substation. As Cornelius hit the buzzing metal structure behind the fence, there came an ear-splitting bang as his two metal springs made contact with the live metal coils on the building's roof.

The massive surge of power had caused the headmasters hair to instantly straighten as the huge current had lit his black nylon cape like a firework. The massive surge of electricity had seen the man's scorched face almost immediately turn the same colour as his black cape. Children stood in open mouthed with awe as the unfortunate headmaster was again propelled skyward by the colossal blast, this time aflame and now heading downward, straight for the crucified Reverend

Lyons.

Cornelius was travelling at such huge velocity that when he had hit the crucifix his impact had managed to instantly uproot the wooden structure from the ground. As the huge wooden cross fell backwards through the school perimeter fence, it took on a toboggan like quality, careering down the steep hill around the school site with the scorched face of the headmaster and the religious zealot clutched together side by side.

The huge wooden religious structure carrying the two men built up great momentum on the journey down the grassy slope, the still flaming gown of the headmaster giving the religious prop the appearance of some huge holy firework as the billowing black smoke plumed outward behind it on its path. The gathering impetus of the steep slope carried the loaded crucifix straight down the hill, over the small grassy bank of a drainage ditch, propelling the cross upward before coming to rest finally in the middle of the main road from the docks.

Both heads turned in unison as the smoking cross halted on the hard tarmac, just in time to see the onrushing flash of the hoofs of a team of six colossal black horses, the galloping beasts whipped into a frenzy as they were driven along behind the shocked face of a driver quite unable to change the path of either the beasts or the massive speeding wagon behind. A wagon ironically packed with five tonnes of donated bibles, ordered by Reverend Lyons for use in the school and freshly delivered off a boat from Germany.

Not a stomach among the watching crowd was able to stand the sight of the gruesome, yet highly paradoxical impact.

It was a graphic illustration of the power of the word of God and even more spectacular than anything Reverend Bentley Lyons himself had yet managed. As the embracing pair of mangled bodies was trampled by the massive horses, a number of children looked skyward and crossed themselves.

Reverend Bentley Lyons (School Chaplin and Biblical Re-enactor) 1899-1978
Cornelius Templeton (Sprung Headmaster) 1923-1978

## CHAPTER 14

## Day Twelve – The Mau Chang Fighters

The queue snaked along the snow-covered path outside the Church Hall, the bodies hugged close to the wall of the building to avoid the blizzard conditions. The well wrapped souls waited, a long line extending out into the frosty darkness, twisting and turning like the body of a huge tweed covered snake along the road curving round the town green. Given the high proportion of the Strathcarnage pensioners in the massed throng however, the snake in question would most likely have been an arthritic and asthmatic cobra with the familiar eye-watering odour of biscuits and stale urine.

The Reverend Aubrey Whisp wiped his wrinkled leathery hand across the condensation on the window inside the church hall, smiling at the size of the crowd outside. Turning away from the scene, he walked across the room with a thin self congratulatory smile, pausing only to exchange greetings with a selection of wheelchair bound parishioners from the local hospice. The churchman quickly glanced along the assembled line and picked the jacket best suited to the drying of a moist ecclesiastical hand, before moving towards him and sympathetically rubbing his palm on the man's back. The Lord's moisture is with you, my child.

The line outside was growing increasingly restless in the bitter cold. All of the publicity material displayed around the town had stated clearly that doors were due to open at seven, and many in the line had been queuing since lunchtime hoping to secure the best seats nearest the action. Some of the real hardcore fans had waited overnight. This was, after all, the end of season finale: the big one.

The shivering masses shuffled from foot to foot, quite unaware of that the sole reason for the delay was Reverend Whisp. The cunning churchman had slipped a quantity of cash to the organisers in return for this delay in opening the hall. The crowd outside was slowly drifting from the poor cash returns of mild inconvenience to a more profitable bounty promised by borderline hypothermia. Whisp was an astute man and had calculated that every minute of delay in opening the church hall doors in the bitter cold night would greatly increase the projected profits of his hyper inflated hot refreshments booth sited just inside the entrance doors. The positioning of the stall and the delay in opening were no lucky accident.

This hot beverage based profiteering idea had come to Whisp partially through necessity. As he had stood in the local bookmakers the previous week and watched the substantial church collection disappear during a close run Strathcarnage wheelchair derby, the churchman again realised he was falling victim to his intense gambling addiction. Whisp's choice, a heavily backed favourite, had fallen heavily at the second cobbled turn into the town market square. However, as fate would have it, the winner's name had proved an inspiration. Peter Coffee had run home to win the race by three clear wheel lengths, leaving the collection plates empty for another week but inspiring Reverend Whisp to muse over a very profitable catering ruse.

Whisp was jerked back into reality by the ringing of a specially concealed phone in the pulpit. Interruptions to services heightened during the summer months, directly related to the increase in Whisp's betting on child shows, but occasionally local sporting updates could also be relied upon to spice up even a winter sermon. It was not uncommon for a bible reading to be halted only for the congregation to be informed loudly of a rundown of the latest scores. More often than not this was usually followed by a barrage of frustrated swearing.

Indeed, the Reverend's legendary halting of a funeral to declare "Strathcarnage Smugglers up two nil. Great. Hairy. Balls." was cited by many of the congregation as one of the favourite Whisp moments. Since no one in the town was overly keen to confront a Tourettes sufferer with a violent temper, raising the matter with the churchman was a never an option.

On this occasion the phone call was from a member of the hall staff informing Reverend Whisp that the main doors had now been opened because of 'safety concerns'. The crowd was already pushing into the hall out of the bitter blizzard. The 'safety concerns', it seemed, were directly related to the incidence of a waiting crowd member setting himself ablaze in what many assumed was a protest at the prolonged delay.

It emerged later that the human inferno was 'Shaky' John Stevens, a local petrol station attendant and long-term sufferer of a rare muscular condition picked up in the town's genetic engineering laboratory where he had previously worked. It was an undiagnosed condition the most notable symptom of which was having his arms shake in a most uncontrollable manner. Owing to the unsteady nature of his handling abilities in the workplace, Stevens was permanently followed by a strong aroma of petrol. His decision to attend tonight's event direct from work, coupled with his decision to risk a quick cigar to warm his hands while queuing in the bitter cold, had resulted in the sudden ignition of the vibrating armed man's outer layer of work clothing.

It was testament to the desperation of the waiting crowd to retain their position in line that those around Shaky had merely kicked the flaming man to the snowy ground and rolled him away from the line's immediate vicinity with their feet, before trying do what they could to extinguish the man with kicked slush while remaining in jealously guarded positions near the front of the queue.

In a further footnote bearing testament to the importance of the event, a lightly smouldering 'Shaky' Stevens had still managed to attend the event, cursing under his breath at having a seat far from the action while spilling quantities of overpriced hot beverages over his black scorched hands.

At the moment, however, the first of the crowd were still surging forward into the hall. Some queued to leave outdoor attire in the cloakroom before rushing into the hall to grab the best seats, a good few frozen souls stopping to buy warm drinks from Reverend Whisp's stall. The seats filled quickly with locals clutching cups of weak tea, the crowd growing steadily, seated under a large gaudy banner describing the special night's proceedings.

The banner read, in bright golden letters on a blue background, 'Third Annual Mau Chang Championships – Colostomy and Drainage bag Fighting: Finals Night."

As Reverend Whisp merrily served overpriced drinks to hypothermic locals from under a similar banner hung just inside the doors, his beady blue eye was drawn to the lengthy queue at the cloakroom and he cursed himself for missing an opportunity to further line his ecumenical pockets.

The history leading up to the night's event is an interesting saga in itself. This tale may be useful to relate, since context helps illustrate the extraordinary fervour of the crowd for such an unusual event, a strange occasion even by the slightly tainted and bizarre values of Strathcarnage.

The entire event had its roots in the travel experiences of a local man, Randolph Braden, who had returned from his annual trip to Bangkok many years ago laden down with his usual armfuls of pornography, drugs and cheap cigarettes. This time however his souvenirs included a lithe young Thai boy by the name Gunter. It was the nubile young tourist trinket who would prove the key to explaining current events.

Gunter was an eager, dark-skinned, adolescent beauty with a lazy eye and few words of English worthy of mention, a native Thai whom the man had smuggled home in his trunk as a souvenir of the trip which had ended a few days before. Tonight was the young boy's first outing in the town.

Randolph Braden was giving his annual lecture and an accompanying slideshow of his yearly expedition to a crowd of interested townsfolk at Haversack Hall. The show, a popular town event, had gone without a hitch until Braden dimmed the lights and began his slideshow lecture. Suddenly, among the pictures of naked flesh and local sights, a strange sight appeared onscreen. On the brightly lit display an unusual slide appeared, the image showing two heavily built and tattooed Thai men in a boxing ring swinging small bags at each other in some sort of rudimentary combat ritual.

Normally the unusual image would have passed unnoticed amongst the other sights promised by the evening's lecturing, a single image lost amongst the more traditional mountain of copulation close-ups, genital detail and the other perverse delights. However when the image had appeared there had been a sudden loud cry of "Stop" from the rear of the packed smoky hall. The unexpected cry had come from a local man known simply to the townsfolk as 'The Major'.

The room fell silent as The Major rose and paced slowly and deliberately from his position toward the back of the hall down the central aisle towards the screen. Leaving a large shadow of himself on the lit screen as he advanced closer, the tweed clad Major stared upward at the image, his journey watched by the impatient assembled collection of Strathcarnage deviants and perverts packed into the dark building.

"This image is simply incredible, Randolph. Quite, quite incredible."

A murmur went round the room, mostly from those disgruntled audience members angered by the ongoing delay to the display of Thai genetalia. A few of the restless crowd were also annoyed at the subsequent delay to the promised presentation of young Gunter and his well proportioned Thai frame. The Major paced in front of the screen ignoring the atmosphere of dissent, studying the image as closely as possible, occasionally pausing to reposition his monocle.

"Utterly unbelievable," muttered the clearly moved greying man, the statements of disbelief aired mostly for his own benefit.

Eventually, one of those audience members keenest to continue with cavalcade of perversion had plucked up the courage to pointedly enquire of the elderly man what "all the bloody fuss was about". The Major turned to the crowd, cleared his throat, removed his now steamed up monocle and began to explain.

"Gentlemen, what we see before us might, to the uninitiated eye, look like some rudimentary tribal combat scene. In many ways, I suppose that's exactly what it is. But gentlemen, what we see here before us tonight, captured on Randolph Braden's travels, is what I believe to be the first, and to my knowledge the only, existing photographic image of a group of men so secretive and so elusive that they have never been witnessed by Western eyes until this very moment."

He turned again to the screen and again shook his head slowly and unbelievingly, totally ignoring the shadow of a random hand caught in the light and making a familiar rhythmic sign to indicate the opinion that the old man was a self abuser of some note.

"Gentlemen, I give you The Piss fighters of Mau Chang."

The audience in the hall looked around at each other distinctly unimpressed. Save from some nondescript grunts and confused murmuring, the assembly remained largely silent. The Major nodded slowly as he recognised the uneasy atmosphere in the room and quickly embarked on explaining in far greater detail why the image had caused him so much excitement.

The Major was a gifted orator and in a matter of minutes, the crowd were transported through an animated and passionately related history of the lost discipline of piss fighting, ritual genital manipulation and the dedication and skill involved therein. Such was the power of the Major's storytelling gift that within minutes the gentleman in the monocle stood before a packed hall of new bright eyed devotees, desperate to know more and to inundate The Major with questions.

Young Gunter had missed almost all of the performance. When the Major had initially uttered the words 'Mau Chang', the young lad had spun around, broken from his harness and ran toward the front of the gathering brandishing his genitals with a cupped hand. Gunter appeared to have taken the utterance of the Thai name as some sort of signal and had sprinted to the hall front only to turn and deposit a jet of urine across the first few members of the front row. The small boy was still in mid-stream as he was knocked unconscious by a swift but vicious blow from Randolph Braden's heavy walking stick.

The Major talked on well into the night, recounting legends of Mau Chang heroes. It was a credit to the man's verbal skills and his deftness of storytelling that only one audience member left his seat during this entire time. That solitary disturbance came from Randolph Braden, his brief movement serving only to allow another swift swing of his cane to stun Gunter when the boy began to stir and look like he may have recovered some degree of consciousness.

The crowd filed out the hall into the darkness many hours later once the Major had finished speaking, the departing crowd talking excitedly amongst themselves as they descended the hall's wide stone steps to began crunching down the long steep gravel driveway toward the distant lights of their homes. Not only had The Major given the men a fascinating glimpse into the Mau Chang piss fighting legend, he had engendered the village with a whole new passion. The Major had delivered a gift to Strathcarnage, almost twenty years to the day since his secretive arrival in the village.

The Major's real name was Mellor Applewhite and he had long ago served as a highly decorated Major of the British Army. However the Major had sustained hideous wounds serving his country, not in the thick of battlefield action as one would expect, but during a particularly gruesome bout of diarrhoea.

A wayward German fifty-pound shell had landed right next to the battlefield latrines, only seconds after a distressed Major had hurried to dispose of a fresh torrent of liquid illness. The subsequent explosion had reduced the entire wooden hut to a mass of splinters in an instant and propelled the entire configuration skyward. The Major, still clinging to the stained porcelain throne with the white knuckles necessitated by the horrific cramps signalling the start of his brown tsunami, had found himself thrown airborne.

Military onlookers had described events as appalling; with one soldier noting that The Major had taken to the sky above the battlefield like a liquid firework, spiralling upwards just as his bowels released their filthy cargo. Such situations, however tragic, tend often to have a tiny glimpse of a silver lining. In this case the gilded beacon of positivism was twofold.

Firstly, although the initial explosion had been substantial, it had not proved fatal due to the white enamel throne protecting The Major from the most devastating of injuries, although this initial good fortune does nothing to detract from the greater physical danger from airborne catapulting. The second positive was the precise location of the explosion, the detonation occurring in a water filled trench running alongside the main supply route. The quantity of wet dirty mud displaced skyward by such a huge blast ensured that many witnesses were blissfully unaware that the subsequent shower of brown fallout they endured was not solely the product of displaced wet earth.

In a terrible irony of Wartime life, the cause of the Major's horrific injuries had little to do with the initial blast, but from his unfortunate landing, bottom first, on the sharpened wooden stake supporting a scarecrow in an adjacent field.

After the emergency services had extracted the thick wooden shaft from the ground and taken the whole construction, complete with the still attached army man, to a field hospital, it had been discovered that the Major had severe internal wounding. Although not immediately life threatening, the massive internal injuries from the impalement meant The Major was destined to wear a pair of rudimentary bags to catch his internal waste products. The proud soldier was now quite unable to have such internal commodities processed naturally by his bodies profoundly ravaged pipe work.

The Major was returned back home to recuperate and then medically discharged from the Army altogether. Unable to face the humiliation of his new disablement in his hometown, the proud man had decided upon a life of travelling. It was this nomadic wandering which would see the Major Mellor Applewhite secretly delivered to Strathcarnage and to subsequently play such a huge role in creating another of the numerous extraordinary town legends.

The ever-unshakable locals of Strathcarnage had welcomed the Major's initial appearance in their town, hearing rumours of the unfortunate man's career as a war hero and tactfully ignoring the steadily gurgling additions to the rudimentary fluid bags hanging on his legs. The major soon felt relaxed and at home in the town and was adopted by that small section of Strathcarnage residents the town could claim as its own high society.

Initially, after arriving in the town smuggled by fishing boat, The Major had been hugely self-conscious of his dual waste collection bags. However, as the local population had showed little interest in his burbling hip accessories, he grew steadily in confidence. The army man slowly grew to take a perverse pride in his twin appendages, often forgetting they existed at all until his attention was drawn by the putrid smell and the wetness of his upper legs.

The bags marked The Major as unique and different, ensuring that everyone in the town knew the man by reputation, without any need for difficult and uncomfortable introductions and explanations. The Major grew to view his twin bags as campaign medals of a sort, proud badges of battlefield honour. His new home offered the army man the added confidence to display his waste bags without the previous guilt and crippling self-awareness he had felt constantly. It had been a constant pain felt on everyday occasions, not merely on the odd clandestine visit to church or an embarrassing appearance in military remembrance parades. In his new home he had found a previously unknown pride in his situation. Even so, on occasion he sometimes grew tired of the sight and sound of them, intensely jealous of other military men's capacity to unpin their decorations and place them out of sight in a drawer.

It was this confusion of pride and embarrassment at his twin reminders of service, combined with his dogged determination to lead a normal life that would lead the Major to an unusual discovery. This bizarre revelation was one which would lead directly to his glorious speech in Haversack Hall, and to all subsequent events in our story.

On his arrival in the village the homeless Major had immediately visited and taken up residence with the new Lord Strathcarnage, the military man having received a hand delivered invite on the dockside inviting him to the family seat of Haversack Hall. When the Major had decided on a life of travel he had sent word of his plans to Lord Strathcarnage, since the historical and military Strathcarnage family and The Major's second cousin, Lord Otis Clamshawe, were distantly related and had often assisted each other out in times of need during family crises. The Major knew Lord Strathcarnage distantly, having helped out with preparations and child entrapment for a couple of the child shows held at the Hall.

The military man's residence at Haversack Hall had proved eventful from the very beginning. Upon The Major's initial arrival at the Hall, Lord Strathcarnage had observed family convention and assembled the entire staff of the house to welcome the new houseguest. The Major had just undergone a lengthy and rough sea journey from southern England and had arrived at Hall along the driveway tired and pretty shaky on his feet. The military man was drunk, having partaken heavily in ship brewed beer while swapping tales with the crew of the small boat carrying him secretly to the village. It was this heavy intake of ship's ale that was later held responsible for those legendary events of his arrival.

Lord Strathcarnage had instructed his staff, on fear of sound and violent beatings, not to stare at The Major's dangling bodily deposit bags, educating the gathering in the facts of that the appendages being a result of The Major's heroic war deeds. When The Major lurched unsteadily into Haversack Hall on his arrival, although the gathered staff noticed that both khaki clad legs were adorned with balloon like swellings now generously leaking foul smelling fluids down his legs, no-one spoke a word. Such was the fierce reputation of Lord Strathcarnage that none of them gave the smallest indication the sight was anything out of the normal.

The reason for the swollen overflowing nature of the bags lay in the simple fact that the dual bagged drainage system was still of the most basic type, medical science having yet to perfect the process to the discreet level of today's modern medicine. As The Major stood unsteadily before the staff line, those staff risking a surreptitious glance could make out the twin pig bladders and sewn in rubber drainage tubes attached to his legs.

Normally even this rudimentary paraphernalia remained unobtrusive. However the combination of the boat trip and the long bumpy carriage journey up the long hill to Haversack Hall had combined with the vast quantities of gassy beer. This had the effect of swelling both of the Major's pigskin bags with both fermented air and waste products. The twin bags now looked like children's party balloons, stretched so thin by the expanding contents that all present were aware of the treacherous volume of the sloshing contents therein.

The Major, having had extensive sections of his internal plumbing removed and redirected, remained blissfully unaware of any feeling of having to urinate or defecate since all such functions were now dependant solely on gravity. While this was a benefit to a man lacking the internal operational capacity to perform such tasks for himself, it also led to a lack of awareness that he was well past the point where he desperately needed emptying.

As The Major weaved slowly along the line of staff, shaking hands and smiling, many present describe the accompanying sound coming from bags on the man's legs as akin to a draining sink. All may yet have gone well had The Major not halted to quiz the Hall's Gamekeeper about the opportunities available around the town for hunting and fishing. During his animated conversation, the Major had forgotten himself and attempted to re-enact his favoured casting motion with an imaginary rod.

The sudden motion and violent twisting of the older man's torso had caused a sudden breach in both the overstretched bladders hanging on the Major's flanks. With a single detonation akin to that of a discharged shotgun, the contents of both fermenting bags of bodily waste ruptured with explosive force, showering the entire assemblage with a fecund mixture of preheated waste products.

In among the sounds of dry heaving from those standing motionless in fear on the now sodden line, there stood a perfectly clean Major, his ruined bladders limp against his side, dripping the few remaining abdominal juices over the expensive buffalo skin rug in the grand entrance Hall.

As the retching assemblage was dismissed by a wave of the hand from the saturated Lord Strathcarnage, the two men stood in the hall exchanging small talk surrounded by a scene of utter filth. There was complete silence in the long wood panelled room, the quiet broken only by hysterical laughter drifting down from the top of the grand wooden staircase. The frenzied hilarity emanated from a deeply wrinkled old woman dressed in black lace ball gown and sitting atop an oversized wooden go-kart.

The frantic hilarity was clearly borne of someone who had witnessed the whole sorry scene unfold below but who had herself failed to be within range of the detonating wall of liquid debris.

As the men gazed up the staircase towards the figure now rocking uncontrollably with laughter, Lord Strathcarnage wiped the remains of what closely resembled, but unfortunately wasn't, a large cigar from his face and with polite formality announced, "Major, I'd like to introduce to you my Great Aunt Agnes."

It was to prove a monumental meeting.

It had taken a later visit from the local doctor to prescribe old Agnes Strathcarnage with sufficient sedation to get her to stop laughing at the incident. Once she had woken, The Major had made a point of finding Agnes. He had both respect and admiration for the fragile, spirited old woman's ability to laugh at the scene of such faecal devastation. She was his type of woman. The elderly Great Aunt of Lord Strathcarnage had found a kindred spirit in The Major and the pair soon began chatting amicably.

Agnes Strathcarnage grew fond of the Major almost immediately. The older man had served his time in the army solving engineering problems and inventing new and more efficient ways of killing men. This job description appealed to Agnes since she was also a keen amateur inventor with a murderous streak for servants, though recently she had concentrated mostly on finding clever and innovative methods of moving her ravaged arthritic frame around the huge Hall. The Major was the only person in the house who did not seem to grow frustrated at her incessant industrial strength swearing, continual engineering conversations and persistent attempts at escape.

Most of the Hall's staff ignored Aunt Agnes. Many were actively encouraged to do so by her frustrated nephew, who himself had grown tired of her continual eccentric behaviour and who was well aware of her reputation. Indeed, in order that he might continue to live without the embarrassment of an aged relative who swore like a dock worker, rolled her own cigarettes and frequently threatened the entire fabric of the ancient Hall with structural damage, Lord Strathcarnage had confined the woman to the oldest section of the home's vast top floor. Agnes was restricted to the East Wing of the hall, given free run of a space that he or the servants rarely visited.

This new opportunity for friendship and companionship saw the lonely Agnes soon form a close bond with the Major; he patiently answering her engineering questions, she talking him through various contraptions and ideas for machines. The ingenuity, technical thinking and violence involved in the numerous inventions the old woman detailed impressed the Major. The engineering man had even pronounced her self-constructed wooden cart "a work of partial genius". Agnes had built the machine around her own body after smashing up an antique French writing desk and a small leather armchair, reconstructing the broken wood around her body to build a wheeled cart. The creation enabled Agnes increased mobility around the huge upstairs rooms and long halls at far greater speed and with much less effort than her now dismantled wheelchair. She could now, she observed, both catch and mow down any servants she found in her upstairs lair with much greater efficiency.

It was the invention of this very cart that was to directly lead The Major to become involved with the Legend of the Piss fighters of Mau Chang.

Agnes had quickly built her rudimentary wooden transport from smashed furniture, crawling around dragging the larger pieces across her room before nailing them together around her body. Only when her project was finished was the old woman to realise that she was unable to wheel the great broad wooden machine through the door frames of the East Wing's lavatories. Desperation saw the old woman smash drainage holes beneath her body with a small hammer as a temporary measure and she set to work immediately investigating more practical options, researching both the Hall's library and her own delivered copies of "Inventing Monthly".

Agnes had spent long days researching her dilemma, eventually happening upon a unique solution.

While investigating a volume on waste gathering and disposal, Agnes had happened upon an essay from an eccentric American inventor working with a new substance called 'plastic' to safely pack food. She had exchanged correspondence with the inventor and the young American gentleman had supplied Agnes with some basic advice and raw materials.

These gifts, combined with her own vast inventiveness, soon lead Agnes to construct for herself an automated collecting, packing and disposal system for her body waste, carefully built and then hidden deep within her mobile wooden base. The old lady was often observed by sprinting staff red faced and straining out body waste. This effort was then followed by a strange collection of mechanical noises from deep inside her cart, before a sudden plume of flames flashed from the vehicle's rear. Agnes would look up smiling and turn her vehicle away noisily down the long wooden corridors, leaving a sealed clear plastic package of waste to drop harmlessly from a trapdoor under the machine onto the polished floor.

The Major was amazed at demonstration of the machine's abilities and had asked to see the invention's workings, realising the new plastic storage system might somehow be adaptable to help the ravaged man build sturdier bags and avoid a repeat of the explosive performance on his arrival.

Agnes had agreed, promising to share those articles studied during her research that might be of further interest to the Major. She agreed too to help him build stronger and less obtrusive bags for his bodily waste. But there was a catch. Not surprisingly given the elderly cunning of Agnes, these might be better described as a series of conditions on which the Major had to agree to before Agnes would help him.

These stipulations saw the Major agreeing to help Agnes both design and construct a sturdier metal bodied cart, strong enough to be driven by a small steam turbine, to show her how to maim and kill a man using only an antique clock and finally, to promise to stay in lifelong contact as her friend. These were the conditions placed on her deal and with broad smiles of agreement the pair gladly shook hands on the contract.

Within a few short weeks Agnes found herself inside the gleaming metal frame of her new construction, lowered into the interior on a pulley manned by the Major and now sitting ready to be welded inside the machine. Agnes smiled contentedly as she stroked the curves of the beautiful silver creation, the new vehicle fully powered by a steam turbine built and carefully mounted by her friend. The Major had helped design and assemble almost every part of the contraption. Everything, that is, excepting Agnes's own newly improved waste disposal device, the invention hidden deep within the bowels of the gleaming machine. The ever suspicious Agnes kept that mechanism a closely guarded secret, afraid The Major might steal the ideas within and leave her before completing construction of the rest of the machine.

Initial testing proved the new invention to be an unmitigated success. Indeed the only minor adjustments required were to Agnes's own improved waste disposal system; since during testing the new steam powered device had fired the wrapped packets of bodily waste at such great pace that they were potentially fatal.

The only other overlooked flaw was the increased weight of the vehicle. The device required eight male staff members to carry her machine down the huge staircase of Haversack Hall to allow Agnes daily access to the wide-open spaces of the grounds to undertake full trials. Lord Strathcarnage had happily agreed to the new outdoor visits on noting a vast improvement in both his elderly relative's violent behaviour towards the Hall staff and a notable downturn in her swearing.

The Major watched on misty eyed from an upstairs window as the old lady fully opened the throttle on the contraption, the pull of her wrinkled hand on the red lever sending the silver vehicle steaming majestically across the grounds, firing sealed plastic bags of excitement induced faecal waste in high arcs above the lawns like a rocket launcher. The vehicle was a resounding success while tearing across the flat green gardens and a delighted Agnes had vowed to reveal her secrets to The Major the minute she had ended her run.

Agnes ended her trials around the grounds early, having accidentally concussed Kwok, one of the home's senior staff, with a launched bag of urine as he pruned Lord Strathcarnage's rose beds. While she was being carried up the wide wooden hall stairs back to her upstairs lair, Agnes shouted to The Major that she was ready to reveal her secrets.

The old woman steamed off noisily along the hall before turning to mount her specially built ramp up the few stairs to the library, where she had arranged to meet The Major for their discussions. Agnes pushed the lever forwards to turn her machine off and waited for the humming turbine to fall silent before removing her leather helmet and goggles ready to address her visibly excited inventing companion.

"Major, these past few weeks, you have helped me in many more ways than I can ever express sufficient gratitude for. So now, as I promised, I have something to show you. I present you with a gift, from me to you. On top of the table behind you, you will find full instructions to enable you to construct special sealed plastic bags for retention of your waste products. You will also find a slim hand printed volume, which I took the liberty to acquire from a dealer in rare books. In it you will find the details of a secret sect in Thailand, written many years ago by the explorer Chinning Park. So far as I am aware, it is the only copy still in existence anywhere in the world. I gift it to you in the hope it may inspire you to great things with your condition. Major, you're a gentleman and a complete shithawk."

The Major began to feel hot tears run down his face for the first time since his anal interaction with the scarecrow. The army man noticed that Agnes also looked close to tears and placed a comforting hand on her thin arm but old lady had quickly regained her usual look of calmness, breathing out deeply before she spoke.

"Major, I hate to correct you, but I wasn't growing overly emotional, I was squeezing out another piss."

At that, her machine again coughed into life with a sudden cloud of steam, and accompanied by a plume of darting flame fired the sealed plastic parcel at great pace towards the room's ornate fireplace, smashing one of a pair of richly decorated Japanese vases. Agnes winked at her friend from behind the cloud of steam, replaced her goggles and as the machine shuddered and groaned into life, she rang the bell to summon the servants and set off again for further testing in the garden.

Reading the slight book Agnes had presented him with had been a revelation to The Major. He devoured the volume in a single sitting, the book containing rich tales of the ancient legends of a fabled Thai village of Mau Chang. The book contained colourful stories of ancient noble warriors worshipping Manu Chan the Urine Deity; of the secretive men passing on their traditions to the next generation, of courage and basic jungle techniques used to fit rudimentary collection bags to be worn with both tribal honour and pride. The tales of the huge ceremonial battles and proud colourful ceremonies of the Mau Chang people were incredibly moving and inspiring, just as Agnes had promised. Within a few hours of finishing the book and re-reading it, The Major had resolved to resume his travels, this time to Thailand, to find for himself these fabled locations and the proud warriors mentioned in the book.

The Major issued his goodbyes the next day and set sail from the Strathcarnage docks on a German freighter heading to India, to begin his long journey. Lord Strathcarnage had asked to accompany his friend on the journey, hoping to pick up some novelty oriental children for his child showing, but The Major asked to make his pilgrimage alone and without companions.

Lord Strathcarnage had reluctantly agreed to the request and the huge moustached man had joined many of the household staff lining the harbour wall to wave the ship off. In a touching final encounter, The Major stood on rear deck of the departing German steamer and saluted the gathered party, before noticing the distant silhouetted figure of Agnes in her new machine, high on the cliff road above the village. The old lady was blowing loudly on her steam whistle and firing bags of excrement skyward across the town as a heartfelt salute to her departing friend.

Nothing more was heard of the Major for three years.

Lord Strathcarnage had attempted to contact his friend through his child show contacts in Thailand on numerous occasions, to update The Major with the news of his elderly Aunt Agnes', and later, of her sad death. Witnesses in Thailand had watched the stranger arrive, the Lord had been informed, but The Major had swiftly taken off into the jungle heading for a secret location somewhere in the north. After this initial sighting the military man had never been seen again. Lord Strathcarnage had watched his Aunt smile broadly when she had heard this news, muttering the words "Mau Chang" under her breath before steaming off on another jaunt in her metal vehicle.

Ironically, Agnes Strathcarnage had met her doom directly because of the very invention The Major had lovingly helped her create. Her friend had been missing in Thailand for a year by the time Agnes had begun regularly extending her trips in the metal vehicle, travelling outside the relative safety of Haversack Hall and down the long driveway out onto the town's roads.

Some weeks after her first few successful trips through the town, Agnes was rattling merrily along the tree lined hillside driveway, then out through the gates leading to the steep road leading down from the Hall into the town when she happened across the local milkman. As she steamed past him, her confrontational nature and obscene gesticulating had provoked a race with the man. It was to be her metal invention against the horse drawn wagon piled high with milk, in a pursuit down the hill and into the main streets of the town itself. As she sped down the steep hill road with the black rock cliff wall to her side, Agnes was managing to hold her own in the race, even moving ahead of the galloping horse on the straighter sections. However, just as she was nearing the end of the duel and the first row of town buildings came into sight, tragedy struck.

As the racing vehicles had reached the foot of the hill without incident, Agnes had sounded her loud steam whistle to signal her delight at the excitement of the chase. The piercing blast had shocked the milkman's horse Glue, provoking the galloping animal to an instant demonstration of distress. The sudden shrill blast had caused the great beast to evacuate his bowels and unleash a flood of fresh horse droppings onto the road surface.

Agnes, now obscured behind the milkman's cart by piled crates, had missed the opening of the equine floodgates. Out of the blue Agnes found her speeding vehicle spinning out of control approaching the sharp bend at the Strathcarnage orphanage, her tyres losing all grip on the wet horse waste. The elderly woman' thin arms fought with her steering, but she was going too fast. The rudimentary design of Agnes' vehicle was never intended for accurate steering at such high speeds, let alone when combined with freshly produced quantities of semi digested grass. The elderly woman lost control and skidded sideways down an embankment and through a hedge, smashing straight through the leafy barrier into the grounds of the Strathcarnage orphanage.

Had she managed to halt the vehicle on the lawn in front of the building, all might still have been well, but such was the momentum afforded her by the journey down the long hill that her silver vehicle had continued travelling at great speed across the orphanage grass, heading directly for the building. Agnes had one final hope remaining. The Major had told her in his letter of farewell that the vehicle was fitted with an emergency escape mechanism. It was a system the engineer had mounted on the front of the contraption and fitted with explosive bolts which, when engaged, would dislodge the nose cone and allow Agnes to roll free in case of dire emergency.

Agnes pulled heavily on the release cord.

The exploding bolts deployed on the speeding juggernaut and the nose cone flew free as designed. However all was not well. Rather than the opening providing a route of escape, the open void of the nose cone only served to complicate matters by channelling onrushing air inside the long metal tube. As the wind blew through the car, Agnes found the whirlwind had covered her legs and lower body with the loose plastic stored inside the body of the vehicle for waste disposal. The roaring current was blowing the plastic up and over Agnes' legs and she found herself trapped by the rippling folds wound round her legs.

Agnes tried to kick against the onrush of plastic, but her frantic actions served only to have the sheets of clear plastic bind her legs further. What happened next remained uncertain but the bouncing motion of the speeding vehicle over the orphanage flowerbeds is thought to have dislodged a quantity of burning coal from the steam boiler deep within the back of the speeding contraption. Horrified onlookers recalled the metal cart suddenly bursting into flames toward the rear; exploding loudly into a huge cloud of steam, flame and smoke, and with a final enormous window-rattling explosion on the lawn, career through the front wall of the Orphanage building.

In one final catastrophic roar of ruined and burning metal machinery, the flaming inferno spluttered into life and fired a massive vacuum packed Agnes upward, throwing her plastic encased body skyward in an long arc. The massive package exploded out through the ruined ceiling and toward the glass roof of the conservatory extension. The shrink-wrapped missile landed directly on a number of the home's children playing in the sunlight inside, frozen fatally to the spot at the fantastical sight. The Orphanage burned to the ground, but curiously, when firemen searched the debris for bodies, they had found Agnes encased in a large vacuum packed plastic bag, virtually unmarked but completely cooked through.

The local paper, The Strathcarnage Porcupine, had with its usual taste and decorum, gone with the headline "Boil in the Bag Pensioner, served on a bed of Roasted Orphans."

The Major had eventually heard news of the terrible accident when he had emerged from the jungle in Northern Thailand. It was now almost two years after the tragic event and The Major was headed back into civilisation a much changed man.

Many had given the military man up as dead long ago. The immense Thai jungle was virtually impenetrable and the numerous rescue parties funded by Lord Strathcarnage had turned up no trace of his friend. It was left to a local hotelier to claim the small reward from local Thai police when The Major had quite casually turned up at his hotel on the edge of the jungle to book himself a suite, quite unaware of the drama surrounding his disappearance.

Thai police had arrived at the hotel to find The Major, grinning broadly and drunk. Since the military man had committed no crime and was discovered to be in perfect health, the authorities questioned him only for a short time before leaving him sitting in the bar, his legs bulging and gurgling curiously under khaki trousers. News was forwarded to Lord Strathcarnage of his friend's sudden re-appearance before the local Thai police force closed the missing persons file and returned to more mundane matters.

Lord Strathcarnage had departed immediately for Thailand on hearing the news.

The local Strathcarnage press had soon been informed of The Major's sudden reappearance and had published a special edition, complete with an eight-page colour pull out supplement complete with the headline "Piss Bag Major Found after Three Years Fannying around in Thai Jungle."

When the Lord had arrived at the hotel, he had been in for a shock. He found The Major a changed man, more serene and displaying an unusual air of thoughtful tranquillity. After caging a few local Thai youths to show back in England, Strathcarnage had bribed the two men a berth on a passing Ukrainian freighter heading in their direction and within days the pair had began the long journey home.

The return journey was strange. No matter how keenly Lord Strathcarnage questioned his old friend about events of the past three years, The Major refused to reveal any detail about his adventures. While stopping somewhere short of outright rudeness, as would be expected of such a cultured gentleman, The Major refused point blank to reveal any news of his time away. The only clue to what might have happened during his strange disappearance came one night after a prolonged evening of opium smoking, two weeks into the ship's voyage.

In a state of drug addled drunken high spirits off the West coast of Africa, The Major announced he had decided to moon at the Captain of the vessel, a deeply unpleasant Russian man called Volkov. Strathcarnage had chuckled at the childish prank and had drunkenly followed The Major as he climbed upward towards the ship's bridge, positioning himself hidden just below the huge windows enclosing the captain behind the ship's wheel. The Major had sprung up and waved merrily at the impassive Russian skipper, smiling broadly as he dropped his trousers and mounted the handrail running below the glass, pressing his bare spread arse cheeks against the window and dragging his backside to and fro across the window with great gusto.

The incredible sight Lord Strathcarnage had witnessed at that moment was the only clue as to what had occurred to his friend during these last three years in the jungle. Even in a state of drunken confusion, what Lord Strathcarnage saw shocked him deeply.

Running over the entire length of the Major's elderly legs were ornate tribal tattoos depicting strange scenes of combat. Gone too were the rudimentary bags for collection of waste matter from the man's ruined insides, replaced by sleek plastic contraptions running discreetly down both legs. Both of the latest bags were also intricately decorated in black tribal symbols matching the leg tattoos. Clearly the Major had a story to tell, but one he seemed strangely determined to keep to himself.

Lord Strathcarnage turned his gaze away from his friend, to respect his privacy as he pressed his nakedness harder against the bridge windows. Turning away and concentrating his stare through the large windows to watch the reaction, the Lord studied the ashen faces of the Russian crew, the vast bearded figure of Captain Volkov vomiting copiously over the side of his padded captain's chair. Strathcarnage followed the gaze of the startled sailors and realised why they were in such deep shock. He had heard rumour of, but had never actually witnessed for himself, the hideous injuries inflicted on the Major's anus by the blunt scarecrow pole. When he focused on the hugely enlarged wound of his friend's exit hole pressed against the glass, the Lord too felt distinctly queasy. It was less the colloquial 'rusty bullet hole' of ordinary men and more 'misshapen scarlet shell crater' of tropical disease textbooks, a quite revolting glimpse deep into those internal caverns of the human body that no man should ever be made to gaze upon.

The shocked Lord helped his drunken, laughing friend down onto the deck, pulled his trousers up over his exposed legs and walked him back to his cabin, wordlessly putting him to bed to sleep off the worst effects of the evening's excesses.

The Major had appeared brightly at breakfast the next morning seemingly with no memory of the previous night's drama. Even the abject look of fear on Captain Volkov and several of his crewmembers seemed not to provoke any recollection of the events. If it had, The Major gave no outward sign, gleefully poking at his grilled tomato with a wry enigmatic smile.

On the afternoon of the men's eventual return to a friendly French port with long established links to Strathcarnage, the men had arranged the final leg of their journey home. Once they sailed quietly through the waterfall hiding the town from the world and docked in Strathcarnage harbour, The Major had left immediately to visit Agnes's grave upon disembarking. He had stood in silent respect well into the twilight of the evening, sobbing quietly for his departed friend. Lord Strathcarnage remained at the ship unloading the children in his cages before returning to

Haversack Hall to grade and catalogue his freshly trapped child beauties and to wait for his friends return.

The Lord had expected the Major to return later that evening, but as the darkness fell around the village's winding streets, the only visitor to Haversack Hall was a messenger bearing a folded note. It was from the Major. He would not, it was announced on the small sheet of stained paper, be returning to resume his residence at the Hall with the Lord. He wrote warmly of his appreciation of everything the Lord had done for him, but that he had chosen to sell family possessions stored with Otis on the mainland and to use the proceeds to buy himself a modest property in the town. He assured the Lord that he would continue to love him dearly, but informed him that the Hall held too many sad memories of his dear friend Agnes to permit a return.

Lord Strathcarnage accepted this decision stoically and made a solemn vow to allow his friend The Major space to settle into his new home and find the peace he craved. He sent a warm reply telling The Major of his decision, adding that should his friend ever require the services of himself or Haversack Hall, then he should avail himself of these freely and without hesitation.

Few people were to see the Major at any point during the next decade. He was occasionally witnessed at the docks, making further secret trips to Thailand, often for prolonged periods, always returning to shut himself away again in his small home and appearing only occasionally in the town's dark winding streets to partake in solitary twilight walks to lay fresh flowers at Agnes's grave. His provisions were always delivered and the man seemed to have become a virtual recluse.

The only visible signs of the Major reported by town residents were the strange sight, after dark, of a bare torso at a window of his home. The military man appeared to be lurching violently around inside, swinging unidentifiable objects wildly around the bare interior of an upper room. This occurrence had become a regular sight when the Major was not absent on his Thai trips, the man passionately screaming strange battle cries in a foreign tongue from deep within the property.

The Major continued this reclusive existence, right up until the occasion of the previously mentioned slideshow of Randolph Braden in Haversack Hall. That night, in addition to being the first public sighting of The Major amongst company in almost ten long years, was also a moment destined to have a massive impact on the life of the village.

After The Major had delivered his speech to the meeting that evening, the hall had been cleared in the early hours of the night. The military man sat exhausted in the middle of the room, mopping perspiration from his brow as Randolph Braden removed his projection equipment from the floor, still shaking his head in amazement at the stories he had just heard.

"So Major, you say these Mau Chang chaps spend an entire lifetime dedicated to the pursuit of battling with rudimentary bags of their own urine as a continuation of some sort of ancient tradition?"

The Major nodded slowly in confirmation.

Randolph shook his head slowly.

"And you say you lived amongst this tribe for three years, learning their ways, skills and their customs? My word, Major, that's such an amazing story."

Randolph stopped what he was doing and walked towards the man, his head down and nervously mopping his brow. Randolph looked around conspiratorially and pulled a chair close. He leaned in and asked the question which was to change the course of the townspeople's evening pastimes forever.

"What if someone, a villager say, was to desire to follow such a path of ancient honour, and to themselves learn the customs and how to train or fight like these warriors? Would you be able to teach them what you know?"

The Major stopped mopping his brow. He raised his head and looked deep into the eyes of the seated Randolph.

"Do you think you have the deep inner fortitude to uphold the discipline and traditions of the Mau Chang people? To both reach and work daily at maintaining such a peak of physical prowess and mental strength to allow your body to undertake the years of training required? Do you think you could uphold a sacred oath to the secrecy of the discipline of piss fighting itself? Until the very day you die?"

Randolph thought deeply for a long time and then nodded his answer, hesitantly at first, but then stronger and with greater conviction. The Major could see that somewhere deep in the man's intensely staring green eyes that he truly meant it and then slowly began nodding with him. The Major stopped nodding and looked back, grabbing his friend's broad shoulders and fixing his steely gaze upon him once more.

"You realise Randolph, that if you are ever to contemplate walking this path, or if any others like you were ever to do likewise, not only will you require years of dedication, but you be required to make an enormous first step medically, itself requiring much pain and sacrifice?"

Randolph looked confused. The Major's eyes fell downward towards the groin of Randolph, before looking back at his face and winking. The younger man followed the gaze, a confused look on his face. As his eyes fell upon his groin area, the bewilderment suddenly lifted, replaced by a look of steely determination.

"In order to become of The Mau Chang, one must become completely like them. Their total dedication to Manu Chan, the piss deity, means all men must be as he is. The Mau Chang referred to this state in their own tongue as "Tamlok Chee Wo", meaning "penis as dry as sand". In the Manu Chan legend this condition was a gift from the gods to mark him as apart from normal men, but since we are mere mortals we must physically change ourselves to meet those physical specifications and to show our respect before we embark on our journey. If you were ever to proceed as a Mau Chang, then so you too must follow."

Randolph nodded his understanding and rose, stretching out his hand.

"Consider it done."

The Major reached for the extended hand but stopped.

"One final thing I must ask of you, before I agree to teach you."

"Anything Major, just ask."

After hearing the request and nodding his acceptance, The Major shook his hand warmly. Randolph lifted his jacket and quietly left the man sitting alone in the middle of the almost empty hall.

After Randolph's departure, The Major roused the unconscious Thai boy and wrapped him in his jacket to carry him home. When the boy awoke and saw his thin frame being covered and lifted by The Major instead of Randolph, he seemed to smile a little before drifting back to sleep in The Major's arms.

Over the next few weeks those who had been present at the talk in Haversack Hall deluged The Major at his small home deep within the town. All of the enquiries appealed for exactly the same thing from him as Randolph Braden had; to be allowed to learn and train in the ways of the Mau Chang Piss Fighters. After a period of reflection and contemplation at the gravity of the undertaking, The Major had proudly agreed to the requests and one by one the new disciples all underwent appropriate surgery.

A steady stream of local men had engulfed the small local Strathcarnage infirmary. The men were all perfectly healthy, but all requested their inner piping be surgically detached, re-routed and fitted with a set of the Major's specially designed clear plastic bags to mark their new lifestyle choice. In most hospitals such invasive and unnecessary surgery would have been refused outright. However the Strathcarnage men had a unique advantage over patients in other infirmaries. The head of Urology, and thus of any such surgical procedure, was one Randolph Braden, the man who had innocently introduced evidence of the Mau Chang to the people of Strathcarnage.

Within weeks, after the townspeople's surgical wounds began to heal, there appeared on the winding streets a significant number of hip bag wearing disciples, proudly displaying their semi full plastic bags of honour on their hips as they paraded themselves around the town. The sight profoundly moved The Major. This new camaraderie he had helped create amongst so many disparate souls inspired him deeply to share with these men his entire knowledge of the Mau Chang.

During the men's recuperation process, The Major had taken time to acquire appropriate premises and arrange facilities. Again he was in luck, because one of those keen to help The Major train the town's men in the Ways of the Mau Chang was Lord Strathcarnage. As a result, the old friend offered him free use of some disused buildings and land within the grounds of Haversack Hall to set up a training camp.

Thus it came to pass that the Camp of the Mau Chang opened high above the town, in the grounds of the Hall, and had subsequently welcomed the first of the disciples sloshing through the gates a mere eight weeks on from the initial slideshow and The Major's inspiring lecture.

As he strolled around the open grass of the parade ground during his first roll call, The Major was gratified to see such a dedicated collection of men. Randolph Braden the surgeon sex tourist and amateur pornographer was there, Gerald Spigot, Peter Fractious and Raymond Dull Jnr. were present from the local law firm, and many other familiar faces the military man had recognised from the Hall on that night of his first speech.

After the initial roll call, The Major conducted a thorough inspection of the men's newly installed bags to determine they were fit to commence training and in order to weed out anyone attempting to enter the camp under false pretences. The local cave miner Albert Steep was one such discovery. Albert hoped that by filling a clear plastic sandwich bag with cloudy apple juice then strapping it to his thigh with a home-made tubing attachment from his aquarium that he might slip into the camp without undergoing the surgical sacrifices of the other men. His attempt at deception was a fatal mistake. Trying to enter a camp filled with such dedicated men under false pretences was a highly risky strategy, and the subsequent discovery led to a tragic finale as those others who had undergone the painful sacrifice had surrounded the impostor and had kicked him to death in minutes, legs sloshing as they rained repeated kicks into his stone dust coated body.

The Major allowed himself a thin smile at the frenzied display of the men's total dedication to the cause.

Training began later in the day, after the carefully concealed burial of the cave digger's body.

The Major was keen to replicate the entire process that Thai disciples of Mau Chang underwent, and before even a piss bag was swung in anger, the well versed army man spent a considerable time lecturing the men on discipline, custom and respect for the ways and legends of the people his pupils had gathered to emulate.

The Major had shared his knowledge gradually, watching keenly for signs that any members had lacked the passion and dedication to follow the entire course through to the end. As it turned out, only one man was to fail at this stage; a homesick Raymond Dull Jnr, who missed his family too keenly to offer the daily proceedings his full attention. After consulting with the local law man and discussing his problem with total commitment and various solutions, The Major had decided to let him leave the course with his blessing.

Unfortunately the other men in the camp saw such departure as a sign of weakness and Raymond was kicked to death, surrounded as he was packing his belongings and soon disappeared under a violently wielded forest of angry sloshing legs before being dragged outside and buried alongside Albert Steep the miner.

Within weeks the rest of the men were deemed ready for the ritual body and bag decoration ceremony. Excitement in the camp grew in the long days leading to the ritual, fully aware that this moment was the first step toward full acceptance to the ancient ways. The men were also excited because they knew that once this ceremony was complete, their group would finally embark on their education in the arts of actual Mau Chang combat.

The tattoos were a time consuming task. However the Major had an assistant to enable the complicated and intricate task to be speeded along. Young Gunter was from the same forest area of Thailand as the Mau Chang and understood many of the complex symbols and traditions.

While not himself an actual Mau Chang member, one of his father's male jungle lovers had spent a few years living close to the tribe and the youngster had gazed curiously on his tattoos and heard frequent tales around the home of the Mau Chang traditions. These stories enabled Gunter to slowly become familiar with the strange tattooed designs, so often displayed on the naked sweating legs which the young man had witnessed thrusting behind his father's own.

Gunter had helped tattoo the men with sharpened bamboo and ink, covering their legs with the various symbols and identifying marks of the Mau Chang. Each man was given a tribal fighting name, arched in black ink just above the pubic hairline, which itself was to be trimmed and dyed in a traditional bright colour using natural plant dyes. The Major had decided to keep the fighting names in the men's own English tongue, to better allow them to familiarise themselves with the ceremonial importance of the act, the actual tattoo merely a traditional Thai translation. Scenes from ancient battles were then tattooed on the men's legs in the dark ink, along with rudimentary tribal symbols and pictures of tribesmen urinating.

Once this task was complete, the men had to perform the final ritual Ceremony of Amok Chi Woo, announcing themselves as newly decorated warriors and designed to ward off Chlymidios or any of the other evil Thai Urine Spirits which might still remain around them.

On the day of the ceremony the flat green tiered lawns of Haversack Hall were heavily populated with the tattooed legs and dyed pubic hair of the crowd of proud men performing the ceremonial dance of the dry spout and shaking their tattooed members in a ceremonial manner at crowds of local villagers, allowed admittance to the camp only for this one special day to witness proceedings.

There then followed a parade where each man would approach the gathered crowd, bow, and then swing their piss bag around their body whilst repeatedly screaming their new tribal name. The crowd cheered each and every man. The local man they had once known as Raymond Spigot the lawyer became Dry Urethra. Randolph Braden became Dripping Sack, so christened by the Major after an early appearance on parade with a leaky bag. All men took part in this ceremony, bowing low in respect before the ceremonial tribal chief, Lord Strathcarnage, who had assembled the Hall staff on the lawn in a naked line in front of the Hall's imposing entrance as a mark of respect.

The final pass of the day was made by the Major himself, the warrior already named by the Mau Chang. As the man reached the front of the crowd, he spun both his piss bag and faeces bag in a wondrously intricate display, pausing only to announce himself screaming as "Dong Tai", or "The Two Bagged One" as the name was translated from the native Mau Chang tongue.

The crowds dispersed and the camp gates were again locked behind the last visitors, the men returning to their life of thoughtful tranquillity. There was a quiet unspoken air of nervousness among the men, who knew the highly difficult and vicious combat training was about to begin. It was at this stage where men would finally prove themselves as worthy of the title of Mau Chang. Were they to fail, as many were destined to do, they would have to return in deep disappointment to the normal life of the village and forever cast aside all hopes of a life as a warrior.

The combat training was ruthless and unforgiving. Each man was required to undertake an intense regime based on physical fitness, hand and bag dexterity and controlled aggression. On the first day, in order to prove to the men the difficult nature of what lay ahead, The Major challenged each man in turn to a combat session in the specially constructed raised fighting area constructed from blessed dirt, traditionally known by the Mau Chang simply as the Toki and based on the shape of a kidney.

The hopeful fighting men had attacked the elderly Major in the Toki quite gently at first, respectful of his age and thin stature. However as he beat man after man, bursting their piss bags in the traditional signal of battle defeat, not a single man in the camp could come anywhere close to providing a challenge to the Major, no matter how hard they fought. The closest the elderly man had come to trouble was when he slid in the hazardous urine soaked mud of the Toki during a battle with the impressive figure of Bubbling Hole, the ex ice cream van owner of the town. However, just as The Major's attacker closed in, his leaping frame closing on the felled man's bag and within inches of defeat, the elderly man suddenly spun and twisted his body across the wet ground like a sea snake, coming up behind his confused attacker only to tear the assailant's swinging bag open ferociously with his teeth.

The Major taught the men an important lesson that day about how tough the task ahead would be: that they still had a great deal to learn.

The military man trained the gathering tirelessly, spending day after day in the sodden earth teaching the rudimentary moves that would save the fighters in combat situations: The Sloshing Parry, The Cross of Piss, The Jabbing Hawk, and The Open Hole. As time advanced it became clear that some men would never reach the standard required to become fully fledged Mau Chang. These men knew their failings and often left the camp in the silence of the night, heads hung in disgrace and swinging their bags in melancholic disappointment as they crunched slowly down the Hall's long driveway, heading home to break the news to disappointed friends and families. After such a long period of training, to be dismissed was a hard blow for many men to take. More than once at the morning roll call the group had been informed of failed colleagues having hanged themselves, bodies found swinging in the roadside trees choked by the sturdy inlet tubes of their bags. Many preferred this sad end to the disgrace of returning home a failure.

The camp continued combat instruction for months and before long only a small group of the most tenacious remained, so skilled and so talented that The Major was unable to deny them the full title of Mau Chang warriors.

In the end only nine men had survived the process from beginning to end but the Major was intensely proud of each one of them. They graduated as Mau Chang on a sunny Saturday afternoon in July, marching proudly past the entire town, gathered again on the flat Hall lawns to honour their achievement and graduation as warriors.

As a special surprise, The Major had smuggled an old Mau Chang friend and tribal leader in from Thailand to be the guest of honour at the ceremony and to present the men with the coloured headdresses and special handmade ball warmers that marked them now as real Mau Chang Warriors.

The Major watched proudly as his newly graduated men had fought ceremonial battles with the visiting Mau Chang dignitary. All managed to hold their own in lengthy fights, although all were eventually beaten. The visiting tribesman, Wan Kim had been highly impressed with the men's proficiency and had presented The Major with a ceremonial shrunken penis as a traditional token of his status as a great warrior and teacher.

The Major and his new troupe performed nightly to packed halls around the village, visiting sailors and fishermen and locals alike entranced by the athletic fighting men. A keen eyed local TV executive visiting one of the shows realised the potential for the sport as event television and soon the tattooed men were household names around the town, with each home adopting a favourite fighter to follow. Townspeople quickly became keen students of the intricacies of the sport and of the traditions of the men. The Major and his Mau Chang warriors soon became heroes in the village, unable to walk the streets without being mobbed by fans.

New trainee fighters put on shows in the town whenever they could and the Major's Mau Chang training school had soon outgrown its small base in the corner of Haversack Hall, using the substantial television money to buy and build a more permanent base on one of the Hall's lower tiers of vast lawns. However, the Major was a wise man and knew that in order to keep traditions undiluted and pure, it must be he alone who trained the men. As a result, the sport became inextricably linked with The Major, and the elderly military man soon became like a god for the growing band of devotees.

All of this history takes us back to the packed crowd in the church hall beside the village green, and to where our story began.

The crowd packing into the local church hall were there to witness the Yearly Finals of the Mau Chang Piss fighters. This was the absolute pinnacle of the piss-fighting year; a cup final, a Superbowl and an Olympic contest all rolled into one.

The Major had maintained the traditions of the Mau Chang even in respect of this finals night. The event had always been held in the small church hall, ever since the event's introduction. Regardless of the cash offered, there had never been any thought of moving the hugely oversubscribed event to a bigger venue. Tickets could have sold out for the finals a hundred times over, but The Major had kept the event in its tiny space as a mark of respect for the traditional values the Mau Chang themselves had held sacrosanct.

The only minor change The Major had made to the conventional Mau Chang ways was to incorporate a category to allow colostomy fighters to compete equally with mono bagged competitors. This had been a decision based purely on personal circumstance and The Major had sent a messenger to the Thai jungle to ask Mau Chang elders for their blessing. The Mau Chang had agreed the request, ruling that any advantage from having two bags would be negated by there being twice the opportunity for a burst. For the first time the Major would be allowed entry as an official sanctioned fighter in the championship finals.

The overall competition rules were simple and the same for all fighters. Both warriors would battle it out in the kidney shaped Toki using guile and skill until one beat the other by bursting his opponent's bag by whatever method chosen. Competition piss bags traditionally had to be made from the lungs of the Thai Water Bison, but could be sewn together and decorated in whichever manner a fighter had preference for. As soon as the signal to begin was sounded by the shrill note blown from the ceremonial brass urinary tract, the bout would commence and then continue without limit of time until a bag was burst.

It was common for spectators to rush to get the seats closest to the action, regardless of the drenching that arrived with the bouts inevitable conclusion. Many of the keenest fans saw it as a distinct honour to receive a face full of Mau Chang fighter's urine, as tradition dictated this was destined to bring their families great luck and strength in the future.

The night's fights began well. A spirited defence of the Junior Colostomy Bag title by a local boy saw him fight impressively to gain an eventual 'slam burst' on the hip of his opponent. A 'slam burst' victory involved getting the opponents bag between your body and his, and then violently and repeatedly driving the two bodies together to fatally breach your opponent's bag. On this occasion, although the bag had burst, it had been with quite impressive force, showering the crowd to the left side of the stage liberally with the sloshing yellow mixture within.

There then followed a number of different weight contests of classic Mau Chang piss fighting, some of which were over brutally quickly, others taking a deal longer owing to the combatants well matched skills. This was expected in the National Championship Finals, with only the very cream of the profession involved in combat. Once these early bouts were over, the crowd began to buzz and grow restless in anticipation for the much anticipated final battle of the evening.

The last fight of the evening was to determine whom the ultimate champion of the year in the Mau Chang discipline. It was great honour to win any bout, but a chance to fight for these ultimate accolades, televised live and now traditionally attended by a small group of original Mau Chang elders acting as official judges, was the highest possible honour. It was traditional in recent years for this final championship fight to be between the highest ranked Strathcarnage challenger and a warrior chosen secretly and transported to the town by the small learned panel of Mau Chang elders.

As the lights dimmed to welcome the two final fighters of the night to the ring, the crowd fell from hectic anticipation to complete silence in respect for the great warriors. It promised, as in every year, to be a master class in the ancient art of Piss fighting.

The first combatant made his way to the oval ring as the crowd erupted in loud cheers. Little could be seen of the man in a sea of raised arms, excepting for his glistening sweaty hands, holding aloft a half full piss bag in salute of the crowd's support. As he climbed into the ring, the reason for the volume of cheers in the packed church hall became apparent. It was The Major.

The military man had been absent from every National Championship so far held in the village, owing to the lack of a ruling on the twin bag rule. Regardless of his age however, he had kept himself in prime condition with his strenuous daily training of other men. He also had retained many secret moves never passed on to the other men and learned from the Mau Chang themselves during his time in Thailand. Many said the only way he would be beaten would be by a supremely talented native brought from the real Mau Chang deep in the Thai jungle.

However, since the native Mau Chang piss fighters were only allowed to travel outside the country to fight this single bout in Strathcarnage, it was agreed by experts that the only thing to halt The Major in a local fight would be the icy hand of death itself. Now the Major had been declared able to fight, the local man faced Thai opposition, and danger, in public for the first time.

The crowd had fallen silent as the lights dimmed, craning to see who the Mau Chang elders had chosen as their challenger this year. The identity was always kept a closely guarded secret until the night of the fight, to deny the reigning champion any opportunity to study his challenger's style. This was a sensible precaution that would ensure fantastic title fights owing to the specialist knowledge of the Mau Chang elders and the surprise nature of the opponent's identity. But tonight was destined to be the greatest surprise yet.

When the challenger made his way through the crowd and climbed into the ring, his silken dressing gown was removed. The Major was absolutely stunned to see who was facing him across the dirt floor of the Toki. Then the crowd too had gasped in shock as they took in the challenger's identity.

As The Major stared across the ring deep into the eyes of his challenger, his gaze was met by that of Gunter, the Thai boy he long ago had welcomed to his home. The crowd was stunned and had fallen quiet, but the silence had gradually built into a fevered roar of expectation. This was truly destined to be an encounter to tell future generations about.

Gunter had visited his native Thailand after his being brought to live in the village, joining The Major on his occasional trips. However Gunter had always returned to Strathcarnage with the older man after a few weeks, viewing the hidden town as his home now and helping The Major establish and run the town's Mau Chang camp.

However one summer many years ago, Gunter had set off alone for Thailand, and had never returned. Although The Major missed his young housemate deeply, he had gradually forgotten about the young boy, news reaching him that the boy had chosen to return to his roots permanently.

Gunter had returned to his Thai village on receiving news of his father's death. Having turned into a young man in his absence in Strathcarnage, it was his duty now to stay as head of the family, helping his mother. However as time passed, the young Thai man's curiosity had drawn him to the jungle to seek out the original Mau Chang fighters for himself. They had been reluctant at first to teach a boy not native to the tribe, but when he had related to the tribal elders his tales and experiences with The Major, the frowning men had relented and trained him as one of their own.

Gunter had had his name changed in the traditional Mau Chang way to "Pok Ni Ni Hoki", meaning, "kidnapped homosexual plaything" in the native Mau Chang tongue. The young Thai had learned the Mau Chang ways but had fought only within

the village in the deep jungle, quickly growing in confidence and ability and gaining a reputation as a talented and ferocious young fighter. The change of name meant that the few tribal reports of the young man's prowess which had been carried abroad to Strathcarnage had never led The Major to link young Gunter with the young man now strongly rumoured to be the tribe's deadliest fighter.

But tonight, here he was, standing across the ring from his one time teacher and mentor; ready to do battle until only one man's piss ran freely in the mud.

There was hardly time for The Major to gather his thoughts before the brass urinary tract signalled shrilly that battle had started.

Gunter was onto The Major in a heartbeat. Springing lithely and athletically around the Toki, the fast young man was difficult to keep an eye on. The Major was chopped roughly to the ground by the young Gunter three times in quick succession, only managing to avoid having his bag burst by the young Thai's heel with some last second defensive rolls. Gunter attacked relentlessly, assault after assault reigning blows around the torso and face of the Major, keeping him unbalanced and unable to launch a counter attack.

The Major weathered the continuous storm as the minutes passed, the young Gunter fighting like a man possessed. Blow after blow fell on the weakening defences of the older man, driving him relentlessly and continually backward.

The Major, however, had not won the respect of other fighters purely by luck and when a tiring Gunter overstretched trying to deliver a knockout head blow, the Major spotted his opening. Instantly the military man sprung up from the mud and used his skill to drop kick the young man heavily to the ground. Although Gunter recovered quickly and was instantly back on his feet attacking, the heavy blow came as a huge surprise and had weakened his attack.

As both men began to tire after the most ferocious battle the Mau Chang world had ever seen, the packed crowd stood and roared approval as the two exhausted warriors took to bag to bag combat. Both men swung their bags of piss furiously and violently, again and again connecting on the opponent's head and face. It was only a matter of time before one man went down stunned, or until a bag burst under the ferocious barrage.

Gunter looked as if he was beginning to tire, and the blows of The Major seemed to be weakening the young man. The Thai looked exhausted by the onslaught, forced backwards for the first time in the contest. He had, however, one last final surge left within him.

With an ear splitting scream, he slung his bag upward with the last ounce of strength remaining and attacked, the blow coming straight down onto the top of the tired Major's head. The Major looked blankly outward and then fell, slowly to his knees. Gunter, instead of the expected rush forward for the kill, himself fell backwards onto the mud, exhausted by his massive effort. The crowd gasped. For the first time the Major looked beaten, but had the Thai fighter the strength left to finish his opponent off?

The young Thai man clambered unsteadily to his knees and grabbed his decorated bag in both hands, raising it again high above his head. Then, with a look of intense anger and pain etched on his young face, he had screamed as loudly as his burning young lungs would allow. He screamed his words in broken English, but the audience got the meaning.

"Old Major dirty man, you bum young boy ass no more."

On the final word of the sentence, Gunter screamed and swung his bag downwards, connecting with the side of the kneeling Major's head with massive force, sending his thin elderly body sprawling sideways onto the wet arena floor. The Major lay unconscious.

Now, as we have witnessed, Mau Chang is a sport rich with tradition and custom. It dictates ancient codes and acceptable behaviour of fighters, teachers and their disciples. However the one aspect that The Major had never been fully taught by the native Mau Chang was the ancient and secret tradition of "Kai Tal", or just revenge.

Ancient tribal laws had dictated that the "Kai Tal" combat of revenge was not merely finished by the simple act of breaching the opponent's bag, but by enacting in the Toki an act of vengeance judged appropriate to the offending act committed. It was this ancient rule that was to end the evening with a finale no one in the crowd who bore witness would ever forget.

Gunter staggered over to his unconscious opponent and turned The Major onto his front with his foot. He grabbed the Major's piss bag, raising the decorated bag aloft to the now silent crowd. Then suddenly the youngster stooped and moved The Major's lifeless body into a bizarre twisted position, raising the older man's backside upward. Then, carefully, the young Thai collected the older man's twin bags and wedged them both between the ravaged pink cheeks of his elderly but muscled backside.

And then it happened.

With another chilling feral scream of "Kai Tal", the young Gunter sprung upwards and with all the power and anger he could muster, whipped his entire body round in a massive kick, landing the blow with huge force on one side of The Major's backside. At the moment of impact, there was a sickening crack of bone as the twin bags exploded their content outwards over the crowd. From the horrific angle which The Major's limp body now laid in the mud of the Toki, it was clear he was dead.

The hall fell silent.

Gunter dropped to his knees weeping, and then fell backwards exhausted onto the wet dirt. Thai elders from the Mau Chang village entered the ring and gathered up the young fighter, carrying him from the hall in their arms, the shocked crowd parting to allow the emotionless men a path from the building.

Gunter looked up tearfully and asked the party to pause only once, to take a long silver tipped walking stick from one of the elderly members of the crowd. As he paused to stare at Randolph Braden, the Thai smashed the stick into Braden's temple, knocking him unconscious to the floor of the hall. Kai Tal. Gunter was then wrapped in a blanket and placed on the back of an open horse drawn cart, the entire Thai party driven towards the small boat waiting at the docks. Those near enough to the cart could hear the noise of the young man under the blanket, still weeping.

In the days that followed the Major's horrific receipt of justice, the appetite for watching and partaking in piss fighting in the town was to collapse. Without The Major, and with his entire reputation tainted, the camp closed its doors within a month, leaving the site derelict. The next year's championships were cancelled due to a lack of interest and Reverend Whisp was left to find other inventive ways of fleecing his congregation.

The television station had received record numbers of complaints from local parents about the content and sheer violence of the finale and keen to keep rating high, The Ox had dropped the sport completely from all schedules. Interest in Mau Chang warriors had died with The Major.

Gunter left the country that night, headed back to his family and his Thailand home. Reports of the young man after his return were sketchy. He was carried off the arriving ship shoulder high by a party of Mau Chang tribesmen, but had slipped away secretly from a ceremonial dinner held in his honour in his home village later that evening. A taxi driver in the north of the country reported a final encounter on a deserted jungle roadside around a week later.

Having picked the young man up on one of the few roads that cut through the dense jungle, the taxi man had driven him to a desolate spot where Gunter had suddenly asked the taxi driver to pull in and let him out. He paid the taxi man and started back along the road as the driver had driven off. When the driver had glanced in the rear view mirror, the young man had disappeared amongst the trees and was nowhere to be seen. The spot in the road that was location of the last ever sighting of Gunter was around a mile from the fabled site of the village of Mau Chang.

In Strathcarnage now, the only reminders of the entire Mau Chang episode which remain are the sloshing sounds from passing male residents of a certain age. Occasionally young schoolboys fighting with each other will cry out during their grappling, "Old dirty Major Man, you bum young boy ass no more", and then erupt into a fit of childish giggles as they burst an empty bag and lay on the ground feigning death, but as time passes, even such youthful exuberance and historical insult is rare.

The Major was buried next to Agnes Strathcarnage where he remains at rest and largely forgotten together in an overgrown tomb, shaped, ironically, like a huge stone pissbag.

The Major 1898-1978

## CHAPTER 15

## Day Thirteen – The Wooden Fuhrer

Herman Schwarz watched from the interior darkness of his shop as the child's face pressed against the cold glass of the window. The small pink oval distorted as curiosity pressed the features harder against the surface; the tiny nose twisting into a crush of flared nostrils while the small blue eyes darted around, marvelling at the display Herman had just finished arranging in the window.

The elderly German shop owner loved seeing local children's faces gaze in awe at his special festive exhibits. However the elderly man had also grown to hate the continual smears left by a steady stream of faces on the small panes of glass that made up the old fashioned curving shop front. With a devious smile he raised the silver handled cane and carefully flicked it from the darkness, the decorated tip connecting with a sudden loud crack at the glass in front of the small face.

The child flew backwards in surprise, toward the safety of his mother. The woman scowled angrily at the old shopkeeper as his face leant forward, illuminated by the small model searchlights that helped make up the display. After a moment considering the mother's reaction, and watching the child hiding his shocked face deep into the woman's skirt, Herman smiled sweetly and raised two fingers at the pair. The woman turned away in disgust, hurrying her child away along the narrow Strathcarnage street.

Herman watched the pair disappear along the cobbled lane into the night with a thin smile, before carefully removing one of the six small figures from their perfect line in the window. He examined the form in the half light from the street outside, blowing small specks of dust from the model, before returning it onto the red and black cotton of the Nazi flag on which it stood. With a few minute adjustments the tiny figure stood again in a perfect line with its five partners, the column illustrating a small section of history of both their owner and of Strathcarnage itself.

The tiny figures displayed in the antique shop window all portrayed Nazi war leaders, carefully carved from wood and intricately painted. The carvings were not only some glorious celebration of a time long past, but were intended rather as a vicious pointed commentary from brave men on a political system that had profoundly affected their lives; not glorious and faithful recreations of commemoration but rather obscene detailed caricatures. The small figures on display in the curving window of Herman Schwarz's Strathcarnage antique shop were the only remaining six pieces of the famous Mannheim Seven.

There in the window stood the carved, painted figure of fat Herman Goering, dressed entirely in women's clothing, complete with an exposed set of mammoth breasts. Then Heinrich Himmler, shown carved completely naked and enjoying sexual congress with a dog. There was the figure of Rudolph Hess, bent over a small carved table with his trousers at his ankles engaged in a disgusting act of sexual depravity with a burly grinning female farm worker. There was a perfect carved representation of Field Marshall Rommel wearing heavily soiled underwear and with his face smeared liberally with carefully carved brown streaks. At the front of the line stood the stern bald figure of Mussolini in full make-up and in black lingerie. Finally, at the other end of the line, bringing up the rear, was the intricately carved wooden effigy of Joseph Goebbels, in a chair and with the perfectly carved wooden members of two Polish soldiers inserted between his painted red lips. These hideous representations of the Nazi party hierarchy made up the Mannheim Seven, or at least the six surviving members of them.

The seventh figure was missing from the set.

The ornate wooden figures had been carved by a group of five German men who had protested, as violently as circumstances at the time had allowed, against the rise of the Nazi regime. However as the party rose to supremacy and had grown all powerful, the small group of dissenting men had been forced to flee from their homes and escape to safety. At the last minute, as angry German forces had closed on the homes of the group hoping to exterminate all resistance to the party hierarchy, they had slipped away from their pursuers and taken refuge in the deep forest outside of Mannheim.

The group remained there, hidden in the dense woodland for the first few years of the war. It was during this period of isolation that these figures were carved as a quiet artistic protest to those events occurring in their homeland without the men's support. Seven figures in total were carved before the men were given an opportunity to escape by a disillusioned German U boat captain.

The Mannheim men had travelled by night with the utmost secrecy to a prearranged point on the coastline before setting off in a small rowing boat to rendezvous with a waiting German U boat. A small but powerful secret group unhappy with the Nazi rule of their homeland had made contact with the men and had arranged for them to be taken to safety in a more friendly neutral country. The men, once boarded, were greeted by a stern faced captain who told the group of their cover story on deck before leading the gathering below. The broad shouldered officer was part of the resistance organisation and had informed the group that he was keen to view the legendary carved figures of the Mannheim Seven later in the safety of his quarters. When that time had come, the bearded commander had marvelled at each of the figures as they were presented to him in his cramped quarters, eventually falling into hysterics when being shown the carved figure of Hitler.

The captain shook the hands of the five men in turn, saluted their bravery and showed them to the best accommodation available on the underwater craft, informing his crew the group were German secret agents who he had been ordered to furtively drop on the British mainland while his ship was out on manoeuvres.

The rest of the crew were not so friendly. While a few shared the commander's disillusionment at the ongoing course of the war, many soon guessed the men's real identities and after a search had discovered the small carvings of their nation's leaders. They viewed the set of engraved figures as a gross insult. Subsequently the crew had argued violently with the captain about providing these enemies of the German Reich a means of escape.

Some had threatened mutiny and had sworn to report the captain on return to Germany. The captain had quelled the revolt by restating his position of ultimate authority and reminding the men of their military duty to complete any mission ordered by their senior officer. The commander eventually suppressed the angry revolt by threatening to report all the men for their own mutiny against an officer, an offence leading to immediate and unquestioning death by firing squad on return home. An uneasy peace fell over the dark claustrophobic interior of the submarine.

Two days later, the crew of the submarine were woken in the middle of the night by sudden screams of sirens alerting them to an attack from enemy shipping. The entire crew quickly swung into a state of high alert. The fugitives remained asleep to begin with, assuming the commotion was another of the endless drills, and it was only when the bearded captain shook them roughly from their sleep that the men knew there was real danger afoot.

Minutes later the dull thud of depth charges began all around and violent rocking of the U-Boat signalled the imminent danger of destruction. As the ship began to spring leak after leak under the intense barrage, the decision was taken to surface and abandon ship before it was too late. As the craft rose through the crashing waves of the stormy sea above, the crew had made preparations to abandon the leaking hulk of the submarine.

The submarine came under fire immediately it surfaced, with the crew throwing themselves off the black hull of the damaged boat into the sea, knots of bobbing men clutching at few tattered life rafts. As the bearded captain helped his crew pull another grey raft from the U Boat deck into the heaving dark water, he sustained a fatal head wound from an enemy bullet, falling limply down the curved side of the submarine and ending up drifting slowly away, floating face down in the water. A number of men died the same way as more and more crew of the sinking ship began sliding down into the lifeboats. But not all of the men aboard made it to the safety of the bobbing rafts.

The remaining German U boat crew, on seeing the captain die, turned on the five fugitives. The men forced the group back down into the dark bowels of the fatally damaged craft at gunpoint, before making sure the hatches were jammed closed and disabled before they too finally abandoned ship. In doing so they sentenced the small party of men seen as traitors to the Nazi cause to a certain death at the bottom of the sea.

As the cold dark water slowly dragged them below to their grave, the men sat helpless, trapped inside the ravaged metal body of the U boat as the cold seawater hissed through breaches in the hull and bubbled around their legs. All looked lost.

Suddenly, in a rush of flailing arms, an idea took hold. The older men grabbed the youngest member of the party and thrust a wrapped package into his confused hands before dragging him through the inside of the sinking boat. From what he could distinguish of the confusion of voices above the roar of onrushing water, he had been chosen to be given a final chance to escape.

The bundle he had been handed was a package containing the wooden figures of the Mannheim Seven and the young man selected as the only member of the party strong and fit enough to save both the figures and himself. Clutching the cloth wrapped parcel to his chest and silently nodding his understanding, the young man was thrust forward through the freezing water of the rapidly filling corridors and past blinking lights to the front of the submarine. Openly weeping, the young man was hugged warmly by his friends and forced into one of the craft's oily torpedo tubes. One of the men reckoned that firing and opening the damaged torpedo tube door was still possible but that the suicidal act would cause the entire craft to quickly flood and sink. The plan would work, but it was only possible to save one of the men.

The man had tears in his eyes as the damaged metal door swung closed behind him to extinguish the final sight of his friends. Before he had time to prepare, a sudden surge of freezing water flooded around his body as somewhere inside the ruined craft the button was pressed to open the outer watertight doors. As Herman fought against the onrushing water, he gripped tightly at his package and began forcing his way slowly out of the narrow opening into the sea. Looking behind him, he watched the black metal outline of the boat slide quickly downward in a trail of silver bubbles, dropping away into the endless darkness behind him.

The young man kicked for the surface, his breath burning inside his lungs. As his head broke the surface, Herman gasped long and deep trying to fill his protesting body with the cold night air. The attacking ship had gone, now barely visible on the horizon steaming away from the scene of its victory. He was now the only survivor of his group of five friends, but he had made it, and he felt the cloth wrapping of the package in his grip with relief.

He drifted with the current for a long time, his limbs growing rapidly numb in the freezing water. The iciness of the surrounding sea told him that he was somewhere to the north, but with no idea where. Frightened of losing his grip on the package, he thrust the cloth down his trousers and began swimming, hoping he would reach land before becoming exhausted or freezing to death. The memories of his lost friends kept him fighting onward, his burning desire to allow his brave comrades some remembrance driving him forward.

Even with such intense passion, he soon grew tired in the cold water, his ability to swim even the most basic strokes a task fatally hampered by repeatedly clutching and rearranging the package beneath his trousers. He knew his only chance of survival was being able to swim freely, so with a sickening feeling of the deepest betrayal to his dead friends he kissed the package, offered a small prayer asking forgiveness, and then cast the bundle adrift, watching as the angry sea gradually unwrapped the material and set the freed small carved wooden figures bobbing away across the water. He watched for a moment as the small carvings floated off in various directions before turning away the sight distraught. After a further hour or so swimming, and now utterly exhausted, the man sighted a rocky outcrop of land.

The sight of those black ragged walls of rock had inspired Herman to fight on against the heavy waves and swim as hard as he could in one final attempt to save his tiring body from certain death. The man laboured on, battling against the endless freezing waves crashing over his exhausted body. Gradually he drew closer and closer to the ragged rock face.

On reaching them, he tried to grab at the sharp rock but his hands, numbed with coldness, could not grip with force enough to drag himself out the water and free his exhausted body from the heavy swell of water and incoming tide. After a number of attempts he gave up and fell back, worn out, into the foaming water. He knew he was so near to saving himself but finding that one final burst of energy needed to haul his body onto the land seemed an impossible task.

Then, as he gasped once more for air in the swell, a miracle happened. As his mouth gaped open in the night air, the German felt a sudden sharp stab of intense pain to the side of his mouth and a red hot jag to his cheek. In the distance he could hear the shouting voice of another human and the intense agony returned as he began to be slowly hauled towards the rocks by his face. Herman reached towards the source of the pain and his hands felt a fishing line. Someone had caught him.

He tasted the metallic tang of blood and felt the pull of jagged metal through his cheek, and realised he was being reeled in towards the rocky coastline. He tried to swim in the direction of the force dragging at him, managing to keep the line slack for only an instant before it snapped taught and the searing agony returned. As he neared the rocks, he turned in the waves and caught sight of the bemused face of a young fisherman, confused by the strange catch he had made. He was soon joined by an older man, and through the crashing waves the hooked Herman heard the astonished cry from the shoreline. "Christ son, you've hooked yourself a man. Reel him in."

These were the events that saw Herman Schwartz caught and landed on the rocky cliff wall just outside the town of Strathcarnage.

In accordance to fishing traditions, and in the absence of any previous protocol regarding an actual man being caught at sea, Herman was stunned unconscious with a heavy wooden baton and dragged to the town harbour to be weighed. When the German came round, he found himself hanging upside down from a set of scales, a large hook through the bottoms of his trousers, an inverted crowd of bemused locals standing staring on at this most unusual catch.

Gently swinging, Herman noticed a small vehicle trundling toward him along the quayside, steam pouring from a stove pipe welded to the top. The crowd parted to make way for the strange vehicle, the contraption halted before him, and an elderly woman driver slowly appeared through the thinning clouds of steam. The woman coughed, waving at the steam with her thin arms before snapping her goggles onto her forehead. Misjudging her technique, the goggles shot off the top of her head and hit a small unsuspecting child just behind her full in the face. He began crying.

Remaining in her vehicle the old woman announced herself as Agnes Strathcarnage, demanding with some authority and some industrial strength language that the crowd cut down the wet man. Herman fell heavily to the stone quayside almost immediately, his weak body winded by the sudden impact. Turning his head, Herman saw an outstretched hand held before him offering to help him up. The thin bony hand was obscuring the image of the woman in her carriage and as the recovering German followed the wiry appendage upward, his eyes met with a set of yellow smiling teeth and strands of grey hair hanging over a wrinkled face.

"Welcome to Strathcarnage. My name is Oliver Trencher, permit me to welcome you to the town."

Herman grabbed the hand and was pulled upright, swaying as he rocked unsteadily on his exhausted legs. Looking around the assembled group with tired eyes, Herman saw the crowd suddenly part and dive for cover as the wooden shell of Agnes Strathcarnage's vehicle began to rumble somewhere deep inside. The German man watched in confusion as people leaped for cover and hid behind piles of crates and boxes around the harbour side. Behind the red leather steering wheel of her car Agnes looked to be straining and in some sort of pain. Suddenly, with a sudden tongue of flame darting from the car's rear, a wrapped yellow package exploded from the rear of the machine at pace, hitting the still weeping boy in the chest and catapulting him straight over the side of the quay into the oily harbour water.

Oliver Trencher led the man off the stone quayside towards the town while various people attempted to rescue the child with a net. Agnes steamed past the men heading back towards the town, the elderly woman waving a thin arm at the wet German and shouting an invitation to visit her in Haversack Hall when he was dried and fed. As the two men drew closer to the town streets Oliver began a conversation, the grey haired local man talking in an uncontrollable rush, watching the German's face intently as he spoke, before losing his bearings and staggering off to one side over the side of the harbour wall, landing out of sight with another splash. The German man stood staring down from the harbour wall at his new friend bobbing in the water, still talking. This, he mused, was a very strange place indeed.

Herman Schwarz later told curious locals the amazing story of his story of escape and was warmly accepted into the community. A few in the isolated town had heard rumours of a war, but knew little of the Nazi party, however locals knew instinctively from the German man's floods of tears and raw emotions while recounting his adventures that they must be a bad thing. With the help of Agnes Strathcarnage the young German was offered use of a small house vacated after a recent local poisoning. Herman had expressed his gracious thanks and soon moved in to become part of Strathcarnage life.

The young man was soon offered a job and began work in the quayside antiques shop of Oliver Trencher. The now dry and most friendly owner had been impressed with his knowledge of wooden carving and his gentle, appreciative affinity with the objects in the shop. A grateful Herman had also listened without complaint to Oliver's incessant talking, a rare talent amongst Strathcarnage locals.

Herman continued to work in the shop for many years, consulting dusty books on antiques whenever a spare moment allowed. Over time the German man became quite an expert in the business of the shop, often helping a jabbering Oliver pick the best pieces from the items frequently smuggled to the town on fishing boats.

Herman had stepped in to the shop owner's frantic and unfocused discussions, quickly negotiating fair deals on those items brought to the shop by visiting crewmen in need of money to spend on the town's women of the night.

The elderly shop owner soon recognised the positive effect of having a knowledgeable partner, who could buy and sell with an efficiency the local man lacked, soon coming to depend on the honesty and dedication shown by his new assistant. As the Strathcarnage dealer grew frailer he began to trust Herman with the task of sailing alone on occasional trips to distant salerooms to find new items for the store. The local man had previously completed these buying trips himself, but his incessant talking had often led to him being thrown overboard by frustrated crews unable to handle the constant noise. As a result, the progressively frail figure of Oliver Trencher could now be regularly witnessed pacing up and down outside his shop, waiting patiently at the harbour for the ship carrying Herman and any fresh cargo home. Such was the growing bond between the two men that Oliver could often be seen warmly hugging his returning friend on the quayside, clearly delighted at both his return and the revelation of some fine new item procured from the trip.

As if to confirm his mounting appreciation for his Germanic assistant, Oliver asked his assistant to move in to his flat above the shop. Herman agreed and as time had progressed the pair began to work closer than ever in making the antiques business below them a growing success. However, events from the German man's past were to again bring tragedy to the lives of those around him.

Whilst on a secret trip abroad, at a large antique fair in the Northern French coast, Herman had attempted to acquire for the shop a number of items of antique French furniture to meet a sudden local demand. A smuggled pornographic film recently aired on the local Strathcarnage Television station and had the final orgy scene filmed on location in a farmhouse in Brittany. The film was shown in the town twice daily and within a few days customers had began calling at the antiques shop demanding rustic French pieces in the same style as those in the film. As demand had grown, it had been decided that Herman should travel and source a quantity of authentic items from sales in Brittany to meet demand.

Herman and Oliver were used to being inundated by demands for furniture shown on the regular stream of pornographic films shown by the local station, customers often complicating matters by requesting clearly visible pieces using only descriptions of the sexual act occurring in the film at the time. Hence the shop quickly ran dry of any stock of chairs, stools or tables resembling those appearing in any newly smuggled film aired in the town, with Herman regularly sent abroad soon after a new title was shown, to source new stocks. He had been nearing the end of this latest buying spree in the French countryside and was paying the dealer for a quantity of farmhouse tables when Herman had suddenly stopped and dropped his pile of fifty franc notes to the floor.

He'd had caught sight of an object in a small glass case behind a display of antique French chamber pots. He moved closer to the case to better peer through the dusty glass at the article which had caught his attention. He could hardly believe his eyes. Staring back at him through the smeared surface was the ornately carved and shocked face of a German shepherd dog, and behind it, the familiar straining wooden face of Heinrich Himmler. Herman knew immediately that he was looking at one of the set of figures he had been forced to abandon to the sea after being saved from his death in the scuttled German submarine.

The Strathcarnage man had exploded with joy, dancing and clapping before the display case in a show of profound delight, before he eventually found the owner of the case in the surrounding crowds and had asked the thin angular Frenchwoman to see the figure, caressing the carving gently in his hands before hugging the object close to his face and kissing it warmly.

The stallholder had backed slowly away from the weeping German man, confused by his behaviour at such a sick carving of bestial intercourse. He had paid the woman the asking price without protest after checking the piece and finding, as expected, his lost friend's initials carved under the figure's pink scrotum. Herman asked the woman if she had ever seen anything like this before but the worried French woman had merely shaken her head and backed away further as Herman had tried excitedly to use rudimentary sign language to describe the other figures in the set.

Herman remained awake all night in his cabin on the journey home, staring at the carving and tracing the carved lines of the tool marks, amazed that he had found the item set adrift so many years previously. The figure was in perfect condition save for some sections where the paint was worn and chipped. By some miracle he had found it. If this had survived, he mused, would there not be some slim chance that the others had been found? Gradually the man became obsessed with the idea of reuniting the seven figures in remembrance of his lost friends. It was the very least he could do to celebrate their sacrifice and bring their story of resistance and courage to others. He decided that once he had returned home to Strathcarnage and delivered this latest consignment of porn related French farmhouse furniture, he would devote himself to searching for the remaining figures.

Arriving back at the village, with the cargo tied in an untidy pile on the top deck of a Polish trawler, Herman found his business partner waiting as usual on the quayside. On being greeted with warm hugs, Herman had wasted no time in telling his partner he had found something very special. Herman had reached into his pocket and withdrawn the wrapped figure, carefully removing a protective covering of red velvet from around the carving before presenting it to his friend. By now Oliver was growing old and weak, and when he laid eyes upon the carving of the bespeckled Nazi crouched and entering the animal from behind, profound shock had sent the man weaving around the harbour side clutching at his chest and making loud gurgling noises. Herman had tried to reach his friend but had succeeded only in grabbing the ornate carving from the elderly man's outstretched hand, his friend disappearing once more over the side of the harbour wall followed by the sickening crash of breaking wood.

The town medical board which had met to discuss the unfortunate death determined the matter as "a broken neck brought on by heart failure brought on by bestiality".

Herman was devastated, blaming himself for his friend's death. Little did

Herman know that the old man had been so shocked only because he himself had owned a very much loved German shepherd dog and had only arrived in Strathcarnage many years ago after being expelled from his mainland village for marrying the animal and living with it as his wife.

The subject of the carving, combined with Oliver's own striking resemblance to Himmler, had caused the elderly shop-owner to assume that his past secret had been discovered. This led to the massive heart attack that provoked his fall off the harbour wall and onto the pile of furniture, where he had broken his neck. Herman was not to be blamed although the deep feeling of guilt was heightened further once the German man had attended the local law firm of 'Spigot, Fractious and Dull' for the reading of the will. There he discovered that he was the sole inheritor of the antique shop and flat above. Oliver had left all his possessions, money and stock to the German man; on condition he laid fresh flowers weekly at an unmarked grave in the local pet cemetery.

After contemplation, Herman saw his friend's death as that of another innocent victim murdered by the evils of the Nazi regime he detested, and so his hunt to reunite the Seven Figures of Mannheim began with a fresh passion and impetus.

The second of the seven figures was found quickly, and in the most unexpected place. Local television news crews had been drawn to the unusual death of Oliver Trencher and had carried the story on the evening news and local press. Herman had remained heartbroken at his old friend's death and had declined any interviews on the matter, but after the story had aired the German had received a strange call one night at his home in the flat above the shop.

It was from The Ox, the head of the local television station, asking for an exclusive interview with Herman over the intriguing story of the carvings. Herman had said nothing and gently replaced the black receiver in its cradle. The TV man had called a number of times, always asking Herman to call him back, but the German had always remained totally silent on the other end of the phone. This might have remained the pattern of communication between the two men, had The Ox not opened a later call with a simple yet moving declaration.

"Herman, I know," said the deep American accent, "where the Goering with the tits is."

Shocked and gripped by excitement, Herman began to speak. After agreeing to the interview, The Ox called at the Antique Shop with his camera crew, his massive hand holding a small parcel wrapped in cloth which he handed to Herman. It was indeed the carved figure of Goering, his massive pink breasts sagging down over his grey Luftwaffe uniform, nipples still as red and erect as Herman remembered. It was the second of the collection. Herman gazed at the TV executive speechless, his eyes heavy with tears.

"No hassles, Herman baby. I found this cute little guy with the tits back home when I was a kid. I hear whispers that it's part of your story. You tell me the whole truth on camera and he's yours. I collect items with a connection to filth and depravity, but I figure this lil' guy means more to you than he does to me, am I right?"

The huge American slapped a slowly nodding Herman on the back and led him to a lit chair as the men had agreed. Once Herman composed himself, he began to unfold his entire tale, telling of the existence of the five remaining figures and how they had came to be lost at sea. It was a remarkable story and Herman told it movingly, breaking down a number of times whilst reliving his escape and the death of his comrades aboard the sinking sub. It made for quality television and The Ox was glad to have some free programming for the local station not involving sex, thanking Herman warmly as the pair hugged at the end of the interview.

The Ox told Herman that he would use his network of connections to ask around about any other figures. The television executive meant his offer genuinely, but as he spoke he was calculating the potential audience for a series of programs following the ongoing search and any future repatriation of the figures with their owner.

Over the next few months Herman's time was taken up by the running of the shop. He sent messages across the seas with visiting boats, requesting they ask around their home ports for help locating anyone who had heard of the depraved carvings, hoping for replies from people who might have some recollection of the striking objects and keen to claim the offered reward. He laid aside all profits from the shop into a separate account, saving them for a day when he might be able to buy back his beloved figures. However after a few months the German man had heard nothing, even going on occasional buying trips himself to investigate possible coastal antique sales abroad. It looked like his lucky streak had gone cold. But then one night, as he prepared for bed, the phone rang again.

Herman had just returned from climbing the long rocky path to lay flowers at the grave of his dead partner's beloved German shepherd wife, and the evening phone call to the closed shop had come as a shock. More so once he had discovered what it concerned.

The call came from a Croatian engine stoker on a coal freighter visiting the town, passing on a phone conversation the crewman had recently engaged in with a heavily accented Albanian dealer in Nazi memorabilia. This dealer had been informed through a network of contacts of requests for information about the carved wooden figures and had sought out the stoker at a portside brothel after hearing he was soon sailing to Strathcarnage. The stoker, speaking in hushed tones, informed Herman that the dealer had asked him to pass on the message to those concerned that he owned a Nazi memorabilia superstore just outside Tirana called "Jackboot And Stormtrooper."

He claimed he was in his possession of a pair of the figures. Indeed, were he to be believed, the Albanian dealer had claimed he was at that very moment staring at both the figure of Mussolini in black women's lingerie and that of Rudolph Hess, complete with supporting table and grinning farm worker.

Herman almost dropped the phone in delight. After hearing a few relayed details from the dealer's call that only a person in possession of the figures could correctly have known, Herman was satisfied the information was genuine and agreed to meet the stoker to hand him cash as part of the reward. Only then did the stoker reveal to Herman the final part of the message he had been told to pass on. The Albanian dealer had arranged a meeting.

The pair met briefly in a café in the backstreets of a shady Belgian harbour town and, with a shake of the hand and the exchange of several concealed parcels of money, Herman was now in possession of four of the seven figures.

The fifth figure, that of a carved Field Marshall Rommel, had arrived anonymously in the post from Brazil a few months later with an attached note in German asking that the figure be taken care of. The figure was wrapped in a blood stained Nazi naval ensign and the note simply signed 'The Hawk'.

The sixth and final figure presently in Herman's possession had arrived a year later after Herman had travelled successfully to a wardrobe and wooden ephemera auction in Warsaw, after a tip off passed on through the Ox. Having outbid a number of elderly German gentlemen who had bid furiously for the figure of a seated Joseph Goebbels engaged inappropriately with two Polish officers, the Strathcarnage man had eventually triumphed and had travelled home in secret from the Polish coast to reunite his figures.

Herman had carefully laid the figures out in a display in the antique shop window on his arrival home and the barbed wire and miniature searchlights of the festive window display had remained a feature of the centrepiece every Christmas since. The figures had been restored to their full glory, the German man lovingly polishing and varnishing them so they looked their very best for the crowds of local people and visiting sailors who would gather around the curved window hoping for a glimpse of the legendary wartime relics. However every year the display was mounted, there remained an empty sadness inside Herman that the most important of the seven figures remained missing.

That final carving, of the Fuhrer himself, engaged in an act of unspeakable depravity with a farm animal, remained lost. None of the many dealers or contacts spoken to had ever heard of even the most fleeting rumour of existence of the final figure or its whereabouts. Indeed many questioned had considered the last carving merely a myth, doubting it had ever having existed. Indeed Herman himself, part of the small group of men who had made the carvings, had only ever seen the Hitler figure once, when aboard the fated German escape submarine. Herman began to doubt it had survived. He knew he was extremely lucky to have gathered the other six figures, eventually coming to terms with the fact this final one must have been lost at sea, never to be seen again. After a decade of Christmas displays, the now elderly German man lost all hope of ever seeing the figure again.

And so it was with heavy heart that Herman turned away from the window after polishing the small incomplete series of carvings. Heading back inside the darkness of the shop, the elderly German found his spirit lightened by the memory of the child's face as he had rapped the window with his cane. He was about to retire upstairs to his flat when he heard a light but continuous knocking on the shop door.

The German man cursed under his breath, anxious to retire to the comfort of his lounge after a long day spent in the drafty shop. He just knew it would be the angry mother returning to complain about his treatment of the child and did not welcome the inevitable shouting match in the cold snow gathering in the shop doorway.

As he opened the door he drew back, shocked and surprised by the figure of a three legged black dog. The animal was carrying a note in its thin mouth, offering it upward to the shop owner. Herman took the note from between the sharp white teeth and read it.

"Herman Schwarz. We have something you want. Something you want badly. If you require it, you must travel to Munich. There you will find the final figure you need."

Herman turned the paper over and read it carefully. On the reverse was an address in a Munich suburb the German man recognised, together with a photograph of the small wooden figure propped against a recently dated copy of a local Berlin newspaper. Herman looked up quickly at the dog, to see if it offered any clues, but the three legged animal was already on his way back along the snowy street, the three remaining paws clicking against the cobbles as it trotted along, eventually turning out of sight from the confused figure in the doorway down a lane. Herman immediately locked and bolted the shop door and headed upstairs to pack for Munich.

Rather than the normal Strathcarnage ritual of long weeks of undercover sea travel, Herman took a small local boat down the channel under the waterfall and then along the coast where he landed and travelled on, first by train and then by air to reach Munich with as much speed as he could muster. The German man felt time was of the utmost importance and didn't want to waste a minute. On landing in the German city Herman had collected his bag and headed straight for the address delivered by the dog. If he not been so caught up in the excitement of events he would have noticed the dark figure carefully watching him in the airport, the pair of blue eyes following the Strathcarnage man's path over a carefully held newspaper. Herman was being followed.

The old man reached the address he had been given by taxi, paying the driver and stepping out onto the street with a sinking feeling in the pit of his stomach. The building standing before him was derelict; windows were boarded up, the door had been nailed closed with planks of wood and grass hung from the broken guttering high above him on a wrecked roof. The building looked as if it had been unoccupied for many years; such was the obvious and advanced state of decay.

A woman walking along the other side of the street pushing a pram with her head bowed looked local. Herman crossed the street and asked the woman politely if she knew anything about the building. The figure raised her head, shrugged, said that she did not and walked on. Herman returned his gaze to the front of the house and carefully examined the ruin as he shook his head slowly at the mystery. He did not hear the woman's soft steps returning.

"Perhaps if you are looking for something, something special, then maybe it might be worth trying the door on the other wall that leads to the garden."

Herman looked up at the woman and met her gaze for the first time. She was even older than Herman, way too old to have a child in a pram. The man stared at her, his eyes examining the elderly face.

"Poor, poor Herman, I really would try the other door," said the woman, beginning to laugh softly, as if to herself.

Herman stepped back and watched her push the pram away, still laughing. He ran after the woman, pulling along side her with a few strides.

"Listen, how did you know my name was ...."

Before Herman could finish his question the elderly woman turned and laid her finger gently on the lips of the man, stopping his question. The words lay heavy in his mouth, pressing towards his lips.

"Quiet or you'll wake my baby."

Herman glanced into the pram, suddenly aware of the child. Sensing his interest and following his gaze, the old woman folded down the hood to allow Herman to see better the loved one within. Inside the pram, sleeping, was a full size black Doberman, teeth bared and with a pink tongue limply hanging between sharp teeth at the side of its mouth. Herman started back at the old lady in shock. Pulling up the hood of the pram she walked off along the street, laughing softly. Before he could turn back toward the house Herman felt two pairs of strong hands grab him firmly from behind and lead him by both elbows towards the gate.

Herman felt himself pushed firmly forward through the opened gate into an overgrown garden, unable somehow to stop himself and his mind still reeling from the encounter with the old woman and her pram. Once in the garden, Herman regained control and dug his heels into the gravel covered path, feeling the hands release from his elbows as he did so. As he turned to confront the men, Herman was distracted by the piercing squeal of an opening metal door ahead of him. Looking around in confusion he took a few paces forward, his gaze drawn by the sudden appearance of an elderly man. He was dressed in full Nazi military uniform. Before Herman could speak, the man bowed, clicked the heels of his shining black boots once and flashed a crisp Nazi salute in his direction.

"Herr Schwarz, we have been expecting you."

Herman looked back for the men who had recently been gripping his arm, but the overgrown garden was empty, the men nowhere to be seen.

"Please, Herr Schwarz, come inside so that we may better discuss our business with The Fuhrer."

Herman was unsure and frightened, but the man certainly knew why he was there. In his dealings with numerous pro Nazi organisations and fans over the years of searching for his figures, Herman had come across many strange obsessives, and this man appeared typical of the type. He knew best results were gained from remaining quiet and allowing this strange delusional role playing to continue. The Strathcarnage man silently stepped forward along the overgrown path, past the uniformed eccentric and through the open metal door. As his eyes tried to acclimatise to the sudden change to darkness, Herman heard the metal door clang shut behind him.

He was in what looked like a corridor, badly lit but heavily decorated in Nazi symbols and flags. It ran straight for around twenty yards before a stair led abruptly downwards, appearing to head under where Herman presumed the derelict building stood. The uniformed man walked past him and held an open hand before him, silently inviting the Strathcarnage antiques dealer to carry on along the passage towards the stairs.

Herman nodded and walked on, descending down a long staircase past portraits of many of the Nazi hierarchy he remembered clearly from the war years. After a long steep descent, the stairs again led into a corridor, this time better lit and more welcoming, yet still opulently decorated with wartime memorabilia and regimental battle flags. Herman stopped and looked back at the uniformed man who had descended the stairs just behind him.

"Herr Schwarz, welcome to our headquarters."

At the end of this new corridor another door opened and another elderly uniformed figure appeared, this time dressed in the uniform of a higher rank. This man was suddenly joined by two shaven headed men who stood on either side of the man like thuggish bookends, their arms crossed to resemble a surreal version of the skull motif on collar of the black S.S. uniform standing before him. The black clad man raised his arm and signalled with two curled fingers that he wished Herman to approach.

Passing the staring blue eyes of the heavily muscled younger men and moving through the door to join the second uniformed man, Herman gasped. He found himself standing at one end of a vast hall with a vaulted ceiling curving high above him. Huge swastika flags hung suspended from the roof along the considerable length of the space and heavy wooden tables and chairs set out in rows filled the entire hall. The uniformed man walked slowly past Herman, his arms wordlessly spread wide as he slowly turned, as if inviting him to proclaim the impressiveness of the space. As the older man turned to stare, Herman noticed his uniform was immaculate and correct in every small detail.

"Welcome Herr Schwarz, to the Kleigenhoffer Bierkeiller. You now stand inside what is now is the last such original hall left standing after the war. It was secret throughout the war and remains so today. I can see you are impressed, no?"

Herman nodded slowly, his mouth beginning to dry with fear. This was more than a tiny group of men play-acting times past.

"I am glad you could make it today, it is nice to see you again after all these years. We have some unfinished business to attend to, my old friend."

The words hit the Strathcarnage man hard and he turned to face the uniformed man, For the first time Herman gazed intently at the man's face, studying the features. Something about it seemed familiar.

"I see you are confused, Herr Schwarz. This is not a surprise. It has been some time after all. My name is Otto Schilling, although you may remember me better as Private Schilling, of the crew of submarine U 563. The last time you saw me I was forcing you and your friends below decks of my ship at gunpoint before sending you to what I hoped was certain death. Apparently not. So nice to see you again."

Herman stepped backwards, mouth fallen open in shock. Now he remembered the man's face, still twisted with hate almost forty years later. Suddenly Herman felt his arms gripped again from both sides as he backed into the hard bodies of the two shaven headed guards. He twisted and tried to escape the firm grip, but it was useless.

"My sons, Klaus and Hans," announced the uniformed man proudly.

Otto Schilling walked off down the red carpet in the centre of the hall, and Herman felt himself pulled forward by the hands of his shaven headed sons. As they walked the considerable length of the hall, Herman noticed what looked like a stage, standing at the opposite end from the entrance through which the men had arrived. Suddenly Herman became aware of a loud moaning sound from his side and turned to see the huge figure of The Ox laid on his side, gagged and bound firmly in the first of a row of wooden seats.

"You already know Herr Ox. It was he who revealed to us your existence. Without his constantly reminding people about those disgusting carvings, we might have assumed you lay rotting at the bottom of the ocean with your little carpenter friends. Once our people brought me the news you were still alive, I could barely believe it. But once I had found Herr Ox here, I soon fooled him into kindly showing me the evidence, the little television film of you crying like a baby while explaining how you escaped. Most entertaining. The power of television I believe."

The Ox mumbled something from behind his gag, but one of the sons delivered a fierce punch to the side of his head, sending the huge man silent as his head lolled forward heavy and unconscious.

"I have lured you both here under false pretences, I am afraid. You see, Herr Schwarz, we both have unfinished business and once I knew you were alive I decided I must fully obey those orders I failed to carry out for the Reich all those years ago.

I plan to complete my orders and kill you, Herr Schwarz.

Your friend here I only needed to ensure I had someone capable of operating the finest high quality broadcasting equipment, in order to carry out the second part of my mission. Your presence here will ensure that he works without any thought of hindrance. You see, a Fourth Reich will begin tonight in this very hall, and you Herr Schwarz, shall watch it happen.

You will witness the re-birth of German's destiny, watch the fatherland emerge from the ashes of the country you and your kind tried to destroy. All this you will witness, just before you die."

Herman stood with his arms firmly gripped on each side as Otto Schilling had paced back and forth before him, explaining the history of his heinous plan.

The Nazi had escaped from the wrecked submarine with five other surviving crew, eluding the British naval ships and swimming eventually to safety. It was as they swam towards an island that they had happened across the single carved wooden figure of Hitler floating in the water. The surviving crewmen had escaped after many adventures through Britain and Ireland, returning to Germany a hero and decorated by the Fuhrer himself after news of the dramatic story had reached Berlin.

Schilling had been promoted immediately into the SS where his loyalty to the Nazi cause saw that he remained part of the Fuhrer's personal guard until the end of the war. Sensing the closing Russian and Allied forces in Berlin in the final few days of the war, Schilling had fled after his Fuhrer's death dressed as a civilian, escaping into those same woods near Mannheim that Herman had used to evade capture in the early weeks of 1939.

After a period in hiding, Schilling had changed his name, acquired false papers in the confusion at the end of the war and moved to America where he had trained and worked as a scientist in California. Returning home after taking an early retirement when his company had been bought over by a Russian firm, Schilling had searched for the remaining five members from that fateful submarine mission. Two had died in battle during the war and one had been shot by the Russians after war trials. However Schilling and his other surviving fellow crew member had begun an underground movement celebrating the Reich and hoping to reinstate the Nazi Party to power in the country.

On hearing word that Herman was still alive, the two men immediately hatched a plot to entice the submarine escapee to Munich using the bait of the carved figure of Hitler. In addition, as details emerged of the close bond between the Strathcarnage man and the head of the local TV station, they planned also to trick the American into bringing broadcasting equipment with him to Germany to allow the Ox to film a final spectacular programme on the discovery of the last carved figure. It had worked perfectly; the arrival and subsequent capture of the Ox providing the men with all the facilities needed to broadcast the forthcoming proceedings live to the German nation.

The plan had worked perfectly until The Ox had grown suspicious of the men's motives during a planning meeting and tried to escape. In the ensuing fight the huge TV executive had killed two of Schilling's group before being violently subdued by the two shaven headed sons. Shortly afterwards they had sent the urgent message to Herman Schwarz using one of the trained dogs of Fraulein Buttress. Now, as planned, the Strathcarnage man had duly arrived, allowing the entire plan to finally reach its glorious climax.

Herman's presence was vital to the entire plan as after the war the story of the escaping men living in the Mannheim woods opposing the rise of the Nazis had taken on mythical proportions. Schilling knew that if his group could display a member of the legendary faction that everyone assumed was long dead, on television and declaring his support for the new Nazi cause, then any opposition to the plan may better be overcome. If Herman refused to read the carefully prepared speech convincingly, both he and The Ox would be executed.

Yet there was to be an even greater and more sinister surprise.

Soon the hall would fill with sympathetic Nazi supporters of all ages, a large crowd recreating the charged atmosphere of the Munich bierkeller gatherings at which the Fuhrer had spoken in the 1930's. The event would be televised throughout the entire country on all TV stations, the entire German television broadcasting network jammed and then over-ridden by technology invented by Schilling's elderly partner.

However Schilling knew he needed a focus for the event in order to create a fervent, unstoppable atmosphere worthy of a return to Nazi party values. The elderly Nazi knew he needed a focus to rival the power of the Fuhrer himself. It was crucial to the plan. Fortunately for the German madman, the Fuhrer was exactly what he had.

At the end of the war, just before his escape, Hitler had shot and killed himself just outside the Berlin bunker where Schilling's group had been based. However, contrary to popular myth surrounding the event, Hitler's body had not been burnt and destroyed. It had been carried away in secret by Otto Schilling. The escaping man had carried Hitler's corpse on his back, dressing the cadaver in civilian clothes until he found a sympathetic undertaker to embalm the body. Schilling had then taken the body deep into the woods in Mannheim where fiercely loyal local taxidermists had removed the internal organs of the Fuhrer before stuffing and mounting him. Schilling had then hidden the prepared body in a secure location and left for America, knowing that one day he would return armed with the knowledge to carry out his plan.

Over the years in America Schilling had studied robotics and animatronics, quickly becoming an expert in the field, driven to learn every last advance and innovation to carry out his fiendish plan. On returning home and finding the body still hidden and preserved perfectly by the dry earth and sand of the specially chosen burial site, Schilling had spent a year hidden away in a remote location performing his hideous technological wizardry. His expertise was to enable the stunning conclusion of a forty year journey leading to this very night.

Hitler was again to walk onto the stage in a Munich bierkeller and give a fierce passionate speech on nationalism to the German people watching at home on TV. Schilling's work was of the highest standard and the animated corpse was indistinguishable from the real thing.

Herman had watched the rehearsals tied to a chair next to The Ox, both men horrified by the accuracy of the animated Fuhrer. The hands thumped on the wooden platform, the black nylon fringe fell over the eyes only to be wiped away by a robotic arm. The body shook with passion all the while the speech was played from a series of speakers built into the pale stuffed neck. There was even a system of minute holes in the forehead and armpit areas to mimic sweating.

Herman had once had the misfortune to have witnessed the real Fuhrer speak and with a chill he realised it was virtually impossible to tell the difference. This robotic Fuhrer was controlled by Schilling from a specially built gallery high above the action, the booth hidden from the crowd's view by the mass of hanging swastika flags. Once the Fuhrer had delivered his speech, Herman would take the stage to renounce his past protests and to symbolically burn the small wooden carving of the Fuhrer onstage while the robot Fuhrer shook his hand and hugged him in a show of mercy. These events would happen with The Ox standing just out of sight at the edge of the stage with a gun held to his temple. Schilling hoped that after broadcast of such a powerful live television performance to the German nation, the Fourth Reich could begin.

The elderly Strathcarnage antique shop owner knew he owed it to his dead colleagues and carving partners to somehow put a stop this madness.

Herman sat backstage with The Ox in a locked room while the hall filled, tied to a chair next to the TV man and watched closely by both of Schilling's heavily built sons. Escape seemed impossible.

As both men sat in dejection listening to the brass band music and the low rumble of voices in the distance, there was a faint knock at the door. One of the sons answered, the open door revealing the face of the smiling old woman with the pram. The woman greeted the two young men by name, kissing them both affectionately on the cheek as she entered the room. She scowled over at the two figures tied to the chairs before hissing a cry of 'traitors' and spitting at them both.

Then the woman asked the two guards if they wanted to see her new 'baby'. It was, she said, a wonderful new puppy which she had named after the Fuhrer's own dog, Blondi. As both men looked at each other and shrugged, they were led toward the pram by the old lady and both men bent over the dark opening.

Suddenly the woman let out a loud whistle and, from the dark hole of the pram hood, two massive Rottweilers exploded out of the canvas and fixed their flashing teeth on each of the guard's soft fat necks. The dog's snarling mouths tore violently at the neck flesh of the pair until they fell, arms flailing, gurgling for mercy, their throats torn out. With another whistle the dogs instantly fell back form their victims, muzzles red and snarling white teeth dripping with blood. The woman bent with a thin smile and patted both the beast's heads.

"Say hello to Charles and Eddie," said the woman happily, clearly delighted at her dog's performance.

"Herman, I am sorry for not revealing myself earlier. I am the wife of the submarine captain who tried to take you to safety many years ago. You never met me but my husband spoke to me often of his plans for your voyage of escape, of your courage and his desire to let you escape our horrible country at that time. After I heard of his death and of the sick hero's return awarded to some of the crew members, I took to training my husband's beloved dogs.

I used our beautiful dogs throughout the remainder of the war to discover fallen airmen and help them to safety. After the war finished, I continued training dogs professionally in remembrance of my husband. When I was contacted by Otto Schilling looking for dogs for his organisation, I decided to supply him with beasts and to join his group undercover. He had no idea who I was.

I was unsure how to stop this madness, but I had to try, in memory of my husband. When I was contacted again asking for a special animal to deliver a message to you, a man I thought long dead, two separate parts of my past fell together and I vowed to do anything within my power to help you, just like my husband had. I found out where this secret base was and once I heard of your arrival in the country, got myself an invite to tonight's spectacle to help you."

Herman mumbled an attempted thanks to the woman, since he was still gagged and tied to the chair. Unable to speak and with the woman looking confused, he shuffled his feet in appreciation.

Untied and free, Herman hugged the woman, the jealous dogs snarling below him. Just then the party heard the music strike up to signal the start of the TV spectacular. It was beginning.

As the group glanced at the wall mounted television, the image of a local football match flickered into snowy interference before being replaced by a clear image of the hall they had stood in earlier; the image accompanied by the loud music they could already hear. The graphic flashed onto the screen, "Der Vierte Reich". They had no time to lose if they were to halt this hideous performance.

Herman untied The Ox and sent him off to discover whether he could find any way of disabling the TV equipment broadcasting the performance, while Herman and the submarine captain's loyal wife made their way towards the control room. As they approached the area, they were stopped by more armed heavily built guards. But even guns were no match for the ferocity of Fraulein Buttress' dogs. Appearing like black streaks of lightning at the sound of the woman's whistle, the dog's sharp teeth closed around the throats of guards before they had even had time to fire their weapons. By the time the dogs were again called off, the men lay twitching and silent, throatless in the bloody corridor.

The Ox, without the advantage of the dogs, had soon returned without luck. All the television equipment was heavily guarded and there was no obvious way of cutting the signals. The heavy American executive suddenly grew pale at the sight of the dogs tearing at the bloody bodies of the guards and had fainted. Herman and Fraulein Buttress tried to rouse the man but had eventually decided that the urgency of their mission forced them to carry on alone. Below them they heard wild astonished cheers rise in the hall and soon after the familiar barking voice begin to give its speech. The robotic Fuhrer had begun addressing the German nation.

As the pair had burst into the control room, Otto Schilling momentarily panicked. The watching audience in homes throughout Germany looked at each other in confusion as the robotic Fuhrer threw both arms aloft, winked, and had executed a brief disco spin at that exact moment, before his controller had regained composure and the robot began speaking again sternly at the microphone. Fraulein Buttress whistled for her dogs again and they stopped feeding at the open necks of the dead guards and appeared at her side dripping fresh blood off of snarling teeth onto the clean white floor of the control room. Schilling had worked with the woman before and knew exactly what the dogs were capable of.

"Listen carefully, Herr Schilling, you will obey completely what I tell you to do, or else Eddie here will tear your throat out before you even have a chance to scream."

The dog snarled at the woman's side, as if understanding the words, wet blood coating exposed fangs.

"Herr Schwarz will instruct you of his wishes and you shall follow them to the letter, is that understood? I have taught him the attack signal. "

One of the dogs moved forward snarling, stopping just in front of the frightened controller and staring into him with lifeless black eyes. The sweating man in uniform nodded his understanding. Fraulein Buttress leaned forward and whispered something into Herman Schwarz's ear and he smiled and nodded. Then the woman bent forward to the dog sitting patiently at her heel and issued it with new instructions. As she pulled the door open the second dog ran off deep into the building, followed by the woman. Herman moved up behind Otto Schilling and placed his hands on his uniformed shoulders.

"Now Herr Schilling, let us begin."

Over the next ten minutes Schilling was forced, faced with the razor sharp teeth of a killer dog, to follow the precise instructions given to him by Herman Schwarz. As they reached the stage, the sound of the barked speech suddenly stopped, only to be replaced by a loud disco soundtrack. Herman looked around confused by the sudden change in mood and caught sight of smiling The Ox behind the lights of a control desk at the rear of the hall, giving him a thumb up.

To begin with Herman had him make the Fuhrer do some basic disco dance moves as he barked out his speech, the audience in the hall growing confused and following the Fuhrer's lead, assuming it part of the ritual. Then Herman instructed Schilling to have the Fuhrer swing his pelvis towards the crowd while winking and licking his lips, before eventually grabbing at himself wildly with a cupped hand around the groin. As the German TV audience had watched at home, most were now in hysterics.

Finally, on a signal waved from the side of the stage by Fraulien Buttress, Herman instructed that the robotic Fuhrer remove his trousers and lean forward over the onstage podium. Then, with her sudden sharp whistle of instruction, the second dog had sprinted lustily onto the stage. What happened next quite rightly left the crowd open mouthed.

The crowd had grown steadily hysterical by this point in the hall and had cheered, assuming that this unusual turn of events was all part of some secret Fourth Reich master plan. With the Fuhrer in position and now fully engaged from the rear by the wild eyed slavering dog, Herman led Otto Schilling from the control room and back down toward the stage.

Herman enquired about a back entrance to the hall and the distressed man in uniform waved a limp defeated hand toward a heavy metallic door at the end of a small corridor partially hidden by more flags. Schilling knew his dream was finally over.

However there remained one final important matter.

Herman asked Schilling for the final wooden carving, that of the Fuhrer. Schilling groped around in his tunic pocket and carefully pulled out the small figure. As Herman reached for the item, Schilling opened his hand and let it drop to the floor. The Strathcarnage man's eyes followed the object and Schilling had taken his chance, using the distraction to suddenly break free. As Herman looked up, he caught sight of Fraulein Buttress watching the uniformed German running towards what they both assumed was an attempted escape. Fraulein Buttress was about to whistle her dogs, but when Herman saw the distraught Nazi heading not for the exit door but for the middle of the stage, Herman had stopped her with a gentle wave of his hand.

The pair watched as Otto Schilling reached the centre of the stage and tried to reach his Fuhrer. Bending over to try and pull the snarling dog off from the partially naked frame of the German leader, Otto Schilling found it was impossible to remove a large muscular dog in heat from its object of desire and the animal had continued thrusting away while the robot held firmly to the wooden podium, the whole ensemble now rocking violently around the stage in time to the thumping beats.

Watching the uniformed Nazi attempting to pull the passionate canine off his beloved robotic Fuhrer had given Herman an idea, and as he leaned forward to inform Fraulein Buttress of his plan. Pulling back he met her smiling gaze turning towards him. She was clearly in full approval. The woman whistled loudly to issue a fresh command to her beloved animals.

In a flash the second dog was onstage and his flashing jaws had ripped off the uniform trousers of Otto Schilling before leaping passionately at the non-robotic Nazi. The TV cameras closed in on the surprised face of the exposed elderly German, now jumping around between snarling canine bodies and the now rocking Fuhrer at his podium. The crowd in the hall cheered again, assuming again that this was another part of the show and many began dancing along, gyrating to the soundtrack being played on the hall's huge speakers. Then tragedy struck.

As the frenzied dog closest to the Fuhrer became more wild eyed in its attentions, it became clear from the TV close ups of the scene that his muzzle had begun to snarl in some sort of bestial sign of intense excitement. The dog rolled his dark brown eyes, let out a howl of final canine release and fell forwards spent and exhausted, still gripping the now damp robotic fiend. As they fell, the pair tumbled over the swastika decorated podium revealing the Fuhrer's exposed and now moistened and shining upturned robotic bottom. As the bestial produce of adoration pooled and then gathered inside the robot with an intense sucking sound akin to a draining sink, strange things began to happen.

The sudden introduction of moisture to the electronic interior of the robotic Fuhrer proved to be an event even Otto Schilling had never anticipated when building his model. As the dog rolled away over the Fuhrer's now jerking legs it howled with animal satisfaction while the Fuhrer's eyes and head had began sparking violently and with a sudden explosion, the half naked black haired robot had burst into flames on the floor.

Otto Schilling had tried to push himself away from the scene, but the frenzied attack of the other passionate dog was driving him toward the now clearly ablaze and yet still repeatedly saluting robot.

As the dog continued to attack and push him back across the stage, Schilling let out a hideous animal scream as a flaming grasping robotic hand clamped itself without warning around his ankle. Unable to remove the vice like grip, the flames began burning the legs of his uniform trousers. The crazed dog had taken this scream as some signal of enjoyment and had increased the ferocity of its sexual attentions, repeatedly leaping up at the man and making any escape from the carnage now impossible. The elderly German held onto the dogs paws tightly, consumed by fear and pain. As the growing pyre began to burn all around it with hideous howls of pain and crackling flesh, lit dog hair spiralled up to ignite the hanging flags. Watching the scene open mouthed, Herman turned to Fraulien Buttress, shouting to her over the noise of the four four beat to escape immediately with him through the steel door. The woman raised her chin and began to shake her head slowly but firmly.

"My dogs and my husband have given their lives to defeat this evil and now I have nothing left to live for. I will remain here and fight. Please, go and take great care to hide the carving of Hitler, for the authorities in Germany will wish to crush anyone who had anything to do with this night."

As she finished speaking, the hall's massive sprinkler system creaked into life and began to shower the vast space with water. As the flood rose over their ankles, the woman dragged Herman towards the door.

"Please leave and lock the door behind you, just as they once did to you. Finally we might finally be rid of the curse of the most fervent Nazi followers in Germany, for tonight they have all gathered in this hall. Leave and be happy that you have continued both mine and my husband's wishes. And thank you for your courage."

With these final words she kissed the man on the cheek and threw herself back into the mass of panicking bodies in the hall, heading towards her still flaming pile of dogs. Herman looked around for the large figure of The Ox, and saw him pushing through the crowd towards Herman. As the pair escaped through the door at his end of the hall, The Ox jammed a large metal pole through the outer handle, using his strength to twist and bend the metal permanently sealing the fate of those inside.

As the men both headed out through the walled garden and made their way through the snow covered Munich streets, a rush of police sirens was approaching the area trying to get a fix on the television signal. As cars and vans flashed past in the falling snow, Herman remembered the final instructions of Fraulien Buttress about being discovered with the carved statue. Before leaving the warren of lanes and entering the more brightly lit streets the Strathcarnage man steadied himself against the massive body of The Ox and with a wince and a momentary squeal of discomfort, the German man inserted the statue into the one place where it was most unlikely to be found.

The pair split up and Herman left the area on foot, eventually heading across country by train for the German coast. Once in Hamburg he had found a fishing trawler heading north that had agreed to carry him as a passenger. Once safely off the boat and after finding another ship to take him safely to his home in Strathcarnage, Herman relaxed. Only when safely home would he allow himself to extract this final carved masterpiece.

Unfortunately, disembarking from the boat on its arrival at Strathcarnage harbour, Herman slipped on some ice on the gangplank and fell heavily backwards on the stone quayside.

The sudden impact caused the anally secreted cargo to splinter, causing massive internal injuries as the wooden shards dug deeply into the man and pierced his lower internal organs. After being rushed to the local hospital the internal injuries were found to be severe and requiring an immediate operation. The old man had never recovered and had died whilst in surgery, the final remains of the carved figure only being extracted after death. The wooden pieces were retrieved by the newly arrived figure of The Ox and given to a local model maker called Crosby Stanton who had happily pieced the fragments back together with great skill and affection.

The antiques shop now lies permanently closed as a tribute to Herman Schwarz and if you should ever be passing the quayside in Strathcarnage, press a face to the window and take a minute to marvel at the courage and dedication of those who died to bring you the fine display of the depraved but beautifully carved figures of The Mannheim Seven.

Herman Schwarz 1920-1978

# CHAPTER 16

# Day Fourteen – The Final Half Chapter

Morgan Kells had been faithfully recording the lives and deaths of Strathcarnage residents since the shipwreck. That fateful night had seen a horrible storm in the area, a tempest during which the S.S. Cloven Hoof and its consignment of mental unfortunates had been driven onto and subsequently sunk by the submerged rocks just off the coast. As the only survivor of the wreck dependable enough to be permitted safe possession of the sharpened writer's quill, Morgan had by default acquired the role of town scribe.

The literate woman had attempted to teach basic literacy to some of the more lucid souls amongst the shipwrecked gathering, but none had ever progressed beyond an angry illegible scrawl, any lessons often ending prematurely with extended displays of brutal frustration. Such impenetrable scribbles and violently subdued pupils were never going to produce the adequate capacity of legible script needed to dispute Morgan's position as town record keeper. However this key role amongst the survivors was not the only notable talent Morgan possessed.

She was also viewed as by many in the group as something of a supernatural prophet, an opinion not based simply on the fact she was the only survivor who could read. The tall, willowy woman also possessed an extraordinary sixth sense.

Some strange power enabled Morgan to feel, both mentally and physically, when someone nearby approached their end. She could feel the slow march of death towards the victim, sensing the dark shadow gathering well in advance of the event, not simply when it suddenly appeared, knocking on the door and welcoming itself inside for tea and last rites. Weeks before any death occurred the tall woman could begin to feel the gradual deep chill of a sinister force, a malevolent coldness passing over her soul. The feeling grew stronger the closer she drew to the person soon to die.

Morgan had led a quiet, gentle existence in her previous village, respected and befriended by all. Nevertheless, as townsfolk learned of her chilling power, the oddly tall, angular figure came to be shunned by anxious neighbours, terrified of those sinister forces at work within. Soon it was whispered that Morgan was possessed by demons and before long locals branded the placid woman a witch.

In due course Morgan was locked up by fearful villagers and put under guard in her own home, before being tried in her absence by local town elders in front of a hysterical throng of superstitious townsfolk in the market square. The woman had been confirmed a heretic and a witch by the village mob and had immediately been dragged from her home in shackles to the shoreline outside the small settlement and set adrift on the ruthless ocean, her arms chained to the sides of a small vessel devoid of oars. In the thin rain of dawn, a ragged group of villagers in black lined the shore and prayed loudly for the woman's soul, eager to witness her being cast out from their number forever. Morgan floated slowly out of the bay sobbing, the small craft carrying her away to sea on the tide, to almost certain death.

Yet the gentle woman had survived her journey, washed aground days later hundreds of miles up the coast. Morgan had lived, but her suspicious rescuers were soon to discover the strange 'gift' that had led such a quiet woman to be set adrift chained to a small craft. A few short weeks later her new kinsfolk imprisoned her behind the thick walls of a local asylum. At the time of the shipwreck of the Cloven Hoof the thin mysterious woman was being transferred by the ship to the mainland, sailing along with other inmates of the remote decaying hospital building to a newly built facility in one of the big cities. During this journey they had encountered the massive storm destined to drive them ashore and smash the craft's wooden hull upon the black rocks.

Morgan helped drag bodies from the massive waves and had watched during the following days as the shipwreck survivors explored the complex of naturally formed caves which lay under the jagged cliffs rising to the sky far above. The educated woman often climbed onto the high ledge of rock by the shoreline to record events, using a dried out and only partially used leather bound book used to register the ships cargo. Sitting surrounded by screeching seabirds and booming waves, the woman began to write these first village records. She kept notes on the search for shelter taking place before her, faithfully recording the names of those survivors mentally stable enough to work and partake in the birth of the village.

Morgan detailed the celebrations on the day the search party had gone behind the waterfall and returned hours later proclaiming they had found a site not only on which to build, but to keep the entire party safe from discovery. It was the tall thin woman who had scratched those first reports of the massive hidden cave behind the waterfall, with the sunlight flooding through a colossal ragged opening hundreds of feet above. It was she who took down notes detailing the discovery of grass and trees growing within, the exited men yelling excitedly about being able to use the light from above to grow crops. It was her slender pen that wrote of those first plans to build shelter, and about the new freedom the site had gifted everyone. All of these first hand accounts are still available now, but only because of Morgan Kells.

It was also Morgan Kells who also christened the place with its new name of Strathcarnage.

Remembering that 'Strath' was the ancient Scottish prefix for 'by a river', and choosing 'carnage' from the pandemonium she witnessed on a daily basis all around her, the tall woman had suggested the name during one of the first gatherings in the vast cave. The shipwrecked survivors had gathered together in a small knot within the huge cavern and surrounded by lamps in the growing darkness within the space those mentally stable enough had voted, deciding upon naming the home of their newfound liberty. The name was passed with murmurs of approval and the site of the yet to be built village of Strathcarnage was born.

However in addition to her documenting the site and the lives of those within, Morgan soon found herself again consumed by the chilling forces of her strange powers of death prophecy. The woman was repeatedly drawn to members of the shipwrecked party ahead of their death, but having learnt her lessons previously, the thin woman began documenting these most important events in total secrecy. Without a word to another soul, Morgan began to record the soon to be extinguished lives of the village for posterity. She took to keeping detailed notes of eyewitness accounts and taking notes of the experiences of the soon to be gone, hopeful that such recordings would someday become significant to the history and remembrance of the place. Should the group fail to survive, her carefully recorded story would be the only remaining trace of these brave people and of the group's struggles for survival. As such, these tales were written carefully by the woman, words recorded faithfully as they passed from the very lips of these town founders, vigilant notes of the details of soon to be departed lives, saved for future generations.

These books were attentively written, Morgan spending much time and mind to carefully catalogue each small detail, scratching these last testaments onto animal skins with her quill, using thick black ink made by crushing the dark black beetles which she had discovered living in plentiful supply in a dead tree on the shoreline. The woman worked alone at night by the light of candles salvaged from the wreck, carefully inscribing and illustrating each of those stories gifted to her.

Each individual in the village was appreciative of the prospect to proffer up significant stories and individual histories to be remembered, sharing key events for Morgan to record, in order to pass on their combined remembrance to curious future inhabitants of the town yet to be born. Morgan gradually recorded each member's story, careful to disguise her terrible power of prediction. Smiling members of the group remained unaware as Morgan wrote that she knew which of the contributors would live on and which would soon die. Unknown to the group, Morgan made sure she concentrated on those records needing to be recorded with most urgency, before they were lost forever.

Once the enscribing of a tale of a 'near dead' was complete, the thin woman would leave the person's shack and allow the teller of the story to more contentedly and peacefully await the icy hand of death, fully satisfied that their existence had been documented and that they would never be forgotten. Morgan always remained totally unconscious of those exact details of how and at what time the onrushing presence of death would visit; only that it was sure to creep silently under the door before long.

Morgan's concluding act was to return to the storyteller's home following their death and cut sufficient skin from the body with which to cover and personalise the bound volume of stories she had produced. This was happily provided by the ship's surgeon, since the skin was one of the few pieces of the fresh dead that could not be easily eaten by the hungry party. As a result, each of these books of the dead were covered in the soft human leather of the person responsible for the content within.

These tomes would then be decorated by red hot metal, the given name of the dead contributor burned onto the spine before the book was placed securely and in the utmost secrecy within a deep cave together with the gradually mounting collection of other volumes. These volumes of books soon grew to be an astonishing testimony of every key event of historical and social significance ever to have occurred in the small town. Soon recognising the work involved as the population grew, Morgan began to concentrate her efforts solely on those she felt were soon to pass from this world.

These early death books, with names scorched less competently on the cover with the straight edges of the raw heated ship's nails, told vivid stories of the original shipwreck and of how the mental unfortunates and crew had been driven against the uneven shoreline wall, the great wooden ship smashed from under them whilst attempting to reach the safety of land.

These original volumes explained how the shipwrecked survivors had found themselves floating in the angry sea, and how they had clambered over the black ragged barrier of rock at the shore to find refuge on the expanse of sunken ground concealed from discovery behind the towering dark parapets.

The testimony told of the first cold nights huddled together for warmth and shelter in the smaller caves, and of how the early settlers had at first searched for a way out of the place. However with every potential rescue vessel liable to turn them in for a reward, and examining the colossal cliffs on every side, the group had rapidly decided on remaining where they were, seeing any escape as nothing more than an impossible dream they could never have fulfilled.

The majority of the shipwrecked feared being sent back to prisons and mental asylums if discovered alive and so the group voted to remain in this location and take their chances at trying to survive on their own. The small number of surviving ship's crew decided to remain too, anxious of being held responsible for the loss of their costly government craft and sentenced to certain death by angry and powerful owners.

Salvaging as much wood and materials possible from the wrecked hull, and discovering plentiful fresh water flowing both from the waterfall and from a river running down through the centre of the cave, the more rational men soon acknowledged continued survival was a possibility and set to work building themselves a new habitat.

Working only with the most rudimentary implements and entirely by hand, the shipwrecked group began to dig and slowly shape themselves an entire new village home inside the massive cave discovered concealed entirely from view behind the cliff waterfall. Sheltered from the sea and wind by the internal location and from the most unpleasant of the elements from the massive arching cliffs above, the survivors soon began to create a larger and larger home. The town of Strathcarnage began to take shape.

Through the older death books you can explore how the town evolved from the earliest basic timber structures along the grassy plain at the cave mouth, to those built after discovery of the massive cave, slowly constructed from the remains recovered from the destroyed ship and from a few others wrecked along that treacherous stretch of coast. The more rudimentary and basic shelters began to vanish little by little as the survivors carved deeper into the cliff walls, creating caves to live in but also using the extracted rock to build more sheltered and sturdy housing on the flatter land next to the small river that ran across the cave floor. Before long the group were slowly creating a new world inside the massive protective womb behind the cliffs.

These earlier volumes also follow the steady community growth and social development of a population entirely cut off from the rest of the world. Careful reading of the death books carries the reader through the various stages of both home building and social growth, observing Strathcarnage's evolution over hundreds of years of seclusion into a recognisable forerunner of the enigmatic and twisted community it has evolved into currently.

There were details of how the town's hidden anchorage had been slowly hewn inwards from the waterfall at the cave's front opening, the river inside the cave channelled around the working men as the surrounding rock was dug out over decades, much of the resulting stone reused to build and pave the rapidly expanding town. Working patiently, generations of the population had created not only a long curved harbour at the edge of the town but had also created a deep channel following the path of the small meandering stream draining the waterfall to the sea. This natural waterway had been deepened and straightened, expanded by the townsfolk into a navigable river leading from the hidden harbour behind the waterfall, out across the plain, before connecting with the open sea through a hidden manmade opening in the seafront rock face that had once been scarcely wide enough to allow a man to pass through. The books told how the town's small secret harbour had gradually developed and expanded into a haven for shadowy trading and smuggling, the slowly growing traffic nurtured by a collection of brutality, robbery, prostitution and good fortune.

The complete history of the settlement was readily available at Morgan's ink tainted fingertips. But her enthusiasm and hard effort at recording the town's goings on had not been appreciated by all.

Following numerous incidents of fights and murders between various opposing factions in the original shipwrecked group, the new village residents had decided it prudent to assign someone from their number to enforce Strathcarnage's perverse set of unwritten laws.

A vote was taken amongst town elders and a suitable man selected from amongst the most trusted villagers. That first lawman in the town wasted no time in securing himself access to the historical town records of Morgan Kells. An overweight Samoan crew member had been selected for the role, and the obese man known to locals only as 'Fat Judas' had swiftly requested the power to confiscate Morgan's books. In being awarded full access, the Samoan man had found himself in possession of the death books and their confessional contents. Eager to demonstrate himself worthy of his new trusted role of authority, the first Strathcarnage lawman scoured the newer volumes of the growing death library for examples of criminal goings-on.

After examining numerous volumes and taking pages of poorly scrawled notes and observations in a hand ironically educated by Morgan herself, Fat Judas had called at a number of homes and detained locals for trial on evidence of offences the lawman had discovered detailed in the pages of the death volumes. A number of lengthy periods of imprisonment in the newly excavated penal complex were only just avoided when the fat Samoan's body had been discovered floating in the harbour the day before the very first Strathcarnage book trials had been scheduled to commence.

The town medical examiner had later ruled the overweight policeman a casualty of suicide, thought to be brought on by the pressures of his new responsible position. The former ship's surgeon ruled that Judas had shot himself 34 times, cut his own throat, before decapitating himself, dismembering his own body and throwing his own remains out to sea. It was, he told the happy crowd buying him drinks after the findings were announced, an open and shut case.

Nevertheless much harm had been done to the fragile trust in the village. Local people, already apprehensive of the rumours that Morgan's sharp rap at their door was followed soon after by an imminent demise, now viewed the existence of such detailed accounts of incriminating information to be a dangerous precedent. Residents panicked to think that information passed to the woman as deathbed memory might one day return to haunt close relatives and others mentioned in tales and still alive. There was always a risk of great damage to the living, they assumed, should any future village lawmakers have chosen to go through the pages of recorded information from the dead. Before long an angry mob had formed outside the book keeper's home and only the last minute involvement of the original ship's captain, now the first Lord Strathcarnage, had saved both Morgan and her collected works from being burned.

After this ugly episode, Morgan locked herself away in her home, fearful for her own safety walking the dark shadowy streets of the steadily growing settlement, and some few village deaths went unrecorded for a period of months during her seclusion. Morgan knew she needed to flee the town for her own safety, and that of her books. Yet even though Morgan appeared to the village to have ended her task, she had not yet fully given up. The tall thin woman, fearful of a repeat of past treatment and exile at the hands of previous superstitious villagers, felt she might yet somehow continue to record, if she could only get out of the town to some nearby location. However this time her forced eviction was to be her own choice and had to be undertaken on her own terms.

So, late one night, once the village was sound asleep and silent, the woman left her home and crept silently, moving like a ghost through the curved town streets and progressively exploring each of the maze of empty caves in the cliff wall. Her journey eventually lead her deep into the caverns at the bottom of the farthest away cliff from the waterfall, a deep but narrow opening abandoned after being hidden behind a fatal and massive rock fall and now thought of as dangerous, cursed and unworkable.

Yet Morgan was dedicated to escape from her latest village rejection by finding herself some new hidden location. So after a number of nights climbing around over the edge of the fallen rocks, squeezing her thin body through narrow passageways into this cave's most deep and dangerous shadows, she had come across a wonderful sight. Exploring the dangerous crumbling depths while her thin candlelight flickered against huge piles of fallen rocks, Morgan had happened upon a great pale seam of sandstone in the innermost cave wall. Pushing at the crumbling soft stone with her thin fingers, Morgan had decided to embark on an attempt to carve herself a path to a secret safe place from which to work and live.

Night after night, hidden deep in the very bowels of the dripping and groaning depths of the rock face, Morgan used a rudimentary hammer and a small crushed tin cup to dig upwards through the layer of crumbling stone, the already softer rock weakened further by a tiny steady stream of running water. The effort was hard and perilous, the slight woman nearly being killed on a few occasions by unexpected falls of rock from above as she worked her way slowly and steadily up through the narrow seam.

As she dug on, moving further upwards, she began to fashion herself tiny elementary steps as she cut through the workable stone, allowing each night's fresh digging to begin from a firm foundation. Although each step took hours to carve in the cramped conditions, she made steady progress.

One hundred and seventy weeks and three days after beginning her work in the subterranean cavern deep under the rockfall at the rear of the town, Morgan swung her hammer at the stone and saw the latest durable flint head disappear through the unyielding rock face.

As she picked away cautiously at the freshly made hole, Morgan saw tiny shafts of moonlight appear. Realising that she had reached some opening on the other side of the solid rock she worked frantically over the next few nights at increasing the extent of the tiny crack, working at the rock with bleeding knuckles until she could squeeze her head and then her thin body through the steadily widening gap, pushing out to the other side like a newborn.

As she looked around at a new cave lit by the faint glow of a full moon, the fatigued woman lay down on a ledge, curled up and slept deeply, contented she might well have found the perfect location for her secret new dwelling.

When she awoke to the echo of the shrieking seabirds, it was fully daylight, and Morgan had to squint against the harsh sunlight flooding into the newfound opening. Pulling her aching body unsteadily to her feet, Morgan walked towards the light and found herself leaving the warm stale atmosphere seeping from the narrow passage. She was now standing upright in cool open air.

The Strathcarnage woman had carved her way inch by inch up within the winding seam inside the rock face and had emerged hundreds of feet above the ground inside another small cave. This new opening was narrow and small, but it led Morgan to a colossal breach, worn into the rock of the cliff face high above the cave.

The cave base had been worn flat and level by a continually running stream flowing into the cavern from above, the running water eroding out this space from a solid mass of rock over hundreds of thousands of years to create an immense jagged cathedral like space. The water still ran down the walls like liquid silver, across the floor of the cave before exiting through a window-like hole on the narrowest wall. As Morgan reached this breach she saw far below the line of the thin strand of grass the shipwrecked had dragged themselves onto after first climbing the massive outer wall of rock on the shore. The green band was now hundreds of feet beneath, nestled behind the deep gutter of black rock. She better understood now from this perspective how the village had remained in effect invisible for so many years.

The cliff grew straight up from the sea on both sides of the site, then right along the coast as far as the eye could see in both directions, rising terrifyingly from roaring waves in a rough vertical wall, but then abruptly, at just this spot, the shoreline bowed outward in a lengthy arc far beneath. At the sea edge laid huge walls of black rock which followed the shape of a long arcing overhang of the cliffs above, another jumble of massive sea rocks hiding the mouth of the river. Morgan could hear the distant rumble of the waterfall pouring out further along the cliff wall, probably through a cavern just like this one, falling hundreds of feet down over the cliff face and disguising the mouth of the cave inside which Strathcarnage lay.

Mirroring the arc of the valley below, a huge overhang sat above the site, beneath which Morgan guessed lay the massive cave inside which the town was little by little being built. From her vantage point Morgan could also follow the grey path of the river exiting from beneath the rock face, outward from the town's newly dug harbour. The river looked silver against the green valley, vanishing with a series of wide twists into an undetectable wrinkle where the townspeople had smashed the gap for the river opening in the black shoreline rock barrier. From this elevated location the woman could see that unless you were conscious of the breach where river flowed into vast sea between the narrow rock passage, the river entrance too would remain wholly undetectable. It was a phenomenon both as extraordinary as it was beautiful.

Over the next few weeks, Morgan had carried her volumes of Death books a small amount at a time up through the steep stepped winding channel she had engraved into the rock, transporting them upwards each night to be stored in the original lower cavern. After piling them and covering them with water-resistant canvas, Morgan began to think about erecting a new home for both herself and her books on the vast grassy ledge high above.

Given that transporting building rock upward through the cliff passageway was both complicated and unworkable, she decided her best plan was to excavate rock from the bare walls of the cavern around her. After some inspection of the site, Morgan discovered the remaining walls were composed of the hardest rock and completely impractical. However, on further examinations of the cave, she realised she was now close to the top of the sea cliff. Soon the ever practical woman found and followed the seam of rock that had initially allowed her to dig upwards from below. She decided to follow the seam further, to excavate herself even more stairs upwards, towards the sky.

Digging slowly and carefully, Morgan soon carved an additional staircase upwards through the rock towards the cliff top. She made certain that the top of the steep stairway was undetectable, carving a small number of the final steps simply as rough invisible rock footholds, concealed under a treacherous looking overhanging ledge above, making any chance discovery of her spot impossible.

Once her hard work was at last complete, Morgan Kells climbed upward and cautiously peered over the grassy cliff edge for the first time. Seeing no-one around, the thin woman pulled herself upright onto the cliff top. Glancing around and seeing only forest, the thin woman smiled at the thought of being the first Strathcarnage inhabitant to have travelled outside the secret cave far below for over two decades.

Far from experiencing an enlightening feeling of liberty and escape, Morgan rapidly grew nervous and became apprehensive of detection and a swift return to an asylum. After another swift glance around, the woman climbed back over the cliff edge and onto her staircase, retreating quickly downwards away from the terrifying world. She would be back, for she needed material to construct a permanent shelter for both herself and for her death books. But she had already decided that visiting the outside world would only be a journey undertaken in the direst of emergencies.

After a few weeks of climbing onto the top of the cliffs and exploring the surrounding forest undiscovered, Morgan could find nothing suitable to employ to build her new home. There was a little random stone, but nothing sufficient to construct anything large enough to house both her and her library. The forest provided potential for wood, but she had no method of cutting down the vast trees and moving the huge load to the cliff edge and down her small winding stone stairs. But then, while wandering far deeper in the forest, a chance discovery had provided the woman with an answer.

Feeling a strange and sudden rush of extraordinary power, Morgan felt guided through the dense woods in the direction of some strange influence. Approaching through a clearing into an open patch of ground, the woman saw what had once been a large walled square, long overgrown and the enclosing structure now broken and derelict. Pushing through the thick weeds and undergrowth, she discovered the site of a long abandoned burial ground. It was quite a large space, and many memorial stones and crosses lay flattened and overgrown by years of neglect. Nevertheless the power of the site gave Morgan an idea. And so it came to pass that little by little, with sacks of material dug out and carried in sacks down the steep hand carved stairs, Morgan Kells would live in a house built exclusively of human bones.

Once her home was finished, the tall woman moved the death books into the small cottage of bone and resolved to continue her work as the town scribe from there, as a mark of respect to the deep power that had given her this unique talent and that had led her to the graveyard.

However Morgan was growing older and she knew that she could not carry on the tradition of the death books forever. She had decided to make certain that her lineage was kept alive by somehow raising a female heir to carry on her work. Having watched her mother fearfully predict both her own death and that of her bewildered father, she now knew her strange power was passed on only directly through the female line. It was a tricky task for a single woman, but not without a solution.

Morgan returned to the village in disguise and hung around the unruly town taverns until she managed to discover a potential father to allow continuance of her line. She remained unobserved in her search, since few of the growing population of locals mixed with the treacherous and feral sailors and smugglers who used the town harbour bars for deals and scheming. The cliff dwelling woman had already searched the village folk for suitable men, examining faces she knew well for those bright enough to both read and write and who looked physically healthy. Morgan had repeatedly drawn a blank.

The woman also had the advantage of knowing the family histories of all the village residents and had found it impossible to select a prospective father from a bloodline unaffected by either sickness or mental fragility.

It was a futile search, for although almost all the villagers still clandestinely used Morgan to pass on their family stories for recording in the death books, to be openly seen with the tall, thin woman in public was looked upon as a serious violation of village custom. The locals, however, remained content in offering the strange woman their personal histories, convinced her records were now being stored in a deeply secret location, said by the woman to be protected by witchcraft.

While Morgan, as an original town founder, was protected in ancient law from open retribution from the village elders, any person knowingly associating with the strange woman was not, with both the guilty party and their family liable to be banished from the village forever. No local man would dare father her child, and this led Morgan to searching the harbour bars among the new phenomenon of visiting smugglers and sailors.

The father of Morgan Kells Junior was the navigator of a Dutch smuggling vessel, a physically powerful, fair-haired man called Gert Tyssen. Morgan had seduced the drunken sailor during a walk along the new harbour side road and, subsequent to getting him to partake in some precautionary light reading and writing, had performed on the sailor a prolonged collection of immoral sexual acts before leaving the exhausted man asleep on the village green before escaping back through the darkness upward to her clifftop home. Impregnated with intelligent Dutch seed, Morgan continued surreptitiously working at creating the death books of Strathcarnage until her body silhouette was too rounded to allow her to safe passage on the secret protracted climbs through her steep cliff stairs to the town.

Sadly Morgan's first born child had been a boy. Since the woman knew that only the female children in her family had been gifted the power of predicting death, the superfluous infant was pickled and set aside on a jar on her fireside shelf, floating around in vinegar while she returned to trawling the bars. Eventually the woman located another potential father and attempted impregnation for the second occasion, this time deep in the bowels of a fishing boat with a visiting Finnish trawler man who was a keen reader.

This time the union was a success, and to Morgan Kells was born a girl. Morgan named the child 'Morgan', after her own mother.

The infant Morgan soon grew and was carefully trained to read and write by her mother, in due course taking over her mother's task as solitary life custodian of the death books. And so this custom continued from generation to generation, the duty of the collection and care of Strathcarnage's death books passed on through the bloodline of the isolated Kells females, all traditionally christened Morgan. The collection in the stone cottage grew little by little over the years, slowly increasing volumes of skin covered books collecting on the groaning shelves of the now extended cottage as each additional generation of Morgan Kells' continued recording histories and important stories from generation after generation of the soon to be departed Strathcarnage population far below.

But then catastrophe had struck.

The most recent of the twenty six generations of Morgan Kells', Morgan's mother Morgan, had given birth to a child only after a elongated and agonizing labour, a complication brought on, many thought, by the drawn out and quite numerous ineffectual attempts to finally get herself heavy with child.

Morgan's mother Morgan had found falling pregnant a near impossibility and had almost given up the search for a father. Having now had intimate relations with the virtually the entire male population of the isolated town and the majority of its seafaring visitors, all without success, Morgan's mother had been forced to set her values lower than those of preceding generations. After unproductive attempts to secure herself a share of workable seed, Morgan Kells had been required in desperation to sexually pair herself with a colossal swivel eyed idiot of a local man called Augustus Fannon.

The mentally unsound 'father to be' had failed all criteria which preceding generations of Kells' had used to determine the quality lineage of intelligent Morgan's. However since Morgan was running out of time and womb efficiency, the latest keeper of the books had been forced to turn to the only male in the village rumoured to have sperm that swam more powerfully than those powerful Russian fishing boats that visited the town even through the harshest winter seas.

Augustus had fathered a regiment of children already among the village's less exacting and more drunken women, and Morgan slowly grew to accept the mentally challenged hulk as her last hope. Sure enough, a number of weeks after her brief eye-rolling interaction with the hulking man against a harbour side wall, Morgan found she was finally pregnant. Luckily however, before Morgan informed the unsightly idiot brute of his success, the man had fallen into a mincing machine whilst working at the local pig processing plant. His fatherly remains had been wrapped and secretly exported to China as meat pie filling, setting sail in the hold of a Chinese tramp steamer before Morgan had even discovered news of her successful impregnation.

Morgan had experienced a terrible pregnancy with the child. Knowing this was her final chance at providing the next generation of Morgan Kells' with an heir, the woman looked after herself carefully and remained safe in her home throughout the full term, hoping all was well. Alas even with such careful precautions, all was not to be successful.

On producing the progeny alone on the stone floor of the cottage, and on seeing exactly what had happened, Morgan let out a loud scream, the ferocity of which had been heard echoing through the streets of the town far below. When she had looked down at her newborn child she had witnessed a sight which would prove fatal to the continuing of the Kells sisterhood and lead, eventually, to the events recounted in this book.

The child had been born a hermaphrodite. Furnished generously with both sex organs, it was the hideous sight of the deformed dual appendages that had caused

Morgan to scream so vigorously. As the new mother examined her child it soon became clear that more was wrong with the child's internal plumbing that had even first been feared.

On emitting the huge scream of disappointment at the unusually equipped infant, the woman's outburst had caused the child to perform a spectacular act of dual incontinence. Morgan had watched on in tears as the unfortunate infant had expelled first urine and then a runny mixture of infant faecal matter from an unfathomable collection of ragged openings. The child's internal plumbing was fatally flawed and Morgan had slid down the cold stone wall crying, destroyed by the knowledge that this child was destined to be remembered as the final Morgan Kells.

Once over the initial shock the depressed mother had nursed her growing baby with all the love and caring she could muster. However, no matter how much she loved her offspring, in the back of her mind she knew that this child represented the end of a noble line of death book keepers stretching back through centuries in the small town. As she sat teaching the young Morgan, just as her own mother Morgan had taught her, Morgan wept at the futility of the task. No matter how brilliant, how eager or how gifted with powers the strangely genitaled child would prove to be, the long tradition was ultimately destined to end finally with her.

Eventually the mother of the latest Morgan had passed away, leaving the strangely designed child alone in the bone cottage high above the village, continuing the task of keeping of the death books. Alone and painfully aware of the finality that her/his birth had brought to the historical role of keeper of the books, Morgan had began to grow increasingly depressed and desolate.

She had wandered the village drunk and with a haunted look, getting into increasingly violent fights with both sailors and townspeople, content that her special powers would keep her from causing any fatalities. She had lost an eye to a travelling Turkish shower curtain salesman in a knife fight in the Ruptured Horse bar, been kicked unconscious at a village fete by angry farmers and made haunted local children cry and vomit when drunkenly exposing her unclad genitalia after staggering uninvited into a biology lesson at the local school watched over by the haunted teacher Cassandra Leech. Nothing could remove the deep pain of knowing she was the last in the Kells line, and feeling that crushing pain of accepting the death of the Kells' line was to be her fault.

But then, out of nowhere, as she grew increasingly aware of that creeping black shadow of her own death finally closing in on her, ready to wipe out generations of Strathcarnage tradition, a miracle had occurred..."

## CHAPTER 17

## Day Seventeen – The Tale's End

"And then what? What next? What was the miracle?" The fat policeman leaned forward excitedly, his plump round face reddening with anticipation as the chair creaked below, protesting at the movement of his massive frame.

"I have no idea."

"What? What do you mean? How can you have no idea? Christ man, you can't tell us half a story now," spluttered the angry policeman.

"I'm not."

"Well then, bloody hell, tell us what happened next."

"I'm not telling you half a story because that's exactly where it all ended. That's when she died, right in the middle of her telling me her own final tale."

The three policemen in the interview room stared around at each other in a mixture of shock and open mouthed amazement. The senior policeman shifted in his chair behind the desk, clearly annoyed at being starved of the tale's conclusion, his gaze turning to the face of younger officer who had recorded every word. The young record keeper was staring at the storyteller open mouthed.

"Did you make sure? Check her, y'know, to see....?" asked the younger man.

"Of course I checked. Once she had fallen all of a sudden to the floor, well, I took my chance and looked. Sweet Lord above, it was like a vast lumpy wound covered in places by tufts of hair, bulges of angry crimson and red flesh hanging all..."

"I think what my colleague means," interrupted the senior officer from across the table, "was did you check if she was actually dead?"

The writer nodded his head slowly.

"Of course I did. I checked her pulse and stuff, before I, you know ..."

He motioned lifting her skirt and made a sickened face at the memory.

"She was about as dead as they come."

"He's making this up, as sure as my name is Findo Gask and as sure as my mother's name was Blodwyn" exclaimed Findo Gask, whose mother's real name, incidentally had actually been Irene. In the tension of the moment, no-one had thought the error important enough to bring up.

Barvas angrily thumped his fist hard into the table, giving the other three men a start.

"Findo, do you honestly, really, for even a second, believe that this whole story, a story we have been sitting here listening to and recording, for thirty six hours may I remind you, do you seriously think this is all some fictional construction? What kind of twisted perverse fiend could come up with such gruesomely detailed and abnormal stories? Do you honestly think he lies?"

The fat policeman sank back into his chair with a fresh squeal of protest at the movement, his face reddening as he sat shaking his head slowly in almost disappointed agreement. The room fell into silence.

"So what now?" muttered the exhausted figure of the young policeman.

The three policemen looked at each other carefully, and at the stranger, each man silently searching the other blank faces for answers.

Each glance, each stare, catches in the other faces a familiar and easily recognised look of utter bewilderment. It is a look betraying a collective incomprehension of just how this collection of four men now find themselves drawn here, sitting together in this anonymous room, to bear witness to these remarkable but unfinished stories.

CHAPTER 18

# The Stranger Arrives

It is three days earlier and at first light in a small Scottish fishing town, an unknown visitor emerges like a ghost from out of the dawn mist. No-one is awake to witness the stranger's arrival, or take any notice of his slow, deliberate footsteps, scuffing steadily along the harbour road.

It is the 30th day of February in the year of our lord nineteen hundred and seventy nine, in this unremarkable little town high on the jagged Western coast of Scotland. The man's arrival is the first act of a sequence of events four men will never forget.

A bestial howl floats across the darkness, the sudden cry breaking the stillness of the night. The townsfolk sleep on in rows of grey stone houses, set in long streets that rise in steps up the curved hill around the harbour. They lie deep in slumber, warm and quite unaware of the single human figure trudging doggedly onwards along the quayside, headed for the worn range of steps outside the police station. The amber eyes of a tattered cat blink open from amid a mound of warm fur on a harbour front ledge to observe. Glimpsing nothing advantageous, they close, return to beneath an arched feline leg, back to the task of staying warm.

The stranger's silhouette advances relentlessly over the cobbled surface, the closely packed stones shining black beneath his march like undertaker's shoes. His feet scuff forward, the noise echoing on the lifeless stone walls, joining in early morning union with the languid slapping of the water against the quayside and the calm creaking of captive fishing boats. All the visitor can hear is his own laboured breathing. A shaft of light from the lighthouse slices through the mist like a blade, casting fantastic shadows of his outline on the harbour side walls. In a split second the beam passes, returning the whole scene to the dim grey light of the approaching dawn.

The old town clock tower chimes doubtfully four times and falls silent, the distant howl comes once more to float across the darkness. Then, abruptly, the animal's lament is cut short by the blunt thud of a shotgun. Seemingly familiar with the noise, or at least the implication behind it, the wise neighbourhood cat springs from his ledge and darts across the road toward the jumbled harbour gloom. The strange visitor pauses at the unexpected burst of commotion in the otherwise motionless night. Shivering, he strides quickly on.

As the lighthouse beam sweeps once more to illuminate proceedings, a pair of seagulls survey the scene with yellow eyes, their hooked claws clicking like typewriters across the granite quayside, beaks stabbing repeatedly into the dead eyes of discarded fish heads. The figure they follow resembles a neglected scarecrow; a zombie in ripped tweed, moving through the grey mist in a purposeful trance, as if stalking some unseen phantom stag.

The visitor halts at the foot of the police station steps, leaning heavily on the stone wall to catch his breath. Illuminated by glow from a solitary lit window above, the full extent of the man's ragged appearance becomes apparent. His once expensive and tailored attire hangs in tatters from his emaciated frame, torn edges of trouser trail after him on the cobbles, his tweed jacket hanging torn and ragged, the frayed cloth flapping in the light sea breeze. The man wheezes with bowed head to strive to fill his lungs with the chill salty air. Thick mud covers both his feet and trousers, thick streaks spattered over the rest of his outfit. A solitary remaining shoe is barely discernible beneath sludge gathered from his trek across the yawning peat bogs that hold the small town edges in shape like a stripper's corset.

The stranger's hollow face is haunted. Dark sunken eyes betray signs of cruel and arduous adventures, the head thrown out of shape by dramatic swellings and his face heavily scratched with thick dotted Morse code lines of dried blood. Despite these obvious marks of suffering the stranger manages a slight reassured smile as he noiselessly mouths the word 'Police', glowing clear above him, picked out in white letters across the blue light.

Pushing upright with fresh effort, the figure continues his steep climb, arm securely planted on the cold stone wall for support. On reaching a level platform at the top of the stairs, he staggers forward, pushes at the doors of the building, his battered hands meeting the blue painted wood with a deep thump. The heavy doors surrender with a loud groan, before swinging gently closed behind the stranger, giving a final gasp as he disappears inside. The whole harbour landscape again returns to stillness, as if the body has been devoured by the town itself.

Once inside the grey interior of the building, the weary face knots in protest at the sudden brightness. Stepping forward, squinting blindly, he stumbles down two sudden steps, propelled forward into the strange room by the change of momentum. Losing balance, as his feet slide on their thick cover of mud, the stranger lurches forwards, losing the struggle to stay standing. Failing to maintain balance, he tips forwards toward the floor, his head catching the edge of the heavy countertop with a nauseating thud as he falls.

Behind the grey painted wooden desk running the width of the room, Sergeant Findo Gask remains expressionless, save for a slight curl of fingers to withdraw his magazine just far enough to avoid the falling head. As the body impacts and crumples out of view behind the counter, Findo pushes the magazine back into its original position with a single thick nicotine stained finger and shifts his wide frame in his creaking chair. Engrossed in the publication and feeling around blindly, Findo Gask finds his packet, slowly removes and lights another cigarette. Blowing out silver smoke with a sigh, the policeman moistens a fat finger, turns to a new page and continues reading, wholly indifferent to events in the room.

Over many years, the laid back policeman had grown accustomed to these unexpected visitors to the station in the early hours. This, his town, typical of many

Scottish fishing towns, was home to a population of hard living males capable of drinking as ferociously as they worked. This lifestyle, especially when combined with the limitless capacity for violence exhibited by the town's long suffering womenfolk, saw many a drunken male resident regularly explode into the station's front office without warning in the early hours, seeking refuge and a place to sleep off industrial amounts of whisky. A steady stream of refugees regularly chose the warm office as a place of sanctuary, collapsing without greeting or apology on any flat surface capable of holding a drunken body for a few hours slumber.

Findo glanced up at the one handed clock, the white face and numbers yellowed by years of cigarette smoke and apathy. It was twenty past sometime late.

Sitting cloaked in sluggish swirling ropes of fresh cigarette smoke, the town policeman scratches absentmindedly at the enormous pale arc of his exposed stomach, still deep in study of his particularly unprincipled Scandinavian publication. The magazine had been one of a number received with a raised eyebrow and an appreciative smirk in the morning post.

Findo was an expert aficionado of such reading material, but owing to stringent limitations imposed by the small print of the Obscene Publications Act (1857) such premium examples of the genre remained a rare luxury on this side of the North Sea. This colourful and morally corrupt reading material had arrived courtesy of a friendly colleague, from a batch confiscated earlier in the week in the clammy hold of a Norwegian fishing boat, seized from a ashen faced crew being subjected to an unwarranted drug search.

Sergeant Gask flicked on through the magazine, smiling contentedly at the knowledge that his colleagues in police stations the length of the west coast were enjoying the same collective fruits of corrupt vice squad action.

Sergeant Gask parted two fingers and traced the line of his slightly greying moustache around his mouth in an unconscious act of appreciation, turning the open magazine askew to better enhance his appreciation of the naked gymnastic contortions of a robust blonde acknowledged only as 'Etta from Helsinki'. The evidently aroused grey pony in the pictures remained anonymous.

The height of the chipped grey desktop hides any visitor's eyes from the worst of the spectacle behind. The police sergeant sits stripped from the waist downwards, his sturdy hairy legs sweating naked against the leather of his cherished swivel chair, then continuing downward to disappear into the discarded police issue trousers pooled at his feet. The pink exposure of his upright male apparatus bears witness to his positive critical evaluation of the open magazine.

Findo Gask had remained a resolutely single man ever since his childhood sweetheart had jilted him at the altar on the day of the hastily organised wedding planned for his seventeenth birthday. His intended and their unborn child had slipped silently from the town on the night before the wedding, leaving only a short tear stained note of justification. The note said nothing of interest other than she "wasn't ready". Findo had run to her house from the church that morning on receiving the news, tearing through the town's narrow streets weeping, breaking her bedroom door down with his massive shoulder thinking his bride might have delayed

her flight. But she had gone forever, leaving only the note. Within a week, and hearing no further news, a broken and inconsolable Findo Gask had walked the many miles across country in the snow, arriving at the nearest large town to sign up immediately to join the police. His intended had never again attempted to make any contact.

Once his training was complete, and Findo had completed long training postings at various stations around the region, he eventually returned home, as sergeant at the local station. Back at home he had gradually settled into his new position of superiority in the town, in the process advancing his encyclopaedic knowledge of seized pornographic material in the vast amounts of free time afforded in such a quiet location. As a now resolutely single man with easy access to the numerous vice squad seizures along the coast, it seemed an ideal diversion.

The other officer on duty in the remote station had also failed to witness the ragged stranger's spectacular entrance. Constable Fowlis Wester lay snoring among the faint urine tang of one of the station's pair of tiny grey cells. The young man had slept on, blissfully unaware of proceedings, his slim adolescent body stirring slightly only once in a while to entwine itself more securely around the well upholstered nude female form of a Dutch hitchhiker, an unexpected bounty discovered earlier in the day whilst on routine patrol along the town's remote coast road.

The freshly qualified Fowlis Wester had originally protested against his relocation to such an isolated rural setting, having hoped for some of the excitement promised to a young man in one of the bigger cities. However the youthful policeman had soon dropped any ideas of transfer requests on discovering the abundant rewards on hand to a handsome young man in uniform in a town on the tourist trail. His was a job that allowed him regular sexual liaisons with a steady stream of adventurous travellers attracted by the area's remote natural splendour. What, he mused, was there not to like?

Even discounting the surprisingly numerous pleasures of the flesh afforded by his position, Fowlis Wester had also enjoyed an additional stream of revenue from the hiring of cine-films, furtive movies shot expertly by Sergeant Gask through the open cell door on each instance the younger man found himself occupied in such encounters. It was lucrative income for both policemen, a financial bonus matched only by their share of returns from the resale of the frequent drugs seizures along the coast.

Fowlis slid a thin drowsy arm across the suntanned Dutch hitchhiker's torso and tightened his grasp on a prominent breast, smiling contentedly to himself and sleeping on soundly.

In the featureless reception area Sergeant Findo Gask had pulled his heavy frame from his chair and shuffled off towards the kitchen immediately behind the desk. The space had been recently converted from an old cell once it had been meticulously and scientifically calculated that the daily number of cups of tea drunk on duty had greatly outnumbered those few occasions the gloomy cell was ever used for any purpose than for furtively shooting films. Conversion had been an undemanding decision to make, helped along by the straightforward technical fact that the room's meagre lighting was totally inappropriate for clear filming. Buyers' always grumbled and demanded refunds if they couldn't clearly enjoy every last detail of the action. Findo Gask, it seemed, wasn't the only local with a well honed knowledge of the pornographic.

As he waddled in tiny undersized steps toward the kitchen, shuffling like a fat penguin trapped in the narrow valley behind the desk, Findo Gask felt his still proud manhood shake under him with each tiny movement. Attention now drawn to the existence of his outstanding companion, Gask lit the gas under the kettle and leaned his sizeable weight against the door frame with a contented sigh, resolved to kill time with a chase to the finish. Slowly closing his fat yellowing fingers round his tumescent appendage, the fat man embarked upon a concerted contest to bring himself to a glorious climax before the kettle whistled.

The sneer of teeth beneath the bushy moustache signalled a narrow victory, a dull grunt marking the crossing of the finishing line just before the arrival of the kettle's steady squealing. Gask smiled smugly at the small victory, gazing around the room with sticky hands.

Spying the station's solitary stained tea towel wilting on a hook, he removed it and wiped both his hands and his lower self clean, replacing the tainted cloth back in its original position with a thin smirk. Returning his attentions to tea production Findo rattled his teaspoon around a chipped mug in time to his tuneless whistling, mixing his six sugars through the tarry water.

Suddenly the black desk phone exploded into life. Gask sighed with mild annoyance, lifting his mug and shuffling back along the valley to eradicate the source of the noise.

Returning the room to silence by lifting the receiver, Gask sipped at his cup and listened as another indifferent and routine enquiry from headquarters spilled from the earpiece. The emotionless voice from afar prompted the flushed faced man to roll his eyes towards the discoloured ceiling tiles above while he mumbled the stock responses to the familiar set of pointless questions.

Without warning, the head of the stranger had gradually began to rise above the wooden horizon of the counter, the face emerging upward steadily, little by little, like a battered and perplexed sun announcing the dawn. Gask watched on with raised eyebrows at the spectacle, continuing to murmur his replies into the warm mouthpiece. The policeman noted with some surprise that the features before him weren't those of a local drunk after all. He had a new visitor. The startled expression drew slowly higher before him, staring back into the round face of the Sergeant still sipping tea.

Gask watched as the stranger's gaze dropped slowly downward over his half exposed body, the expression gradually changing as it registered the spectacle of the policeman opposite completely naked and fully erect below the creased edges of his white shirt. The stranger's features twisted into a look of bewilderment, suddenly noticing the open magazine and craning his head to scrutinize the finer details of the naked Etta and her intimate rapport with equine livestock. The mouth of the man opened and moved as if to speak, but no words appeared.

Sergeant Gask took another sip from his cup, holding his gaze on the new face as he gradually closed the magazine. The Sergeant asked his colleague on the other end of the phone to hold the line and, smiling pleasantly at the stranger, had smashed the heavy black receiver against the man's temple, sending him back to the floor in a lifeless pile, back out of sight behind the counter. Findo Gask wiped the receiver carefully on his shirt, returned the phone to his mouth and continued mumbling his answers.

On completion of his call, Findo Gask shuffled around the counter to the public side, squeezing his girth carefully through the narrow hatch to avoid chance splinters in sensitive exposed areas. The shape of the strange visitor lay sprawled before him in an unmoving bundle, lifeless on the worn red paint of the stone floor.

Sergeant Gask stood with his hands planted firmly on his hips while examining the unresponsive body, moving forward after a while to roll the heavy pile of humanity over with his foot. Gask remained convinced in his initial impression that whatever the visitor's identity, he most definitely was not a local. The expensive city man's idea of country attire, out of place in this most frugal and rural of settings, were now torn to rags and covered in mud. The upturned face looked battered and covered in scratches, freshly marked with a livid spherical contusion where the impacted phone had recently made contact with his temple. Sergeant Gask craned his head to one side for an improved view, shrugging at the unanswered complexities of the mystery before bending over to better poke around the unconscious man's trouser pockets.

It was at this stage in proceedings that young Fowlis Wester had appeared topless and freshly awake behind the counter. The bright faced young man stood for a moment inspecting the scene, his blue eyes screwed up tightly in protest against the sudden brightness. As he watched on the youngster had ran a metal comb through his disorderly blonde hair, smiling broadly at the panorama which had greeted his appearance.

Fowlis had entered from the cell corridor, sleepily opening the anonymous grey door only to be met by the disturbing apparition of the considerable width of a semi naked Sergeant Gask bent over an unconscious man. The senior officer's great naked fluffy buttocks pointed in Fowlis Wester's direction, the sound of rhythmic grunting drifting towards the younger man as Findo Gask rocks to and fro over the comatose form in an ongoing fight to wrestle a wallet from the stranger's trouser pocket.

"Shall I get the camera, Sergeant? This sort of thing may sell well to the specialist gay uniform fetish market. "

Sergeant Gask twisted and scowled at his juvenile colleague, his expression making apparent his distinct lack of humour at the comment. Findo raised a single fat fist into view of the youngster, unfurling a nicotine stained middle finger in a sign of critical response. Fowlis shrugged and smiled back with an expression of mock innocence then continued to busy himself with the comb. In his best camp voice he responded.

"Ohhh look at her, getting all offended. Suit yourself loverboy."

Gask stood upright, clutching the newly extracted wallet in his hand.

"Got it. Nice of you to join me son, I take it you're finished with your little windmill admiring, tulip picking acquaintance then?"

Fowlis nodded slowly before saluting.

"International relations work complete, Sergeant. Inge, that's my new Dutch companion, has just left the building. And worry not Sarge, I made sure I used the back door."

Gask laughed at the remark, his naked gadget shuddering below the hairy overhang of his stomach at the sudden burst of amusement.

"Oh, I'm well aware of that son. I did pretty good coverage of all that stuff on reel three, if you want to check my angles and close ups."

Both men sniggered as Fowlis ambled around the counter to join his half naked superior officer. Amused at the sight of the body sprawled before him, the younger man finished attending to his hair and had replaced the metal comb into his pocket. As the pair swapped theories about the potential identification of the figure, both men were suddenly distracted, attention drawn by the pained moaning of the slowly stirring shape on the floor.

On partially reviving and being greeted with the inopportune sight of Sergeant Gask leaning over him half naked, smiling, and most worryingly, still visibly erect, the stranger noticed the fatter man had now been joined by a younger man. He too, half naked and smiling broadly. Fowlis Wester winked at the stranger knowingly. The stranger's face took on a sudden look of intense horror, his eyes slid back into his head and he promptly fell back, again unconscious.

"I think we both better get dressed," laughed Gask, "or we might well be here all night."

Returning themselves to a rough approximation of full uniform, the men reconvened at the rear at the counter, passing a recently acquired Dutch herbal cigarette between themselves as they occasionally craned their heads to muse over their unconscious visitor. Fowlis Wester leaned forward and examined the figure more closely, his young brow furrowing in bewilderment at the fresh circular bruise on the side of the stranger's head. Before he could ask, Fowlis turned to find the older man looking back, smiling broadly and with the joint still in his mouth, displaying the phone receiver in his hand and swinging the object in a hitting motion by way of clarification.

"He must have fallen and struck his head somehow. Clearly an unfortunate accident."

Fowlis Wester nodded, a knowing smile playing on his face as he returned his attentions to examining the prostrate body.

"Obviously. He certainly looks as if he's been through a rough patch. Don't recognise him. Any ideas on who he is or where he came from, Sergeant?"

"Well, interesting you should ask that, Constable. I strictly followed police guidelines and searched his person for clues to assist identification. All he had on him was this wallet."

Findo removed the wallet from deep in his pocket and began to wave it, the square of leather shaken in the air between two huge fingers.

"Which reminds me…"

Reaching into the folds, Sergeant Gask withdrew a bundle of notes, carefully counting out half before handing the money to Fowlis Wester. The young man counted his unexpected bounty, raising an eyebrow in satisfaction before waving the money at Gask in recognition while stuffing it into his shirt breast pocket.

"In addition to the wallet being empty of any monies, I observe that we have a driving licence with an address in a city far away. If it's his, and the likelihood is high if we bring into play our police training and use the attached photo as a basic but reliable clue, then our unconscious friend here is one Reef Mogg. There's nothing else here of note except an old iron house key and a battered picture of some pretty gruesome woman."

"Let me see?" asked Fowlis Wester.

Gask held up the dog eared photograph in the direction of the young man.

"Oh my sweet lord, that's practically an affront to the laws of nature. Are you sure it's a woman? Or human even?"

Gask shook his head at the young man, returning the photo to the wallet.

"So cynical for one so young. Although I should maybe keep this, just in case I need to scare any children away from the fire in the pub on a Sunday afternoon."

"No money at all then?" asked Fowlis Wester winking, drumming his fingers on his shirt pocket.

"Not a single penny. Strange that."

"So do you think we should wake him Sergeant? I mean following strict procedures and all?"

"Of course, I'm not having him lying about here all night here making the place look untidy. But, as you point out, we have to carefully examine the situation and follow our strict medical training to wake him gently, especially if we suspect evidence of a head injury."

"So will I go and get the fire hose then?"

"Indeed Constable Wester. We'll make a fine policeman of you yet."

The two policemen stood peering through the open hatch of a cell door, smiling broadly at the soaked figure, now dripping and shivering, head bowed under the folds of a threadbare grey blanket. The shape had grunted once to accept a cup of tea, which he now held between his hands as if in prayer while perched on the edge of the raised sleeping platform. Otherwise Reef Mogg had remained totally silent to any enquiry or effort at conversation from the two policemen.

Turning his head towards the faces framed in the small door opening, the purple swelling from the recent telephone impact has become even more apparent. Reef Mogg glanced at the two men for a moment and had returned his gaze to the floor, failing to find amusement even in the heavily endowed naked female form drawn life size onto the door below the small hatch. The artwork gave the appearance, from his point of view, of a large breasted woman with two policeman's heads.

Without returning his gaze at the design, the saturated man spoke.

"Sergeant Gask?"

The fatter man flashed a worried glance at his colleague before returning his full attention to the cell interior. Gask slowly nodded his response, all trace of his broad smile abruptly gone from his lips.

"We've already established, albeit unconventionally, that you know how to handle a phone. Is there perhaps any small chance you could employ the object in a more unadventurous manner? Say perhaps to contact your superior officer? I have an extremely important statement to make involving a sudden death, and I would much prefer to entrust such information to someone far more responsible and far less violent than you. If you could be so kind. Oh, and incidentally, that 'hideous affront to nature' in the photo was my mother."

Gask swallowed hard before slamming shut the hatch, cursing under his breath as he retreated with Findo Gask towards the front desk.

Once back in the front office the two men had prepared fresh cups of tea in the warmth of the kitchen, mutely pondering what course of action should be taken next. Sergeant Gask had winced as Wester dried both cups with the station tea towel but decided it best to keep quiet. The younger policeman was the first to break the silence as he lit the gas and shook out the burning match.

"We'll have to phone headquarters Sarge, won't we? He sounds like he's not like our normal local idiot, and as soon as someone comes, he'll tell them everything."

Sergeant Gask mused on the point and had given his best thoughtful look. Suddenly his eyes widened in a moment of revelation.

"No doubt he will, young Fowlis, no doubt he will. So, with that course of events more than a distinct possibility, instead of directly involving headquarters, I'll bypass procedure with a little used shortcut. I'll phone Barvas at home instead."

" What? Barvas? THAT Barvas? Chief Inspector Bastard!! Are you joking Sarge? I've heard about him, he's a psycho. I met a young constable who once worked in the same station as him when I was transferring a prisoner up the coast. He told me that neither the officers nor prisoners bother to use his name, they just call him 'Bastard'. To his face. The guy told me he actually prefers that to Barvas."

Gask nodded, deep in thought.

"Yup. Probably all true right enough, but you just leave Barvas to me Fowlis m'lad. We go back a very long way. He might not be greatly amused at being woken this early in the morning, but he'll most probably be fine with me. He's a hard man alright, and he is dangerous, but right now it still beats phoning those assorted idiots at headquarters and getting them involved."

Fowlis Wester lifted his cup to his lips with an unsure hand. Suddenly he looked very worried.

"Listen Sergeant, I know he'll maybe be ok with you, but, well, I like it here and I don't want, y'know..."

His voice trailed off into silence.

Sergeant Gask nodded and laid a reassuring fat hand on the boys arm.

"It'll be fine, son. Barvas and I are old acquaintances. I'll make sure it's all fine."

The young constable didn't give any impression of the words having steadied his nerves.

"Listen, son, I like you being here too. Ok?" added Sergeant Gask, his fat discoloured fingers pressing comfortingly as they gripped the white cotton of the younger man's shirt.

Fowlis felt the encouraging contact and had examined the optimistic and honest face nodding back at him.

Fowlis Wester forced a thin smile of his own to show appreciation and understanding. While he didn't doubt his superior would try his best to look out for him, from all information gathered on Barvas he doubted even the lengthiest of friendships meant anything much at all in the face of the senior officer's renowned ferocity. Still, since Sergeant Gask seems clearly familiar enough to phone Barvas at home and wake him, maybe some faint hope remained. Fowlis relaxed himself slightly, his forced smile slowly changing into something a little more natural.

The younger man hoped shifting the focus might help him relax into being more convinced by this dangerous idea.

"Must be something wrong with the milk, Sergeant, this tea tastes terrible. There are funny bits floating in it."

Gask nodded and smiled unconvincingly as he crept off towards the front desk, lifting the phone and dialling while Fowlis Wester stood behind him in the doorway sniffing at the open milk bottle. Findo Gask closed his eyes and muttered a silent prayer to himself while listening to the phone ring out at the other end. Then from the receiver came the sound of fumbling, before the stern bark of what Gask recognised as a familiar yet perpetually irritated voice.

"This, my friend, had better be good..."

## CHAPTER 19

## Barvas Arrives

Barvas arrived less than an hour later, his shapely Daimler rumbling over the cobbled street and pulling up on the harbour front outside the station. He struggled slowly and painfully out of the black car, looking around as he pulled himself to his full height and turned his collar up against the cold sea wind and thin rain of the morning. He glared ahead at the police station building, his jaw muscles tensing repeatedly under the pale skin on the sides of his face. There was no-one to witness this second arrival of the morning. The town still remained silent and dead.

The tall policeman lifted the solid handle of the car's back door and pressed the inlaid silver button until it clicked softly. Pulling the door open with a low creak of metal, he stood back and watched as the strange animal within climbed down and onto the cobbled surface, paws clicking quietly on the shining stone. Barvas bent and adjusted the battered brown leather helmet on the dog's head, before running his hand along the soft hair on the dogs back, gently patting its muscular hind quarters.

As the pair set off toward the stations nearby stone steps, the beast caught sight of a scrawny ginger cat and stopped to stare and growl with terrifying menace and bared teeth. The cat shot off for the second time that morning in panic, back towards the harbour side shadows. In the distance Barvas heard a skittering sound of claws losing grip on stone, then a loud splash. The dog looked up at Barvas with a single eye as if satisfied with his work and the policeman smiled thinly and nodded back his approval before moving off again through the morning mist towards the stone police station steps. The tall man limped as he walked, wincing all the time in pain as he made his way across the black cobbles and then slowly but deliberately up the ascent. The dog followed loyally, always keeping pace a few steps behind.

The heavy doors closed softly for the second time that morning, swallowing more strange visitors from the street.

The sudden appearance of Barvas plunged the room into silence. He stood staring ahead, his thin stern face and piercing grey eyes moving between the two intently watching faces for a few moments before settling his piercing gaze on the younger officer. Beside him, the dog appeared and stared intently into the room with his single eye.

"What's your name, son?"

"Fowlis, sir. Fowlis Wester. "

"That's nice, I'm very pleased for you. Now Fowlis, do you think you could do me a favour?"

Fowlis Wester nodded a little too hurriedly, finding himself gripped by a strange fear.

"First of all, can we drop all the 'sir' horseshit, it doesn't really suit either of us. Then, once you've realigned your cosmos to that request, you could challenge my first impression of you and attempt some further giant leaps towards the more pleasant side of my nature I'm rumoured to have by making us all some tea. And bring some milk for the dog."

Barvas patted the dog's huge head.

"And make sure it's fresh and on a clean saucer. He doesn't like filth."

Barvas limped across the room and gently lowered himself onto the battered public bench facing the counter. The dog followed and curled itself on the floor under the bench, next to his master. Reaching down and rubbing his own leg with a grimace, Barvas spoke again.

"And make sure you bring me a big plateful of his special chocolate biscuits, from his secret stash. If you haven't found them already then my guess is they'll be hidden somewhere on the top shelf of a cupboard. In all probability concealed behind your cereal boxes."

Fowlis Wester glanced at Sergeant Gask open mouthed, only to find the fat man leisurely nodding back with a slender smile.

Barvas rose slowly and paced the room, stretching his leg whilst examining the limited highlights of some ripped local police notices, his back to the desk. Without turning he added final details to his order, just as the young man had returned into the room to ask.

"Milk and four sugars, son. And I've just thought, put the dog's milk in a cup, he enjoys the challenge."

Fowlis Wester stood, perplexed for a moment at the superior officer's apparent psychic abilities but then had dutifully nodded at the man's back before vanishing off into the side room, the sound of running water and rattling spoons confirmation he was obeying instructions. Barvas turned and stared at Findo Gask.

"I'm hoping you're still eating those big thick chocolate things, Findo, though by a quick glance at the load being exerted on those shirt buttons I'll be thinking I'm not going to be too upset."

For the first time since his arrival, a thin lipped smile broke on the harsh angular face of the superior officer. Sergeant Gask soon followed suite.

"Nice to see you too, Barvas. Who's your not so little friend?"

Barvas nodded to the dog.

"This? This is my new partner Stubbs. He was in that wreck up North, the one where the train hit the car on the level crossing in the middle of the night? You probably heard about it."

Findo Gask nodded. He had. Five dead.

"Stubbs here was the only thing that survived. He was all smashed up, trapped inside the wreck and they planned to just put him down. I heard about it and phoned the recovery team, said I wanted him. Sent a couple of vets up to get him. You know how I am with lost causes and car wrecks."

Findo nodded and watched his friend's back.

"Speaking of car wrecks, Barvas, how's your leg?"

"Still wooden. Still fitting badly. Still provoking a dire mood and abundant angry outbursts. But I'll live. How are you, Findo? Been a while."

Findo Gask smiled and clapped his open hand against the spread of stomach with a loud slapping sound.

"Can't complain."

Barvas' eyes narrowed and his smile receded. He never had come to terms with his friend settling for life in this stagnant rural backwater.

"Can't, or just can't be bothered? Though I suppose you must have come across something important for once in this godforsaken place, or at least important enough to give you good reason for daring to phone me at such a ridiculous hour of the morning sounding all 'secret service'. I know we didn't train as spies, Findo, so let's cut to the chase, what's up?"

"It's a strange tale, but I'll wait until you get your tea and biscuits down. I know you better than to make requests on your limited supply of goodwill before you've had your first cup of tea of a morning."

Barvas turned to face Findo Gask with the beginnings of a grin on his bony face. He had grown bored of the oppressive atmosphere of wide-eyed fear that usually greeted his appearance. It was nice to meet an old friend again and be exposed to that recollection of an ancient familiarity. Barvas lowered himself back onto the narrow public bench and winced as he idly rubbed his wooden foot.

"Bloody rain and damp."

"Rheumatics?"

"Not exactly, the wood expands and digs in. Take my advice Findo, try hard not to mislay a leg."

The fat policeman grinned, thankful his old friend still retained the dark humour that had once provided him with such an agreeable roommate back at Police College.

"I'll bear that in mind. Are you sure you want tea and biscuits? Or would rather I have the lad bring some hot varnish and a length of rough sandpaper?"

Barvas looked up, his expression suddenly deadly serious, grey eyes staring darkly at the fatter man. Findo Gask gulped and his Adams apple bobbed beneath his dirty shirt collar, worrying that he had misjudged the informal mood of his old friend.

It was almost two decades since they had last met for anything longer than a few passing moments, and Findo was acutely aware of the man's terrifying reputation throughout the force. Barvas leaned down and returned his attentions to his foot without comment. Findo Gask felt his insides knot and his clenched palms begin to sweat. He closed his eyes for a moment to curse himself for his casual familiarity.

Opening his eyes again just in the nick of time, Findo Gask found himself instinctively flicking his head sideways at the last possible second to avoid the launched lump of wood headed directly en route for his face. The false limb just missed making contact with his skull, whistling just past to the left before hitting the glazed panel behind with an huge explosion of noise, embedding its length in the glass right up to the foot.

Stubbs woke up with a start from his position beside Barvas' single remaining limb and sprung up, instantly ready to attack. Sensing no immediate danger of assault on his master, he lay cautiously back down, single eye wide, and returned his head to the warmth of the paws.

Sergeant Gask turned to examine the levitating limb, complete with shoe and sock, sticking out from the shining flat surface like a modern art installation. He turned back to see Barvas now grinning broadly at him from across the room.

"You're still one fat, disrespectful bastard Findo, but it's nice to see you've not lost your reactions."

Behind the glass, having almost suffered a heart attack at the explosion and the subsequent appearance of a mystery lower limb, Fowlis Wester steadied himself against the counter, only relaxing his white knuckles on hearing the two men's laughter suddenly echo noisily around the room outside. He sighed in deep relief and returned to making tea with trembling hands. It was going to be a long day.

After serving refreshments, complete with a spotlessly clean cup of milk and a plate of the concealed biscuits discovered exactly where Barvas had predicted, Fowlis Wester clutched his cup and sat on a stool at the far end of the desk watching events uneasily. During a lull in conversation Barvas suddenly nodded his head toward the younger man. Findo Gask followed his stare to observe what had provoked the attention. The two older men stared at Fowlis in silence, suddenly causing his agitation to intensify.

"What?"

"You look like you've seen a ghost, son," remarked Barvas over the top of his cup.

"Not a whole one. Just got a bit of a shock with the unexpected appearance of the random wooden leg, that's all," replied Fowlis, nodding in the direction of the levitating foot still embedded surreally halfway up the glass.

Both older men again laughed enthusiastically at the reminder, Fowlis Wester joining in with a thin unconvincing smile, quite incapable of mustering any reaction anywhere near natural laughter.

The three policemen drank their tea, Barvas and Gask exchanging old police stories while the younger man listened on in silence. Feeling both uncomfortable and excess to requirements in the room, it wasn't long before Fowlis Wester made his excuses, lifted his empty cup and retired back to the protection of the kitchen. He felt better out of sight, but curiosity soon drew him to the gap in the open door to secretly observe Barvas from his unseen position.

Fowlis listened as Gask recounted to Barvas concise details of the night's events, his deep rumbling baritone recounting the story while Barvas listened on intently, his face set in a thoughtful scowl. Fowlis noted that Gask was more frank than even he had expected, but noticed that he had still chosen to skip a few of the more 'interesting' passages.

Fowlis realised with discomfort that even Sergeant Gask seemed afraid to tell Barvas all. It seemed that even though the men were undoubtedly friends, Gask too feared Barvas. Somehow that recognition was at the same time both strangely reassuring and mildly upsetting. Fowlis glanced back at the embedded wooden limb with a slight shiver and returned his attention to examining the thin face of Barvas.

Fowlis replayed to himself the legend of how Barvas had lost his leg, a horrific accident during a high speed car chase trying to arrest three rough local brothers from a big town up north. The man who was both his partner and mentor had died in the crash and most were of the opinion that it was this tragedy which had turned the then young Barvas into such a bitter man. A few weeks after Barvas had been discharged from hospital following the incident, the three brothers involved in the chase had been found crucified. Each fugitive had been discovered and brought back to the village, then nailed to one of the doors of the triangular bank building in the middle of the town's market square, right next to where the car had crashed.

Findo Gask had been one of the officers ordered to remove the nails from the men's dead hands and remove the corpses from the scene, and the event remained legendary among both the town population and the wider police force. Barvas was never formally charged but had been questioned at great length about his movements on the night of the murders. He was finally released due to lack of evidence, but even while under such intense suspicion the policeman had still attended all three funerals, keeping his distance in the churchyard watching over each of the burials with a contented smirk.

Fowlis Wester had once asked Sergeant Gask about the episode, but instead of the expected angry denial of his friend's involvement, the fatter man had merely shrugged and smiled at the enquiry. Fowlis Wester felt a chill run down his spine now as he watched Barvas swallow tea and smile, the young man unable to take his eyes off the figure at the centre of the gruesome legend, now sitting just across the room.

Fowlis watched as the man drained the last of his tea, tipped his cup upside down over the open mouth of his dog Stubbs, the beast pushing his head out from under the bench to catch the last few drops. Barvas then nodded towards Gask.

"So Findo, are you ready?"

"Yeah. One thing before we go though. Why does Stubbs wear a that helmet? Does he have a lazy eye?"

Fowlis could feel tension in the silence, even in another room.

"He doesn't wear it for himself, Findo, he wears it for other people. It was an appalling accident." Barvas bent down out of Fowlis Wester's view behind the counter, presumably to remove the dog's head covering.

Fowlis heard Findo Gask take a massive intake of breath and then mutter a religious curse, loudly and distractedly, to himself.

A short silence gripped the room, before Barvas again bent down out of sight, presumably to return Stubbs once more to the dignity afforded by the head covering. The uneasy silence was broken by the shaking voice of Findo Gask, shouting demands on the younger officer to ready the interview room.

Fowlis Wester knew little very work was needed to ready the small room for its first interview in years. He slipped out the room and obeyed the request without question, removing all the offending evidence of late night gambling sessions and setting the chairs to face each other across the table in a more traditional manner.

He set about the removal of some tattered packs of playing cards, brimming ashtrays and a few drained bottles of whisky collected in the corner.

Fowlis returned and nodded to let his sergeant know all was organized. On receiving the signal, a pale Sergeant Gask left the room to extract the soggy figure of Reef Mogg from the cell, returning to quietly instruct the young officer to recover and return the embedded leg to its owner in the interview room.

Barvas took the leg from the younger man, staring at him without expression while he reattached the limb. The two men waited in the tiny interview room for the return of Findo and the mystery visitor.

Silently watching the young officer, Barvas slid his limb onto the smooth skin of his curved red stump. The distant sound of a one sided conversation echoed into the room along the corridor from the nearby cells. Stubbs sat on the floor by his master's side, the dog's moist single eye staring intently at the young man. Fowlis felt uncomfortable alone in the room with Barvas and his silent beast and was thankful when the door eventually swung open to reveal the bedraggled figure of the visitor.

On entering the room, Reef Mogg shuffled over to the seated figure of Barvas and the two men stared at each other intently. The bedraggled man offered his hand to Barvas. The policeman remained motionless, gazing up from his seat impassive and unmoving. The blanketed stranger broke off the gaze, lowered his hand and shrugged before sitting himself at the table directly across from Barvas, bowing his head without a sound.

"Are we ready to talk yet?" asked Barvas.

The stranger's battered head turned deliberately towards the figures of Fowlis Wester and Findo Gask and nodded slowly in their direction.

"Not them."

Barvas tightened angrily.

"Listen, my damp friend, I have no idea who you are, or who you might think you are, but I am Detective Inspector Barvas. These are my men and I am the superior officer within fifty miles in any direction. Since we are the only three people who matter in your slowly rotating world right now, that automatically makes me the most important person in existence. I'm your king. I make the laws, I break the laws. I say what happens and what gets ignored. I acknowledge your request, but guess what? It's currently sitting right on top of today's list of 'things most liable to be ignored'."

The man stared intently at Barvas, unmoved.

"Not them."

The two men glared on at each other in silence, Fowlis Wester noticing Barvas' jaw tendons tightening and releasing, slowly contorting beneath the pale skin in barely controlled fury. Fowlis stole a look at Sergeant Gask to check his reaction, only to find his colleague utterly hypnotized by the drama.

Barvas and Reef Mogg remained staring, the room soundless but crackling with tension as neither man's gaze wavered or retreated. Even Stubbs had noticed the sudden change in atmosphere and had raised his huge head off his paws to watch.

Suddenly, without warning, Barvas exploded upwards, kicking his chair over behind him with a crash as he slammed both his fists down on the table with massive force, directly in front of the stranger. The unkempt stranger jumped back, mouth suddenly thrown open in shock and trepidation. Within seconds the stranger had regained his composure, but it was already much too late.

Barvas stared intently at the man, teeth bared in a grimace and now leaning in closer over the table. Then, slowly, his expression changed and he smiled, the arrogant smile of a man used to being totally in control.

The one legged policeman stood upright with a slight grimace and a murmur of suppressed pain and turned to Fowlis Wester and Sergeant Gask, the two men themselves still recovering from the unexpected explosion of action. With a slight nod towards the door, he let both men know his decision. The pair shuffled out the room and closed the door behind them with a quiet click.

Outside the room in the florescent light of the grey corridor, the men leant against the cold painted brick and exhaled deeply, releasing the claustrophobia of tension. The two turned to look at each other, finding themselves both wearing the same expression of relief. Sergeant Gask nodded in the direction of the front desk and the men retreated away to safety for the second time that morning.

In the room, Barvas recovered his upturned chair, positioning it slowly and deliberately back at the opposite side of the desk from the battered stranger. Stubbs rose and clicked across the room to take his place on the floor beside his master. Sitting and pausing to pat the dog's head before returning his attention to the man opposite, Barvas cleared his throat to announce that he was ready to proceed. Before taking his chance to speak, the stranger interrupted.

"I think you'd make a good king Mr Barvas. Really. And if, as you say, this is to be my kingdom, and you my unconditional ruler, then so be it. But I have something of tremendous importance to tell you, and I must tell it without any diversion from your attention, hence my wish to tell you the initial details alone. As strong as my distaste for your men's methods may be, my sole reason is to allow myself the chance to speak to you without any interruption. Trust me, my tale is one that requires full concentration."

"So I take it you are finally ready to tell me what this is all about, this great secret story you seem to be so careful to share with only the chosen few?"

The man nodded slowly and looked up, his face now more relaxed but yet with a look of deep foreboding suddenly in his eyes. Barvas was interested. Whatever this story was destined to be, it looked bound to be out of the ordinary, given that the very prospect of retelling was obviously filling the man with such a deep and profound fear.

Barvas eased himself back in the chair and folded his arms, preparing to listen.

## CHAPTER 20

## Barvas Reacts

It was over an hour later when Barvas appeared back at the front desk with Stubbs at his heel, the click of paws and the heavy unbalanced thud of the shoeless wooden limb attracting the attention of the waiting policemen. Barvas' face was now colourless and deeply lined, the expression that of a man disturbed and profoundly distressed. He was sweating heavily, even though it was a cold February morning and the interview room unheated.

Sergeant Gask and Fowlis Wester glanced at each other uneasily as Barvas crossed the room to sit again on the public bench. He sat heavily, leaning forward and dropping his head in his hands with a horrible sigh. Stubbs stood before his master, lovingly nudging his arm with his head, checking all was well. It was Gask who dared speak and break the silence, the younger man still largely dumbstruck by the man's reputation.

"Well, what does he have to say for himself?"

Barvas raised his head and wiped the sweat from his brow with a pass of his wrist, before patting Stubbs on the head to reassure him. Then, still staring at the covered face of the dog, he laughed, low and awkwardly.

"Findo, we've known each other thirty years, correct? We've both been policemen for almost all of that time. Never, not once, in all those three decades have I heard a story so fantastical, so bizarre and as outlandish as the one which I've just borne witness to in that interview room."

Findo Gask glanced between Barvas and the younger officer again, a nervous look creeping onto his face. He had known Barvas for all that time, but never once in all that time had he seen the confident man look so uneasy.

"What is it then? Is he lying to you about something we did? Is he feeding you some line, looking to report us?"

Barvas looked up impassively at his friend and then began to laugh again.

"That's just it Findo. In all my years listening to scumbags, deviants and lowlifes trying to construct elaborate tales that stunk worse than a dead body in an open summer grave, I've never been so utterly convinced that the man sitting in that room is telling me an entirely truthful tale. And no, he didn't mention you or the boy. The truth is though, the whole story he *is* telling me is beyond incredible. It not only defies belief, it defies all logic and any possible reason."

Barvas stood and slowly limped across the room to the counter, where Sergeant Gask stood fully upright, chilled by what Barvas seemed to be saying. Gask was disturbed by the change the stranger's statement had brought to the normally immovable façade of his friend. He had only once seen Barvas frightened so deeply and completely, on the night a much younger Findo revealed to his friend that he knew with total certainty of his responsibility for the three crucifixions in the town square. That day he had seen this same look very briefly, just before he had pressed the cold metal of the bloody watch discovered at the scene into his friend's hand. It had been discovered at the scene but quickly hidden by Findo Gask.

"Shall I phone headquarters and get us back up or an expert or something?"

Barely were the words out of Findo Gask's mouth than Barvas exploded into a sudden rage, smashing his hand into the wooden countertop and upsetting a cup of tea. The mug skittered across the wooden surface before disappearing over the edge and smashing loudly on the floor, causing Stubbs to spring behind his master, surveying the scene with his one eye from the gap between his legs.

"NO !! Do you hear me? No-one hears a word of this, Findo, not today, not ever. This incident will never leave the walls of this station; no one will hear a word of this other than the three men in this room. Not a living soul."

Barvas leaned heavily forward on the desktop as if exhausted by this furious outburst and sunk his head back into his hands. The two policemen behind the desk again looked at each other, confused and frightened. Gask felt a chill as Barvas raised his head and gazed at the two men with wide grey unfocused eyes. Without a word Barvas regained his composure and returned across the room to the bench followed by the ever loyal figure of Stubbs.

"Sorry, but I don't want anyone else involved in this Findo. Not now, not ever."

Barvas paused, as if to let the words fully sink in and be fully understood.

Findo Gask nodded, slowly at first and then firmer and with more conviction. This seemed to calm Barvas and he leant back, his body losing its angry inflexibility.

"Tell me, Findo, how many men do you have at the station here?"

"Right now? Just me and the boy here. Normally there are four of us, but Hestace Creel is in Spain on holiday for two weeks as of yesterday and Watt Avery is off on indefinite sick leave after he broke his back while he was trying to change the van's engine in his garden. We phoned headquarters for extra staff to cover, but they phoned back yesterday morning and told us they'd checked records and, since there were no crimes of any significance reported here in the last twelve months, we were being left alone to just muddle along. Young Fowlis here and I are sharing all the shifts between us for the next two weeks, until Creel comes back."

This information seemed to relax Barvas further and he smiled distractedly and nodded.

"Some good news at last. Ok Findo, get me headquarters on the phone."

The two men listened to Barvas as he took the receiver and requested his superior. Barvas asked for two weeks immediate leave starting from this morning. After a cold exchange and a short wait for a final decision, Barvas thanked the voice unemotionally and hung up.

"Ok, that's that settled. Now we can get on."

Sergeant Gask and Fowlis Wester looked at each other and then back at Barvas. Again Gask spoke for them both.

"Barvas, can you tell us what in God's name is going on?"

Barvas sighed, as if mystified at where he should begin any explanation, pushing himself upright and moving unsteadily around the counter on his wooden leg to join the other officers. He planted himself into Findo Gask's empty swivel chair and spun to face the two men with a loud squeal of metal, leaning forward to address them both.

"Just after we both left Police College, Findo, do you remember I was posted to a town about 50 miles north of here? It was in the middle of nowhere. And by god they hated me, Findo, you remember that?"

Sergeant Findo Gask nodded at his remembrance of the events.

Barvas had got on the wrong side of every single instructor at their police training college, having displayed an overconfidence that quickly marked him an unpopular student. But he had passed every test with flying colours and in spite of the hatred he had provoked amongst the teaching staff they had little choice but to acknowledge his talents.

However, when the course ended and Barvas had finished top of the entire year, they took their revenge.

Expecting the long-established and traditional reward for the head of year of a prestigious posting to one of the bigger cities, Barvas discovered he had instead been posted in a remote town in the very north of the region. His new placement was one of the quietest and least satisfying postings available for presentation. They had their revenge on him.

Barvas was devastated by news of the posting, but had portrayed no emotion as he read of his fate, keen to deny his detractors any shred of satisfaction. He had simply examined the list, noted down the contact name and number of his new superior and walked without a sound out the hall, returning through the crowds of excited graduates back to his room to pack for his new posting.

Findo had been at Barvas' side to discover his fate. After checking his posting calmly and then that of his friend, Barvas had stopped only to shake Findo's hand and offer his best wishes before leaving. Findo Gask watched the man exit with solemnity and dignity, his every step followed by the narrow eyes of superiors impatient for a response, their faces growing incensed by the lack of reaction. By the time Gask had returned to their shared room to offer his friend private commiseration, Barvas had already gone.

After a few weeks in his new posting, Barvas had applied for a transfer, but his every request was flatly denied without any word of explanation. News of his college reputation had spread through the senior ranks and grudges were being passed down through the system. Findo had visited his old friend a number of times in his remote northern outpost and had instantly recognised the posting as totally incompatible for a man of Barvas' enormous natural talents as a policeman. Gask found his friend introverted and progressively more difficult to reach, and gradually the two friends had lost touch.

Many years later, Findo had again come across his friend following the crucifixion incident. Findo suspected that this brutal retribution owed a great deal to the fact the three brothers were paid informants, protected from prosecution by senior officers, rather than purely revenge for the crash and loss of his leg. The night Findo had returned his friend's watch was the last Findo Gask saw of Barvas for many years. Until, one day, many years later, Findo had picked up his local newspaper and saw the thin memorable face staring back out at him.

"Is this about that newspaper thing?" asked Gask, reminded of the story.

Barvas nodded back slowly.

"One night we got a call to the station, Findo, phoned in via Headquarters in the middle of the night reporting some strange lights in the forest on the coast road. The two officers I worked with went off to investigate, leaving me in the station to look after things. As you well know Findo, they were never seen again."

Findo nodded as he recalled the details of the strange incident.

"The next day the car was found empty with both doors open, abandoned on the main road in the middle of nowhere. There was no trace of either of the men, or any indication of a fight or struggle. The engine was still running when they found the car. Or should I say when I found the car. I was the first one to realise something was wrong. I couldn't raise any signal on either man's radio or from the one in the car, just interference, so I locked the station and took the other car out to look for them.

All we ever found was a scrap of paper on the empty driver's seat, with a single word written on it in illegible pencil scrawl. Everyone examined it but no-one could make out what the scribble was, or even if it was a word. It was checked against known criminal's names and nicknames, signatures, farm names, even towns and streets but not even the experts could work it out. They searched for the missing men for months, but not even the most minor trace was ever found. They were both good men Findo, really good friends, and they had just vanished. Twenty years ago now and nothing, never even a trace or a clue as to what had happened."

Findo nodded back with understanding at his friend, recalling the facts of the case that had appeared in the newspaper. Findo had himself been briefly ordered to the area to assist with the search in the initial stages, but no trace of anything or anyone was ever discovered. Findo remembered the area's complete isolation, and the later disappearance of three mountain rescue men searching the area. Findo knew all the details but couldn't connect those events with Barvas' behaviour in the last few minutes.

"So what's the stranger got to do with any of this?" asked Findo Gask.

Barvas looked up and smiled.

"This? Well, the strange man you found unconscious on the station floor this morning, the guy sitting through there in that interview room of yours, he's just spent the last hour telling me all about another sudden death, right in the same area. Another death, another mysterious set of events, and then he handed me this..."

Barvas dug around in his pocket before withdrawing his hand to hold out a small scrap of paper. On it was unreadable pencil writing, which Gask knew instantly from memory was exactly the same as in the note discovered in the abandoned police car years before.

"And do you know what it says Findo? What that word is? It's just the same unreadable scrawl as all those years ago in that empty car. But now *I know* what it says. Our visitor Reef Mogg told me. It says 'Strathcarnage'."

Fowlis Wester let his cup slip out of his hand and smash below him on the floor. The very sound of the name gave the young policeman a horrible deep chill. Stubbs, who had been dozing under the bench opposite, sprung up at the fresh noise and then as if he too could sense the dark threat of the word, retreated back into the shadows below the counter, his ravaged head pressed tight against Barvas' false leg.

All three men had grown up in Highland villages much similar to the one where they now stood and knew the tales of Strathcarnage well. It was a mythical place of dark legend, spoken of in tales passed down beside remote firesides. The stories, even the very name itself, had been evoked to intimidate and strike fear into unruly children for generations. The mythical name stood as a promise of unspeakable horror and great evil, uttered to strike immediately silent both the loudest children and adults.

These were legends handed down over generations, filled with characters and events so grotesque that even the very name was viewed a word too powerful to be uttered without the greatest reverence. It was a name that had fuelled many a child's nightmare in remote Highland village homes. Rumour had it that the tales were once collected and written down in a book, but that the church, on discovering its existence, demanded the book confiscated, exorcised and then burnt, the remaining ashes spread out to sea by a specially organised party of senior churchmen.

Over the years, rumours would emerge of brave souls seeking to find some trace of the strange place, but it was said none were ever allowed to return from their quest. As time passed and evil of the myth had intensified, people had preferred to leave the name unspoken, the word gradually disappearing from consciousness and into whispered legend, only rarely mentioned by a few of the older storytellers.

The area's people were very superstitious, and mention of Strathcarnage had long been rumoured to bring a dreadful curse to the door of anyone who dared speak the name. Some claimed that even writing the word would raise a most dark evil upon you. With such rumours common, people quickly chose to forget the legend, and it had grown into a secretive but still pervasive myth. There always seemed to be someone still willing to repeat the tale on dark nights around a glowing winter fireside, keeping the ancient legend alive like a shadowy family secret.

Findo Gask leant back against the counter and recalled many of the same tales, his own grandfather having whispered them to him at his bedside as a small child, claiming to be passing them down exactly as his own grandfather had done to him in front of the smouldering peat fires of his croft more than 70 years previously. Findo remembered with a chill his grandfather's account of the sudden appearance of another stranger in a remote seafront village, a ragged female stranger claiming to be from a distant village called Strathcarnage.

According to his grandfather, the whole village had fallen into a terror at the news. Locals, familiar with the evil fable, had fallen on the old woman and dragged her from the town, locking her away within a remote cottage high on a hillside far outside the village. She was to remain there until village elders were gathered and it was determined what her fate should be. That same night, before the elders could be assembled to pass judgement, a ferocious storm had torn through the town, ruining buildings as huge waves pounded relentlessly over them from the sea, as if God himself wanted to tear open the very walls of the town searching for the woman.

According to his grandfather the remote cottage prison of the old woman had been hit repeatedly by lightning during the storm, and villagers had watched in terror from the battered town below as the building caught fire and burned, the colossal flames visible high on the hill in the distance.

When locals had reached the house the next day, and the flames had burnt out, it was discovered that every living soul and animal in the cottage had perished; their twisted bodies burnt black in the smouldering ruins.

But one body was missing.

The room where the old lady had been imprisoned lay intact, still padlocked. When the melted iron lock was broken open the room was found to be totally unharmed by the fire, and yet empty.

Gask shivered at the memory, remembering the wide eyed terror of his grandfather as he had shared the tale with the young boy. His grandfather was a resilient man who had lived a long tough life never paying heed to any of the area's traditional superstitious tales. All apart from this one. His terrified elderly eyes had darted around the dark room as he told the tale in a hushed voice, as if afraid of being overheard passing on these myths of such terrible evil to his young grandson. Now, decades later, Gask still remembered that abject look of utter fear and saw it anew, glinting in the eyes of Barvas.

"It's true Findo, I've heard the outline of his story and I trust he's telling the truth. Now I want you both to hear it for yourselves."

Findo Gask found his logical sceptical side slowly reasserting itself.

"Ok, listen Barvas, I don't doubt you, really, I mean I've known you for a very long time. But what if this guy is just a crank, lying and spinning you a pretty good tale? Maybe he's making it all up and he's studied all the old Highland fables and decided to come here to freak us all out? Maybe he's a lunatic who likes superstitious tales and telling a good story to scare people?"

Barvas looked intently at Findo Gask and reached behind him, pulling a rectangle of cardboard from his back pocket. It was a postcard. He held it up toward Findo Gask, hand shaking slightly as he did so.

"Look at this Findo. Look very carefully. Tell me what you see?"

"It's a postcard. A black and white picture of two old bearded men on the front. They look like gnarly old fishermen."

"Yeah, it is. It's a postcard. Black and white, two old men. Now look closer. Look at the faces…"

"Yeah, so, you've seen one fisherman you've seen them a….oh my god. Holy Lord above…"

The face of Findo Gask was frozen, open mouthed, the colour rapidly draining from his cheeks.

"Yes, that's right Findo. Look at them. It's them, my two lost friends from my station. It's them and they've grown old. Now look at the wall behind them, at the name on the little sign..."

"But.. but it can't be. Oh please no. It can't..."

From behind the head of Findo Gask, the pale face of Fowlis Wester appeared, his hair hanging untidily about his traumatized face as he examined the postcard over the fat man's shoulder. It was he who found the courage to speak out loud the name written on the sign above the two men's heads.

"Holy god," the young man gasped, " It says..... Strathcarnage.."

Without another word, Barvas led the three men back towards the stranger in the room.

## CHAPTER 21

## Day Four – The Men React

"Fowlis, have you written down everything you have heard here in this room? Every word?" asked Barvas.

The young policeman nodded slowly.

"All of it?" asked Findo Gask from the other side of the room, wanting to make sure.

"All of it," the young policeman repeated, holding up the thick wedge of paper as if to prove his honesty.

Barvas turned and looked at the men assembled in the room with a serious face.

"Well, as far as I can see we have no choice now. Fowlis, think of somewhere to hide all that paper safely while we take a rest for a while. Go have a sleep in the cells yourself after you hide it and meet us out front of the station in the car in two hours. We're going to try and find this godforsaken place."

Findo Gask felt his jaw fall open.

"Find it? Are you mad? This is obviously some.. some crazy elaborate practical joke. That place is nothing more than an evil legend. This man is making all this up."

The fat policeman walked over to the table and grabbed Reef Mogg by the shoulders. Shaking him violently and desperately he began to yell in the man's face, demanding he admit to the others in the room he was the creator of some sick fantasy.

"Tell them. Tell them it's all nonsense, admit that you made it up. This has gone too far. Tell them !"

The man looked straight into the fat policeman's face and slowly shook his head.

"I can't. It exists. I'm sorry, but I've seen it with my own eyes."

Then Reef Mogg lowered his head and began to softly weep as Findo Gask moved back and released his grip.

The other men looked around the room at each other, drawn into individual space by the deep shock of all they had heard. Barvas was the first to move, standing, to help the weeping figure of Reef Mogg to his feet before leading the man silently out the room. Findo Gask left next, shuffling off pale and terrified, leaving Fowlis Wester in the room alone to gather the scrawled collection of papers together.

After gathering the bundle and placing the papers in an old box file, the young man sealed the box and searched around the station for somewhere safe to hide the collection. After contemplating and deciding against numerous hiding places, he settled on what he thought a brilliant idea. Dragging Sergeant Gask's chair back behind the front desk, the young constable stood on the seat and slid aside a polystyrene ceiling tile, pushing the packed box onto the supporting metal in the cavity above. Pulling the tile back into place, he stepped down from the chair and stood, smugly satisfied that the hiding place would remain undiscovered and the box would be safe until their return. Walking away, he paused for a moment and returned, again removing the tile and taking some unmarked paper from the box.

The young man walked through the empty station to the police cells, carrying the few blank sheets of paper and a freshly sharpened pencil, locking the heavy steel door behind him. A couple of hours later and his task completed, he returned one last time to his hiding place carrying the few written sheets, secured the spot and joined the other men at the car.

The group, stood around the car waiting for the young constable to return, were never to be seen again after that day.

A local man, Herbert Spencer, had known Findo Gask well and had been out enjoying his daily walk along the harbour-side road on the morning in question. He watched seen Fowlis Wester locking the station building and as he drew nearer the group, had asked his fat friend whether there was trouble and why the station had been closed for the past couple of days. Gask had shaken his head silently at the man and climbed inside the car with the young constable whose name Herbert Spencer would later fail to recall during questioning. Herbert had remembered the strange haunted look of Findo Gask as the fat policeman had gazed out the car window and given the man a single wave as the vehicle had moved away. Herbert had walked on mystified, watching as the glow of the car's red tail lights had vanishing ahead of him into the fog.

Herbert Spencer was the last man to see any of the men alive.

Three weeks later the black Daimler was found abandoned, partially hidden in trees on a forest track forty miles north of the town. All four doors were left open. Tracker dogs were employed to search for the men, as well as intensive searches by sea and by Navy helicopter. No trace of the men or any indication of the direction they had taken was ever discovered. After a few weeks the search was scaled down and then, over time, abandoned.

A thin official file on the men's disappearance remains formally open, but lies hidden in a forgotten box gathering dust somewhere, lost now under a pile of other abandoned cases in the dark basement of an anonymous police archive building somewhere in Scotland.

The mystery has never been solved.

# CHAPTER 22

## Footnote

These handwritten transcripts of events in the small police station, complete with the thirteen and a half tales dictated from the death books of Strathcarnage which make up the body of this book, were discovered a number of years ago during renovation of the interior of a former police station, somewhere on the west coast of Scotland.

On removing ceiling panels during the building's conversion into residential property, a builder working on the development had found a sealed box containing a thick bound pile of papers handwritten in pencil. After reading the first few pages, he had resealed the box and carried them to his van. The builder later delivered them to an old writer friend of his acquaintance in the city whom he knew was keen on Scottish history, to let him examine the contents and to see if they might be of any possible use to him.

That writer is me.

I have faithfully duplicated the entire contents of the box, precisely as written, and I have retyped the entire script here faithfully from the originals, for you dear reader.

Final additions had been added to the beginnings and end of that part of the paper which I now presume makes up the original visitor's statement, detailing a brief history of how the statement came about.

These later additions seem to be a hastily handwritten account of events by an author signing himself F.W. The handwriting is the same as that of the statement; therefore I feel it safe to assume that the entire contents of the box were written by the same hand.

After lengthy examination of the thin case file held in the police records office concerning the sudden unexplained disappearance of the three officers, I have added identities to the three men, already suggested in the papers by initials used by Fowlis Wester.

I have also spoken to a now frail Herbert Spencer in a remote Northern nursing home, the last witness to see the men alive, driving out of the town, and he confirmed to me the presence of a previously unidentified strange dog.

I have in addition examined maps, studied aerial photographs and both sailed and explored the surrounding coast, exploring the whole area in minute detail from both sea and land.

I have found no trace to date of any site which matches that mentioned in the stories.

The complete evidence that exists concerning the mystery is contained in those writings discovered in the box, now fully transcribed and detailed in this book, with the addition of a postcard found on the bottom of the box and postmarked 'Strathcarnage', dated three days before the recorded date in the notes of Reef Mogg's strange late night arrival in the police station. The postcard's appearance matches exactly the description contained within the handwritten notes.

The postcard is of a basic design, featuring a black and white picture of two heavily bearded men. The message reads simply, "Do not worry about us, for we shall remain where we will never be found." This message is followed by an unidentifiable signature and two kisses.

I have questioned at great length the builder friend who delivered me the box and he assures me the package was fully sealed and covered with years of undisturbed dust on its discovery. I have known the builder personally for decades and his honesty is above reproach. He wishes to remain anonymous.

The police building concerned has since been demolished and replaced by a block of six modern seafront luxury flats.

On a final strange note, after I had received delivery of the box, opened it and fully examined the contents, the builder had returned a few weeks later and presented me with a different postcard he had found hidden in an old cupboard in the basement of the building. This item was found behind mouldering packets of cereal and an ancient half empty pack of chocolate biscuits in a kitchen cabinet, removed before the item was removed and smashed up. This postcard had no address or stamp of posting, only containing a shakily written message in what appeared to be the same hand as the original notes.

The postcard had on its front a single blurred black and white image of a man I now know from my study of the original police files to be the image of a much older Fowlis Wester.

The card read simply "Never find us."